BIG KNOT ENERGY

SHADOWVERSE

BOOK TWO

RAELYNN ROSE

TWISTED HEART PRESS LLC

❀ Created with Vellum

CONTENT WARNINGS

Big Knot Energy includes kidnapping, violence, family trauma, abuse (mentioned and not by MMCs), and MMFMM and MM. There might be others I have forgotten. You know your heart and mind - please take care of yourself. I try to approach any delicate matter with tact and respect.

CHAPTER 1

Issa

Six months ago

"*D*id you think I wouldn't find out?" Antonio bellowed, his hand clenched around my jaw so I was forced to look into his eyes when all I wanted to do was cower.

He released his hold on me but only long enough to draw his hand back and whip it across my face. My head was thrown to the side from the force and tears welled in my eyes. I'd stopped trying to make excuses, stopped begging him for mercy, stopped begging him to stop.

I wasn't sure I could even form a coherent sentence anymore. My lips were swollen and a split down the center of the bottom made it throb to my racing heartbeat.

"Who the fuck do you think you are?" *Slap.* "A fucking *beta.*" *Slap.* "*Nothing!*"

That last word was followed by a closed fist punch that sent me stumbling back until I landed hard on my side. Pain ricocheted through my hip, my back, my elbow, and my shoulder before my head slammed against the hardwood floor.

Stars danced around the edges of my darkening vision, Antonio's curses and threats sounding so far away.

Maybe I was dying. Maybe I would finally get away from him, away from my family, away from this life that I hadn't chosen.

I supposed I should have been afraid of dying, but all I felt was relief. I would finally find peace.

I'd been texting my sister's pack as often as I thought I could get away with, trying to warn them of various ambushes or even when my fathers planned to steal from their shipments.

And Antonio had found a way to uncover the texts I'd thought were permanently deleted.

Now, I laid in a heap on the floor, my eyes closed as my heart thundered harder than I'd thought was survivable. Surely, it would give out at any moment and send me into cardiac arrest. That might not be the most comfortable way to go, but it would still set me free from my alpha's torment.

Not my alpha. I might carry his bonding mark, might have stood at the front of a room during the bonding ceremony my parents had planned, but he wasn't someone I wanted, someone I would *ever* want. He didn't give a shit about me.

We'd had another beta in our little fucked up pack, but at least he'd been able to get away after that first week together. He'd slept with me because that was required of us, then split. Neither Antonio nor I had heard from him since.

Although, I highly doubted my alpha would tell me shit about anything, even Carlos contacting him.

I'd thought about Carlos a few times through the years, wondered if he was happy, if he'd found a better pack, better alphas, or if he'd merely moved away and stayed off everyone's radar.

Darkness filtered in and out as consciousness tried to escape me.

Whether I died or was no longer awake, at least I would escape the pain igniting the nerve endings across my entire body.

In the past, Antonio would only hit me where my clothes would cover. That way, I wouldn't have to apply so much makeup to cover the bruises and cuts. He would also inject me with sedatives or slip them into my food and drink to keep me docile, to keep me from speaking my mind, to keep me from fighting him when he tried to have sex with me...

When he tried to knot me.

For a while, I'd wondered if I simply didn't like sex. The mere thought of Antonio so much as touching me made my stomach turn and my skin crawl.

But I was beginning to think I wasn't opposed to sex in general, but sex with Antonio.

I wasn't an omega. My body wasn't made for an alpha's knot. Not that he gave two shits about what I wanted, whether I enjoyed myself, or whether he caused me intense pain each time.

My lids fluttered when the sound of a door slamming shut shook the floor and sent a fresh wave of adrenaline through me. Was it possible Antonio had left? Was I alone?

And what were the odds I could get to a set of keys and take the car that was mine from when I'd first come here and been allowed to come and go as I pleased?

I had to get to Cora. Had to warn my sister and her pack. Had to warn them that our parents had made plans to kill the alphas of Pack Rivera and their unborn child.

The room spun and my stomach lurched as I pushed to a sitting position. Where was my phone? Whether or not I could find my keys, I had to find a way to warn Bain, to warn Cora and her mates not to trust my mom.

No matter how doped Antonio kept me, I was still able to hear everything that was said around me. I always wondered if my alpha thought the sedative disabled my hearing or caused memory loss. But he and my fathers had always spoken freely in front of me.

They thought I would remain the dutiful daughter. They thought I would remain loyal to them, to the alpha they'd forced me to bond with, that I would put them and their power-hungry ways above my sister and future niece or nephew.

Why was the room swaying so much? Or was that me? I couldn't force my eyes to focus, could barely see through the swelling, and there was a constant ringing in my ears.

But I had to warn someone, damn it. I would never forgive myself if something happened to my little sister and her baby and I'd had the information that could keep them safe.

Pushing onto my knees and grabbing any piece of furniture I could to steady myself, I finally found my phone across the room. The screen was cracked and barely readable, but I had to try.

My vision swam in and out as I typed then hit send. No point in deleting it this time since my alpha had been able to find all the others.

Phone still in hand, I used the side of the couch to pull myself to my feet, blinking slowly to try to clear my head enough to drive. I had to do something but was starting to worry I might kill someone else when I passed out behind the wheel.

Pack Rivera's estate wasn't far. I would simply have to stick to the backroads and hope I didn't veer off the road or into the other lane.

My legs felt like a newborn foal's as I swayed side to side and hit every piece of furniture and even the walls on my way to, *hopefully*, grab my car keys.

They still hung in the exact same spot they had since the day I'd been moved into this house by my parents.

Antonio didn't want me. Didn't love me. He loved the connection to my family, the power and money he gained by working for my fathers, for being a member of the infamous Pack Alvarez.

But I was his property, at least in his mind. Forget the fact I was a beta, forget the fact there was absolutely no guarantee I would ever be able to carry his heir. Forget being faithful to me or showing me the smallest scrap of respect. I was a tool for him to use at his will.

The keys jingled against the fob on the keychain as I put my hand to the wall and slid along to the garage, nearly tripping down the three steps and over to where my newer model Mercedes Benz sat.

My beta siblings and I might not have been favored by our parents, but at least they'd cared enough about appearance to ensure their kids all drove nicer cars.

Not that prestige or appearance ever meant a damn thing to me. I was just happy I had a car that would actually start and get me where I needed to go without it breaking down on me.

The garage door seemed like it took an eternity to rumble up enough for me to finally back out and head down the driveway and to the roads that would lead me to Cora.

I had no idea whether she was home yet, but from what I'd heard from Antonio, there was an attack on her pack planned for when she was visiting the obstetrician. Pack Rivera's guards would be at their home, though. They could contact Bain or one of the others and warn them.

My vision was still doing that weird in and out thing where the edges were rimmed with sparkling black, narrowing my sight down to a pinpoint. I had no idea whether it was from a head injury or from the swelling in my eyes. I was terrified to so much as look in the mirror for fear of what Antonio had done to me sending me into a panic attack. No way could I drive then.

Not much further.

I just had to hang on long enough to get to Cora's house, to warn one of her alphas or their guards, then...

I didn't care what happened to me after. I didn't even care if one of my sister's alphas decided to execute me. After all, my own alpha was behind all this bullshit. In my head, I deserved death. I'd earned a death sentence merely by association.

The rapid, reverberating thud of the warning strip snapped me back to attention. I'd had no idea I was drifting off the side of the road until those vibrations sounded through my sedan and rattled my seat.

"Just a little further," I said aloud, trying to keep myself awake and alert.

It couldn't be more than another ten minutes. *Please don't let it be more than another ten minutes.*

I wasn't sure I had much more than that left in me. It was a struggle just to keep my eyes open and my thoughts clear. Or clear*ish*.

There. Up ahead, the first of the tall gates surrounding the estate of Pack Rivera came into view. I'd made it. I was here.

Foot on the brake, I slowed my vehicle, or thought I was as I approached the manned front gates. I could barely make out bodies clad in all black, but they were blurry and out of focus.

The closer I got, the more those bodies moved in a frantic motion, waving their hands in the air like those blow-up dancing advertisement balloon men in front of car lots or businesses closing shop.

Oh shit. Oh no. My pinpoint vision was becoming more of a blurry dot.

I was almost there. Just a few feet more.

My head drooped forward a second before my entire body was thrown against the seatbelt and the airbag deployed, my face planting against it and the burn along my cheek blaring through the rest of the pain for the briefest second. The scent of whatever the hell they used in those safety implements filled the car and stole my breath.

Voices boomed around me. Something tapped beside me over and over. But I could barely open my eyes or lift my head.

Blinking hard, I forced my head to raise with the last few ounces of energy I had left and turned my eyes toward a man whose face was framed in the window.

"Open the door," the man ordered. He had dark hair and gray eyes and reminded me of Cora's alpha, Bain. Could this possibly be the brother, Enzo?

I blinked a few times, trying to clear my vision and thoughts, but finally lifted a hand to hit the button to unlock all the doors.

My side was yanked open, then a man with pretty green eyes lowered in front of me, his hand cupping the back of my neck before smoothing it over the back of my head.

"Is anything broken?"

"What?" I asked. *Was anything broken? Anything like what?*

"Can you tell me if anything's broken? Do you have a headache? Any dizziness?"

I continued to stare at him as I tried to make heads or tails of what he was asking me. That wasn't important. None of that was important. I had to find Cora. Had to warn her.

My hands felt like they were made of rubber as I tried to push him out of the way and climb from the driver's seat but tripped over my feet. Or the ground. Or maybe it was the air that threw me off balance.

The man with the pretty green eyes, the one who kept touching me and asking me questions, lifted me from the ground. I swayed, my head rolling against his chest as he carried me.

"Call Bain," he ordered.

"Can you tell us why you're here? Who hurt you, Isabelle?" the one I thought might be Bain's brother asked me, his tone far gentler than any I'd heard from an alpha, especially one who was supposed to be the enemy of my family.

"Corazon," I managed to groan out.

"She's not here," Cyrus said. "Call a doctor. Is Henderson still working for Bain?"

A doctor? Were they calling a doctor for me? And who was Henderson?

"No idea. And Bain's not answering his phone."

"I'll contact the doctor," another man said. A door opened then closed.

I was set on a soft surface; I assumed a couch. Feet thundered against the floor, then someone was thrusting a glass of water into my hand and said, "Here."

A wet cloth was dabbed at my face, pulling a hiss from between my teeth when the cloth irritated a cut there.

"Tell Corazon," I managed to push out as I wrapped my hand around the wrist belonging to the person tending to my wounds.

His brows lowered and he looked from me to the guy standing over us then back again.

"What do you want me to tell her? You want her to know you're here?"

I shook my head, trying to remember what exactly my sister needed to know. "Not mom." The words came out slurred.

My eyes refused to focus, my lids constantly lowering as sleep or unconsciousness beckoned me forward. Sleep sounded so good right now.

"Not mom. Not *your* mom?" the pretty eyed alpha asked, cupping my face in both of his big, warm hands. He was definitely an alpha, but I'd never seen one be so gentle, especially not with a beta.

My lips felt numb as I said, "She's lying. Mom...my mom. Tell Corazon."

"Your mom is with Corazon today. Did you want us to call her?"

Panic gripped me as I tried to focus on the man hovering over me. "Stop her. Tell Corazon. Mom...the baby." Why did my words sound so slurred? "She'll hurt Cora."

And the last of my energy depleted. I heard the men muttering around me, heard them making orders, hopefully calling Cora or her alphas.

But blackness swallowed me into the abyss. And before the last of reality faded away, my final plea was that I wouldn't wake up.

That I would finally be free from the world my parents had forced me into.

CHAPTER 2

<u>Cyrus</u>

Four months ago

I'd arrived at the estate of Pack Rivera under the guise of delivering some stuff I'd bought for our soon to be nephew. Or soon to be *born*? I wasn't sure how the hell that would be phrased.

And, technically, he was Enzo's nephew by blood, but since we were a pack, that made Cora our family and her baby our family. I would protect either of them with my own life.

That family extended to Cora's beta sister, Isabelle.

Since the day she'd crashed into Pack Rivera's gate – that had already been fixed and was like new – she hadn't left my thoughts.

I couldn't get the way she'd looked that day out of my head. Her face had been battered, bruised, and swollen. There was fresh and dried blood on her lips, her hairline, and trailing down her temple. And her abuse had been at the hands of her fucking alpha, the man who was supposed to protect her above everyone and everything else.

She was shy, quiet, and demure. But it felt more like she was afraid. She was afraid of alphas and had every right to be.

Until her sister had become bonded to Pack Rivera, the two of them hadn't had good experiences with those of my designation. Bain, Ford, Valen, and Cohl were doing their best to make sure she was eating well, getting enough rest, and had regular visits from Doc Henderson. But she needed more than that to fully heal.

She needed her own pack. Her own home. Somewhere to decompress, somewhere she truly belonged.

And with alphas who were growing obsessed with her in the most profound way.

Didn't matter what Enzo or Ax said – it was obvious by how often they talked about her and checked on her they were as interested in her joining our little group as I was.

Even if she had no romantic interest in us, I knew it would make all three of us feel better if she was under our roof, under our care, and our protection.

Not that Pack Rivera couldn't keep her safe. Their home and property were a damned fortress and guarded by armed men around the clock. Since they were involved in...less savory activities, they tended to gain enemies. The protection was as much for them as it was for their omega. Or rather, *more* for their pregnant omega and extending to them.

We'd all noted the increase in the number of guards posted outside the gates, around the property, and at all entry and exit points since Pack Alvarez and Cora's originally arranged pack had attempted to assassinate all of them. A few of the guards had even made me, Enzo, and Ax wait at the gate a few minutes while they got the okay from their boss to let us onto the property.

Ax had grown impatient during those times, but I fully understood. If we had someone in our life, I would be just as protective.

Especially if that someone was carrying our child the way Cora was carrying the first heir of Pack Rivera.

If we had Issa in our pack, I would make sure she was safe. That she *felt* safe. I would let her make the choices and decisions about her life she'd never been given before. If she only wanted us as packmates, as *friends*, then we would give her that space. If she wanted another person romantically, we would add them to the pack if that made her happy.

"Hey," Corazon said from her place on the couch. Her belly was round, and she had that pregnancy glow that made women look so beautiful. I wasn't one to fetishize pregnant women, but I'd always found that glow to be damned near ethereal. "What are you doing here...again?" she asked with a wry smile.

Lifting my hand, I showed her the bag I'd carried in that contained several sets of stupidly priced baby clothes. It was stupid because the baby would outgrow each of these items within weeks. But hey, it was our job to spoil the shit out of our nephew.

"I come bearing more gifts," I said, setting the bag on the coffee table as I tried to inconspicuously look around for Issa.

She wasn't sitting on the couch with Cora and Cohl, and I wasn't about to start roaming room to room in search of her.

"She's on the patio," Cora said.

My gaze darted to her face and my cheeks burst into flames at the wide grin on both her and Cohl's faces.

"Dude. It's pretty fucking obvious. Just tell her you're into her. Or seduce her or whatever," Cohl said as his hand made slow circles on Cora's swollen belly.

Craning my neck, I looked around as much as possible to ensure we wouldn't be overheard, then lowered onto the coffee table across from where the two sat, ignoring Cohl's possessive growl. He knew I didn't want Cora but was the least stable of the four alphas. He even tended to growl at his own packmates when they tried to cuddle with their omega.

"You know her better than the rest of us—"

"Not really," Cora said, cutting me off. There was sadness in her eyes, even as she smiled softly at me.

"Would she…do you think she'd be up to staying with us? Just for a while. She could decide if she wanted to stay. You know we'd never force anything on her and wouldn't demand anything of her."

"I know," she said with a nod.

And then she went silent, her lips pursed to the side as though she was chewing the inside of her cheek.

"She might not want to be bonded," she finally said.

"That's fine. I just…we want her to be happy. And safe—"

"She's safe here," Cohl muttered as he lowered his head and nuzzled Cora's belly.

I'd never really thought a whole lot about being a father. It wasn't that I wasn't interested in having a child one day, but, unlike so many alphas, it wasn't a driving force to my life. If one day we added an omega – or a beautiful Italian beta – and he or she was willing to carry our child, I would love and dote on him or her.

But watching the way these four alphas fawned over Cora, the way they couldn't resist touching her belly or talking to their unborn child made me almost wish for the day when it was my turn to wait impatiently for my mate's belly to swell with the life we created, for the day when I would hold my child in my arms. And no, I didn't give a shit which of us fathered the child – he or she would be ours and would be loved and protected, regardless of how they presented in the future.

"I won't answer for her. *None* of us will make the decision for her," she said, gripping Cohl's hair tight and earning a throaty purr from her alpha. "Talk to her. See if she would want to stay with you. And then, if you all get along, the four of you can talk about forming a pack."

The sisters had been estranged at best, and that was primarily because of the way they'd been raised. Since Corazon was the only omega child, she was treated like a prize, though she was still raised by someone other than her parents. The entirety of her upbringing had been how to please her future alphas, to produce heirs to inherit her fathers' empire, and to continue their delusions of grandeur.

But I'd seen the sisters trying to talk, trying to reconnect. Corazon had made sure her alphas treated Isabelle as a member of the pack, even if it was temporary. Even if she would one day leave.

And hopefully, one day join our pack.

Looking toward the kitchen where Isabelle would be sitting on the patio just outside the sliding door, I gathered my courage and took a few deep breaths. Why the hell was I so nervous? If she said no, she said no.

But if she said yes…

So many possibilities. There was the possibility of these feelings that had sprung to life at the first sight of her battered body growing stronger. There was the possibility of developing a full bond with her.

There was the possibility of rejection.

The fear of that sting would be worth it, though. At least it would be worth it if she didn't turn down my offer.

I hadn't come out and directly asked my packmates whether they wanted Isabelle in our home, but all three of us had been talking about her nonstop. And if they were thinking about her half as much as I did, it was a wonder we were able to get shit down or run our club without burning the fucking place down.

"Just go talk to her. Be calm. Out of the three of you, you're the least likely to freak her out." Corazon watched me push to my feet and shove my hands through my hair twice. "Or you would *normally* be the calm one. Dude. Seriously. She's already on pins and needles. Just tell her…whatever. How you feel or something. Ask her if she'd be willing to stay at your pack house. Tell her…I don't know. Tell her you're worried about her safety and want to help keep her safe."

"They leave for long hours to work the club," Cohl muttered against Corazon's belly where he was still nuzzling it and pressing kisses over her maternity shirt.

"Not helping, alpha," Corazon said playfully.

With another deep breath, I straightened my shirt, pushed my hand through my hair once more, and forced my feet to carry me from the living room and into the kitchen.

Isabelle was stretched out on a recliner, her head tipped toward the sun, her eyes closed as she soaked up the warm rays. It was still chilly outside, so she wore a sweater and had a throw draped over her legs.

How often had she been able to do something as simple as relax in the sun, to have a little quiet time to herself?

After one more calming breath, I slowly opened the door so as not to startle her. Her lids lifted and her eyes settled on me...

And she tensed.

"Hey," I said, closing the door behind me. "Mind if I join you?" I asked.

She looked past me and into the house then back to my face. "Um...sure. Yeah."

When she moved as though to sit up, I held out a hand. "Relax. You don't have to...move for me or whatever."

Smooth, Cyrus.

Internally rolling my eyes at myself, I lowered onto a recliner beside her so I wasn't towering over her and intimidating her.

She wasn't as small or petite as her sister, but she wasn't exactly tall. She was thin, *too* thin, and looked frail. A small scar was fading along her hairline and shadows underlined her haunted eyes. She always seemed as though she was watching for one threat or another. Even though she was behind a secured gate and surrounded by armed guards.

"I was talking to Corazon. And my pack. Enzo and Ax..." Damn it. I was rambling and stumbling over my words.

"I know who your pack is," she said, a ghost of a smile playing at the corners of her pillowy lips.

While Isabelle and Corazon resembled each other in that sisterly way, the beta sister held something that called to me, to my alpha, in a way I couldn't define nor deny. Not that Corazon wasn't a beautiful woman. But I'd never once weaved a single sexual fantasy around her the way I had around Isabelle – Issa – on nearly a daily basis.

Who the fuck was I trying to kid? It was more like hourly.

"We'd like you to come stay at our house." I held up my hands when her eyes widened, and her lips parted. Her warm, sun-dried linen scent spiked and was tainted with a slightly bitter smell as her fear ratcheted up. And why wouldn't she be afraid? I was another alpha, just like the ones who'd made her life a fucking nightmare.

"W-why?" she stammered.

Sitting up and turning my body to face hers, I hunched my shoulders a little and clasped my hands between my spread knees in hopes of appearing less intimidating and a little smaller.

"I'm only going to speak for myself, but I promise the others feel the same way. We feel responsible for you. We want to know you're safe."

"I'm safe here," she said. Her eyes flitted to the closed door then back to me again. "Do *they* want me to leave?" Her voice sounded so small, so sad that it broke my fucking heart.

"They never said anything about you leaving. *We* want you in our home. And, if you'd like someday, in our pack. As a member."

She crossed her arms over her chest and blinked rapidly and I feared the moment those beautiful hazel eyes grew glassy.

But she never so much as teared up.

"I have no desire to carry your children," she said, lifting her chin and leveling what I assumed was supposed to be a glare on me.

"That's not...we haven't discussed having a family. Not that we won't want a child or two someday. But...we just..."

Fuck. I was screwing this all up.

"I like you. We like you. And we want to make sure you're safe. We want to help you grow. We want to help you gain your independence."

From what we'd been told, she was still reluctant to leave the house, even when the entirety of the pack left the estate for one reason or another. And even when there would be plenty of firepower to protect both women.

"All we want from you is your happiness. You're free to get a job if you want or just...live your life. We make more than enough that you won't have to worry about feeling as though you need to earn your keep or whatever."

Maybe I should have waited and let Enzo have this discussion with her. As pack lead, he might have been able to give her better reasons, or at least been more articulate.

No way would I have allowed Ax to be the one to ask her. He would flirt with her and make sexual innuendos that might have ended up turning her away before we ever had the chance to show her who we really were. How safe she would be. That we were nothing like the fuckheads she'd known her whole life.

"Give us a shot. A week. Two tops. If any of us make you uncomfortable, I will personally call Bain to come kick all three of our asses and bring you back here."

"I don't really have anything to bring with me. I've been borrowing Cora's clothes and stuff."

That wasn't a no. Hope bloomed so bright in my chest I had to fight the urge to jump up and start doing a jig.

"We can order anything you want or need. You'll have your own room if you aren't comfortable sleeping with any of us or in the pack bed."

"I'm not great at cooking, either."

"Not expected of you. Nothing is expected of you except…I *would* like it if you would consider seeing a therapist. Not a requirement," I tacked on quickly. "But I think it could help. Other than that, we just want to see you heal from your ordeal. From your past. And we want to help show you most alphas are nothing like your fathers or that mother fucker who hurt you."

I winced as my anger pushed forward, but relaxed when a small smile stretched on her lips.

"I've heard curse words before, Cyrus."

Why the hell did my name rolling from her tongue wake up my dick?

Doing my best to remain quiet when her eyes left my face to stare off into space, I clenched my hands together so hard my knuckles were white from the lack of blood flow.

"Okay," she said quietly.

"Yeah? You'll give us a shot?"

Her smile was bigger, brighter this time, and I noticed her eyes grew a little greener as she nodded. "Yeah. I'll give you guys a shot."

CHAPTER 3

Issa

Three months ago

Cyrus hadn't been kidding when he'd said they would order anything I needed. My closet and dresser drawers were nearly bursting at the seams and my bathroom held several scents of bodywash and bubble bath, along with any and every type of makeup and hair product I could ever want or need.

The pack was…the alphas were crazy. In a good way.

No. That wasn't true. Of course, everything was good, and the alphas were as sweet as they'd been when they'd checked on me over and over after the day I'd rushed to Cora's to warn her.

Ax…he was the crazy one.

And Cyrus hadn't been bullshitting me when he'd said they weren't expecting me to lay on my back so they could rut me when they felt like it. In fact, the only time anyone touched me was when I would wake up screaming from a nightmare and one of them would be wrapped around me, holding me and talking in low, comforting tones.

Then there was Ax. He teased me relentlessly, flirted in the cutest way, even ruffled my hair like I was his little sister rather than a single, unclaimed beta sleeping in a room right by his.

They had made me sit on the bed while they'd fussed about where all my new belongings should go and argued over who bought the best stuff. It was all beautiful, but there was no way I would or could ever wear that much.

Especially since I was still nervous about actually going into public.

Since Antonio had vanished after my sister's pack had executed my fathers and mother, it felt as though there was a threat around every corner, like every shadow in the yard was a hiding place for my former alpha to lie in wait so he could drag me back to the hell I'd been living through since I'd graduated high school.

At the moment, I was wandering my bedroom in the dark, stopping near the window to look down onto the moonlit yard. For three bachelors, they'd kept their yard tidy and well-manicured. Their house was pretty, too, but definitely decorated for a pack of men with the darker colors and leather couches.

This wasn't the first night since I'd officially moved in here that I either couldn't fall asleep or woke up in the middle of the night and was too scared to sleep.

I knew it was stupid. Antonio wasn't here. My fathers were dead. No one could get through any of the windows or doors without setting off the alarm and there were cameras everywhere. I'd even noted the red blinking light of one in my room, though I tried to ignore it. I hated to think one of the alphas might watch it when I slept and would hear me snore or mumble something embarrassing.

With a frustrated sigh, I pushed from the windowsill and made my way from my room. A snack sounded tempting, even something as simple as a glass of wine or maybe some hot chocolate. Anything that would give me that warm, fuzzy feeling enough to make me drowsy again.

The moment I stepped into the hallway, soft, masculine moans met my ears.

Turning my head, I stared down the darkened row of doors. Two of them were open and the sounds weren't coming from that direction. They were coming from downstairs.

Had Ax or one of the other two brought someone home? And being as I'd been upfront and blunt about not wanting any of them to expect me to hop into their bed on demand, I was shocked by the level of jealousy coursing through my system at the prospect of one of them having sex with another beta. Or even an omega.

Especially an omega.

My siblings and I had been raised to believe we were nothing special because of our designations. Alphas were the rulers and leaders while omegas were fucking royalty. The only reason my fathers had deemed me and my brothers worthy of an arranged bonding was because they'd chosen packs that would further their criminal empire and agenda.

Keeping my steps and breathing as quiet as possible, I padded down the hall and toward the stairwell, peering over the railing and into the living room.

Cyrus was on his back, Ax between his knees. The muscles in Ax's back and ass bunched and rolled beneath his skin as he rolled his hips forward, making love to his alpha packmate while kissing him deeply.

I'd assumed the three of them had been or were currently romantically involved, but this was the first time I'd had a front row seat to it. And everything south of my belly button was warm, my core throbbing, and my panties growing damp with arousal.

This was…they weren't fucking. Ax wasn't rutting into Cyrus the way Antonio used to with me. He was making love to someone he cared about, someone he loved.

My chest rose and fell with deep breaths as I stood there like a voyeur. I kept in the shadows so as not to be detected, but it still felt wrong to encroach on this special moment between them.

Or it could simply be a way for them to sate a primal need since the broken beta they'd brought to their house wasn't interested in sex.

Though that wasn't true. I'd just been scared. Still kind of was.

Memories of the times Antonio had caused tears and pain down there when he'd forced his knot into me caused nothing short of terror to squeeze my heart anytime I contemplated having sex with another alpha.

They wouldn't do that to you.

That little voice had grown louder and louder lately, reminding me these alphas were not the men of my past. They had never and would never hurt me, not intentionally.

When Ax's pace picked up and he threw his head back on a low moan, I began to back away.

Not only did I not want to get caught watching them, but I felt like I was about to catch on fire. It wasn't quite like how I'd heard omegas describe their heats, but damn if my body wasn't warm and my skin too tight.

And an undeniable urge to rush down those stairs and join the two alphas, maybe to wedge myself between them, straddle Cyrus's hips and ride him while Ax took him was almost overwhelming.

It wasn't that I was never turned on or horny. It had just been a long damn time since I'd actually wanted an alpha to take me the way Ax was taking Cyrus. I wanted to know how he would feel pumping into me, how Cyrus's hands would feel on my body, how Enzo's mouth would feel on my breasts or pussy.

Taking a step back, then another, I turned quickly and jogged as quietly as possible back to my room, closing my door with a quiet *snick*. Then I stood staring at the door as my heart raced behind my ribs and my breathing sawed in and out of my lungs.

I could no longer hear the moans or the heavy panting from Ax and Cyrus, but that image was burned into my corneas.

Replaying the scene on loop in my head, I let my hand trail down my body, cupping my breasts before trailing to my sleep shorts to touch myself over the fabric. So much pressure had built in those short moments that I was sure I would combust if I didn't find a release … immediately.

On shaky legs, I headed for my bed and climbed under the blankets, closing my eyes as my hand moved under the blanket, under my shorts, and directly between my legs. I pretended it was Ax's hand or Cyrus's. I pretended I was the one lying on that couch, I was the one Ax was pumping his cock into.

Dipping a finger into my core, I circled my arousal around my clit as the tight bundle of nerves throbbed to my heartbeat. A whisper of a moan left my lips before I could stop it, but I refused to stop teasing myself, pushing myself closer and closer as those first tingles of release built in my abdomen.

My mouth parted and I swallowed back the cry as I came harder than…ever. I wasn't sure I had ever come while with a man, but that had been, by far, the strongest, most earth-shattering orgasm I'd ever experienced, and it had everything to do with the erotic display I'd seen downstairs.

* * *

WE'D FALLEN into a fairly comfortable pattern. As in, I was comfortable around them, and they were comfortable being themselves without worrying about scaring me.

Honestly, after spending the past few weeks with them, I wasn't sure how anyone could fear any of these alphas. Enzo could be a tad intense, but only because he truly cared about his pack. And me. They'd alluded to me officially joining as their beta, but no one had come out and actually asked if I wanted to join.

It wasn't that I was expecting to be courted; I was a beta, not an omega. They weren't required to perform any grand gestures, there would be no bonding ceremony, no soft, sparkly gifts.

But I didn't need any of that. I'd had a bonding ceremony. I'd had an alpha buy me shit when he was trying to impress my fathers. And look how that turned out.

No. I just wanted a pack to care about me simply because of who I was and not what my family name could bring them.

I laughed inwardly as I poured my first cup of coffee. My family was dead. Or at least my parents were dead. And with them went the power. My sister was the only omega and she'd bonded with an equally powerful pack of alphas.

A wave of shame rolled over me at the memory of gunmen converging on the car carrying Cora to her bonding ceremony. Antonio, my brothers' packs, and my fathers all ran while Cora was left alone. We hadn't known for weeks whether she was dead or alive, whether she'd been assassinated or sold into omega trafficking.

The shame really shouldn't be in my heart. I hadn't been driving. I'd had zero control over Antonio's actions. In fact, I barely remember that day, the events more like a hazy memory from the sedatives my alpha had injected into my bloodstream.

Smiling at Cyrus as he breezed past me, stopping to press a morning kiss to the top of my head, I filled my mug and carried it to the living room to wake up while watching some reruns of *The Andy Griffith Show*. None of the guys grumbled about my love of old TV shows or movies, though they often teased me about it.

"Morning," Enzo grumbled as he dropped onto the other end of the couch, his laptop under one arm, a steaming mug in his free hand.

"Good morning," I said, giving him a soft smile before returning my attention to the ever so perfect town of Mayberry.

As I sighed at the easiness of the fictional town and its people, the soft thud of music bumped through the floor.

Turning a frown on Enzo, I asked, "Is that Ax already?"

It wasn't exactly early at ten in the morning, but the guys tended to work late. Which meant I tended to either wait up for them to get home – I was still too scared to sleep in this house alone – or was woken up when they came through the door since I stayed on the couch until I was no longer here alone.

"Sounds like it. Unless Cyrus is working out."

"Not me," Cyrus said, his hand wrapped around what I assumed was a protein drink by the packaging.

The alphas owned a few clubs but primarily focused on a higher end one that happened to showcase a male dance review. *Not* a strip show, as Ax argued over and over again. Probably because he was one of those dancers.

I'd been informed he'd been formally trained from the time he could walk, but being as I was too scared to leave the house let alone set foot into the club, I'd yet to see it.

"Is he working out or...?" I let the question trail and hoped I didn't sound like a horndog when I so desperately wanted to sneak down there and catch him shaking his hips while sweat glistened on his – hopefully – bare chest.

Yep. I'd developed a hardy crush on Ax. And Cyrus...and Enzo.

Ax was such a flirt, but it was obvious he saw me as simply a packmate. He wasn't shy about changing when I was in the room and had even openly talked about other women when I was in the room.

Cyrus was so freaking sweet, always trying to anticipate my needs before I was even aware of them. It tended to be him who woke me from my nightmares, holding me against his strong body, gently restraining me to keep me from hurting him or myself while muttering sweet and comforting words until I'd calmed down enough to go back to sleep.

It had taken a few times to convince him to stay in the bed with me. I trusted he wouldn't try to take advantage of me or make me uncomfortable.

Enzo. I mentally sighed. He was so...dominant. But not in the jackass way. He could easily command respect and rarely used his alpha bark on his other two packmates. *Never* on me. In fact, his expression and tone tended to soften when he addressed me.

Yeah, I was crushing hard on these three men, but I didn't have the courage to tell them I was ready to entertain the idea of not only joining their pack but actually asking for more than the chaste kisses to my forehead, temple, or top of my head, or the gentle hugs.

Cyrus smirked in my direction, then faked a serious expression. "You'd better go check on him. Wouldn't want him working out without a spotter."

"Yeah. Because her ninety-pound self can do shit if he drops a weight."

I scoffed. "Trust me when I say I do not weigh ninety pounds." Although it wasn't much more. Unlike omegas, I wasn't blessed with the wide hips or the big butt and boobs. Not that I was rail thin or shapeless, but I was...average.

My hair was twisted up in a messy bun and I was wearing one of the pajama sets they'd ordered for me, but we'd all just woken up. None of them even hinted at me so much as applying mascara since all I did was sit around the house and the only people I saw beside these three were my sister and her alphas.

With my hand wrapped around my mug, I grinned. "Should I change the music when he's not looking? Put on some nineties pop?"

"He likes nineties pop," Enzo said with an eye roll.

Because of course Ax would like nineties pop. He also liked what Enzo referred to as chick flicks, which was any movie that had a romantic storyline and no explosions.

Cyrus winked at me as I passed him, trying to keep my steps light to avoid my approach being heard over the music.

The stairs didn't so much as squeak under my feet as I snuck downstairs, lowering my head to look the moment I was low enough.

He wasn't working out.

And, as I'd hoped, he was shirtless.

The basement spanned the length of the house with the home gym in the corner closest to the stairs and the rest open with mats and mirrors hung around the room so Ax could create different routines for the guys who danced at the club.

Lowering onto a step, my eyes began to water from the lack of blinking while my heart began to race, and I was instantly warm from the neck down.

I'd known he could dance. He'd even pulled me to my feet a few times in an attempt to get me to dance with him. But this? This was unlike anything I'd seen him do before.

He would roll his hips, his eyes on the mirror, then spin with so much grace it was like he was part cat. He leapt through the air, his legs spread in the splits before landing and rolling on the ground to pump his hips while holding himself up on one arm, simulating having sex with someone.

My mind started playing tricks on me as I pictured myself beneath him, my legs spread as that wickedly beautiful body of his writhed and gyrated and ground against the floor.

By the time he finished, I was breathing nearly as hard as he was.

His eyes met mine in the mirror and a salacious grin spread across his face. "Whatcha doin' there, creeper?"

"I'd planned to change your song and throw you off but...you can really dance, Ax." After the words left my mouth, I felt stupid for voicing them.

Of course, he could dance. Not only had he trained his whole life, but he danced in front of hundreds of people on a regular basis.

"Thanks." He grabbed a towel from a pile stacked on a table and rubbed it over his face and head before moving it down his pecs and stomach, my eyes following his every move.

It was a feat to keep from licking my lips...or crossing the room and licking the spiced rum scented sweat covering that perfectly chiseled body. He looked like he belonged on the latest cover of Alpha XL.

"That for me?" he asked, nodding his head at my mug.

It took a few moments for my brain to catch up to his words and for me to stop ogling his half naked body.

"What? No. It's mine. Get your own."

He stuck his tongue out at me, so I returned the gesture, then giggled the whole way up the stairs.

CHAPTER 4

<u>Ax</u>

Two months ago

"We need an omega," I said, leaning my head against the seat as Enzo drove the three of us home in the pack SUV.

"Why the fuck would we need an omega? We have Issa," Enzo said.

"We don't have her. She simply lives with us," I grumbled. I swore I'd been walking around with a case of blue balls since the day she'd walked through our door with the understanding she was willing to give our pack a shot. And, thankfully, she hadn't left.

"She'll come to us when she's ready," Cyrus said, turning his upper body to look at me over his shoulder.

"Or we find a male omega for her. She's comfortable around us but is still wary of other alphas. And we don't want her to feel as though she's being replaced or like her place with us is threatened. A male omega wouldn't be a threat, could actually help her lean into her natural beta instincts, and…maybe rev up her libido."

"What makes you think she doesn't have a libido? Not everyone wants your dick," Enzo grumbled around a yawn.

"Just because I can't smell her arousal doesn't mean she doesn't want me, asshole. And yeah, *everyone* wants this dick." I smiled to myself as I dropped my head back again. "But you both know I'm right."

"An omega wouldn't scare her. And it would be someone to hang out with while we're at work. She's got to be bored out of her mind when we're out," Cyrus offered, always the voice of reason.

"She's scared of being alone, too. She won't sleep in her bed unless we're home," Enzo pointed out.

"See? If we found an omega, there would be another body there so she wouldn't feel alone. And omegas tend to be more outgoing and could help her break out of her shell."

Cyrus nodded. "She's been doing a lot better with her nightmares, but mainly when she coerces me into sleeping in her bed."

"Oh, I'm sure there's a whole lot of arm twisting there," I said with an eye roll. I had to bully my way into the room and declare a pack cuddle just to have her pressed against my body.

"She didn't freak out at the grocery store the last time she let me drag her along," Enzo pointed out.

The first time she left the house after she'd escaped the claws of her former alpha, she'd nearly had a panic attack when a trio of alphas moved down the aisle toward where she and Cyrus were shopping.

She really was doing an amazing job at working through her trauma, but we would all prefer she saw a licensed therapist, someone who knew how to help her with the kind of issues she suffered after her fucked up bonding with Antonio.

"Do you realize how fucking rare male omegas are?" Enzo pointed out as if I hadn't already thought about that.

"We have time. Not like we're in a rush to create heirs or some shit. We put out some feelers, maybe even approach an agency, then find the right person for her. We let her decide. If she's not up to another member joining the pack or doesn't get along with the omega, we throw the whole plan out the window," I said.

Exhaustion was settling in my bones now that we were finally on our way home for the night. And we had actually taken the next two days off to spend more time with Issa.

We'd been working nonstop lately, and I wanted to try to get her out of the house again, but this time on a date, maybe to a nice restaurant or something. Especially after all the grumbling she'd done about not needing the fancier clothes since she didn't go anywhere.

Personally, I was dying to see her in one of the dresses I'd bought her, especially one of those I knew would cut high on her thighs and give me glimpses of her cleavage.

She was comfortable around us, had even changed in front of me – while keeping her tits and lower half covered under panties and a bra – and was fine with puppy piles. But that didn't mean she was ready to take anything further than that.

But fuck me if I wasn't more than ready to feel that body under my hands, to finally feel how soft her lips would be against mine, to taste how sweet her cunt would be on my tongue.

Reaching down, I adjusted my cock before it ended up punching its way through my slacks and tugged on my pants to make room for my half-swollen knot.

Enzo pulled the SUV into the secured garage and killed the engine. We ambled toward the door, the twelve hours we'd put in at the club weighing us all down. Even though Issa was a beta, her soft scent had permeated the house and I could smell her the second we stepped into the mud room that doubled as a laundry room and through the kitchen.

She was asleep on the couch, the blanket over her legs, the tank top she'd donned for bed riding up her stomach and showing off a slice of skin that I wanted nothing more than to reach down to run my fingers over the olive hued skin…then follow my fingers with my lips.

"Told you," I said.

"Told me what? I was the one who pointed out that she's uncomfortable going to her bed when we're not here," Enzo grumbled before rounding the couch and gently touching her shoulder to wake her.

She hadn't even bothered turning off the lamps or the TV, just dozed off while binging a show we'd seen her watch a few times. Something about two brothers hunting demons and monsters and shit. I had a feeling she was watching for the dudes, but whatever...I was hotter than both of them combined.

Cyrus had attempted to lift her and carry her to her room the first time we'd found her asleep on the couch, but she'd woken up screaming and swinging her tiny fists. Not that she'd actually hurt Cyrus, but she'd felt terrible after.

So now, we all made sure to wake her carefully and gently, purring for her so she woke peacefully.

"Hey," she whispered, her voice groggy as she pushed up to sitting and rubbed both eyes with the heels of her hands. "You're home."

"We're home," Enzo said. And I didn't miss how soft his face and voice got anytime he dealt with her. I'd caught him more times than I could count simply staring at her with a love sick expression when she didn't know he was watching her.

We all wanted her. But we'd all agreed anything that might happen would be decided by her and on her timeline.

She stretched her arms over her head with a yawn, that damn tank top raising higher until my knot became fully engorged, and my dick tapped the back of my zipper as though to remind me he still hadn't had any loving.

For the first few days she'd been here, I'd fucked Cyrus – and vice versa – damned near daily. It had been more of a necessity than a luxury. She was used to us walking around with boners *now*, but none of us had wanted to make her uncomfortable by showcasing the tents in our pants or boxers when she had first moved into our home.

Even when I woke up with my rock-hard cock pressed against her ass, she didn't react or say anything. Though she was usually still sleeping by the time I rolled out of bed for a quick breakfast, work out, and dance practice.

We all waited until she was on her feet and heading toward the stairs – more like shuffling toward them – before we all filed behind her.

"Pack bed?" I called out behind the other three.

"That works for me," she said before yawning again.

I hoped someday she would feel comfortable and safe enough to go to her own bed when we were out. We had alarms everywhere, cameras pointing toward every inch of the house and property, even sensors to let us know if our property was breached from any direction.

As the three of us headed to our bedrooms to wash off the day and change into clean boxers or shorts, Issa headed toward her bedroom where one of two pack beds was located. The other was in the empty and never used omega quarters. But if my plan worked, perhaps it wouldn't be long before five of us were cuddled together in a puppy pile every night.

* * *

"WHAT ABOUT THIS ONE?" I asked, turning my laptop toward Cyrus and Enzo.

All three of us sat at the kitchen table with the local Omega Center's page open, scouring through the omegas interested in finding a pack.

Enzo leaned to the side and scoured the page. "Nope. See there? He's not interested in a pack with betas."

"Fuck him, then," I said, clicking through the one page of male omegas.

Omegas were rare enough. Male omegas were as rare as female alphas. But hey, one of our bartenders, Aryn, was a female alpha. Therefore, I was determined to take that as a sign from the universe that we were meant to have a somewhat abnormal connection with the various designations.

Cyrus didn't even glance at my laptop, his face mere inches from the screen in front of him. Dude refused to see anyone about getting glasses for computer or close up work.

"I think I found one," he muttered, almost to himself.

Even though we'd gotten in late, we had all snuck out of the bed at the butt crack of dawn this morning so we could do some digging while our sweet Issa was still asleep.

Enzo and I pushed our chairs closer to him on either side. There was only a head shot of the male omega, but from what we could see, he was hot. Unbonded, unclaimed. Still living with his parents, only omega child with three younger sisters. No information on his family pack. A few hobbies and interests listed.

But what got all of our attention was the fact he had zero limitations on his preferences in a pack, meaning he didn't care whether it was all alphas, all betas, or a mix. In the spot about willingness to carry a child for his future pack, he entered *willing to discuss*. That wasn't a deal maker or breaker for us since we'd never really bothered having that conversation. Personally, I wasn't in a hurry to become a parent. I was having entirely too much fun.

He also lived fairly close.

Before the other two could say a word, I lifted my phone and dialed the number he'd added to his profile. Although, it could very well be the number to the center, but I didn't care. I wanted to try to get in contact with this man and see whether he'd be willing to do a casual meet and greet with us and Issa, see if she liked him, if they would get along.

And I wanted to try to make it as organic as possible.

After leaving my name and number on a generic voicemail, I turned a grin on my packmates.

"She's going to hate the whole blind date thing," Cyrus said, his attention still on his screen as he scrolled through the exact same list the three of us had been scouring. There had only been a few that looked remotely interesting, but nothing as intriguing as the one omega I'd contacted.

"So we don't tell her. She's finally getting out of the house. We convince her to join us at the club. She caught me working on some new choreography again—"

"She didn't catch you. She heard the music and rushed through the house to watch," Enzo said with a smirk.

That first time I'd found her watching, she'd looked shocked and in awe. After that, she didn't bother hiding her approach as she made her way down the stairs to plop herself on the floor in front of the mirrors to watch me. And if she noticed how hard I got from her eyes on me, she never made a single comment about it.

"Whatever. We tell her I want her to see the full show. Tell her she needs to finally wear one of those dresses or whatever. Get her out of the house. Introduce her to Aryn and the rest of the crew so she'll know she's completely safe even if we have to retreat to our offices or tend to other business."

"When did you become so…mature and organized?" Cyrus teased.

I lifted my hand and flipped him the bird.

"And poof…he's a man child again," Cyrus mumbled with a soft laugh.

CHAPTER 5

Issa

"But why do I need to go?" I asked, sitting on the end of Ax's bed as he rummaged through his closet.

"Because you haven't left the house in weeks. And because I'm dancing tonight. And because I'm your favorite alpha in the world." His head peeked around the corner of his closet, his brows raised. "Enough reasons or did you want me to keep going?"

After a cheeky grin, he disappeared again, the sound of hangers clacking against each other mixing with his frustrated huffs and complaints that he really needed to find some *new shit to dance in.*

I had moved in with Ax, Enzo, and Cyrus months ago after I'd finally escaped my abusive asshole alpha.

Not *my* alpha. I didn't choose Antonio. Nor had I chosen the beta I'd only seen twice after the bonding ceremony.

Unfortunately, Antonio's bite mark was still on my shoulder, something I did everything in my power to avoid looking at after every shower and ensured it was covered by clothing. I wasn't proud of that mark. I wasn't proud of that bond.

And I sure as hell hadn't enjoyed the sensation of the bond opening in my chest. He felt heavy. Oppressive. Dark. After that first night, I'd locked down the bond to keep him from feeling my emotions and to avoid feeling an ounce of his evil nature.

At least I did when the asshole wasn't dosing my food or drinks with sedatives. I'd walked through my life in a haze, like every moment of the last two years was a dream.

That asshole had threatened my sister, had sided with my parents when they'd plotted to take out Cora and her pack simply because she refused to fall in line and obey the rules they'd put in place for all six of their kids. I was one of five betas, Cora being the only omega. She'd definitely had it worse, being trained like a show dog. My parents had made some fucked up deal to sell her off to another powerful pack.

And their plans had blown up in their faces.

Now, the two of us were making our own rules, living our own lives. Or I was trying to, anyway.

"You know I hate being in public," I called back, leaning back on my elbows as Ax stepped from the closet in a pair of worn jeans that hung low on his trim hips and showcased his round ass.

All three alphas were…well, nothing short of absolute perfection. And saw me as the poor beta who needed protection.

He stepped into the bathroom and my cheeks heated at the sound of the toilet seat lifting a second before liquid trickled into the toilet. The fact he was peeing with the door open while I sat on his bed told me exactly how this beautiful man saw me – as a sister. A friend. A roommate.

When he came back into his bedroom, I quickly averted my eyes as he pulled up his zipper, a wry smirk pulling up one side of his mouth. "Shit. You can look. You know how much I like to be admired."

Of course he did. That was why he danced on stage with the others at the club he and his packmates owned. He definitely didn't need to, but he loved it, loved to perform, loved having people fawning over him.

Rolling my eyes, I pushed back to a sitting position and crossed my legs under me. "How about I squeal and clap my hands for you now, then watch movies until you boys get home?"

I would have preferred to be waiting in the pack bed for the three to return, for them to climb in and smother me with their scents...and other things.

Instead, I got the joy of constant sexual frustration every time I heard them moaning from one of their rooms as they fooled around with each other.

Ax leaned back against his dresser and crossed his arms. "Okay, here's the deal – we're supposed to meet someone tonight. And we want you to meet them, too."

My dark brows pulled together. "Why would I want to meet one of your one-night...*oh*. An omega?"

His head dipped once.

"You guys are meeting with an omega tonight?"

Another nod.

"Then...why would you want me to meet them?"

The look he shot me made me chuckle. He looked at me like I'd just insulted his favorite pair of vintage Nike Airs. "You're pack. We all decide together."

My brows shot up to my hairline and I blinked a few times. "What?"

"What?" he said, only his tone was confused.

"You said...but I'm not pack. I have..." I turned my head and pointed at the mark on my shoulder.

A soft growl rumbled from Ax. "That thing means abso-fucking-lutely nothing. If it'll help, I'll cover it with my own right now."

My core fluttered with the thought of his teeth sinking into my shoulder. But he'd said nothing about bonding me as his mate, but rather simply making me a packmate, as in...a member of his family. None of the three alphas had so much as tried to kiss me in the three months since they'd requested I live with them.

"You don't need to...what about Enzo and Cyrus?"

"What about them?" he asked, opening a drawer and pulling a t-shirt out before tugging it over his head. Shame. I really did enjoy ogling his body as much as any other red-blooded human. He was hot and was fully aware of that fact.

"They've never said they saw me as pack."

He crossed the room and grabbed my hands, pulling until I had to put my feet on the ground and stand. "You live in our house. You carry our scents around every day. You're pack, little beta. You're stuck with us. If you want our marks, say the word. But that doesn't matter to us."

Something tightened in my stomach, a mixture of affection and fear. I didn't like the thought of another alpha declaring ownership over me. Not again.

But these three hadn't done that, hadn't demanded anything from me. In fact, they told me I could take my time looking for a job or refrain from working all together. They'd also offered me a job at The Vault, but I wasn't sure I was ready for that just yet. Antonio was missing, but I highly doubted he was gone for good. He'd lost out on a lot of money when my sister's alphas had killed my parents as well as another rival pack. They currently controlled the majority of everything that was imported or exported from the region.

And one of the alphas in this house just happened to be my sister's brother-in-law.

"Well?" Ax asked after a few moments of me chewing on my bottom lip. "Will you go? I want you to meet them. We want you there. And you haven't seen me dance in forever."

"I see you practice here. Doesn't that count?"

I'd had the privilege of watching him perfect his choreography on many occasions since I'd moved in, though I hadn't yet seen him perform ballet or lyrical.

The big, broad, tattooed alpha had been put into several dance classes the moment he could walk. His parents had been convinced he would present as an omega...like the rest of his siblings.

Unlike my own family, his didn't treat him or any of their children any differently. I'd met the entire brood and wasn't sure I'd laughed as much as I had the night they demanded he brought me to his family pack's home for dinner.

Huh. Maybe I *was* pack. I hadn't thought much about it that night, but his mom kept referring to me as Ax's beta, or the pack's beta.

I supposed if I would be saddled with another alpha – or three – this was practically a dream scenario.

Or it would have been. Because now they were interested in adding an omega, someone who would be guaranteed to get pregnant when they decided to add to their family.

"Please?" he said, batting his ridiculously long and dark lashes at me and sticking out his pillowy bottom lip in the cutest faux pout ever.

"I have nothing to wear," I said, grasping at straws as he adorably tried to destroy every reason I couldn't go.

"Bullshit." He wrapped a hand around mine and tugged me behind him until we stepped into my room and into my closet.

After a few seconds of pushing various pieces aside, he pulled a dress free that still had tags attached.

There was a reason I hadn't worn it – the damn thing cut so low my boobs would practically hang out and the hem was only a couple inches below my ass.

"No way, Ax. I'll be naked in that thing."

My breath caught in my lungs when a dark blond brow raised, and his pupils blew wide. "We can get to the naked part later tonight," he teased, quickly averting his gaze.

Teasing me about being naked wasn't uncommon, not with Ax. I was pretty sure he would walk around with his dick in his hand, offering it to anyone interested if it was allowed.

"You're wearing this. And makeup. I want every single person in that room jealous of my beta."

My belly instantly went crazy with butterflies and my heart thumped wildly in my chest.

My beta.

Why did that sound so damn good coming from his mouth? And

why couldn't I be more than another housemate, another member of the pack?

Once an omega was added…

With a sigh, I nodded. "Fine."

I knew the three alphas wouldn't care if I slept with other people. Why would they when they participated in that activity together on a regular basis? I'd never begrudged presenting as a beta, and the fact they couldn't smell my arousal every time I'd touched myself to the sounds of them making love made me appreciate my designation all that much more.

They would be meeting with an omega tonight; someone they might end up courting. Maybe I would spend a little time getting cute and look for my own conquest. Even being bonded to Antonio for two years, we didn't often have sex. And when we did, it was quick and usually painful; the alpha had never given a shit about my pleasure, simply pumped into me until he found his release, then went to his own bedroom. As in, we didn't share a bed or a room.

That had never bothered me.

But living here with Ax, Cyrus, and Enzo, there had been many nights when I'd woken with nightmares of my abuse at my alpha's hands and wanted nothing more than to climb into bed with one or all of them and let them hold me.

Pushing all those thoughts and fantasies aside, I took the dress from Ax's outstretched hands and headed for my bathroom.

After stripping and stepping into the shower, I tilted my head back to wash my hair, then moved on to showering, washing, and exfoliating.

"Curl your hair tonight, too. I love when it waves down your back."

I squeaked and slapped my arms around my body the best I could when I looked through the glass door to find Ax leaning against the vanity watching me.

"What the hell are you doing?"

"Getting ready. Just like you," he said. I couldn't see his face, but I could hear the smile in his voice.

"You have your own bathroom. Get out, perv."

His chuckle followed him out as I tried to will my heartbeat to a normal cadence. How long had he stood there watching me? My cheeks felt like they were on fire. Had he watched me shave my armpits and bikini line? Watched me shave my legs?

Rinsing quickly, I ended the spray and reached around the glass door for the towel. I could hear the alphas' voices rumbling through the house as I dried off and stepped in front of the mirror to start my skincare routine. Being the daughter of ruthless criminals might have had a lot of downfalls, but I'd always had the best of everything from skincare to clothes. Even as a beta I'd been a bit spoiled, and this pack definitely kept me in that spoiled princess category.

Huh. Maybe I had been pack this whole time and hadn't registered that fact because I still carried Antonio's mark.

There were ways to break the connection, to permanently remove his mark. But I refused to ask Ax, Enzo, or Cyrus to bankroll such an expensive procedure. I would simply do as I'd done all this time and keep the bond locked down and ignore the mark.

Except the dress Ax had chosen would put both my shoulders on full display.

Full coverage concealer for the win.

After an hour, my hair was waved around my shoulders, my makeup was dark, smokey, and evening ready, my lips were plumped with gloss, and the dress Ax had chosen hugged my curves. It literally felt as though a sneeze would flash my butt at anyone within twenty feet.

Slipping my feet into a pair of heels, I huffed a sigh when Ax yelled, "Hurry up, beta!" through the house.

A tube of gloss, my ID, phone, and some Valium were tucked into a clutch, and I was ready to go.

A long whistle cut through the air as I carefully descended the stairs, my hands clutching the railing tightly to avoid rolling down the last few steps. It had been months since I'd crammed my feet into anything more than a pair of sneakers or house slippers.

"Damn, girl. Where has this hottie been hiding?" Enzo said, moving toward the stairs and taking my hand, holding it up and urging me to spin. "Why the hell would you hide a body like that from the world?"

"You look beautiful, Issa," Cyrus said. "There will be plenty of our people there tonight, so if you get overwhelmed and want to leave early, just let one of us know. We'll get you a safe ride home."

"Oh, hell no. We're partying tonight. I want to see this girl drunk," Ax teased.

"You're meeting your omega–"

"*An* omega. Not *ours*," Cyrus said, cutting me off.

"The last thing you need is to babysit your drunk roommate."

Cyrus's brows creased as he shook his head.

"I told her she's pack but she doesn't believe me," Ax said, escorting me through the house and toward the garage.

Instead of the three climbing on their Harleys like they often did on warmer days, we climbed into the Land Rover parked beside my little Miata. That vehicle had been Enzo's idea. I would have been perfectly content with a used sedan since I didn't often go anywhere alone except to my sister's.

Enzo turned in the driver's seat as I pulled my safety belt on. "You think you're just a roommate?"

I shrugged up my shoulders and tried to keep my face neutral.

"Do you not want to be pack?" Cyrus asked.

Well, shit. This was supposed to be a fun night out and now I was feeling a little emotional and extremely on edge. Honestly? I wasn't sure what I wanted. It had been a long damn time – as in the entirety of the years I'd been alive – since I'd been asked what *I* wanted.

"You know what? We don't have to talk about this now. That was shitty of us to start a big ol' heart to heart conversation when we won't be able to talk after we get to the club," Cyrus said, reaching over to pat my leg from where he sat beside me.

I opened my mouth to thank him but couldn't form the words. Honestly, I wasn't sure what to say. Yeah, I wanted to be a member of the pack. But what I didn't want was to be owned. And I really didn't want to be just a background member. I wanted…

Well, hell. I wanted them to look at me the way Ax did when we were in my closet, the way Enzo had looked at me as I'd walked down the stairs to find them waiting in their button up black shirts, worn jeans, t-shirts…yeah, they looked good in anything they wore.

But they looked best when they wandered the house in nothing but their boxers.

When Cyrus pulled his hand away from my leg, tingles were left in its wake, and I instantly missed the warmth of his touch.

An omega. An omega would arrive at the club to meet these alphas. An omega they might very well be interested in courting and adding to the pack. What would she look like? Would she be dark-haired and curvy like my sister? Or was she a stunning blonde with big boobs, wide hips, and a round butt?

I swore every omega I'd ever met was the epitome of a Barbie doll, only petite. I wasn't exactly tall at my whopping five feet and five inches, but Cora barely stood at five feet two inches. Even the rare male omega I'd met in my life had been small.

That was what alphas wanted, the soft, curvy type, the omega who would submit and serve.

Nah. Even as I thought it, I could taste the lie. These alphas didn't want someone to submit to them. I couldn't picture them with a woman who wouldn't sass them, challenge them, force them to put in the work to earn her as their omega.

Because strong alphas, strong *men* didn't require their partner to be a doormat. And they sure as hell didn't drug them to keep them quiet, compliant, and docile.

Nope. Not tonight. I refused to allow all the bad memories to ruin a night out with this pack.

My pack?

Okay, fine. For tonight, I would think of them that way, as my pack. I would let the fact they would be there watching over me keep me from going into a full panic attack the moment I was bombarded with any oppressive alpha hormones.

CHAPTER 6

The club was already packed when we parked around back and entered through the employee entrance. Ax tried to talk me into letting him escort me through the front door so he could watch all heads turn my way. He said he wanted to show me off.

I, on the other hand, wasn't quite ready for that type of attention.

Even as I sat on the barstool near where Cyrus was pouring drinks, I kept fidgeting, pulling the top of my dress up while trying to keep the hem from riding up my thigh any further.

A martini sat in front of me, barely touched. I wanted to drink. I wanted a buzz so I could squash the nerves over meeting this person who could make my alphas forget I existed. But my stomach was turning with nerves.

"Here," Ax said, setting a shot glass in front of me as he slid onto the stool beside me.

"What?" I asked, looking at the liquor then to his face.

"You look like you need this. Ready?" He held up his glass and waited for me to do to the same with mine. "To meeting new people." I forced a smile and threw the drink back, almost choking on it when he added, "And getting my beta drunk so I can take advantage of her later," before tossing his own shot back.

Coughing, I slapped his arm then took the napkin Cyrus offered to wipe my lips and chin. "You're a jerk."

"Had to say something to make you smile. You're over here looking like we forced you to clean the bathrooms. This is a club. With music and dancing and hot people. Have fun. We have plenty of bouncers and employees to make sure you're safe." He pointed overhead. "And those things are working overtime to keep the hormones and perfume under control. You're safe here."

He pushed to his feet, ordering two more shots from Cyrus, offering me another.

"To an amazing show by the hottest alphas in town."

"Including you," I said with a smile and a shake of my head.

"Well, duh."

We threw back our shots, with me wincing at the burn as it went down my throat, then he kissed the top of my head. "I expect you front and center when I get on that stage."

He pointed at me as he backed away, a wide grin showcasing his straight white teeth, before he disappeared through the crowd, leaving me to my own devices.

It only took about ten minutes before I began to feel the effects of the alcohol warming my stomach and chasing away the nerves.

Ax was right – I'd needed those.

So what if they were meeting an omega. So what if she would join the pack. That didn't mean I couldn't be friends with her. That didn't mean they would mistreat me just because they'd found their mate.

Being as I only had one sister and had only recently formed a close relationship with her, it might be nice to have another sisterly type in my life. We could become best friends and gang up on the alphas.

A smile pulled up my lips as I made my thoughts turn from dreading the addition of an omega to actually looking forward to another female in the mix.

Fingers trailed along my shoulder, and I jerked away. An alpha sidled up beside me, leaning sideways on the bar, his eyes on me. Or rather on the almost vulgar display of cleavage from my dress.

"Dance with me," he said. Not asked. *Said.* Like he was trying to use his alpha status to influence me. There were only three alphas on this planet that made me actually want to obey, and this smarmy jerk wasn't one of them.

"No, thank you. I'm waiting for someone." Not like I was lying. My pack *was* waiting for someone.

I raised my eyes to the bar, leaning to the side in search of Cyrus. He was currently leaning forward, his head tilted as though trying to hear the order of the group in front of him over the thumping of the music.

The alpha ran his fingers over Antonio's mark, and I couldn't help jerking away. The pink scarring had been covered with makeup but there was no way to hide the raised ridges.

"Hmm. Is someone looking for a little fun away from her pack?"

I curled my nose at him. "No. I'm not. I literally just said no thank you and told you I'm waiting for someone."

"And here I am," he said, holding his arms out and grinning as though he'd made the best joke. "Just one dance while you're waiting."

"Sorry I'm late, baby," a male said from behind me, turning the stool so he could cup my cheeks and plant a kiss directly to my lips.

Even with the scent filtration system working overdrive, I inhaled the most delicious chocolate covered strawberries. The taste was even better when his tongue touched the seam of my lips and I opened immediately for him. I hadn't had much more than a glimpse of seafoam green eyes and wild, long, curly hair before he'd slanted his mouth over mine.

The alpha growled in frustration, but eventually, I felt more than heard him leave my side.

"I think the coast is clear," the man – the *omega* – said against my lips.

All I could do for a few seconds was blink at him, my eyes devouring every inch of his beautiful face. He had a strong jaw, straight nose, thick, dark brows, dark lashes that lined a pair of eyes I could stare into for hours, and the most beautiful hair that suddenly made me feel a little self-conscious about my own that I'd only recently started to grow back after fleeing Antonio. I no longer felt the need to keep it shorter since the three alphas I lived with would never grab the tresses to hold me still while they beat me senseless.

"You okay?" he asked, bending at the knees to see eye to eye with me.

"Huh? Oh. Yeah. Yes. Thank you." I raised my hands and touched my fingertips to my lips. I swore they tingled and my whole body was warm.

This man was absolutely an omega, yet he was so tall. Not quite as big as Ax, Enzo, or Cyrus, but at least close to six feet tall. And he was ripped and solid. I wasn't sure I'd ever seen an omega so...big. Even the male omegas tended to be on the smaller and softer side. Not this guy.

He was...holy shit, he was hot.

Or the alcohol was officially kicking in. I was definitely feeling buzzed and now, after that toe curling kiss, I was definitely feeling horny, as well.

"Amir," he said, offering his hand, then bringing mine to his lips to feather a kiss to my knuckles.

A giggle tore from me as I ducked my gaze a second. I'd only ever seen a man kiss a woman's hand in the damn movies. No one I'd ever been with had ever done something so sweet and romantic.

"Isabelle. *Issa*," I said.

I glanced over my shoulder again, looking for Cyrus, but he was with another group, pouring drinks into a row of shot glasses.

"Want to dance?" he asked.

"Uh..." I wasn't sure where Enzo was, and Ax was getting ready backstage. But they'd assured me there was plenty of security here to make sure I was safe. Surely, being on the dance floor couldn't be seen as risky being as I would be surrounded by so many people.

And, it might have been stupid, but Amir didn't feel like a threat, and not only because he was an omega.

"Yeah. Actually, I'd love to dance."

When was the last time I'd gone dancing? When was the last time I'd truly let myself just...be? I literally couldn't remember. Whether because it had been so long, because the alcohol was officially screaming through my veins, or because my body was hyper aware of everything Amir did from the moment he wrapped his hand around mine to pull me onto the dance floor to when his body pressed close to mine and began to move to the beat, his moves as smooth and sure as Ax's.

One of his big hands was pressed to the small of my back, the other held my hand. Our lower halves were pressed so firmly I could feel his hard length against my belly.

Between the alcohol, my unrequited crush on my pack, this omega's delicious scent, and the beat, I began to wonder if this was how an omega felt before going into heat.

Tilting my head back, I smiled up at him, pressing myself closer. I had never been good at coming out and asking for what I wanted, probably because it had never mattered to anyone in my life.

But in the three short months since I'd moved in with Enzo, Ax, and Cyrus, they'd shown me alphas and the opposite sex of any designation could be kind and caring and generous. They'd taught me it was okay to be myself.

Problem was I was still trying to figure that out. I had no idea who I was if I wasn't the daughter of Pack Alvarez, if I wasn't the beta of Antonio Rossi.

Amir's striking green eyes bore into mine as the sexiest smirk pulled up his pillowy lips. Did he have a pack? Did he have alphas somewhere in this club or at home waiting for him? And how free it must have been to simply be able to go out without either someone hawk eying your every movement or dictating your every step.

The music slowly faded out and the lights dimmed until only the bar was lit.

"Ladies and gents, put your hands together for the men of The Vault!" someone called over the big speakers all around the room.

Amir didn't release his hold on me, instead moving me to stand in front of him and wrapping his arms around my waist to keep my back to his front.

And yep, he was still sporting a rather impressive boner that rested against my ass through his pants and my skimpy dress.

Oh, how easy it would have been for him to release his cock, lift my skirt, and take me right there on the dance floor while everyone was distracted by the men who were filing onto the raised stage.

It took me a second to find Ax. His eyes were on me, a wide grin flashing in the dark. A second later, the opening music to *The Saints* by Andy Mineo started and I squealed. I'd seen the choreography for this particular dance but had only seen my alpha practicing it alone. I couldn't wait to see all of them dancing together.

The men began to move, some darting forward while another line moved back. It didn't matter how many times I'd seen Ax dance – the way he rolled his hips made me wish he would see me...differently. I wished he would look at me the way Amir did while we danced. I wished he would see me as someone more than a packmate.

I wanted him to see me as *his*. I wanted them all to want me to be theirs.

But I would remain thankful the three alphas had taken it upon themselves to not only give me a place to stay where I would be safe but took it upon themselves to protect me on a daily basis. They were patient with me, taught me to speak up for myself, and gave me the support I needed to heal from the years of conditioning by first my fathers then my alpha.

Not my alpha. He was never my fucking alpha. He'd been someone my parents had chosen for me, regardless of what I wanted for my own life. It didn't even matter to them that I wasn't an omega like my sister. They had arranged the packs for all six of us, including my beta brothers.

Ax was back in the front, his eyes on me as he smiled and winked a second before doing this move where he jumped then dropped to the ground, rolling his hips like there was someone below him. With his body moving like water and Amir pressed against me, his scent wrapping around me and going down my throat with every breath, his arms tight around me and his cock pressed against my back…

I was going to combust. There was no way around it. I either needed to find a way to ease the constant sexual frustration or I would go out of my damn mind.

As the music came to an end, the men all stepped to the front of the stage in nothing but low-slung jeans or sweats and smiled as the crowd erupted into catcalls, screams, whistles, and applause.

Ax tossed his shirt at me, smacking me in the face with his yummy, spiced rum signature.

"Damn, girl. I think that man is flirting with you," Amir said in my ear, his lips grazing the outer shell and sending shivers down my spine.

"He's my…he's a friend. I live with him and his pack."

"He's your alpha?"

"No…he's…no. He's my roommate."

Yeah. They'd declared today that I was pack, had almost looked disappointed that I didn't see myself that way, but it always felt like I was their kid sister with the way they touched me in chaste ways, the way they ruffled my hair and teased me.

The way they would have sex in the other room while I laid there each time trying not to be a perv, only to end up touching myself to the sounds and their increased hormones on the air.

As the dancers left the stage, the overhead lights started flashing again and the music thumped a seductive beat through the room.

And I could have sworn that same beat was thrumming through my body straight to my clit.

Amir turned me in his arms, swaying his hips with mine again. "Fuck, you're sexy," he said, his sweet breath brushing over my lips to land on my tongue.

Had anyone ever referred to me as sexy? Cyrus told me I was beautiful tonight. Ax and Enzo both teased me, saying I looked good.

But sexy?

"Let me buy you a drink," he said, leaning his mouth close to my ear.

"I'm a beta. Aren't I supposed to buy you the drink?"

He waved a hand through the air, giving me a look as though I'd said something ridiculous, before leading me to the bar. Cyrus wasn't behind it anymore, but I recognized the bartender who'd been working alongside him earlier and flagged him down.

"Honey, the last thing I have ever or will ever do is go by rules made by stupid people. There isn't a way in hell I'm letting some-one..." His eyes roamed me from head to toe slowly and I swore it felt like he was physically caressing every inch of my body. "Who looks like you spend her money on me."

The beta was already pouring me a new martini before I bothered telling him, then asked for Amir's order.

"Can we have two shots of..." Shit. What had Ax ordered for us earlier? It had burned going down, but I swore it had been pure liquid courage. "Do you know Ax's favorite liquor?"

With a smile, Jaden nodded and got to work, pouring a beer from the tap for Amir, then setting two shot glasses of dark liquor before us.

"To the most beautiful woman in here," Amir said, holding his glass up with a beautiful smile that caused tiny creases at the corners of his light eyes.

"To the most beautiful *man* in here," I countered.

Yep. One hundred percent pure liquid courage. Because no way in hell would I have ever been brave enough to dance with some random man, omega or not, had Ax not plied me with booze.

And I sure as hell wouldn't be flirting so openly.

We finished off our drinks. Danced some more. Then headed back to the bar for two more rounds of shots. And I was officially tipsy. Or maybe drunk.

Definitely horny.

Amir had kissed me on the dancefloor, his tongue teasing mine, tasting me. His body had been pressed so close to mine, one of his hands dangerously close to the swell of my ass, the other cupping the back of my head to hold me in place.

There was a voice at the back of my head telling me to check for my alphas, find out if they'd met their omega yet. Especially since the point of me coming tonight was to meet her. But I was having entirely too much fun with Amir. And just because they found someone they might want to add to their pack didn't mean I couldn't find someone who wanted more from me than another friend.

"I want you so badly," Amir growled into my ear. Or maybe it was a purr.

Didn't matter. I wanted him, too. And because my boys owned this place, I just happened to know a few rooms where we could be alone long enough to play.

"I need to taste you," he said.

Pulling back, I gave him what I hoped was a sexy smile, wrapped my hand around his, then began to tug him through the crowd and to one of the offices that not only locked from the inside but was rarely used.

Punching in the code to enter, I pulled Amir in behind me then turned the deadbolt into place. Just because it was rarely used while the club was full didn't mean I wanted to run the risk of one of the employees catching me in a compromising situation.

Like bent over the desk with Amir pumping into me from behind.

CHAPTER 7

Issa

The moment I turned toward him, Amir cupped my face in his big hands and slammed his lips against mine, pushing me against the door. It was a bruising, claiming kiss, and I couldn't get enough. His hair was so soft in my hands as I tangled my fingers in the curls, trying to get closer as if that was at all possible.

His hands left my face and smoothed down my throat, my shoulders, to cup my breasts through the dress. He rubbed a thumb over one of my pebbled nipples, tearing a gasp from my throat.

"Fuck, you smell good," he murmured against my lips.

When he pulled away, I swayed a little, both from the alcohol and the lust, but he pressed a hand to my stomach to hold me up as he dropped to his knees before me, shoving my dress up my hips to bury his face against my thong covered pussy.

"I need to taste you," he said, his breath warm against my sensitive skin, even with the barrier of the cotton and lace.

His fingers shoved my panties to the side as I gripped his hair, dropping my head against the door. The bass vibrated against my back as Amir purred against me, the deepest sound I'd ever heard come from an omega.

His tongue flattened against my core and made a long, slow swipe, earning a guttural moan.

"Holy shit," I breathed out as he began to focus his attention on my clit, sucking it between his lips, flicking it with his tongue. When he slowly pushed a finger inside of me, my insides began to tighten.

I'd orgasmed before. But only when I was alone. This omega had barely spent five minutes expertly playing my body and already I was coiling tighter than a spring and ready to explode.

"You're going to make me come," I moaned.

Who was this wanton person? I barely recognized my own voice let alone my thoughts and actions. I had never taken a stranger into the back room of a public – and packed – place to fool around.

Who was I kidding? I planned on getting fucked by this omega, not just fooling around.

"Good," he said against my folds at my declaration. "I want to taste you on my tongue for the rest of the night."

His finger pumped in and out of my core while the other held me to the door. Had he not been holding me up, I was sure my knees would have buckled until I crashed to the floor, especially when he added a second finger then teased my back entrance with his pinky.

Unintelligible words began to spill from my lips as I babbled and moaned. That spring that had tightened exploded, my inner walls clenching around Amir's fingers.

He pulled his mouth from me, still fucking me with his fingers, and launched to his feet, claiming my mouth with his and stealing my moans.

As I finally began to come down from the release and the after-shocks slowed, he pulled back and smirked down at me. "I wanted those moans all to myself."

"And I want you inside of me. More than your fingers."

Yep. I'd gotten off by his mouth and fingers. And now I wanted to feel that bulge that had been teasing me all night bared to my hand, my mouth, and my body. I wanted to feel him stretching me, filling me. I wanted to fall apart around him again, to hear his sounds of pleasure.

Instead of waiting for him, I reached between us and fumbled with his button and zipper, my numb, drunken fingers slipping a few times as we giggled.

"Bend me over the desk," I said, my voice throaty, husky, and completely alien to my own ears.

I squealed a giggle when he pulled me from the door and whirled me toward the desk that smelled heavily of Cyrus's warm, wet wood scent. And for some reason, being taken by a stranger over his desk made me wetter than I'd known was possible for a beta.

Any plans I'd made of stroking him with my hand, of taking him into my mouth, went right out the window when one of his hands gripped my hip so hard, I hoped it would leave bruises while the other shoved my panties to the side again so he could press himself against my core, the smooth head nudging against my entrance.

Glancing at the omega over my shoulder, I said something I had never thought would leave my lips.

"Fuck me hard."

A very unomega-like growl rumbled from him a second before he whipped his hips forward, slamming into me, his cock stretching me almost to the point of pain. He was so thick, so long.

I'd never been with an omega, but from everything I'd ever heard, male omegas tended to be tender and sensitive and small... everywhere.

Either Amir was an anomaly, or all those people were full of shit.

There was nothing small or tender about the way his hips smacked against my ass, causing my own hips to hit the edge of the desk as I scrambled for something to keep me steady and only causing a mess on the desktop as I knocked over a cup of pens and sent loose papers fluttering to the floor.

"Holy fuck," Amir growled. "You are so fucking perfect."

Something else I'd never heard from a single person in my life. And I didn't care whether he was as drunk as me, if he was saying what he wanted me to hear, or if his hindbrain had taken over. At this moment, all I cared about was how he was making me feel, the sensations he stirred in my body, in my mind, deep inside my chest.

We weren't using protection, but omegas couldn't impregnate anyone. Not that he couldn't have some kind of scary disease. But my brain was equal parts desire and liquor; there was no room for forethought or logic. Only want. Only desire. Only need.

The grunts coming from Amir was like gasoline on a flame, sending me spiraling, spiraling, spiraling, until I threw back my head and cried out with another release.

"Your cunt is squeezing my dick so perfectly. I want to come in you. I want you to walk through that club smelling like me for the rest of the night."

"Yes. Please. Fill me. Come in me," I cried between nonsensical sounds and words.

Both hands gripped my hips hard, he slammed into me hard enough I wondered if he hadn't actually bruised my cervix, then the sexiest guttural moan floated around me as heat filled me with each twitch and jerk of his dick.

As we stayed the way we were, my forehead resting against the cool wood, his big body draped over my back, and his cock still deep inside me, the beeps of the outside lock came a second before the knob turned, then a heavy fist pounded against the door.

"Issa?" Enzo's deep voice came through the door.

Shit. This was not how I wanted them to see me, some wanton slut fucking a stranger in one of their offices at the club they owned.

"Your alpha?" Amir asked, quickly pulling from me and helping me fix my dress before tucking his cock away.

"Yeah," I said instead of once again explaining our living situation.

Running my fingers through my hair and swiping them across my lips to fix my makeup, I hurried to the door and turned the deadbolt out of place before opening the door to find Enzo smirking at me with a raised brow.

His eyes rose over my head, a look of surprise and something else flitting across his face before he stepped further into the room and closed the door behind him.

"Guess I don't need to make introductions," Enzo said.

I frowned at him, then turned to look at Amir.

Amir's brows were raised up his forehead. "This is one of your alphas?"

"He's not—"

"Yes," Enzo said, cutting me off.

A deep chuckle rattled from his chest as his eyes roamed me from head to toe. Even if he hadn't smelled the perfume exploding from Amir, there was no way he couldn't tell what we'd been doing in here.

"I'm glad you two are getting along so well already."

Like someone had thrown ice water over my head, I turned to look at Amir.

"Were you here to..." I looked at Enzo. "This is the omega you were meeting tonight? Who you wanted me to meet?"

That smirk was still on his face as he nodded. "I didn't know he was going to be early or I would have arranged a table in the VIP section."

Oh no. I'd just fucked the omega my pack was hoping to court, hoping to add to the pack. I had literally thrown myself at him, begged him to bend me over Cyrus's desk like some needy...

Lifting my hands, I covered my face as my cheeks felt like they would burst into flames.

Gentle hands pulled them away and I was surprised to see a concerned look on Enzo's face.

"Why are you embarrassed? He's hot. And he obviously wanted you. You can't think you two are the first to utilize one of the offices."

"Okay, picturing the three of you getting busy back here is not helping," I said, jabbing a finger at his chest.

We teased and play flirted, but little did they know...my flirting was real. It wasn't an act when I told them they were hot or that I was jealous of their one-night flings. I wanted them in a way that...well, in a way Amir would have them if things went well.

"I'm sorry. I didn't know he was...shit." I was still buzzed from the shots and drinks, but my embarrassment over the situation was making things both clear *and* more confusing.

Because I really, really wanted this omega.

Yet he'd come here to meet the alphas, come to see whether they would be compatible, to see whether they were all interested in the whole courting thing.

That concept was still a little foreign to me. In my world, in my family, alphas simply took what they wanted. They didn't bother asking the omega or even beta what they wanted or whether they were interested in joining the pack.

But Enzo was the brother of my sister's alpha. While Corazon's pack hadn't exactly courted her in the beginning, they'd made damn sure to make up for lost time and constantly smothered her in gifts and affection.

It didn't hurt that the five of them were expecting their first child.

Neither Cora nor I had any idea what loving parents looked like, yet the alphas of Pack Rivera were so damn loving toward her and had bought far more than any child would ever need before the pup was born.

"What the hell are you sorry for?" Enzo asked, his brows pulled together in confusion as a very amused look glittered in his eyes and his lips quirked as though he was trying and failing to hide a smile.

"If you're sorry, I definitely didn't do any of that right," Amir teased.

I looked between the two of them, looking for...I wasn't sure. Disapproval? Judgment? Anger?

Amir looked content, sated, relaxed.

And a little aroused.

His pupils were blown again, and his sweet scent was filling the air and making it hard to focus.

Or maybe that was the booze swimming through my veins.

"You definitely did everything right," I said, wincing at the feeling of his release leaking from me. I really needed to rush to the bathroom and clean up. We'd barely finished, had only started to catch our breath when Enzo had knocked on the door.

"Does that mean you're okay with us courting him?" Enzo asked. He leaned against the door, crossing his arms and legs, and smirked at me. "If Amir is amenable, that is."

"Amir still needs to meet the other two," Amir said, looking from Enzo to me before winking. "But this little vixen does live with you, right? She's pack?"

"No. I'm–"

"Yes. She is," Enzo said, all playfulness missing from his face as he cocked a brow at me. Because he wanted me to put Amir at ease or because I once again denied that I was a member of their pack?

"When can I meet the other two?"

"You saw one of them on stage," Enzo said, that sexy smirk back on his lips.

Amir turned to me and raised both brows.

"He was the alpha who threw the shirt at me after he was done dancing."

"Oh, damn. He smelled amazing. Or at least his shirt did. Who's the third?"

"Cyrus. He's been behind the bar off and on, but I can text both of them to meet us in here. Unless you two would be more comfortable out there–"

"No," I blurted. And I wasn't quite sure why I was suddenly reluctant to leave this room.

Part of me felt as though every single person out there would instantly know that I'd screwed a stranger in the office. The other part of me didn't want any of those people out there to so much as get a glimpse of this incredibly beautiful omega.

Mine.

I was only a beta, yet I was ready to stake my claim on the man, to rub against him like a cat to leave my scent on him, but also to smother myself in his.

I couldn't exactly mark his flesh like an alpha, but I sure as hell could find other ways to stake my claim.

CHAPTER 8

<u>Ax</u>

"Did you know she could dance?" I asked Cyrus as we hurried to Cyrus's office where Enzo, Issa, and the omega waited for us.

"How would I know that? I'm still surprised we even got her out of the house. And how the hell did you convince her to wear that dress?"

We had all taken plenty of time filling her closet and drawers with new clothing after she'd agreed to stay with us.

Issa hadn't been given the opportunity to live her own life because of her fucked up parents, who had been killed by Enzo's brother and his pack, and that apparently included being allowed the luxury of a full closet. She wore whatever they deemed appropriate, or what her piece of shit alpha, whom she'd been forced to bond with, wanted to see her in.

Neither Issa nor her sister Corazon seemed the least bit phased their parents were dead, but they still had a lasting effect on both women … especially in the way they saw themselves when they looked in the mirror. Issa was beautiful and majestic, yet we could tell even though she tried to hide it that she didn't believe she was worthy of true affection from anyone.

I knew I wasn't the only one struggling to restrain myself around the gorgeous beta. We were constantly visiting each other's rooms on a regular basis. From the moment the gorgeous dark-haired beta filled our home with her soft, clean scent, I'd walked around with a chubby.

But she needed time to heal. The last thing I or the others wanted was to make her uncomfortable by pawing at her or for her to think she owed us a damn thing.

As far as I was concerned, she was already ours, whether she carried our mark or not, whether she ever allowed us into her bed or her body or not.

"You know they fucked on your desk, right?" I teased as we pushed through the crowd of dancers. A few people patted me on my shoulder or back and told me I'd done a good job on stage. And yep – I ate that shit up. I would never deny I was a bit of an attention whore, but I also really loved to dance.

And might have intentionally asked Issa to watch me rehearse a few times under the guise of needing her opinion when really...I was hoping to make her want me.

Enzo had texted us letting us know where he'd found Issa and with who and that they'd both appeared as though they'd had the fucking of their lives. Arousal and jealousy crashed through me. But if this omega was half as tempting as Enzo had declared through our group text, then there would hopefully be a time – hopefully sooner rather than later – that I would get the chance to feel him under my hands. And if we could talk Issa into joining us? All the better.

From the corner of my eye, I caught Cyrus adjusting himself as we neared the door. I knew the feeling; I'd been hard as stone since I'd watched Issa shower like a fucking voyeur.

I don't know why I kept flirting with her. Nah. I totally knew why – I was hoping to get her to see me as more than the guy she lived with, more than the alpha who'd helped her after she'd escaped her abuser. I wanted her to see me as her packmate, as her alpha.

As we neared the closed office door, the heady, sweet smell of chocolate and strawberries tickled my senses and sent blood rushing straight to my cock.

"Damn," I muttered under my breath.

Cyrus punched in the code then pushed open the door. Enzo was seated in a chair across from the desk, Issa sat on the edge, her thighs clenched together tightly, and her arms wrapped around her middle. And the omega…

"Wow," Cyrus said under his breath as I closed the door behind us. Clearing his throat, he stepped forward, extending a hand. "I'm Cyrus. Thank you for taking the time to meet with us."

"Are you kidding?" the omega said, pushing a hand through his thick mane of curly hair. He was masculine yet there was a softness to his eyes, the perfect specimen of an omega.

He wasn't petite or dainty, yet his lips were full and pillowy, and I had to fight from picturing those lips around my cock…or on Issa's body.

The beta in question was having a hard time making eye contact with us.

"Tonight was a blast. Your beta is…sorry, girl, but you are hands down the sexiest woman I've ever met."

Issa smiled and ducked her gaze as her olive complected cheeks blushed bright red.

"And you move like a cat. I swear you had every single person in the room purring or perfuming," he said to me as he shook Cyrus's hand.

"Does that mean you're down to letting us court you?" I asked.

"As long as this little vixen is part of the package, you can court me 'til you're blue in the face."

Issa's cheeks went even brighter as she fidgeted with the short hem of her dress. She smelled heavily of chocolate covered strawberries and her clean sheets dried in the sun scent. We had cameras in here, and I didn't give a fuck if it made me a perv, but I had every intention of reviewing the footage from their time in here the second I could wrap my fist around my cock.

"She's pack. She's definitely part of the package," Enzo said, winking at Issa.

Cyrus was the only one who didn't outright flirt and throw out sexual innuendos at Issa. But no matter how much we teased and flirted with her, she acted as though she wasn't interested. It was so much harder with a beta because her scent wouldn't give her away; we wouldn't be able to smell her arousal like we would an omega, wouldn't scent her slick.

I wanted to bristle at the thought there was a woman out there who didn't find me irresistible, but I supposed I would remain content as long as she stayed under the same roof with us. She might never want us romantically, but we could still keep her part of the family and keep her safe.

"Then I'm down with you courting me," Amir said.

We hadn't bothered telling Issa anything about the omega, hadn't told her Amir was a man. We hadn't wanted to influence her one way or another, although I could tell she'd become insecure the moment we'd told her we were meeting with someone tonight and wanted her approval. Because if she hadn't gotten along with Amir, if the two of them hadn't clicked, the whole thing would have been off. Issa came first, whether she realized it or not.

Amir turned to Issa. "As long as you're okay with that."

She blinked a few times, her attention roaming to each of us as though surprised she had a say in this.

"You have the deciding vote, beta," Enzo said, leaning back in the chair until the two front legs came off the ground.

"I...what?"

Amir closed the small distance between them and took her hands into his, bending at the knee to look into her eye. The three of us were several inches over six feet, but Amir wasn't small and delicate. He looked as though he stood somewhere close to five-foot-nine or ten and towered over our sweet beta who'd taken months to come out of her shell.

"This is your pack, *Habibi*. I would never come between you and your alphas." A sexy soft smile quirked up one side of his full lips. "Although, I would ask that I get the chance to continue seeing you."

Issa's head twitched like she'd been shocked, and her eyes went wide. "You would still want to see me? Without them?"

"Well…yeah." He released one of her hands to push the hair from his face. "I mean, I would love to be a member of your pack someday, but you were the one who caught my attention first. Your alphas are just a bonus."

"Damn. That stings," I muttered but couldn't wipe the smile from my face.

Issa glanced at me and rolled her eyes with a smile. "Yeah," she finally said.

"Yes? You're okay with the four of you courting me?"

"Betas don't–"

"Nope. Stop with the rule bullshit. We've already discussed this," Enzo said, cutting her off before she could spout more nonsense she'd been fed by her fathers growing up.

She looked to Enzo, and I tried my best to decipher the look she shot his way. She looked equal parts confused and overjoyed.

"Then, yes. I'm more than okay with them – *us* courting you."

"Fuck yes," I said, pumping my fist in the air like a complete douche.

But the smile on Issa's face made my excitement grow even more. It had taken weeks for her to stop asking permission for simple things like eating food from the fridge or pantry. Weeks for her to stop asking permission to do mundane things. Weeks for her to accept the little gifts we bestowed on her – although to me, they were all necessities. She'd come with nothing but clothes her sister had loaned her. We'd had to buy her a whole new wardrobe, along with all the toiletries and beauty products women loved.

It had taken even longer to get her comfortable with leaving the house and that was only if at least one of us with her, even if she was simply being driven to her sister's to visit for the day.

But here she was decked out and looking like a fucking goddess, her skin glowing from her time with Amir, and finally allowing herself to admit she was not only a member of our pack but had a say in what happened in our lives.

We'd never sat down and had some heart-to-heart conversation about her place with us; to me, it had all felt natural, from the moment I'd laid eyes on her slumped in her wrecked car to the moment she'd agreed to stay with us. Although, I think in her mind, she'd thought we'd meant temporarily.

We hadn't had a conversation with her, but the three of us – me, Enzo, and Cyrus – all agreed she belonged in our lives. And my pack-mates were falling as hard for her as I was. I was sure there were ways we could have won her over, some romantic gestures that would have helped her to see us as her alphas rather than alphas she lived with, but...none of us really had a clue what the fuck we were doing.

Even this whole courting thing with the omega was new to us. We'd wanted an omega, sure. Most packs of alphas wanted an omega in the mix. But we'd wanted things to be right, especially after bringing Issa into our lives. Whoever joined the family had to love her as much as we did. They had to accept her as much as they accepted us, cherish her the way she deserved.

"Now that we got that out of the way, would you prefer to stay at your own home during the process or with us? We have plenty of room. Don't we, Issa?" Enzo said, turning a flirtatious smirk toward our beta and making her blush again.

Damn. We had seen her in nearly every state except sexual. We'd all seen her naked at one point or another, but none of us had yet to actually touch her. None of us had heard the sounds she would make while being pleasured nor how she would sound when she got off.

Oh, but I absolutely would hear those sounds the moment we got home and I was in my bedroom. And I had every intention of rubbing one off while watching the sexy ass beta fucked by the equally sexy omega right there on Cyrus's desk.

CHAPTER 9

<u>Issa</u>

There was a part of me that had hoped Amir would agree to stay with us while the alphas...while *we* courted him. But I knew his time would end up being monopolized by the sexy as hell and dominant alphas.

But that also meant if I wanted to see the omega, I either had to get over my fear of leaving the house solo, or he would have to come here. And with him being here, we were right back to that very same problem. Unless he and I scheduled our home dates for when the alphas were away at work.

Amir was an omega. There was zero doubt about his designation, but he was far from some helpless damsel. Had that alpha continued to harass me after Amir had pretended to be my date, I knew he could have held his own in a fight. He wasn't small, his body was rippling with muscle, and he carried so much power that it was physically palpable. Had I not caught his scent, I would have actually assumed he was like Ax, Enzo, and Cyrus.

"You're sure you're okay with this?" Cyrus asked as we all walked through the kitchen after coming home from the club.

The cool thing about them owning The Vault was the fact they could hand the closing duties off to their employees. As they had tonight so they could get me home before four in the morning.

"I'm okay with it," I assured him for the fourth time since we'd left through the employee entrance and climbed into the Land Rover.

"So..." Ax started as we headed up the stairs. "You and the omega on Cyrus's desk."

"Seriously, Ax?" I said, swatting at his hands as he ran a finger along the neckline of my dress. My face felt as though it would go into flames.

He held his hands up and followed me into my room instead of retreating to his own. In fact, all three of them had followed me in and were watching me with varying expressions on their stupidly good-looking faces.

"We're just happy that you're finally putting all that bullshit behind you. I, for one, was starting to wonder if you no longer had a measurable libido," Ax said, flopping back onto my bed hard enough to bounce.

"For fuck's sake," Enzo said, but I'd noted the increase in his coppery scent. Any time he was in the mood, his signature went from the sweet, tangy scent to more of a burned, frayed wire smell. And I loved it. I wanted to bottle it so I could carry it with me. Or pour it on my bed and roll around in it until every inch of my body was covered in his essence.

Or the scents and release from all three of them.

What the hell was going on with me? The alcohol had left my system, leaving me tired, so I could no longer blame my wanton thoughts on the buzz.

"I have a libido, jerk," I said, moving to the dresser and rifling through until I found my favorite tank top and shorts combo to change into for bed. But I needed to wash all this makeup off.

I should have probably showered, too, wash off the sweat from dancing and...other activities. But I wasn't quite ready to lose the sweetness that clung to me after my time with Amir.

"You could have told me it was a male omega," I called through the open bathroom door as I pulled out my skin care products and started the process of not only removing the makeup and grime from the night but slathering my skin in oils and serums and moisturizers.

"And ruin the surprise?" Ax said from way too close.

I jerked upright and glared at him in the mirror, my eyes resembling a racoon as I scrubbed away the eyeshadow, liner, and mascara. "You weren't content stinking up my bedroom and bed with your odor so you thought you'd follow me in here?"

Leaning down, I splashed the warm water on my face to rinse the cleanser and squealed when he leaned over me and wrapped his arms around my waist.

"Oh please. You love my odor." He then proceeded to run his cheek and chin anywhere he could reach without either knocking me over or getting my product all over him.

Yep. Teasing me like a big brother.

If the whole thing with Amir worked out, at least I knew *he* didn't see me as a sister. And if he did...nope. Not the kind of man I wanted in my bed.

Chuckling at my own thoughts, I grabbed a towel, patted my face dry, then bumped my hips back to dislodge Ax's tight hold around me.

"Ooh. Foreplay," he said, but moved away and leaned against the doorframe, watching as I went through each step of my routine.

"We wanted the meet and greet to be organic," Cyrus said, still in my bedroom instead of crowding me in here like Ax.

"Instead, it ended up orgasmic," Enzo said with a chuckle.

Ax turned wide eyes and a wider grin toward his – *our* packmate. "That was awesome! I wish I'd come up with it."

He finally left me alone to finish up. I closed the door and locked it so I could change into my pajamas, then stepped out to find them all piled on my bed in nothing but their boxers.

"Sooo...are we having a slumber party or something?"

"We're bonding tonight," Cyrus said, lifting the comforter and waiting for me to cross the room.

"Bonding?"

My body instantly ignited at the concept. Because I'd done nothing but fantasize about these three men for months and they were in my bed. In fact, they'd invited themselves instead of me having to blurt out how I really felt about them.

"You need a reminder that you're pack. We're snuggling tonight. You're going to hold off showering until tomorrow night. Then we're going to take the omega on a date," Enzo said as though it made total sense.

And deflated my hopes. Because they merely wanted to leave their scent on me, assert their earlier claim that I was a packmate and not a temporary roommate.

"*We're* taking him on a date, or *you* are?" I asked, climbing under the blanket beside Cyrus and sighing when he tugged me closer, turning me so my back was to his front.

"Hey! Why do you get to snuggle her?" Ax whined, climbing from the far side and jostling all of us as he scooted and crawled until he was lying directly in front of me, a teasing smile on the lips I constantly dreamed of kissing. "Much better," he said as he lined his body along my front, although the position was a little awkward.

I wasn't used to sleeping beside a man when I'd first come here. I wasn't used to sleeping beside anyone.

Antonio and I had had our own rooms, our own beds. The beta who'd been forced into our pack only spent a few nights with us before he'd disappeared into the ether. I was unsure whether he was alive or dead.

So having so many warm, hard bodies around me could be both comfortable and unsettling.

We'd slept together in my bed in the past, but it seemed as though it was always Ax calling for a pack cuddle. Not me.

The urge to push my butt against Cyrus, to wiggle my hips as an invitation warred with the urge to slide my hand under the sheets and touch Ax.

But slow, steady breathing and the light rumbling of a snore told me everyone had fallen asleep within minutes of the lights being turned off.

And I laid there staring into the dark.

So many things had happened tonight, so many changes were coming, and my mind wouldn't shut down. I'd always preferred to read before bed or even watch a show I'd seen dozens of times to get my brain to at least slow enough to rest.

These alphas had completely wrecked my nightly routine.

I couldn't complain, though.

I loved being wedged between them, even in such an innocent way. I had fantasized about being sandwiched between them naked while all three of them used my body for pleasure while making me cry out with release.

At least they were here with me tonight. If I woke with a nightmare, I could snuggle into their warmth and let them chase away the darkness.

With nothing else to occupy myself, I let my mind wander back to the evening's events, to meeting that beautiful omega, to feeling his lips on mine and how that kiss had felt natural, as though we had kissed a thousand times, while also setting my body aflame.

I still couldn't believe I'd led him back to Cyrus's office, that I had willingly spread my legs while he'd knelt and eaten me until I'd come on his tongue. Then I'd begged him to take me hard against Cyrus's desk.

I wasn't sure I'd ever truly been the kind of person who would refer to herself as overly sexual, but damn if Amir didn't bring something wild out in me.

Not just Amir. Ax and Cyrus and Enzo constantly made me overly aware of their every move. I was constantly aware of the way their back muscles or biceps would bulge while doing mundane chores around the house, the way their jeans encased their firm assess, or their sweats perfectly outlined their long, thick cocks.

Turned out it wasn't that I didn't dislike sex, I just didn't like the thought of Antonio touching me. Didn't matter if he doped me - I always knew after that he'd used my body without bothering to ask whether I was in the mood, or to take his time to prime my body, or to make sure I found my release before him.

With the alphas surrounding me, I couldn't reach for my phone to check the time, but it sure felt as though I'd been lying in bed for over an hour, waiting for sleep to find me. My body and mind were both exhausted, yet I couldn't seem to make either shut down enough to rest.

"What's wrong?" Ax whispered, startling me.

"Can't sleep," I whispered back.

I opened my eyes to find him staring at me, only a sliver of moonlight across his face illuminating the sharp angles of his cheekbones and his square jaw.

"Are we making you uncomfortable? I can wake them up and tell them to go to their own beds."

Wake *them* up. Tell *them* to go to *their* beds. He didn't volunteer to move away. And I sure as hell didn't want him to, not yet.

"No. Just a lot on my mind. Tonight was..."

"Amazing? Hot? Spank bank worthy?"

I lifted a hand and clapped it over my mouth as I began to chuckle. "Spank bank worthy? Really? How would you know whether it was hot or not?"

"We have cameras everywhere. I haven't watched it yet, but I have every intention of jerking off to that video later."

A gasp pulled from my lips. I tried to come up with some witty retort, but my brain short circuited as it was taken over by need, desire.

There would be footage of everything Amir and I had done in that office.

And whether Ax was joking or not, it would be easy for any of the three of them to watch every moment. And yeah, I liked the idea of them being turned on by it, by watching as Amir licked my cunt, as he'd bent me over the desk, only pulling my panties out of the way so he could slam his long, thick cock inside me over and over until I'd practically melted into a puddle.

We both went quiet again, but Ax's breathing hadn't gone slow and steady like the two alphas at my back.

"Can I ask you something?" I whispered.

"Of course," he whispered back. He shuffled until his face was only inches away, his lips barely a breath from mine. It wouldn't take much for me to move forward to finally taste his spiced rum on my tongue.

"Why did you think…oh man. This is kind of embarrassing."

He wiggled a little until he could slide one of his knees between mine. "Now I really need to hear your question."

I swore this alpha was never serious. Even when I'd seen him come back bruised and somewhat bloody from playing bouncer at the club, he still had a smirk or a smile on his face like life was nothing but a game to him.

"Why did you guys think I wasn't interested in sex?"

I was glad the lights were off and he couldn't see how red my face had gone.

But I also wished I could see him as he answered. Someone could lie with their mouths, but there was no way to lie with your eyes.

I swore I felt his shoulders shift as though he'd shrugged. "You never seemed interested in the three of us."

I blinked. Then blinked again. "You guys are always screwing around together in your own rooms. Why would I think you were interested in anything more with me?"

"Girl. I flirt with you nonstop. You've literally caught me watching you shower on more than a dozen occasions. Why do you think I hang out in your room so much?"

"I thought…it felt like you saw me as a sister or something?"

"Ew. No. I have sisters and trust me when I say I've never once watched them shower or dress nor have I picked out skimpy dresses for them to go out to the club. If I had my way, all four of them would walk around in turtlenecks and snow pants until they were forty. Or longer."

The bed shook lightly as I giggled.

"You really had no idea we wanted you? As in wanted you in our bed?"

"You've never said anything. Or touched me. And yeah, you flirt with me, but you flirt with anyone with a pulse."

"Oh please. I am not that bad," he whispered.

"Yes. You are. And if you two are going to fool around, could you do it in another room so I can get some sleep?" Cyrus muttered, his voice scratchy and hoarse with sleep.

My eyes widened and I sucked in a breath a half second before Ax chuckled deeply.

"He's crabby when he's horny," Ax said, no longer whispering.

"Dumb ass," Cyrus said before hugging me tighter to his chest.

Sure didn't feel like he wanted me to leave the bed so Ax and I could fool around.

And, even if this embrace wasn't technically considered sexual, it confirmed what Ax had said. I'd been looking past all the little signs, all the teasing and flirting and ignoring the fact the alphas not only wanted me as a packmate. They wanted me to be their beta romantically.

CHAPTER 10

Enzo

Cyrus pulled the Land Rover we used when we all needed to ride together – or when Issa was determined to look her best for this first date – onto a long, dirt driveway.

"You sure this is the right place?" Ax asked from the backseat beside Issa.

It had taken every ounce of my control to pretend to be asleep as I'd listened to her whispered conversation with Ax. And I'd had this sick, voyeuristic need to hear them fucking around.

But then Cyrus had gone and opened his big, fucking mouth and they'd both clammed up.

She hadn't realized we were attracted to her? Did she not see herself when she looked in the mirror?

Issa and Corazon – my brother's omega – were similar, yet different. Where Corazon was petite and curvy with big tits, a big ass, and wide hips, Issa was a couple inches taller and…shit, that was about where their body differences ended. Issa had amazing tits, wide hips, and a bubble ass that all three of us had ogled more times than she would ever realize.

Both women had thick, dark hair, but Issa's was growing out from just above shoulder length when we'd met to now past her shoulders. She'd never said as much, but I couldn't help but wonder whether the shorter cut had been her idea or that shit stain ex alpha of hers.

And no. I didn't give two fucks that she still carried his bonding mark.

He was nothing. And if he ever dared come near her, dared to lay some fucking claim on her, I would relish in every second of pain I inflicted on him before ending his life.

Corazon had chocolate brown eyes, but Issa's were closer to the color of honey or fine whiskey. There was no way anyone could look at either woman and not get a boner.

"This is where the GPS said to turn," Cyrus said, glancing at the digital map on his dash before turning his attention back to the bumpy road.

After a few seconds, the trees gave way to an open expanse of land and a beautiful two-story house. Or rather a barn that had been turned into a house, complete with a covered wrap around porch.

There were chickens roaming the property, a horse walking along a fence line about an acre back, and someone was bent under the hood of a 1963 Thunderbird.

That particular someone was a tall, muscular omega wearing what I could only describe as a sundress. His hair was pulled back in a bun I'd seen both Corazon and Issa wear when they wanted their hair out of their face or couldn't be bothered to spend any time on their locks.

"Is that Amir?" Issa asked, leaning between our seats to get a better look.

The omega in question lifted his head when he heard us approach.

"Yep," Cyrus answered, amusement in the single word.

"Is he wearing a dress?" Issa asked, a tinkling laugh filling the cab of the SUV.

Amir wiped his hands on the dress that hung to his knees, adding to the smears of grease and dirt, then glanced at his phone.

Cyrus and Ax were out of the vehicle first with me and Issa directly after.

"Sorry. I lost track of time. Been trying to get this damn thing back on the road for months," he said.

He took a step forward as though to hug us or shake hands, but then glanced down at himself.

"Would you be pissed if I took a minute to shower and change?"

"Do you often work on your car in a dress?" I asked, trying and failing to hold back an amused grin.

Amir's shoulders rose and fell as he smiled. "It was the first thing I grabbed from the basket with all the work clothes in it. But Mom's going to kill me when she finds it ruined."

He lived with his mom? What about his father? Or fathers? He appeared to be in his early twenties, but that didn't mean shit when it came to living with your family. Especially for an omega.

And being as Amir was one of those rare male omegas, he could have ended up at risk out there in the world without a pack to watch his back.

When he lifted his arms to pull the elastic from his hair, causing his biceps to bulge, I mentally took back that last thought. Amir looked as though he could handle himself, as though he would put up one hell of a fight if any asshole got it in their head to attempt to manhandle him or take him against his will.

Fuck, he was hot. Where Issa was soft and feminine, Amir was strong and masculine and obviously completely secure with his designation, sexuality, and appearance. Maybe he could rub off on Issa a little and help her pull out of her shell even more since she'd seemed surprised the three of us found her attractive.

He was hot, but he was also a bit...odd. But in a good way. Seriously. The dude had pulled on one of his mom's dresses to work on his car. I wanted to ask why he didn't just wear a pair of shorts, but part of me wondered if he was wearing anything at all under the dress.

And now I was hard.

"Take your time. We're in no rush," Cyrus said.

"Would it be okay if I go look at your horse?" Issa asked, the sweetest smile on her pretty face. She'd been so badly bruised and swollen when she'd arrived at my brother's estate that day. The only thing that lingered was the lightest scar over her eyebrow and it was nearly invisible when she wore makeup.

"Of course. Actually, hold on." He jogged to the porch and grabbed a small bucket. "Here. These are some apples Mom was going to give them later. Feel free to bribe her with treats."

"What's his name?" she asked as she took the bucket, her gaze dropping shyly for a second.

She'd been bold when booze had been in her system. We'd all seen the video of them dancing and kissing on the dancefloor, had seen her drag him to Cyrus's office by the hand.

Now, she was having a hard time meeting his eyes in the most innocent moment.

"*Her* name is Princess Fancy Pants."

A sweet giggle tore from her lips and her eyes went wide. "Tell me you're kidding. You did not name that beautiful animal Princess Fancy Pants."

The smile Amir shot Issa was full of nothing short of affection. "Technically, my little sister named her. My girl is somewhere in the pasture. She might come up to the fence if she sees Princess getting a treat without her. My horse's name is Pearl. She's solid white and salty as hell. Watch your fingers with both of them."

He gave her a toothy grin, then turned and jogged into the house to shower and change.

A part of me was tempted to ask if he needed help washing his back, but I had no idea whether his family was inside or not. We were courting Amir, but I didn't exactly want to make a bad impression with his mom or dads.

We didn't know much about him, didn't know how many siblings he had or whether it was only the one sister, didn't know what designation his parents were. All we knew was the few paragraphs he'd written on his bio for the Omega Center website.

I would have lost money if someone had bet me that Issa would have been the first to be with him.

We followed Issa across the property to where the horse was watching us, shifting her weight from one foot to the other as though it knew Issa had sweets for her.

Ax and Cyrus hung back a little with me, but all three of us kept a close eye on Issa. The animal was behind the fence, but that didn't mean she couldn't get bit if she wasn't careful.

As we watched her, though, it was obvious this wasn't her first time around one of these animals as she laid her hand flat with the apple, then rubbed her free hand along the horse's head and down her neck.

"Why was Amir working on that car in a dress so fucking hot?" Ax asked as he leaned against a post aways down from where Issa glanced in our direction periodically. "I don't know if it was the dress, his dark skin covered in grease, or the whole fucking scene, but I'm about to burst through my damn jeans," he said, adjusting his bulge.

She smiled and shook her head, but her cheeks went pink before she turned her head at the sound of hooves hitting the ground hard and fast.

"Hi, Pearl," she said sweetly as an all-white horse appeared and shoved her way closer for a treat.

"Did she have horses with her family pack?" Cyrus asked.

"No idea," I said.

Because Issa wasn't exactly open about her past, like she refused to think about her previous life. Or maybe she just didn't want to relive it by talking about it with us.

"We should get her one. We have the property for it. We'd just need a few things," Cyrus said.

"Like a barn, saddle, food…" Ax started, but cut off when Amir's steps caught our attention.

He hadn't been exaggerating when he'd said his shower would be quick. His hair was damp and hanging in wet curls around his face. His warm, brown skin was free of grease and sweat, and he'd pulled on a pair of fitted jeans and a t-shirt.

"Sorry. I wasn't sure what the dress code was for today. I can change if this is too casual," he said, stepping closer to Issa and pressing a kiss to her cheek before giving each of us a quick peck on our cheeks.

Not all male omegas were actually attracted to men; they only accepted a male alpha in their bed during the heat to help with the pain and fever.

It might have been wishful thinking, but it sure as fuck seemed as though Amir was attracted to all four of us and not only our beta.

"You're dressed fine. Issa declared we make our first date casual," Ax said, winking at her when she turned a forced frown on him.

She'd donned a pretty sundress that covered her shoulders – and the mark she hated – but was short enough to give us all a display of her long, beautiful legs. The dip in front also gave us a hint of her cleavage.

Yep. I was a boob man.

Then again, I was also an ass man. I didn't discriminate; a beautiful body was a beautiful body.

Issa gave each horse one more scratch, then joined us, leaning into Amir when he wrapped an arm around her shoulders as we walked toward the SUV.

Damn it. I had hugged her, had even draped my arm around her the way the omega was now, but she never seemed as though she was as relaxed in my arms as she was with Amir.

Maybe after her little chat with Ax last night, shit would start to change.

I still couldn't believe she didn't know we wanted her. I supposed we could have been more overt about it, but we'd wanted to give her time to heal after the bullshit she'd endured, hadn't wanted to rush her or make her feel pressured into anything with us.

Amir glanced over his shoulder, then reached out a hand when Ax picked up his pace to catch up. The omega smiled as Ax took his hand.

Cyrus turned raised brows to me as we followed behind the trio.

This was a good sign, right? The omega was definitely into Issa. And he'd greeted us each with a peck to our cheeks after he'd showered and changed. Now, he was seeking touch from one of his – possible – future alphas.

Omegas were all about comfort and touch. Then again, most omegas wouldn't have been outside working on a vintage Thunderbird, either. At least none of the omegas I'd ever met.

I'd also only come across a few male omegas and they'd all been petite, small, and a little on the meeker side.

I liked that Amir was bigger. Meant he wasn't fragile. I liked that he'd had zero problem flirting with then fucking Issa even though he'd come to The Vault to meet us. He wouldn't have recognized our scents on Issa since we hadn't met before that night, so it had merely been Issa's beauty and appeal that had reeled him in.

Shit. She'd reeled us in before we'd even truly gotten a real look at the woman beneath the bruising and swelling. For someone who'd been mistreated by alphas her whole life, she seemed to trust us. And fuck if that didn't make me swell with a pride.

"So where are we going today?" Amir asked, offering his hand to Issa as she climbed into the backseat. The big dude didn't act like a needy, demanding omega. Yet another brownie point earned in his favor.

"Well, we were going to have a picnic, but after meeting Princess Fancy Pants," Issa started, shaking her head with a smile at the name, "and Pearl, I thought…there's a rodeo the next town over. I've always wanted to go to one. Any chance I can talk you boys into it?"

"I'm down for whatever," Amir said, lifting her hand to his lips. "What do you think, alphas?"

My dick twitched at the honorific coming from his full lips.

I had never been to a fucking rodeo. Being on his family's property was probably the closest to country life I'd ever experienced.

But when I turned to find the sweetest look on Issa's face, I knew there wasn't a chance in hell I could turn her down.

"We'll need cowboy hats," Ax teased.

"Really? We can go?" she asked, her smile growing wider.

Fuck me. She looked so excited over something as simple as us agreeing to her change in plans.

I really hoped Amir would agree to join the pack, but all I could see in that moment was the glow on her cheeks, the excitement in her pretty honey-colored eyes, or the way all four of us men were watching her like she'd hung the fucking moon with her dainty little hands.

CHAPTER 11

<u>Issa</u>

I wasn't sure what I was expecting at a rodeo. The closest I'd ever come to seeing one was in clips on social media or on TV.

The real-life experience was so much different and way more fun.

There were booths selling kettle corn and funnel cakes, others selling barbecue, nachos, or hot dogs. So many choices. If I had the stomach space or time, I might have asked to try everything.

I still hated that the alphas – *my* alphas – had to foot the bill for everything since I still didn't have a job.

It wasn't that I didn't want to work or that I didn't want to actually look for a job, I was just…well, I was still terrified of leaving the safety of the pack house.

Antonio was still out there, and I was sure he wasn't overly happy about the fact that I'd warned Pack Rivera of the actions of my fathers and another rival pack, nor the fact that since my parents were dead, he would no longer inherit shit.

"I'm so getting a funnel cake," Amir said, guiding me to that particular vendor with the alphas close behind.

I hadn't missed all their shared smiles, the thoughtful looks they exchanged, nor the way they felt as though they were constantly flanking Amir and me to keep others from getting too close.

There wasn't really much of a risk for me, at least not the way it could be for Amir. I didn't perfume. I wouldn't inadvertently send my hormones into the air if I got turned on and send any alphas nearby into rut.

Amir, on the other hand, was not only an omega, but fucking gorgeous. Big and strong as an alpha, ruggedly beautiful, and smelled like the most erotic dessert.

"Share with me?" he asked, pulling me closer to his side and kissing the tip of my nose.

This was the first time we'd seen each other since the night at the club. And he sure as hell didn't act as though he regretted it nor was he behaving awkwardly. He acted as though tonight was one of hundreds or thousands we'd spent together.

Glancing at the alphas, I felt a twinge of guilt.

Enzo, Ax, and Cyrus were left wandering behind us, following us like they were our bodyguards instead of important members of the pack. It felt as though I'd taken over the date completely when the four of them were the most integral parts. I couldn't ease Amir through his heat cycles. I couldn't get him pregnant.

And, although I hadn't bothered mentioning it to them, I had no desire to carry a child. Ever.

It wasn't that I didn't like kids; my own experiences growing up made me want to avoid bringing another person into the world who could end up mistreated by their future pack.

But if the pack wanted to have a kid with Amir, I would never treat the child the way my siblings and I had been treated, regardless of their freaking designation.

I was getting ahead of myself. Other than our extremely passionate – though short – time together, this was our first pack date.

"I feel like I'm stealing all your attention," I said to Amir, nudging him with my shoulder as we walked hand in hand through the vendor alley.

The events I was interested in seeing wouldn't start for another hour, giving us plenty of time to sightsee, people watch, and spend money on things we didn't need.

Like the white, felt hat Ax plopped down on my head.

"Ax...really?" I said as he pulled my hair over my shoulders and the rim of the hat down further.

"We are definitely getting you a horse. Especially if you'll wear this and dresses while you ride," he said, stepping back and letting his eyes roam me from head to toe.

"I actually agree with your alpha on this one. You look hot in that hat," Amir said, smiling at Ax when he nudged him with his shoulder and raised a hand for a high five. "Look," he said, nodding toward a mirror sitting among dozens and dozens of hats in different styles and colors.

Okay. It did look cute. But where and when would I wear a hat like this?

"Wait...did you just say you were getting me a horse?"

"You looked happy with, uh, Princess what's-her-name and Snowball," Enzo said.

"Princess Fancy Pants and Pearl," Amir said with a chuckle.

"You can't just buy me a horse. They don't live in a yard like a squirrel. And I know literally nothing about keeping a horse other than they need food and water."

"Oh, *Habibi*. I can teach you any and everything you need to know if these alphas want to get you a horse. The thought of seeing you on top of a beast, gripping it with your thighs..."

His pupils blew wide, his perfume lifted on the air, and he licked his bottom lip as though he wasn't talking about me riding a horse...

But riding him.

My body grew warm as a cloud of heady alpha hormones mixed with Amir's perfume. My nipples were pebbled under my dress, and I had to clear my throat twice before I could speak.

"I don't need a horse. Don't be ridiculous."

"I'm still getting you the hat," Ax said as he handed cash over to the vendor.

I wasn't sure what had happened from the moment Ax decided I needed a hat to when we started to head toward the main show, but I was now under Ax's arm while Amir walked hand in hand with both Cyrus and Enzo.

No one had said a word, no one had decided it was time to swap partners.

Like we'd all spent our whole lives together we'd just naturally gravitated to different partners until we climbed the steps to search for seating with a clear view of the dirt oval circled with tall gates.

Time flew past entirely too quickly. We all cheered and clapped for the races, laughed at the rodeo clown.

And then…it was over. In a blink of an eye, our date was over.

Or at least this portion was over. Because I was far from ready to call it a night.

I'd gone from being afraid to leave the house, to dancing and drinking with Amir – among other things – and now I was reluctant to go back home.

I loved the pack house, I really did. For three bachelors, they'd made the home cozy and warm. It was mostly modern, but not overly masculine. And a part of me wanted to show it off to Amir.

Or maybe it was the fact I wanted his scent mingling with the alphas to hold me over until the next time we could see him.

"What's wrong?" Cyrus asked, sidling up beside me and pulling my hand through the crook of his elbow as we descended the rickety metal stairs with the rest of the crowd.

"I'm having too much fun. I don't want the night to end," I admitted.

It had taken some time, but the three alphas never made me feel stupid for speaking my mind or asking for what I wanted.

Okay, I didn't *always* say what I wanted. I hadn't bothered mentioning the crazy crush I'd carried since I'd barreled into their lives.

But they hadn't bothered mentioning they were attracted to me, either so I figured we were even.

"Want to go to the club? Do some dancing?" Ax offered.

He had an arm thrown around Amir's shoulders and clasped my hand in his free one.

I looked down at my flowy sundress. It wasn't exactly club attire. And we were all covered in dust from the horse hooves kicking up clouds of dirt as they'd raced around the ring.

"I was thinking more like, um, maybe we could invite Amir back to the pack house. Show him around. Have a couple beers."

"I'm good with that," Amir said. My face flushed when he winked down at me.

I swore my body had been tight and warm since the moment we'd pulled into his driveway to find him bending over the engine of that muscle car.

Lie. I'd been a little...*excited* for weeks.

The alphas tended to walk around the house barely dressed, their muscles constantly on full display.

Throw in the fact Amir's mere presence made it feel as though every erogenous zone in my body was being touched and stroked nonstop...

Maybe inviting him back to the house wasn't the best idea. Because there was a good chance I would either end up throwing myself at the omega and making a fool of myself or end up with my feelings hurt when he spent the night with the three alphas.

We all stopped near the base of the bleachers as the crowd moved around us.

Amir pulled away from Ax and stepped in front of me, taking both my hands in his and bending at the waist a little. "We can do something else if this feels like it's moving too quickly, *Habibi*."

A smile pulled at the corners of my mouth. "You've called me that a few times. What does it mean?"

"It's a term of endearment. Like saying my love."

It was his turn to blush as a faint hue darkened his light brown cheeks.

"If you want to go dancing, we'll go dancing. I wouldn't mind having you in my arms again."

"We can stop by the house to change if you're worried about what you're wearing. But for the record, I still say you look hot as fuck," Ax said.

Cyrus cuffed the back of his head. "Smooth, jackass."

"What? She is." Ax looked to Enzo for backup and shrugged when the pack lead shook his head with a smirk.

I stared up into Amir's green eyes and felt myself get lost for a moment, as though the rest of the world had simply faded away.

"This is your pack. I don't want you to think I'm trying to steal them away from you. I want you...in case I haven't made that obvious."

Damn it. He sent another of those winks and my lower half tightened as heat pooled low in my belly.

"I would love to spend more time with you, with all of you," he said, turning to glance at the alphas before looking back at me, "but not if it'll make you uncomfortable."

It had been my idea. And now I was acting erratic and insecure.

Nope. I wouldn't let years of conditioning by my parents and asshole alpha make me think I wasn't deserving of Amir's attention or of Ax's, Cyrus's, and Enzo's affection.

"No. It's okay. I do want to spend more time with you. I'll leave it up to you boys. If you want to go out, I'll want a quick shower and change. But I'm just as happy with lounging around the house and binge watching some cheesy horror movies."

Amir's brows shot up his forehead. "You're a horror girl?"

"And action. And black and white TV shows. The cheesier, the better," Cyrus teased.

I wasn't sure what it was about horror and action. I hated violence in real life. Hated blood and gore.

But watching something I knew as a fact was make believe felt...it felt comforting. Almost like I had some control over the moment. I could turn it off or close my eyes if something got too intense unlike in real life.

"Oh, I'm so going back to your house for scary movies and snuggles," Amir said, tugging me closer and rubbing his cheek against me.

He was scent marking me. And damn…it felt so damn natural. So right.

I couldn't wait until all five of us were snuggled on the big couch, our arms and legs entangled until I went to bed smothered in the scents of these four delicious men.

CHAPTER 12

<u>Amir</u>

I had known this pack had a beta. I'd known she was a woman.

What I hadn't been prepared for was how badly my omega would pine for her after that first moment I'd heard her voice at the club.

Enzo had warned me she could be a little shy, that her past made her leery of strangers, mainly alphas. I wasn't an alpha, but I wasn't small like most omegas.

Yet...she hadn't shown an ounce of fear from the moment I'd pretended I was her boyfriend to when one of her alphas had caught us in the office.

And then she'd gotten a little closed off when she'd mentioned continuing our little date somewhere else. The last thing I wanted was for her to think I was encroaching on her place in the pack.

Although...

She'd sounded like she was going to deny Enzo was her alpha

when he'd come into the office at Vault. He'd cut her off, affirming that he was, indeed, hers, that she was his.

There were some questions I needed answered before I allowed myself to get too close to these people. The last thing I wanted was to let myself fall for a pack who was unstable.

They seemed close, seemed to care for each other, but I'd noticed the alphas didn't touch Issa as much or as intimately as I'd assumed they would have.

Again, did she not feel a part of the pack or had the alphas done something to make her feel as though she was on the outside looking in and how would my presence affect their relationship as a whole?

We were all piled in the SUV, Issa between me and Ax as Cyrus drove, and Enzo took shotgun. The guys would occasionally ask a question or tease each other, but Issa felt tense beside me, even with the smiles and giggles from the alphas' banter.

"Are you sure this is okay?" I whispered in her ear.

She turned her head to look into my face, the only light touching her coming from the passing streetlights.

After a few seconds, a slow smile stretched across her face.

"Yeah," she said with a nod. "It's more than okay. I'm sorry I'm acting all…" She waved a hand in the air as though searching for the right word. "I swear I'm not moody or possessive of these guys or anything like that."

"It would be okay if you were," I said, gently touching her face with my fingertips.

Fuck me hard.

Those were the words she'd said to me when I'd turned her to take her over the desk. That woman, the beta who'd fallen apart first on my tongue then around my cock, was so different than the woman who was watching me as though she was unsure of what to do or say.

"Can I ask you something?"

"Sure," she said.

"It's kind of personal."

I swore I could feel all three alphas tense and hold their breath in unison.

"I saw that bite on your shoulder at the club. And I'm assuming it wasn't from one of these alphas."

Her hand raised to cover the mark hidden under the pretty blue dress she'd worn for our day date. It wasn't the typical silvery crescent scars left by an alpha but more like her flesh had been ripped by someone.

"No. It's not from them."

I really hoped I wasn't pushing her too far. But I needed to know how carefully I needed to tread with her, with her alphas, with this pack.

"They hurt you?"

"*He.* Only one alpha. And yeah. But, uh…"

She was blinking a lot and fidgeting with her purse strap as her anxiety rose. I didn't need to scent the change in her signature to see this wasn't a topic she wanted to discuss.

"It's over. And these guys…they saved me. Took me in. They keep me safe."

"You saved yourself, beta," Enzo said, turning to look at her over his shoulder.

I looked at him, at Ax, then caught Cyrus's eyes as he watched me in the rearview mirror.

This sweet woman had apparently been through some shit. I'd noted a small scar over her eyebrow but had assumed it was from some old injury.

Now, I wondered if it had been caused by the same asshole who'd left that mark on her shoulder. It had been obviously covered by makeup, but the raised ridges were obvious, like the alpha had ripped through her skin then hadn't bothered to tend to it so it would heal properly.

Anger built in my chest and tore a growl from my throat before I could swallow it down.

"Please tell me you three beat his ass."

Ax huffed a laugh. Enzo smirked. Cyrus sighed as though we all exhausted him.

"Fucker disappeared before we had the chance," Enzo said.

"So that's how you met? You guys rushed in like knights in shining armor?"

"Actually, um, his brother is mated to my sister," she said, pointing at Enzo.

"That's kind of cool."

Except the mood seemed to have shifted from my question and now I felt like the biggest dick for bringing it up.

But I wanted to know more about her, know why she kept shutting down. She would behave as though she was having a great time, then it was like she'd catch herself smiling too much and would retreat into her shell.

Instead of pressuring her with more questions, I came up with a plan in my head to break through her walls and keep her from rebuilding them. I could tell there were far more layers to this beta than she let the world see and I was determined to peel them away one by one until I found the diamond hidden underneath.

Clasping her hand and bringing it to my lips, I feathered a kiss to each of her knuckles before lowering our entwined hands to my thigh.

"No more shitty talk tonight. We've got time to reveal all our deepest, darkest secrets."

I waggled my brows at her and earned a dick hardening giggle.

"Do you guys have something to eat, or should we order out? My treat."

Enzo scoffed. Ax leaned forward to frown at me past Issa. "We're courting you. No chance in hell are you paying for shit."

Issa had a slight smile still on her lips as she shook her head and rolled her eyes. I'd caught her doing that a few times when it came to Enzo or Ax, as though they entertained her in the most annoyingly fun way.

I was so curious about the dynamics of this pack and found myself wanting to spend as much time as possible until I'd learned everything I could.

Like, other than owning The Vault, what did the alphas do in their downtime? Did Issa work?

Who was I kidding? What I really wanted to know was the background behind her failed bonding and whether her previous alpha was a threat to the beautiful, sexy as fuck beta.

Holding my hands up in surrender, I let the alphas follow their instincts to care for an omega and pay for the food.

Issa and I voted for Chinese delivery.

Enzo, Ax, and Cyrus didn't bother voicing their choices for dinner – they would end up getting whatever the omega and beta wanted regardless of whether they preferred the meal or not.

Good alphas. Issa was a lucky woman. I could only hope this would continue and wasn't them putting their best faces forward to win me over.

I wanted a pack of my own. I'd always wanted a pack of my own. I wanted a big, loving family like my parents had, even if we never chose to have children.

But I wasn't so desperate as to choose the first group of alphas who came along.

Actually, this was the sixth pack this year alone I'd allowed to court me. The first two hadn't gotten past the first date. They'd made it obvious the only time I would receive any affection – or attention – was during my cycle. No thanks. I didn't want a relationship built around convenience. I wanted love.

The other three...there wasn't anything inherently wrong with them, I just hadn't felt the same kind of connection with them as I had that first night with Issa then with her alphas today during our unorthodox day date.

All three alphas were easy and open with their affection. I might not look like a stereotypical omega, but I still thrived on attention and touch. I still craved the gentle caresses, the warmth of their hands around mine, and I even loved the way they teased and loved on Issa.

What confused me was the way she had first tried to deny they were her alphas, then the way she was almost tense any time one of the alphas would wrap their arm around her shoulders or hold her hand.

She didn't act as though she was afraid of them, but it caused those questions about their dynamics to continue to rattle around in my head.

The pack house was large, but not pretentiously so. It was a sprawling two story with dormer windows. Was that a livable attic? A third floor? Or could it be the omega wing?

Butterflies erupted in my stomach, and I tried to ignore them. The last thing I needed right now was to get excited over the prospects of being mated to this pack before I had all my questions answered.

"Your home is beautiful," I said as I climbed from my side of the vehicle and offered a hand to Issa after the vehicle was pulled into the four-car garage.

"Thank you," Cyrus said.

We walked as a unit toward the door leading inside. I kept my hand wrapped around Issa's and smiled when Enzo's eyes dipped to our clasped hands then rose to my face before he winked.

The garage led into what I assumed was a mud room complete with a fancy washer and dryer, then into a massive kitchen. I could absolutely cook up a feast in here.

There were two doors leading from the kitchen, but we went through one that led into a large family room with vaulted ceilings that showcased exposed wooden beams.

It was almost like the house had a cottagey feel; it was warm and cozy and inviting with enough masculine elements that it was obvious alphas lived here without being overly macho or cold.

I couldn't find any hints of Issa in the house other than her scent that seemed to float along with the warm and spicy scents of Enzo, Cyrus, and Ax, like her signature amplified or complemented theirs until I found myself wanting to faceplant into the nearest surface to pull all the yumminess into my lungs.

"Get comfortable. I'll order the food," Cyrus said.

"Do you want a tour while we wait?" Ax said.

And I might have been seeing things, but I swore he and Enzo exchanged a mischievous look.

"I'd love to see the rest of the house."

My family lived modestly. It had nothing to do with finances; my fathers made plenty of money.

But my mom was the omega, and she loved the whole home-steading lifestyle. And, of course, her alphas couldn't deny her of a damn thing.

That was how we'd ended up with chickens, horses, and how my parents had ended up with four kids so spaced out in age. Each time they'd thought they were done my mom would decide she wanted another.

"Issa. Why don't you give Amir a tour while we get the couch set up?" Ax suggested.

Yep, he'd definitely glanced at Enzo from the corner of his eye.

These two were trying to give me some time alone with Issa without embarrassing her.

"Sure. Um, you saw the kitchen and the living room."

Her cheeks grew pink under my attention, and I so desperately wanted to peel away that first layer to see who she was or could be if she simply let herself go the way she had at the club.

Twining my fingers through hers, I smiled warmly at her and let her lead me to a dining room that was off the kitchen. That was apparently where the second doorway in the kitchen led.

Then, she dragged me upstairs and started pointing out bedrooms, going so far as to open each so I could get a peek inside.

"This is Ax's room. Across is Cyrus's," she said, pushing each door open and flipping on the light so I could step in and look around.

Cyrus's room was immaculately clean. Ax's looked the way I thought it would, clothes everywhere, bed unmade, and a towel laying on the floor near the hamper instead of inside of it.

The door beside Ax's was Enzo's. His room was tidy, but nothing like Cyrus's.

Each of their rooms smelled so strongly of them, of wet wood that had sat out in the sun warming all day, of spiced rum that made me want to lay on a beach and listen to music, of sweet, tangy copper.

We left Enzo's room and she pointed to a door. "That leads upstairs to the omega wing." She started walking that way, but I pulled her to a stop.

"Nope. I want to see my beta's room."

I hadn't meant to let the possessive term slip from my lips, but there was no reason to hide the fact I was highly attracted to her. As much as I would love for this pack to be the one for me, I would be as content to have Issa in my life.

If she would accept me without the full pack being onboard.

She rolled her lips into her mouth and that sweet pink hue washed over her cheeks again. "It's nothing special."

"It's yours. That makes it special."

Glancing over her head, I eyed the door she hadn't opened. Then, without waiting for her, I reached around her and turned the knob, pushing the door open and stepping inside, pulling her along with me.

The light flipped on and illuminated a room that was...well, lacking. As in lacking personality. The walls were white, the bedding was plain, the dressers and other furniture looked as though it was already here when she moved in with the pack.

The only way to know it belonged to Issa was her clean linen scent and a few pieces of clothing lying on her made bed as though she'd had a hard time deciding on what outfit to wear for our date.

"No art. No family photos," I muttered, turning in a slow circle.

She carefully pulled her hand from mine and fidgeted with her skirt. "This was supposed to be temporary." She shrugged and forced a wobbly smile.

"Do you want to talk about it?"

She shook her head.

"Can I ask another personal question that has nothing to do with your past?"

Her brows raised. "Sure. Can I plead the fifth if I don't like the question?" Her smile was more genuine this time.

Crossing the small space separating us, I pulled her closer to me. "You want those alphas."

She blinked a few times, and her eyes went wide.

"But when I asked that first night whether Enzo was your alpha, you started to deny it."

"It's kind of...it's a long story. Complicated."

"I like to think I'm intelligent. Give me the abridged version. Or at least as much as you feel comfortable telling me."

She sighed and rubbed her cheek against my chest in an instinctual move, though I wasn't sure whether she was scent marking me or borrowing mine to settle her nerves.

"I told you Enzo's brother is my sister's alpha." I nodded. "Well, I was…hurt. And I went to Cora's house – that's my sister – to warn her. These alphas were there. They took care of me. Then offered me a place to stay while I got on my feet."

I waited for her to continue.

When she pulled away and sat on the sofa on one side of the room, I followed her. And waited some more.

"And?" I asked.

I didn't want to push her too far, but I had a feeling Issa was the kind of person who needed help stepping outside of her comfort zone until she could truly discover who she was outside of whatever box she'd been shoved into before meeting this pack. And me.

"And *what*? That's how I came to live with these alphas."

"But that doesn't explain the fact you denied they were your alphas, or the fact all four of you are obviously head over heels for each other but I've yet to see…anything other than casual touches."

"They're just flirts," she said.

But I noticed the way her eyes darted to the side as though she was either lying or didn't quite believe her own words.

Turning so one of my knees rested on the couch and I could fully face her, I tilted my head.

"Either you're in denial or completely blind."

Her brows shot up her forehead. "Excuse me?"

"Those three alphas watch you like you hung the damn moon."

"They do not," she said, that sweet pink brightening her olive cheeks again. Her complexion was only a tad lighter than my own.

As I watched her, I realized it wasn't that she was in denial or blind. She didn't believe someone could truly see her, that they could truly care about her.

And the urge to find out who the fuck had hurt her, who had

caused her to believe this way about herself was nearly as over-whelming as the urge to drag her onto my lap and wrap my arms around her for the next few hours.

Nah. I would rather run my hands and tongue across every inch of her skin, to worship her the way she deserved, to show her exactly how perfect she was.

But that would do nothing about the doubt she carried about her alphas' feelings for her.

"Have you never had a conversation about your place in this pack?"

She'd been so strong and confident that first night, had asked for exactly what she wanted from me.

But I was an omega. Not an alpha. I wasn't a risk to her. She had no reason to fear me, regardless of my size.

"Ax…" She ducked her gaze and a smile pulled up her lips.

"Yes?" I asked, drawing out the word.

"We all crashed in my bed that night. After the club."

Yep. Her cheeks were definitely growing darker with a blush.

"I couldn't sleep. I kept thinking about…everything. And Ax–"

She cut herself off and covered her face with her hands for a brief second as the sweetest giggle escaped from her lips.

When she dropped her hands, she refused to look in my direction.

"He'd said they thought I wasn't interested in sex. Said I acted as though I wasn't interested in them. But I thought they weren't inter-ested in me. They're always fooling around with each other. And I got the privilege of lying there and listening to all the moans and sucking their hormones into my lungs with only my own hand to–"

She cut herself off again, turning wide eyes on me as though she hadn't meant to speak those words out loud.

Oh. This girl was so sheltered and not in a good way. I'd seen the way she could let loose, the way that, once her inhibitions were lowered, she could go after exactly what she wanted.

And, in that moment, I made it my personal mission to teach her how to get exactly what she wanted from these alphas every moment of the day.

CHAPTER 13

<u>Issa</u>

Why the hell was I so embarrassed talking to Amir about this? He'd tasted me. He'd been inside me.

Yet admitting that I had zero game without liquid courage or that I hadn't known my alphas wanted me here, not only permanently but romantically, was kind of humiliating.

But not like I'd been able to go out there and date, to flirt and tease and find another beta or an alpha to call mine.

Nope. Just like my sister and brothers, my life, my future had been planned out for me from fairly early on. And I was absolutely positive my fathers and my mother were aware Antonio abused me, that he kept me drugged so I wouldn't fight him when he wanted to use my body for his own satisfaction.

I hadn't seen my beta packmate, Carlos, since shortly after our bonding ceremony. I had no idea whether he was dead or alive, whether he'd found another pack of people he actually cared for, or whether he'd done what I'd always wished I could and turn my back on my family and carve out a life of my own.

Yet…I had that very choice now and was doing nothing short of existing. It took damned near arm twisting from my alphas to get me to leave the house.

It had only been a few nights since Ax had more or less told me the three of them wanted me on a deeper level. And none of them had done anything more than hold my hand or wrap an arm around my shoulders.

Were they really waiting for me to make the first move? Did they expect me to just…what? … jump at them like a flying squirrel and wrap my legs around their waist? Because it would take a whole lot of booze before that would happen.

Or at least a modicum of self-esteem.

Even before I'd gotten tipsy at The Vault, being around Amir had been easy. But, since he was an omega, I didn't feel as though he was a threat. I'd never met a single omega who'd abused another person, who would demand anything from me, who would hurt me for their own sick pleasure.

I still couldn't believe my alphas – it was still hard to admit they were mine, even to myself – had believed I wasn't interested in sex or a sexual relationship with them. They weren't naïve enough to think they weren't the physical embodiment of masculine perfection. And while they were alphas, they'd never made me nervous or uncomfortable. I knew they would never do a thing to hurt me, not intentionally.

Those three alphas watch you like you hung the damn moon.

That was a bit of an exaggeration. And not only because I was merely a beta. They cared about me; I knew that. And just because they were sexually attracted to me and wanted me to officially be their beta didn't mean they were in love with me or anything of that sort.

The bigger question was would I even know how that looked or felt? Would I have a clue how it felt to be loved by an alpha? Would I know how it looked for an alpha to gaze at me with nothing short of affection and awe in their eyes?

"Okay. Let's go with some easier, less squirm inducing questions. Why haven't you made this room your own?"

"I told you. I really did think this was a temporary situation. I'd thought they were simply being nice and letting me stay here because of my sister and her pack and all that."

"That's the only thing holding you back?" Amir asked.

My shoulders rose and fell. "Well, that and the fact I don't have a job yet and have zero money."

He waved my words off as though swatting at a bug. "If those three are like every other alpha in my life, they'll jump at the first chance to spend money on you."

My eyes darted to my closet of their own will. The first day I'd woken here, I'd found them circling the kitchen table with laptops open in front of them, ordering clothes and toiletries and necessities along with some luxuries like makeup and skincare products. Honestly, though, even the clothing could be considered luxury being as they'd made sure almost every single thing in the closet or drawers had higher end labels on them.

It was my turn to wave off Amir's words. "That's just frivolous spending. Why would I ask them to buy me stuff for the bedroom when I have what I need?"

"Oh, girl," he said, reaching forward and taking my hand, giving me a faux sympathetic look. "I am so going to teach you the ways of the omega. By the time I'm done with you, you'll have those three crawling behind you on their hands and knees, begging for your attention."

A giggle tore from my chest at the imagery.

Then his words hit home. "Wait. What do you mean by the time you're done with me?"

He moved closer until we were touching. "I saw the woman behind the walls you've built around yourself, the fortress you've built to protect yourself. You're a queen, Issa. And I can't wait to see how you rule your kingdom. I will do anything and everything it takes to help you come out of your shell, to help you see what the rest of us see when we look at you."

My mouth opened then closed. I wasn't sure what I was trying to say or what I was even thinking at the moment.

I was a queen? I was a fucking beta. There weren't packs out there vying for my place in their pack.

The only reason Antonio had wanted me was because of my parents, because of my fathers' business, their power and wealth.

Amir was an omega. I was supposed to be chasing him. The alphas were supposed to be chasing him.

Okay. So yeah, they kind of were, but they'd been more concerned that I approved of him rather than seeking out the first willing omega to add to the pack. They'd wanted to make sure I got along with him, that I was okay with him even before I'd known the omega was male.

Male omegas were as rare as female alphas, yet here he was, adamant that I see myself in a different light, adamant that I was royalty in his eyes.

"My parents…" I started but was unsure of how to finish my thoughts. How the hell did I tell him about how I was raised? Enzo, Ax, and Cyrus were fully aware of my background. They'd done what they could in the past few months to help me get past all that bullshit, to accept that my upbringing was abnormal.

And then there was the whole thing of how Amir might see me after finding out the kind of people who'd raised me. Or rather, birthed me, being as we'd all been raised by nannies.

"What about them?" He rested an arm along the back of the couch, lazily toying with my hair.

I could ruin everything with just a few words. Amir could learn about my parents, about my past and decide I wasn't worth the risk, that the pack wasn't worth the risk.

His fingertips brushed along my cheekbone as he ducked his head to force me to look him in the eye. "Your past doesn't define you, *Habibi.*"

My love. He kept calling me that. And yeah, it was far too early for that four letter word, but the term of endearment sent a frenzy of butterflies fluttering in my belly every time.

"Have you heard of Pack Alvarez?"

His dark brows shot up his forehead. "Yeah."

Rolling my lips into my mouth, I hoped he would connect the dots so I wouldn't have to put them into words.

"That was your family pack? You're Issa Alvarez?"

"Isabelle Alvarez, one of five beta children. My younger sister is the only omega of the six of us."

"Weren't your parents killed in a freak fire?" he asked.

That was a piece of information I wouldn't divulge. There wasn't a chance in hell I would get Cora's pack in trouble, not when they'd done so much to protect first my sister then me. And also because the pack lead was the brother to one of my alphas.

"Yeah. They were."

His brows lowered until a crease formed between them. "The alpha who mistreated you...he was chosen by your fathers. Arranged bond and all that bullshit."

His beautiful eyes seemed to darken as his anger grew.

"Yeah. All of us had our packs or alphas chosen for us. Except my sister...did her own thing." Yet something else I wouldn't divulge just yet. No reason to tell an omega we were courting that Enzo's brother and his pack had kidnapped my sister on the day of her bonding ceremony and then fell in love with her.

His eyes narrowed. His arm rested on the cushions behind my head. He was no longer gently stroking my cheek or toying with my hair. He simply watched me with various emotions flashing through his eyes.

"That actually explains a lot," he finally said.

A knock on my door startled me, and I glanced up as Cyrus peeked his head inside. "Am I interrupting?"

"Of course not. This is your–"

"Stop," Amir said, surprising me.

"What?"

"You were going to tell him he wasn't interrupting because this is his house. Or did I guess that wrong?"

"How..." How the hell had he known what I was going to say? Yeah, I'd said that very thing to all three alphas dozens of times since

I'd moved into this room, but there was no way Amir could possibly know that.

Cyrus grinned and raised a brow as he stepped further into the room. "The living room is set up whenever the two of you are ready. Did you show him the omega quarters yet?"

"Not yet. She was telling me how she came from a pack of assholes who convinced her she wasn't important because of her designation. I'm paraphrasing, of course. But you get the gist."

My mouth hung open as my wide eyes went from Amir to Cyrus and back.

Of the three alphas, Cyrus had always been sweet, quiet, gentle, and calm. Where the other two were constant flirts and had short fuses when it came to those they cared for, Cyrus was gentlemanly.

"Accurate on both accounts," Cyrus said with a smirk.

My brows lowered.

"I meant that you were wrong and his paraphrasing was correct. You know what, I'll be downstairs. You two take your time."

I leapt to my feet, calling out to Cyrus before he could close the door. "Don't you three want some time with him?"

"First of all, I'm right here," Amir said, grabbing my wrist and yanking me back down to the couch beside him. "Second, you are *all* courting me, so we need time together, too."

"And third," Cyrus said, smiling as he backed from my room, "we'll have plenty of time to get to know each other later."

With that, he closed the door behind him, but not before I caught the grin on his stupidly gorgeous face.

"Like I said, wrapped around your little finger," he teased before returning to running his fingers through my hair.

"I believe you said they watched me like I hung the moon."

One of his shoulders shrugged up as he smiled. "Eh. Same thing. Either way, those three are obsessed with you. I can't believe you haven't been riding them nonstop. They're fucking hot."

Tilting my head to the side, I ran my gaze over his face from his high cheekbones to his square jawline, over his straight nose, to his beautiful light green eyes. "So you like men, too? Not just during your heat but…Sorry. That was super rude and intrusive of me."

"I don't discriminate. Beauty is beauty." And the way he was staring at me now, the way his voice pitched a little lower, made me think he saw me in the beautiful category. "And you can ask me anything. I'm seriously hard to offend."

Why did I constantly doubt him? I doubted anyone who told me I was beautiful or sexy or desirable in any way. But, until I'd finally escaped Antonio and began to build a life of my own outside of my fathers' rule, I'd never been treated as though I was anything more than either a nuisance or a rung in the societal ladder.

For a few moments, we simply stared into each other's eyes until I felt as though I was drowning in the beautiful seafoam green. His gaze dipped to my lips, and I couldn't help but hope he would lean in for a kiss.

Because this man could kiss. Even the fake kiss at The Vault had curled my toes and rendered me speechless and fuzzy brained for a few moments.

"You want me to kiss you," he said, as though reading my mind.

"Yes," I whispered.

"You know you can kiss me, right? You don't have to wait for me or the alphas to initiate affection."

"I'm not an omega. I don't thrive on touch."

Lie. I had been touch starved for years. But the only time anyone had touched me throughout my life had usually been to either cause pain or to bring themselves pleasure while completely disregarding whether I was enjoying myself. Especially since I was usually drugged by my fucking alpha.

His fingers combed through my hair. "Does this feel good?" he asked as his short nails scraped against my scalp.

"Yes," I whispered again.

His hand trailed down until his fingers grazed my cheekbone then my throat. "What about this?"

I nodded.

When his hand drifted lower and the pads of his fingers barely grazed over my pebbled nipples, I had to swallow hard to avoid moaning and making a fool of myself. Such a gentle touch yet it felt as though the sensation made my clit throb and my inner walls clench with need. As in a need to be filled. Immediately.

"Touch can be beautiful. It can be arousing," he said as he trailed his fingers along the swell of my breasts before moving further down my ribs to my upper thighs. "Or comforting. It should never hurt… unless that's your kink." The sexiest smirk pulled up one corner of his mouth before he winked at me. "In that case, I'd be more than happy to bend you over my lap and spank your round ass."

Heat rushed my cheeks and my core. I wasn't sure whether I was embarrassed by his offer or turned on.

Maybe I was embarrassed that I was so turned on by the thought of Amir's big hand slapping against my bare ass.

His big hands gripped my hips and pulled me onto his lap until my thighs straddled his and my core rested over his engorged cock. "Touch should never hurt. What happened to you before…that's your past. Let me show you how beautiful you are. Let your alphas show you how much you mean to them."

Sucking my bottom lip between my teeth, I worried it a few seconds as my gaze bounced between his eyes. "I don't know how," I admitted barely above a breath.

Amir's smile was slow but beautiful as he leaned forward and rubbed his nose against mine. "Good thing you have me to teach you." And then his lips pressed to mine in a chaste kiss that still managed to send my heart galloping behind my ribs.

CHAPTER 14

Cyrus

$\mathcal{I}$ stood outside Issa's door a few more minutes and eavesdropped on their conversation. Some of it was too quiet to hear, but for the most part...Amir was fucking awesome.

It was generally an alpha's job to dote on and cherish their omega. And of course, we would totally do that with Amir. But we'd wanted to do the same with Issa from pretty much the day she'd agreed to stay with us.

Over and over, she'd acted as though she wasn't a part of the pack, as though she didn't believe we wanted her as our beta and her time with us wasn't just temporary.

But...had we bothered to actually show her how we felt? I knew I was doing my best to give her time and space to heal after the bullshit she'd endured through her life before us. Had we managed to make her feel more like a roommate instead of a woman who'd crashed her way into our hearts the same moment she'd crashed her car into the gates of the Rivera estate?

With my back against the wall beside her bedroom door, I inhaled deeply, dragging the increased pheromones into my lungs, Issa's warm fresh linen mixing beautifully with Amir's chocolate covered strawberry.

My dick thickened until I had to adjust myself before my fucking zipper bit into the flesh of my shaft.

I had no idea whether they were fooling around or having sex, but standing out here like a voyeur would do nothing to quell my hard-on. This was supposed to be a date, a chance for Amir to get to know us all.

And yeah, it was for *him* to get to know *us*. It didn't matter how we felt about him – Issa liked him; therefore, we would do whatever was needed to convince him to join our pack.

The small, broken beta had all three of us wrapped around her dainty little finger. She held so much power over us three alphas yet had no idea how to wield it. Shit. I wasn't even sure she realized how much control she had over us.

Pushing from the wall, I quietly made my way down the hall, descended the stairs, and lowered onto the couch where Enzo and Ax waited.

"They coming?" Ax asked.

I nearly barked out a surprised laugh. "Um…one way or another," I said, and grinned when Ax and Enzo turned raised brows on me.

"Damn, dude. How the hell does he get her to lower her damn walls? I would give my left nut to feel her under my hands," Ax said, dropping his head against the couch.

"Have either of you actually…tried anything with her? Tried to kiss her or make love to her or anything?"

"I did but you cock blocked me," Ax said.

"You tried to fuck her with us both in bed," Enzo said, rolling his head to look at Ax from the other end of the couch.

"So? You could have either watched or joined in," Ax said with a shrug.

"Yeah. Right. 'Hey, Issa. I know we haven't done nearly enough to make you feel like an important part of the pack, but enjoy this gangbang'," I retorted, shoving Ax's head when he waggled his brows like that was exactly what should have been said that night. "You're an idiot."

There was no force behind my words and a grin stretched across my lips as I tried to picture Issa's face had one of us actually said that.

We had finally seen the footage of her with Amir in the office and she absolutely had a libido. Which meant we'd been depriving our girl this whole time.

But what if she wasn't attracted to us, or only one of us? What if she only saw me as a packmate and friend? I would still have Amir, Enzo, and Ax, but I wanted Issa as badly.

Possibly more.

I'd fallen in love with her almost from the start. Not that I'd bothered to tell her – or my packmates – that little nugget of information.

There were cameras all over the house including in our bedrooms. But we didn't tend to check those. It felt like an invasion of privacy, especially when it came to Issa who'd had her entire life controlled by alphas. We wanted her to feel safe with us. We wanted her to know she had control over every aspect of her life.

But in this moment, as their combined scents began to filter down the stairs and into the living room, I was more than tempted to open the app to see if we should get comfortable instead of waiting for them to join us.

"Fuck it," Ax said, pulling his phone free and opening the camera app as though he'd heard my own internal battle. "Ho-ly shit," he growled out.

In unison, Enzo and I leaned toward him to get a view of his screen. Issa hadn't changed out of the dress she'd chosen for the day date at the rodeo. It was currently up around her waist as she rose and fell on Amir's cock, one of his hands gripping her hip while the other appeared to be cupping a tit, his head leaning forward, more than likely sucking and nipping at her nipple.

Copper, spiced rum, and my own wet wood scents exploded into the room, mingling and mixing with the pheromones from our beta and our omega. And fuck anyone who tried to say otherwise – Amir was ours if for no other reason than what we were watching on the phone.

He obviously made Issa happy. He was shattering all those walls she'd built around herself, smashing through the ice she'd had protecting her heart.

Now I was torn between finding a way to control my near rut level need, pulling my cock free and jerking off to the sexiest fucking thing I'd ever seen, or begging one of my mates to suck me off.

"I vote gangbang," Ax said. But his voice didn't hold the normal teasing tone but was deeper and huskier than normal. Yep. All three of us were fighting our alpha instincts to rush into that room, fuck both the beta and omega, and mark them as ours. "We need more cameras in that room. I wish I could see her tits bouncing."

Once again adjusting my boner, I turned my attention away from the screen. "Give them some privacy. We'll all be together eventually."

"Dude. Amir said his next heat is a couple months away. Can you wait a couple more months to feel her wrapped around your cock?" Ax said.

Enzo snatched his phone and ended the feed. "We've waited this long. We'll wait as long as she needs."

"She told us she wanted sex. I wasn't the only one who heard her, right?" Ax said, turning his head to look from Enzo to me then back.

"And she'll let us know when she wants one of us to fuck her. Until then…we let her set the pace." And this was one of the reasons Enzo was pack lead. He might be a flirt like Ax, but he was able to keep his shit in check where Ax…well, the fucker followed wherever his dick led most times.

The three of us had been lovers for years, but that didn't mean we hadn't enjoyed flings with betas through the years. Until Issa, I'd never felt the need to remain exclusive to one person. Or in this case, two people.

There had never been jealousy when one of us fucked someone either in one of our offices or brought them home.

But for the first time, I found myself jealous. Only I wasn't sure whether I was more jealous of Amir or Issa.

Nah. Bullshit. I was definitely more jealous of Amir. He'd gotten through to her in a way I hadn't achieved. He'd been with her twice now, had tasted her, had felt that sweet little body against his, had felt her cunt wrapped around his cock.

"Fuck," I ground out, pushing to my feet when my thoughts kept my dick at full mast.

"Where you going?" Enzo asked, watching me over the back of the couch. Or rather couches since we'd pushed them together so we could all cuddle together while watching a movie.

"I need some air before I shove my cock down Ax's throat."

Ax barked out a laugh.

Enzo shook his head. "He's rubbing off on you."

I lifted a hand over my shoulder as I moved through the kitchen and out the back door to the patio. It wasn't so much that Ax was rubbing off on me as I was feeling…unstable. Out of control. Those were two things I didn't suffer from, two things I'd never struggled with.

But after seeing someone take Issa in a way I'd dreamed of for months I was fighting my instinct to rut into the first person I could.

And my girl deserved more than a quick, hard fuck from me, especially for our first time together.

No. When I finally got Issa into my bed, I planned to take hours memorizing every inch of her body, to learn every one of her sounds, what made her moan or whimper, what brought her the most pleasure.

And then I would bury myself as deep as possible short of knotting her.

CHAPTER 15

Issa

Three days after our rodeo date and I was still floating on cloud nine. Amir was…

My cheeks heated until I pressed my cool hands against them. Amir was amazing. He was flirty like Ax, sweet like Cyrus, dominant like Enzo…and played my body like a well-tuned instrument.

Three days later and I was still glowing from the three orgasms he'd managed to pull from me while we'd made love on the couch.

Or fucked. Had sex. Whatever. It was too early to refer to it as making love. Right?

When we'd finally left my room and I'd given him the tour of the rest of the house, including the omega quarters and nest, he'd demanded a test run and eaten me until I'd cried out and almost collapsed onto the cushioned floor of the nest.

Four freaking orgasms from Amir. Four *that day*. I wasn't counting how he'd made me feel the night we'd met.

Since that day, my alphas had become more affectionate, running their fingers through my hair, hugging me from behind, dragging me to sit on their lap on our downtime when we were able to relax and watch movies.

Amir and I texted or talked on the phone several times a day as we tried to figure out another time for a group date. The two of us could always hang out around the house or I could even go to his house, but I'd felt bad about stealing so much of his attention that night when all four of us were supposed to be courting him in hopes of him joining our pack.

Our pack. *My* pack. That night was the first night I'd finally allowed myself to accept the fact these alphas cared about me, that they wanted me as their beta, that this wasn't a temporary solution until I could get past my trauma enough to leave the house in search of a job and get my own place.

HAVE YOU SAID ANYTHING YET?

I SMILED DOWN at my phone, rolling onto my stomach and kicking my feet like a teenager.

THEY'RE AT WORK.

YOU CANT TELL me theyve been at work for three days straight.

AMIR HAD BEEN COACHING ME – translation: he was trying to give me the courage to ask the alphas for a few changes to my room since I planned to stay.

Honestly, even if the alphas hadn't been adamant about me being theirs, their beta, about living here with them and being pack, I would have had a hard time picturing myself anywhere else. With or without the romantic connection, I'd felt more at peace and safer in the few months with them than I had my entire life.

No they havent been at work three days straight. Smartass.

Talk to them tonight.

Itll be too late. I dont wanna nag them when they worked all night.

After a second of those little bubbles dancing, a face palm gif popped up on my phone and made me giggle.

As much as I wished he was here with me, texting like this made me feel...normal. I was a little old for this kind of relationship, but it was something I'd never had the chance to experience in my younger years. My parents had sold me off to Antonio practically the day after I graduated high school. And I sure as hell wasn't allowed to date before then.

Losing my virginity to someone like Antonio...I'd wondered if I would ever actually enjoy sex with another alpha.

I still wondered that, honestly. It scared me. The thought of Enzo or Ax or even Cyrus losing themselves to their hindbrain, forgetting I was a beta and not built for a knot...

The fact a knot actually caused me pain never stopped Antonio. That was something I'd never told my new alphas. And probably never would. Why dredge up the past when all it would do was make them angry?

Not at me, of course, but *for* me. Not that it made a difference. Regardless of the fact I knew the three men in my life would never hurt me, my fight or flight actually kicked into gear when an alpha showed even a hint of anger.

. . .

KNOW WHAT THATS CALLED? An excuse.

I SENT him an emoji with its tongue out.

WHAT ABOUT THE OTHER THING?

I STARED down at the little conversation bubble and chewed on my bottom lip. He'd been coaching me on how to approach the alphas, how to just walk right up to them and plant a big kiss on their lips. Or to crawl into their bed and seduce them.

No matter what Amir or the alphas said, I still didn't see myself as sexy. And I sure as hell didn't see myself as seductive. Where my sister, Cora, had been raised and groomed to serve her alphas, I was more or less an afterthought, even though I was older than my sister and the first-born daughter after four big brothers.

I'd known my parents would arrange my bonding as they had for my beta brothers, but I'd thought they would at least prepare me for life a little better.

Who was I kidding? Cora had been sent off to school for omegas. I'd finished high school after being raised by nannies, then all but forgotten. Most of my memories of life after I'd left my family pack were hazy due to how often Antonio kept me doped to the gills with one sedative or another. I'd even suffered some withdrawals the first few weeks living with Cora and her pack.

Apparently, Amir got tired of waiting for me to respond. My phone vibrated with an incoming FaceTime call.

Unable to wipe the smile from my face, I accepted the call.

"Fuck, you're beautiful," he said the moment our faces came onto the screen.

My cheeks heated and I dipped my eyes for a second. When he said those words, I actually believed them, believed *him*, believed he thought I was beautiful and worth something more than my past experiences.

"Thank you," I said when I finally looked back at the screen.

He was on his bed, his back against the headboard, his long, curly hair pulled back away from his face.

The memories of running my fingers through his hair as he'd knelt in the nest and licked me until I'd almost screamed his name sent fire licking through my veins.

"I'm going to tell you something my mom told me – people can't read minds. That includes alphas. And since you four aren't bonded yet– " He cocked a brow at me as though to remind me of speaking my mind and asking one of them to cover Antonio's mark. "They won't feel your emotions, won't feel your needs. You have to use your words, *Habibi*."

Tilting my head, I let my eyes drink in the sight of him. He wasn't wearing a shirt, but the screen cut off around his shoulders, so I didn't get a full view. I still hadn't seen him fully naked yet and I wanted to… badly.

"What language is that? Habibi?"

"Arabic. I'm a Greek Arab. Mom's Greek. Dad's family is from Syria. My grandparents came over here as refugees before they had my dad and uncles."

That explained why his skin was even darker than my own olive complexion.

"Do they know about me?" I asked, suddenly feeling shy. Which was stupid being as he was inside me twice. And had tasted me… twice.

"Of course. They know all about you and the guys. They're dying to meet you. But I had to reel them in. Because trust me when I say you won't walk out of our house. You'll roll. Mom's love language is food. Like I said…she's Greek."

I chuckled and we fell into an easier topic of his family. He was the only omega in a long line of alphas and betas on both sides. While they'd doted on him, they hadn't treated him as though he was better or lesser than his siblings or cousins. His family sounded…well, perfect. He had the family I'd always dreamed of when I was a young girl.

"Quit changing the subject," he said with narrowed eyes and a smile when I started asking questions about his aunts and uncles.

"What? I'm just curious."

"Really? So, if I told you to be waiting naked when the guys got home?" He raised one dark brow.

My cheeks went up into flames. I knew I had to look like a tomato from how hard I was blushing.

The camera angle changed on Amir's end until I could see more of his chest. His pecs were chiseled, there was a dark smattering of hair, his nipples were dark against his tanned skin and pebbled as though the conversation had either turned him or it was chilly in his room. I preferred the former.

"What time will they be home?" he asked. And his sexy voice definitely sounded deeper.

Checking the time at the top of the screen, I said, "In about an hour. Maybe less if it wasn't too busy tonight."

Being as it was a weeknight, I didn't think they would be as late as they normally would. I tended to be asleep on the couch by the time they rolled in then would shuffle up to bed once I felt safe with their presence.

But since the night of our date, I'd been staying up chatting with Amir and was usually still awake when I heard the garage door rumble up.

"Hmm. I wonder how I could possibly get you worked up enough to jump your alphas' bones when they walk through the door."

The camera moved again and the outline of his long, thick erection through his sweats came into view before his face filled the screen again.

"You're a tease. Anyone ever tell you that?"

"Oh, honey. A tease is someone who doesn't follow through. And I'm pretty sure I've proven I always follow through on my flirting."

That he had. And I was already addicted and fiending for more.

"Sit up for me," he said.

My hand shook as I gripped the phone and rolled over so I could sit up.

"Show me what you're wearing."

My face went hot again. "I'm just wearing a t-shirt—"

"Show me," he said, so much authority in his voice I wanted to obey. He was an omega, for fuck's sake, but that demand felt more like an alpha's bark.

Turning the phone, I slowly revealed my body in an oversized t-shirt.

"Trail your hand up your thighs and push that shirt out of the way. I want to see what's under the shirt."

If I was an omega, slick would have already dampened my thighs. Omega or not, I was growing wetter by the second and there was currently no one here to help me with the ache in my lower belly.

Doing as Amir asked, I trailed my hand up my thigh, hooking my t-shirt and dragging it up to my belly so he could see my purple boy shorts.

"Fuck, you're so sexy," he said.

I swore his voice sounded shaky, as if he was…

"Look what you do to me," he said, turning the camera so I could see his hand wrapped around his cock he'd pulled out of his boxers.

A very omega sounding whimper tore from my lips at the sight of his big fist slowly pumping his cock.

The sexiest purr rattled through the phone at the sound and the camera turned back to his face. "I can't decide whether I want to see you slide your hand down your panties and get yourself off or if I want to watch that beautiful face while you fall apart."

Those words alone sent my hand sliding down my stomach and into my panties. The moment my fingertips brushed over my clit, I sucked in a shaky breath and laid back against the pile of pillows.

"Mmm. Are you touching yourself?" he asked.

I nodded, my lips parted as pleasure rippled through me and over me.

"Show me, *habibi*. I want to see your fingers plunging into that tight cunt."

Setting the phone down long enough to slide my panties over my hips, I propped myself better on the pillows and set the phone on the nightstand to give him the perfect view of both my pussy and my face.

Amir took my lead and set his phone up to give me a view of his body, including the way he slid his hand up and down his cock in slow movements as though savoring the moment and refraining from coming too soon.

Not that he needed to hold back. Amir had some kind of mystical talent where he could hold off even while fucking into me until I got off. Only then had he allowed himself a release.

I wished he was here. I wished it was his hand or mouth on my body.

"Let me see your cunt swallow your finger, beta."

My nipples were pebbled and straining against my t-shirt as I slowly pushed first one then another finger into myself, pumping in a rhythm that matched the way he stroked himself and pretended it was him inside of me. Though my fingers could never come close to match his size or skill.

My alphas were helping me find my inner strength. But Amir was showing me how fun sex could be. I'd enjoyed myself in ways I hadn't known were possible with another man more since I'd met him than I ever had. Sex with Antonio sure as hell had never been enjoyable.

"Can you make yourself come with your fingers? Or do you need your vibrator?"

"I don't have a vibrator," I said, my voice shaky with need, lust, and pleasure.

He hummed as though in deep thought, although his hand never stopped stroking along his length. "We'll have to go shopping, then. So many toys I want to introduce you to, so many fun things I want to show you."

"L-like what?"

Amir began to describe what exactly he would get me and how he would use it on me, how he wanted to watch me fuck myself on a dildo, how he wanted to fuck one of my holes with a long, thick dildo while he fucked the other.

Lowering my other hand, I rubbed my fingers along my clit as I continued to fuck myself with my fingers, every word out of his mouth pushing me closer and closer to the edge.

"Come with me, Issa. I want to hear those sexy ass moans fall from your mouth."

"Yes," I breathed out as tingles started at the base of my spine and rippled through my lower belly until stars danced behind my closed lids.

Throwing my head back, I continued rubbing myself as my body tightened and I cried out, Amir's name falling from my tongue as his own grunts and moans filled the room.

I had to force my eyes open so I could watch the pearly ropes of his release coat his stomach, his chest, all the way up to his throat. I'd never been with an omega before him and had had no idea how much they actually came nor how sweet their release was on my tongue. If I was there in his room, I would have run my tongue along every inch of his body to savor that chocolate strawberry sweetness, savor his essence, coat my tongue and fill my senses with his delicious signature.

A sharp intake of air jerked my eyes toward the door to find Ax standing there wide eyed in nothing but his boxer briefs, the outline of his long, hard cock straining against the fabric.

CHAPTER 16

<u>Ax</u>

onight had been slow, even for a weeknight, so I'd decided to try out some new choreography on the stage, more or less putting on a one man show for the patrons who'd come in for the night.

Now, I was tired as hell. I wanted nothing more than to take a quick, hot shower and drop face first into Issa's bed.

We'd all taken to sleeping together. It was normal now. Natural. And she no longer stiffened when one of us draped an arm over her waist to tug her closer, melding her back to our front, her knees over ours.

It had been three days since Amir had spent quite a bit of time entertaining our beta in her room and again in the nest. I didn't blame him – Issa was hot.

I also didn't blame her. For a male omega, he was far from dainty. His body was firm and tight with rippling, toned muscles, he stood around five feet ten inches, and had a deep, warm voice. Then he offset all that pure masculinity with his beautiful wavy hair, full, kiss-able lips – that I'd yet to taste – and beautiful green eyes framed with thick black lashes.

And yep, I'd noticed all that shit from the moment I'd spotted him dancing with Issa that night in the club when he had come in for the initial meet and greet.

Kind of like how I'd noticed the green flecks in Issa's honey brown eyes, or the way there were hints of auburn when the sun shone on her hair. Or how she couldn't lie for shit and would look to her left when she was trying to come up with an excuse for something. I'd also noted that she chewed the inside of her cheek when she was uncomfortable, causing her plump lips to purse in the cutest fucking way.

What could I say? I was a man lost to my beta.

We'd given her time to grow to trust us, to begin to heal from years of trauma. And sure, I knew it took far longer than mere months to overcome shit like that, but I was fucking dying to have Issa Alvarez...scratch that – Issa *Rivera* in my arms. Her sister was bonded to Pack Rivera. It just so happened our pack lead was the brother to the head of that pack. Not confusing at all.

Or it was and had earned us a front row seat or a spot at the head of the line on several occasions.

Didn't care either way, honestly. Enzo's brother ran...businesses. We ran a club. It had been the eldest Rivera brother who'd been able to finance the club we now ran and had built into an extremely successful place that catered to those with alternative tastes and lifestyles. The Vault also gave me an outlet for my obsession with dance. Not that shaking my hips or making men and women scream was what I'd been trained for since I could walk.

It struck me as ironic that just a few months ago we were perfectly content with the life we'd built. We could fuck each other or bring home a one-night stand. We could earn a shitload of money and... well, spend it however we saw fit.

There had been zero desire to add anyone else to the pack.

Until Issa. Until the day she'd crashed into our lives.

Even with the beautiful beta now in our pack, there hadn't been this deep-seated need to add an omega. We hadn't really had the conversation, but the three of us had never really expressed the desire for children. At least not anytime in the near future. We were only in our twenties. We had plenty of time for all that shit.

But our girl was intimidated by alphas. She'd grown to trust us, but she was still leery. An omega was no threat to her. And since Issa hadn't shown any interest in women, we'd intentionally sought a male omega. Not an easy feat being as they were the rarest of their designation.

It had felt like fate when we'd come across his profile. His profile had said he was open to a pack with a beta, that he was interested in bisexual relationships outside of his heat when his body would demand the relief only a knot could bring.

Oh, and he was hot as fuck.

And then I'd watched the way the two of them had interacted on the dance floor as they'd watched me onstage. Before I'd even met him face to face, the way Issa had been instantly drawn to him cemented my plan to meld him into our pack through any means necessary.

Okay…maybe not *any* means. Unlike Enzo's brother, we had no intention of kidnapping an omega for any reason.

But fuck…I'd pay Amir to stick around for Issa, as long as she was happy. Although yeah. I wished I was the one who made her happy, who elicited those adorably shy smiles, who she wanted to ride the way she had the omega three days ago.

Cyrus pulled the SUV into the garage and killed the engine as Enzo and I pushed from our doors. Slow nights ended up being the most tiring. Not only was I physically exhausted from all the dancing, but I was mentally exhausted because of the lack of stimulation. Not to mention I hated that my servers didn't make nearly enough on slower weeknights.

We all trudged through the mudroom, kicking our shoes off as we went, then made our way to our individual bedrooms for a shower before bed. Since meeting Amir, she'd grown more comfortable with going to her bed when we worked late instead of waiting on the couch as she'd done the first few months.

We'd all been sleeping with Issa and, regardless of what the other two had planned, I had every intention of climbing under the blankets with her and tugging her to my body.

Amir's sweet chocolate and strawberries scent still clung to every surface, mixing with Issa's warm, sun-dried linen as well as our scents. It felt...fuck, it felt perfect. I wanted that combination here permanently, but we were still currently courting Amir.

Well, *Issa* was courting him since they talked or texted nonstop like a couple of teenagers while Enzo, Cyrus, and I worked the club.

Her scent rose above the others, but that was more than likely due to my absolute obsession over the introverted beta.

Would she still be an introvert once she finally got over the bull-shit she'd been fed her whole life, when she fully accepted us as her alphas and Amir as her omega?

I couldn't wait to see her shine like the diamond she truly was.

Stripping my clothes on my way to the bathroom, I dropped them wherever they fell, then let the hot water sluice down my body, washing away the sweat and stress of the day. My muscles loosened with every minute I stood there soaping up until I was more than ready to drop onto Issa's bed and let sleep drag me under.

The three of us had invited Amir to the club again tomorrow. Friday nights were when we introduced new choreography from the male dance review...*not* strippers as my packmates liked to call us. We didn't dance in thongs; we didn't swing around a pole. And to me, that was what separated us, regardless of whether we brought someone onto stage or removed our shirts.

After drying off, I tugged on a pair of boxers and padded barefoot to Issa's room...

And froze in the doorway.

Her phone sat on the nightstand, Amir's face and body filling the screen as he jerked off. Issa laid on the bed in nothing but a t-shirt she'd snagged from one of us, her fingers thrusting into her cunt while her other hand rubbed her clit in quick circles until they both got off simultaneously.

As if the sight wasn't enough, the sound of their moans filling the room sent every drop of blood in my body straight to my cock until I was dizzy.

I sucked in a gulp of air as my lungs constricted and my alpha pushed to the forefront, demanding I charge across the room, rut into my beta, and clamp my teeth into her flesh.

Instead, I gripped the frame of the door until my knuckles cracked under the pressure.

Issa's eyes went wide when she spotted me, and she scrambled to end the call and pull the blanket over her lower half.

A growl ripped from my chest the moment she was covered.

Fuck. *Don't move. Do not fucking move.*

Because if I took a single step toward her, my hindbrain would take over and I could never hurt my beautiful girl.

"I'm sorry?" she said, the statement sounding like a question.

"For what?" Damn it. My voice was deep, the vibrations of the growl rumbling through each word.

Her mouth opened but nothing came out. Her sweet and warm scent was strong on the air and was as fucking boner inducing as any omega's.

"You have nothing to apologize for, baby girl."

Once I felt like I wouldn't lunge at her the moment I put one foot in front of the other, I moved further into the room, my eyes going from her to the phone then back. "You two were having phone sex?" It was meant as a tease, but even I could hear how deep my voice sounded.

Her head nodded quickly up and down, and her throat moved on a hard swallow.

"I don't blame you…or him."

Her full lips fell open and her chest rose and fell in heavy breaths. When her eyes travelled from my face down to the tent in my pants, her warm, sun-dried linen scent turned sweeter and floated on the air and landed on my tongue, sending even more blood to my cock until my knot throbbed with the need to be buried inside of her.

But she was a beta. Her body wasn't built for a knot. And I would never hurt my sweet girl.

When she blinked a few times and started to chew the inside of her cheek, I knew her nerves were strung tight. I should leave. I should back out of the room and let her…

What? She'd already gotten off. Maybe she'd want to call Amir back and explain the abrupt end to their call.

I'd caught the smirk on his face when he'd spotted me standing near the door just before she'd ended the call, so he knew I'd seen enough.

Just as I'd made up my mind to force my body to turn and give her some privacy, she pulled the blanket away from her lap and pushed to her knees. Her hands shook as she grabbed the bottom hem of her tee and slowly peeled it over her body, revealing those tits I was obsessed with but had yet to feel or taste.

"Issa…" But any other words dried up on my tongue when she rested back against the pillows and spread her knees in invitation.

"You don't have to…I don't want you to think…" Fuck. I couldn't think straight let alone form a coherent sentence.

"I want you, Ax. You guys thought I had no libido…" I rolled my eyes and shook my head as she threw my words back into my face. "But I've wanted you for a long time. And Amir said he thinks you three are waiting for me to make the first move. I trust you. I'm not afraid of you. Of any of you. I know you would never do anything I didn't want."

"We would never hurt you," I forced out through my tight throat.

"I want to be pack. Officially. I want you to mark me. I want you to cover this," she said, gesturing toward the ruined flesh left behind by that piece of shit Antonio.

As slowly as I could, I approached the bed when all I wanted to do was rush to her, cover her with my body, and thrust into her core hard and fast while chomping down on her shoulder.

Fuck yes, I would cover that fucking mark. I'd never said a word about it, but every time I'd caught a glimpse of that scar, red hot rage burned through my veins. It was obvious he hadn't tended to her to help with the healing. The skin was ragged and raised instead of the beautiful silvery crescents that should have been left after she was bonded.

"What about a bonding ceremony?" I asked. My voice sounded guttural and forced as I struggled against the trembling of my body.

"I've had one. I hated it. Hated all those people staring at me. Hated everything my mother picked out. Hated…well…it might not have been so bad had it not been with Antonio and Carlos. But still."

Carlos. The beta who'd been packed with her and her alpha before he'd disappeared shortly after their ceremony. From the little she'd told us about him, they were more roommates than anything, hardly talked, and only slept together once after they were officially bonded to Antonio.

He might not have been a threat to her, but I still wouldn't let the cocksucker anywhere near her if he someday reappeared.

The longer I stood there staring at her, the more tense she appeared to grow until her knees began to close.

Nope. *Hell* no.

Moving close, I put one knee on the bed and began to crawl toward her. "If you only want my mark, I'm more than happy to give it to you." *You can have every part of me.*

I kept that last part unspoken. No reason to freak her out when she was finally letting herself feel something for me, for us. When she was finally allowing herself to feel free, to accept she was an integral part of our pack.

No. We didn't need an omega. We didn't need Amir. Sure, all three of us alphas wanted him. How could we not? He was sexy as fuck.

But it was more than that. He made Issa happy. He'd helped her smash through whatever walls she'd built around her heart. Had helped her realize how beautiful, how sexy, how fucking perfect she was.

"I want you. I'm…" Whatever else she'd planned to say never left her mouth. I pretended she wanted to tell me she was in love with me, that she loved me.

Because fuck...I loved this woman so much it hurt. I would have continued to live exactly as we had the past few months if that was all she wanted from me. I would continue to flirt with her, to buy her pretty shit, to protect her. But I would never have pushed her for more than she was willing to give.

Though if she wanted more...I would literally give her my heart and soul on a diamond encrusted silver platter. I would crawl on hands and knees through hot coals to officially have her as mine, to have her feel even an iota of what I felt for her.

Yeah, I loved Enzo and Cyrus, but it was nothing compared to the way the mere thought of Issa made my dick instantly stand at attention and my heart race.

Instead of saying anything else, she pushed up onto her elbows and smiled at me. "Are you...we don't have to do anything else if you just wanted to mark me–"

Her words were cut off by a squeal as I lunged for her, my mouth slamming against hers hard enough I'd worried I might have hurt her or bruised her plump as fuck lips.

When her arms snaked around my neck to hold me closer and her tongue teased the seam of my lips, any fear I'd had of hurting her disappeared.

Her legs wrapped around my thighs, pulling me closer to the heat between her legs. The only thing keeping me from plunging my cock into her tight, wet heat was the fucking cotton of my boxers.

Slow. I had to take this slowly. I wanted to savor my first time with her after fantasizing about this very moment for so fucking long.

Except she apparently didn't want any foreplay. One of her hands left the back of my neck and trailed down my chest, tickling my abs, before sliding below my boxers. Her thin fingers wrapped around my cock and my hips bucked forward of their own volition.

Her mouth pulled from my mine and nipped and kissed along my jaw and throat before rubbing her cheek across my scent gland. A satisfied growl rumbled from my chest, mixing with a moan as her fingers tightened and she began to slowly stroke me from base to head.

"I need to tell you something else," she whispered against my skin.

When I tried to pull back to look into her eyes, she held me in place with the hand still cupping the back of my neck.

"A couple things." Her voice was barely above a breath as she pulled my cock free from my boxers and guided the flared head toward her opening.

She didn't wait for me to push forward, instead raising her hips and taking me in slowly, one agonizing inch at a time.

"I'm in love with you. I have been for a while, but I was scared... I didn't think you wanted me like that. But I'm in love with you. And I want Amir to be our omega. I want you guys to win him over, mark him, and bond him to us."

I could barely think past the way her wet cunt squeezed my cock as she took me fully inside of her until my knot pressed against her opening. It took every single fucking ounce of control I possessed to keep from shoving forward and locking us together.

For now, I would let her control this moment. I would keep my face buried against her neck if that was what she needed to speak her mind, to tell me what she'd been holding back for as long as I had been hiding my own feelings.

My arms wrapped around her and held her closer, her tits pressed against my hard chest. Yeah, I was the flirty alpha. But every second I'd flirted with Issa had been genuine, it had been the only way I could release some of my feelings for her without overwhelming her.

"I've loved you from the first moment I saw you, Issa."

Pulling my hips back, I pushed them forward again, clenching my teeth against how tight she was, how wet and warm and perfect she felt wrapped around my cock and in my arms.

I'd known being with her would be life changing. And I didn't give two fucks how sappy that sounded. I'd never met anyone so beautifully broken and yet as strong as Issa. Through everything she'd been through in her life, she was still determined to build a life of her own. She was fighting tooth and nail to work through the trauma, to accept the fact an alpha could love her, could want her for more than prestige or her last name or even what she possessed between her legs.

Her feet locked around my thighs and urged me to pump into her faster. Fuck. I was trying to hold back. Trying to make this last. But between the overwhelming scents, the fact the woman I was obsessed with actually loved me back, and the way her cunt was practically strangling my cock…there was a good chance I would blow my load before she got off.

And that sure as fuck couldn't happen. I didn't care if I had to edge myself, pull away from her anytime I felt the first tingles of an orgasm and lower my mouth to her core to devour her pussy until she came on my tongue.

Fuck. I needed to see her face. I needed to look into her beautiful brown eyes, to see those pretty flecks of green and gold in the dim light from the lamp she'd left on for her little show with Amir.

And the fleeting image of the two of them masturbating together, of having phone sex while the three of us were out caused my balls to tighten.

Nope. Hell no. Fuck no.

Pulling from her, I smiled at her frustrated groan that quickly morphed into a moan when I licked one of her nipples and sucked it between my teeth, grazing it lightly before moving further south.

I could smell her arousal, the warmth of her scent stronger near her soaked pussy. She was so wet. It wasn't like being with an omega, no slick coating her upper thighs or dampening the sheets below her. This was a mixture of the release she'd given herself and her body's reaction to me.

And yeah, that definitely gave my ego a boost that simply the sight of my hard cock and bare chest had been enough to prime my girl's body to be fucked.

Flattening my tongue, I ran it from her tight little back hole up to her clit, my hands clamping around her thighs to keep them open when they began to close around my head. I wasn't sure whether she was trying to keep me in place, but there was absolutely nothing short of death that could make me stop licking her cunt until I tasted her cum on my tongue.

Her fingers tangled in my shoulder length hair, holding my face to her core as her hips began to writhe, fucking herself on my tongue. My hips began to rock against the mattress, almost fucking myself against the bed.

"Ax," she moaned out as her breathing grew faster, heavier.

I looked up her body, at the way her back was arched off the bed, her tits pushed together by her arms as she kept a death grip in my hair, her lips parted, her eyes closed.

Perfection. Absolute and utter perfection. She was everything I'd never known I needed. Until we'd met her, until that day at Bain's estate, I hadn't realized I'd been missing a part of my heart and soul, that our pack was missing such an integral part.

Pushing a finger into her, I curled it and rubbed that spongey spot that would make her see stars as I continued to feast on her like a dying man, and she was my final fucking meal. I could live off her flavor on my tongue alone, breathe in her scent instead of oxygen.

All I needed was Issa.

CHAPTER 17

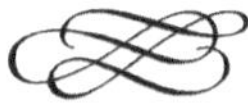

<u>Issa</u>

I'd said the words. I'd told Ax how I felt. One down, two to go.

Maybe I hadn't been able to look him in the eyes when I confessed how deep my feelings for him were, but at least he knew. And he'd said them back. He loved me. He and the others had given me time to heal, had waited for me to decide when I was ready to trust and allow another alpha inside my body.

Ax, Enzo, and Cyrus were the first alphas I'd ever allowed in my heart. And all I could do was hope and pray they didn't make me regret that decision.

Ax's wickedly talented tongue stroked my clit, his lips suctioning around it as he added a second finger to the first and pumped them into my core until my body felt as though it would combust. Like my times with Amir, it wasn't mere tingles that rippled through my body.

Nope. It felt as though explosions were rocking through me from the inside out, stealing my breath as I opened my mouth on a silent scream and fell apart on Ax's tongue.

He continued to work his fingers into me, lapping slowly at my clit until the aftershocks began to slow to light fluttering of my inner walls. Only then did he pull away, his chin and lips glistening with my release before he swiped the back of his hand across his face, then rose up my body, his cock sliding inside me with ease, only stopped by his swollen and throbbing knot.

I wished more than anything I could give him everything, including allowing him to knot me, to lock us together until his knot deflated. But my experiences with an alpha's knot weren't exactly something I looked back on fondly.

Ax's beautiful blue-green eyes were on my face, so many emotions flittering through them even as his pupils remained blown with lust. I had no fear he would lose himself to rut and hurt me. I trusted him. I trusted all three of my alphas more than I had ever trusted another living soul.

"I love you," he breathed out as he began to pump his hips in a slow, deep rhythm, rubbing all the right spots until my breath was once again frozen in my lungs. "I've loved you this whole time."

His words held so much emotion I felt tears burn the backs of my eyes.

There was a part of me that had known all along how Ax felt about me, how they all felt about me. But another part, the louder and bigger part, didn't believe I was worth an alpha's love and devotion. I was nothing but a beta. In my family, a beta couldn't exactly be used as a bargaining chip to climb the ladder or gain more power. Not that that had stopped my fathers and mother from arranging packs for all five of their beta children, not just their one omega daughter.

"I love you, too," I whispered back.

He lowered his head and pressed a kiss to my lips before pulling back, his face barely a breath from mine. "Are you sure?"

Was I sure about the mark. Was I sure about being bonded to him. I knew exactly what he was asking without him voicing the words.

I couldn't think of a single moment in my life I had been surer about anything as I was about believing these three truly saw me as *their* beta, *their* mate.

"Bite me, Ax. Bond me to you. Make me pack."

"You're pack with or without my mark, baby girl. Please know that."

I raised my head to stop anything else he might say with my lips. Pulling back, I cupped his face in both my hands, my gaze bouncing between his. "I want nothing more than to proudly display my *true* alpha's mark. I want to be bonded to the three of you." A wry smile tugged up one side of my mouth. "That way, you can never get rid of me."

A heart melting smile lit up his beautifully rugged face. His thrusts became faster, harder, tearing more moans from my mouth as his purr rumbled against my chest. He was barely holding his weight off me on his elbows, his forearms framing my head as he continued to stare into my face.

"I'm going to make you come all over my cock and then I'm going to show you how fucking much I've wanted you. You're mine, Issa. You're ours."

Widening his knees, he forced my legs open wider, giving him room to slam into me harder, faster, deeper. Within seconds, another orgasm built and slammed into me like a fucking bulldozer. I screamed out his name and squeezed my eyes shut as wave after wave of the most delicious tingles rippled through my body, and I swore my body was seconds away from catching on fire and burning the bed below us.

Ax's body hovered over mine, his chest pressing against mine as he continued to thrust into me. His lips brushed along the ugly ragged mark Antonio had forced on me a second before he slowly bit down, his teeth breaking through the flesh and sending my body soaring into a fourth orgasm of the night.

By the time he pulled his teeth free and slammed his cock into me until his muscles went taut, his eyes squeezed shut, and he grunted with his own release, my body felt as though my bones had turned to jelly. I couldn't have stood if my life depended on it.

His tongue was soft and warm as he lapped at the blood seeping from the puncture marks on my shoulder. It would take a few days to heal, and his bite didn't quite cover Antonio's, but already, I could feel Ax blooming to life in my chest.

His presence was like the sun – fiery and bright. It warmed me emotionally and physically and, if my body wasn't so tired from how many times I'd come in the past two hours, I might have rolled him onto his back and ridden him until we both forgot our own damn names.

No wonder he was always flirting – it was like his very presence inside me was yet a new erogenous zone, as though he was a walking, talking aphrodisiac.

He was still inside me, his knot nudged against my opening, but he didn't push for more, just gently tended to his mark.

"I can feel you," he whispered, his breath warm against my torn flesh.

"I can feel you, too," I whispered back, running my fingers through his shoulder length hair, carefully working out a few tangles as he purred in contentment.

No. That wasn't the right word. I could feel his beaming joy and warm affection down the invisible thread in my chest tying us together.

"Where are Enzo and Cyrus?" I asked when he pulled from me and shifted some of his weight off my torso while resting his head on my shoulder and pressing kiss after kiss to any part he could easily reach.

"I assume in their rooms. We all headed for our showers when we got home. I just happened to be the lucky one who got to your room first."

I lifted my head and looked toward the open door. My other two alphas would have heard every noise we'd made in this room. Yet I didn't feel a bit of embarrassment. Especially since I planned to enjoy them, as well, as soon as possible.

"Aren't they sleeping in here tonight?"

I'd grown to love the pack cuddles at night. It made me feel so safe, as though the alphas formed this big force field around me while we slept. Even my nightmares didn't dare appear while they were in the bed with me.

"We were all heading your way. They must have turned back around when they spotted us fucking."

My cheeks burst into flames at his words. That had been far more than fucking. That had been…damn. That had been life changing, and not simply because I'd finally felt Ax inside of me. It was as though something deep in my heart and soul had finally clicked into place. It sounded corny, but being with Ax, feeling his presence explode in my chest made me feel like I could take on the world, like nothing could hurt me, like just being Ax's beta formed a force field around me and my heart.

"Your beta wants you!" Ax yelled, causing me to start with surprise before giggling.

"I could have just texted them."

He rolled fully off me, his head resting on my chest, his warm breath breezing over his bite and sending the most delicious shivers down my spine.

Heavy thuds sounded down the hall as my other two alphas left their rooms and entered mine. A sweet smile stretched across Cyrus's face. Enzo looked…intense. I was tired, but not too tired to be with another of my alpha's tonight.

"Let her rest," Cyrus said as though he could read Enzo's mind, and climbed into the bed on the other side of me. "Are you okay?" he asked, gently running the pad of one finger along Ax's mark.

"I'm perfect." I sighed, reaching for him and pulling his face down for a kiss.

But he didn't deepen it, didn't settle between my thighs and push his thick cock inside of me. He didn't even doff his boxers before climbing into bed as if he needed that barrier between us to resist the temptation of doing exactly that.

"I'm finally pack."

Cyrus feathered his lips across my forehead, my eyelids, my nose, cheeks, then finally my lips. "You were already pack, Issa. But now, you're officially ours."

CHAPTER 18

Amir

The alphas had invited me to the club tonight and I planned to stay the night at their house whether I was invited or not. Watching Issa fuck herself with her fingers had been one of the sexiest things I'd ever seen in my life. I wasn't sure I'd ever come so hard in my life, covering my chest, stomach, and hand in my release, the two of us moaning together as she fell apart.

When I'd spotted Ax at the door, his eyes wide and his lips parted as though he was panting, I chuckled as Issa lunged at the phone and ended the call. I would have bet a hundred dollars she'd immediately covered herself, too.

Two weeks and I was beyond obsessed with the beta. No one had officially invited me to join their pack but fuck me...I would do anything to join if for no other reason than to be with Issa every day for the rest of my life.

I'd been blessed with the most amazing parents. They didn't give a shit whether I joined a big pack or fell in love with one person. They didn't care whether I bonded with a beta, an alpha, or even another omega, as long as I was happy.

Poor Issa had had the complete opposite family life, and I was slowly helping her to see not only how amazing she was but how wonderful pack life could be when mated to the right people.

And fuck…those alphas were not only gorgeous but treated her like the queen she truly was.

Pulling up to the valet, I handed my key fob over, told the bouncer my name like I had the first time I'd come here, and smiled at him with a nod when he pulled back the rope and let me in.

Immediately, I began to search for my girl. I found her sitting at the bar in a black dress that showed off her back and shoulders…and a beautifully fresh bonding mark from one of her alphas.

As though she felt me staring, her head lifted and turned in my direction, a warm, wide smile pulling up her red painted lips.

Her makeup was a little different, darker, smokier, and sexy as fuck.

Issa turned and hopped off the stool as I approached, her red heels giving her a few more inches yet she was still short enough I had to bend to press a kiss to her lips.

"Sorry," she said with a sweet giggle when she raised her hand and wiped away the lipstick from my lips.

"Should have left it. My own temporary bonding mark for the night," I teased, gently running the pad of my index finger along the mark covering the one from her first asshole alpha. She shivered under my touch and her nipples strained against the silk of her dress. "You look so beautiful," I said loud enough for her to hear me over the thump of bass filling the club.

The room wasn't completely packed yet, but it was full enough it would be a tight fit if we were to head out to the dance floor. It would definitely happen, though. My girl could fucking move.

"Is Ax dancing tonight?" I said, bending to speak into her ear.

"Yeah. He came up with a new show. I think that's why he invited you tonight specifically. He wants to show off a little."

Enzo and Cyrus approached wearing jeans that looked soft and high dollar, and button-down shirts. Enzo was wearing black, Cyrus a hunter green that made his eyes look even brighter. I had an overwhelming urge to rip those shirts open and leave bites and hickeys across every inch of their bodies. How the hell did I earn the attention of such a sexy pack?

"Glad you came," Enzo said, leaning forward to press a quick peck to my cheek.

"Good to see you," Cyrus said. When he went for my cheek like Enzo had, I turned my face so I could feel his lips on mine, then smirked with a raised brow at his almost shy smile. The alpha was the sweetest of the three, yet I could see the heat in his eyes as though he was constantly holding back from what he really wanted.

I didn't want him to hold back. Didn't need him to. My body was built for alphas, and I was more than ready to be with all four of them if for no other reason than to see my girl fall apart around their cocks while I took a knot from one of them.

They usually wore slacks while working the club. "Are you two officially off the clock tonight?" I yelled over the music.

"Technically, but we're never really off when the doors are open," Cyrus yelled back.

Sure, it would have been nice to hang out without having to constantly yell back and forth, but this place was amazing. As were the dancers who performed a few times throughout the night.

One could say I was biased since one of my prospective alphas was one of said dancers, but the show was actually really cool.

"This place is amazing," I said, leaning closer to Enzo.

"They own a couple strip clubs, too," Issa said with a smile, squeaking when Enzo poked her ribs. "What? You do."

"We own them but don't work them," Cyrus said.

"Strippers as in naked women? Or…"

"Both," Issa said. "But I haven't been to the others yet. I only come here with them."

And from what I'd learned from her through our phone conversations and texting, that was usually rare.

She'd admitted to having borderline agoraphobia, but mostly

because she'd been afraid of alphas, afraid her former alpha might see her in public, just…afraid.

But Enzo, Ax, and Cyrus were gradually teaching her to trust them to protect her.

"Guess what?" she said, leaning into my side.

I tilted my head down, my grin stretching at the beatific smile she gave me. "What?"

"I got a job."

My brows shot to my hairline. She'd wanted a job since she'd never been permitted in her past, but her fear had kept her from even driving herself anywhere or going out alone.

"Where?"

She pulled away and stretched her arms wide. "I'm the new server. I'm going to work three nights a week when they're here," she said, jerking her head toward Enzo and Cyrus, and I assumed Ax was included in that.

"That's awesome! I'm so fucking proud of you!"

I drew her closer, wrapped my arms around her back, and lifted her feet from the ground. Her sweet giggle in my ear was the most beautiful music.

When I set her down, she wrapped her arms around my waist. "Will you come in on the days I work?"

"Hell yes, I will."

She'd told me a little about her family, about her youngest and only sister Cora, about how her only omega sibling had actually had the opportunity to go out to clubs and have friends.

Issa had never had that opportunity since her parents had bonded her straight out of school. She was only in her mid-twenties but was finally getting the chance to experience a real life, a life with people who cared for her and wanted her to have anything and everything she could have ever dreamed of having.

And my sweet beta didn't dream of luxury trips or expensive clothes. She wanted freedom and independence. She wanted love. She wanted to figure out who she was away from the claws of the Alvarez name.

"Oh! And did you see?" She tilted her neck and pointed to the mark.

"Of course, I saw that. It's like a fucking beacon." I pressed my lips directly over it before pulling back. "I can't wait to see you wearing a necklace of bonding marks."

I winked at Enzo and Cyrus, who were watching us with matching smiles.

The lights dimmed, and a different beat mixed with the music playing through the giant speakers around the room.

"I want to get close," she yelled, taking my hand, then reaching for Cyrus.

The two alphas smiled at her and let her pull them along with us to the dance floor. Enzo shoved his way through the crowd, making a path for Issa to get close enough to see Ax's performance.

The beat gradually morphed until the first notes of *Boom* by iBenji filled the room, the beat sultry and primal.

The dancers filed out in varying formations, their bodies moving like snakes. Gradually the song bled to *Sail* by AWOLNATION and the real performance began. But I couldn't see Ax anywhere.

"Where is he?" I said, bending to speak into Issa's ear.

Her shoulders shrugged up, but her head was craning and turning side to side as she sought her alpha, as well.

After a few moments, Issa was tugged from my hold. I frowned and was prepared to start throwing fists, but Cyrus and Enzo had her by her arms and were gently guiding her to the steps that would lead up to the stage.

Her eyes were wide, and her lips moved as she shook her head, no doubt telling them she didn't want to go up there. But the two alphas merely smiled.

The dancers were positioned around a platform in the center of the stage as Cyrus and Enzo urged her to lie back, ensuring her dress was pulled down and she wasn't flashing anything at the crowd.

Somehow, they'd managed to remix the songs until *All the Time* by Jeremih filled the room and a single spotlight shone directly on Issa like she was a sacrifice to the crowd. It was both unnerving and boner inducing because I wanted nothing more than to jump up on that stage and fuck her for the world to see she was mine.

Another red tinted spotlight lit on a body floating down from the ceiling. Holy shit! It was Ax. He was strapped to something and was slowly being lowered down until he hovered only inches from Issa.

Dipping his head, he kissed the tip of her nose, his lips moved as though he was telling her something – probably reassuring her – before he spun until his crotch was over her face and they were in a beautiful and graceful sixty-nine position.

He spun again and rolled as the ropes pulled him away from her body. He moved like water, dancing in the air like a fairy. Although I couldn't imagine a fairy being nearly as sexual or muscular as this alpha.

After a few more moves, he lowered back down until his knees bracketed Issa's hips. A couple dancers rushed forward and removed whatever had kept him attached to the ropes.

And then it felt as though I had a front row seat to the most erotic show in the world. Ax would roll his hips against her, then spun them so she was straddling him, his hands keeping the dress from riding up and flashing her lower half at the feral crowd watching him, screaming and whistling nonstop.

I couldn't make a sound. It was like every bit of oxygen had been sucked from the room.

With Issa still straddling him, he bent his knees, lifted onto his hands, then began to thrust upward as though fucking her right there on stage.

Issa's smile was...fuck. It was like looking into the sun. It was hard to see from here, but I knew damn well both their pupils were blown wide. There wasn't much separating them from fucking with an audience.

Ax continued to maneuver Issa around as part of his routine until he wrapped her legs around his waist and escorted her off the stage while the remaining dancers finished off the show.

Reaching down, I adjusted my cock and winced at the slick leaking from my ass and dampening my boxers. If I wasn't careful, I'd end up with an embarrassing wet spot on my fucking jeans.

As the song ended and the spotlights shut off, the crowd went absolutely insane, the noise nothing short of a roar.

Enzo and Cyrus grinned at me, and Enzo jerked his head for me to follow.

They led me to the same office where I'd fucked Issa for the first time and we all walked in to find Issa straddling Ax's lap, their lips locked as they made out. But at least they were still dressed. Had I walked in on Issa riding Ax's cock, I was pretty sure there wasn't a chance in hell I could control myself. One way or another, I would need to get off.

"Do we need to go home?" Enzo teased.

Cyrus shook his head and pushed a hand through his hair.

Ax's shoulder length hair was disheveled both from dancing and from Issa's fingers running through it. His lips and around his mouth were stained red from her smeared lipstick.

She pulled back and looked at us over her shoulder. "Not yet. I want to dance. And drink. A lot. I can't believe you did that," she said, slapping Ax's chest playfully. She turned to me. "Did you know they had that planned?"

"Uh...no. But I definitely volunteer if you ever do that performance again."

Ax winked at me while Issa carefully wiped away the crimson smears around his lips. Her makeup was all over the place, too, and would need to be touched up.

A flash of her on her knees, leaving that red lipstick all over my cock pulled a whimper from my chest. All three alphas tensed, their heads whipping in my direction.

Holding up my hands, I swallowed down the whine from the increased alpha hormones permeating the air.

"I'm fine. Just horny."

Ax laughed loudly. Issa smiled sweetly as she grabbed a tissue and a mirror to fix her lipstick. Enzo's eyes burned a path along my body while Cyrus pushed his fingers through his hair again. I was beginning to think that was his nervous tick. It was endearing as fuck.

I wanted Issa. There wasn't a single doubt in my mind she was meant to be mine. I was meant to be her omega.

But these three alphas…fuck.

Not only were they gorgeous, not only were they successful and strong, but they treated Issa the way she deserved. They'd been there for her to heal, had protected her, had given her space to grow and let her set the pace for their relationship. I'd told her they looked at her as though she hung the moon, and I'd meant it. They practically shot hearts from their eyes every time they so much as glanced in her direction.

That alone made me want them as my alphas. I wanted to be their omega. I wanted to be pack.

I wanted to be Amir Rivera.

CHAPTER 19

I didn't dance. That was Ax's wheelhouse. But when my sweet beta and the delicious omega begged and dragged me onto the floor…how the fuck could I say no?

Cyrus had disappeared into his office to take a call, so I was currently swaying to the thump of bass with Issa sandwiched between my body and Amir's. More than once, the two of us would lock eyes over my beta's head and an intoxicating cloud of chocolate covered strawberries would rise, stronger than the scent filtration system could control.

I swore my dick had been hard since I'd heard the telltale sounds of Issa being fucked by Ax. And yeah, I probably should have charged into that room so I could feel our beta's cunt wrapped around my cock, but I'd sat on the edge of my bed, my fist around my shaft, and fucked my hand until I shot ribbons of cum over my hand to dribble on the floor. At least we had hardwood floors; it was a lot easier to mop up messes that way.

My boner had instantly returned after seeing the way Issa was dressed tonight, watching her on stage with Ax, and now having both her and the omega so fucking close, their scents drilling into my very being and coating my tongue.

By the third song, I had to beg for mercy. It was too fucking hot out here with all these bodies pressed together. Or maybe it was the way I was struggling to stop myself from pulling Issa's skirt over her ass and taking her right here in the club in front of over a hundred people.

"Let's get a drink," I called over the music.

She nodded and smiled, sliding her hand into mine while reaching back for Amir.

She'd changed so much in the past few months, even more so since the night she'd met Amir. I loved watching her grow, loved watching the way she refused to cower even when alphas crowded around us.

Loved the way she trusted me to keep her safe from any possible threat.

Raising my hand, I got the bartender's attention and put in an order for the three of us. Issa had grown more adventurous and moved from only wine to various mixed drinks and even shots. Like the night she'd gotten a little drunk and dragged Amir to the office for a quick fuck.

Had he been anyone else, that might have pissed me off, scared the shit out of me, and yeah…made me jealous as fuck.

Luckily for all parties involved, she'd just happened to be drawn to the very person we were interested in integrating into the pack.

I might not have had to pay for the drinks at my own club, but no fucking way would I not tip my staff. Slapping down a twenty for Aryn, the bartender tonight, I took the drinks with a nod and passed them to Issa and Amir.

"Can we do shots? When Ax and Cyrus come back?" Issa yelled.

"You sure?" I asked. She was small. She had put on a little more weight during her time with us, but she was still nearly as petite as most omegas.

"We're celebrating!" She lifted her dirty martini and waited for Amir and me to do the same.

"What are we celebrating?" Amir yelled.

"I have a real pack and a job!" She tilted her drink back and gulped it down instead of sipping on it.

I couldn't help the frown that crossed my face or the anger that built in my system at her statement.

It took her a second to notice I hadn't taken a drink or that I was currently scowling at her.

"What?"

"You *had* a fucking pack, Issa. Just because none of us had bitten you until last night meant fuck all. We've been yours the whole time, you little brat."

The anger that had bloomed hot in my veins changed to a different kind of heat when her confused and mildly concerned look turned playful.

"Did you just call me a brat? Because I have absolutely no problem living up to that title."

"Holy shit, Issa!" Amir said with a burst of surprised laughter. "How do you get hotter by the second?"

She lifted her drink to take another sip before remembering it was empty. Raising her brows to me, she gave me a flirty smile until I motioned for Aryn to make her another.

I liked this side of her. I liked watching the stunning butterfly emerge from her cocoon. We'd done what we could for her, but all three of us alphas knew it was Amir's influence that had finally held a mirror up to her face.

"Slower this time," I warned her half-heartedly as I passed over her new martini.

Ax finally joined us, dressed in a pair of jeans and a t-shirt. He was probably still burning up after that performance. I'd only danced with my beta and – hopefully – future omega and was sweating my ass off.

"That was so cool!" Issa squealed. "But maybe a little warning next time."

"Nah. I liked the surprise on your face. Glad you made it," Ax said to Amir, leaning forward and pressing his lips to the omega's.

Between Ax's natural tendency toward wanting to fuck any hole he could find, Amir's natural omega sex appeal, and Issa's newfound confidence, I was going to end up having to buy new pants when my dick ripped through its fabric prison.

"Text Cyrus and tell him to get his ass out here. I want to do shots!"

Ax's brows shot up his forehead and he turned wide eyes on me. "The fuck happened since I went backstage?"

"She wants to celebrate," I answered with a shrug.

He looked at Issa, Amir, then back at me. "Okay. But since when is she so..." He waved his hand up and down toward Issa. "Bubbly?"

"Because my whole pack is in one place, I have good alphas, I finally told you how I felt...well, one of you." Her eyes dropped for a second and a bright pink blush darkened her olive cheeks. "And I'm finally ready to start working. Oh, and you were awesome up there. Shots!" she yelled again.

"Is she drunk?" Ax asked with a chuckle.

"She's only had that one drink."

"I had one while I was waiting for Amir, too. But no, I'm not drunk. I'm happy. For once in my life, I'm so happy. And you're horny," she said, pointing at Ax. She was yelling to be heard over the music, so when the sound dropped right as those last three words fell from her mouth and anyone close enough could hear her, that old shy Issa returned for a second as she turned and buried her face against Amir's chest.

"Is everyone staring at me?" she asked with a giggle.

"Not *every*one," Amir said, wrapping his arms around her shoulders and rubbing his chin along the top of her head to scent mark her.

Ax threw his head back and laughed loudly as I chuckled and shook my head. I'd thought I had my hands full being pack lead over someone like Ax. Now, Amir and Ax were rubbing off on Issa.

"What makes you think I'm horny?" Ax asked as he signaled for Aryn to grab him a beer and five shots of American Honey.

"I can feel you, remember?" she said, turning her head to peek at him.

The way she'd looked when we'd entered the office, her lipstick smeared from kissing Ax, the way her tits rose and fell with each deep breath...

Nope. No way could I last all night without burying my cock in someone, preferably Issa. Or Amir. Or both.

Cyrus finally returned from the office, tucking his phone into his back pocket. I couldn't gauge anything from his expression or body language as to what kind of call he'd had to rush to take, but since he didn't look pissed or motion for me to join him, I figured it was business or personal.

Just because we were a pack didn't mean we had to know every single thing about each other or how we filled every minute of our day. Although, every minute of my day was filled with work or Issa... or thinking about Issa.

And now Amir.

"We're celebrating!" Issa repeated to Cyrus when he sidled up to the bar and leaned one hip on a bar stool.

"What are we celebrating?" he asked with an amused quirk of the brow.

"Don't ask. It'll piss you off," I said with a roll of my eyes.

"Lots of things," she said, narrowing her eyes at me. Grabbing a shot glass, she raised it high and yelled, "To a full pack."

Just before she put it to her lips, she hesitated, turning to look at Amir with wide eyes.

"Um...I don't think I was supposed to do that."

"Do what?" he asked.

I frowned at Ax and Cyrus, wondering if they had any clue as to what she was talking about. Ax had a direct link to her emotions but couldn't exactly read her thoughts through their bond. He shrugged. Cyrus shook his head.

"I called you pack," she said to Amir. "But I'm not your alpha. I'm not...I'm just a beta."

Amir wrapped an arm around her shoulders, careful not to spill his still full shot, and kissed the top of her head. "You're my beta. And I'm your omega." And then he lifted his eyes to Ax, Cyrus, and me, waiting for confirmation as to whether he was our omega, as well.

"As long as you continue to make her smile like that," Ax said, gesturing toward Issa with his shot glass, "you are absolutely pack."

"Um…aren't you supposed to claim him?" she asked, a wide grin bisecting her beautiful face.

"We're not biting him in the middle of the bar, baby girl," Ax said.

But fuck me if the mere thought of claiming him then fucking them both where everyone would see and know exactly who these two belonged to didn't make my dick hard as granite.

"So…to pack?" Issa asked with raised brows and the sweetest, widest grin.

"To pack!" Ax yelled, lifting his drink high.

All five of us tossed back the shot, four of us chuckling at the face Issa made as the whiskey hit her tongue then burned its way down her throat.

Her nose was still wrinkled as she started collecting our shot glasses and setting them on the bar. "I'm practicing for my first day," she said with a shrug when I raised my brows in question.

"You realize you can't drink on the job, right?" Cyrus teased.

"Duh." She threw her arms over her head and yelled, "Another shot!"

Tonight would only go a few ways if she kept drinking. She would either end up drunk and horny, drunk and puking, or drunk and passed out.

I was totally down for option one but didn't want drunk Issa to make any decisions sober Issa would regret in the morning.

And one of us had to stay sober to get the rest of the pack home.

She'd declared Amir pack without technically asking us, but I wouldn't deny my girl a damn thing. If he was willing, I was more than ready to move him into the omega wing tomorrow if for no other reason than to see how much more he could pull her further out of her shell.

"Why don't we take this party home, instead," I offered. "That way, we won't have to keep yelling over the music and one of us won't have to be the parent of the group."

Cyrus smiled softly and shook his head. Because he knew he would end up the parent of the group. I might have been pack lead, but Cyrus was the one who always made sure we were all taken care of, made sure there was always enough food in the house, even before Issa had joined us. He was gentle and caring yet would rip someone to pieces for fucking with his family. Just like a momma bear.

Or...poppa bear. I was pretty sure he wouldn't appreciate being compared to a female bear.

I almost laughed aloud at my own rambling thoughts. I wasn't drunk; far from it. But the realization that Issa had publicly declared Amir as our omega, the fact he'd agreed, and the fact we were all heading back to the house together...

I was fucking nervous.

I didn't get nervous. Why the fuck would I? I didn't get on stage like Ax. And I'd yet to meet a single person who intimidated me. With the way Bain and I had grown up, with the people who'd been in our life, it was hard to find much to be afraid of...short of losing someone I loved.

It seemed that tiny circle was growing by the day. I might not be in love with Amir – yet – but I loved him for how good he was to and for Issa. Because I was crazy in love with my beta.

CHAPTER 20

wo shots later, and I'd ushered our little ragtag group through the club and out to the SUV. I'd made sure to have one of my employees bring it to the curb since Issa was in heels and a little...wobbly.

I had never seen her so loose. She acted as though she'd broken free from those chains her family had wrapped around her heart and mind. I just hoped it wouldn't fade with her buzz.

Enzo and Ax weren't nearly as drunk as Issa and Amir, but there was no point in risking them getting behind the wheel. I'd only had the one shot with them and had nursed a beer. Issa had dragged each of us onto the dancefloor at some point, even all five of us once. Although, Enzo and I pretty much just swayed a little to the music.

Ax, Issa, and Amir? I could have propped a chair in the middle of the floor just to watch the way the three of them moved. My dick had been rock hard for hours.

Yet...I couldn't fuck Issa or Amir. Not tonight. Or at least not until their brains weren't flooded with booze. I didn't want either of them to regret anything in the morning.

Amir and Issa sang to the music playing through the radio at the top of their lungs. I glanced over at Enzo and shook my head with a smile. Ax was being nearly as loud as they were, except the bastard was actually on key.

Issa really had become a completely different person since meeting Amir. She was blooming right before our eyes like a fucking daisy or rose or some other beautiful flower.

She trusted the three of us, but she'd still remained closed off to outsiders, had been nervous around alphas, and was nervous to leave the house even with one or all three of her alphas.

Although she was only finally accepting that she was our beta after months of living with us.

But how much of that was our fault? Had any of us bothered to tell her exactly how we felt or asked whether she wanted a permanent place in our pack? I knew I sure as fuck had never told her my heart was hers, that I'd fallen hard for her within only days of knowing her, that I would literally give my life for her as long as she was safe and happy.

The three were still singing along to the radio as I pulled the SUV into the garage. We would have to take Amir back to the club tomorrow to get his vehicle, but he was definitely staying the night tonight. He and Issa drank entirely too much tonight, and by the time he sobered up, it would be closing in on dawn. No way would I let the omega be at risk when he could make my sweetheart smile so wide and so often.

"It's like we have a chauffeur," Issa announced, lunging forward and wrapping her arms around my throat before pressing her red painted lips to my cheek in a messy, loud kiss.

"We need to get her drunk more often," Ax said as he pushed from the door and guided her out his side. "I like drunk Issa."

"Because you're drunk, too," she announced, wrapping her arms around his neck and her legs around his waist, letting him carry her into the house.

He pressed a kiss to the tip of her nose, and I had to swallow back the twinge of jealousy. He'd been inside her last night with both his cock and his teeth. He'd felt her cunt wrapped around his dick while he'd bonded her to him.

I wanted that. I wanted both. I wanted her body below me, under my hands and mouth, wanted my teeth sinking into the soft flesh of her shoulder. Or maybe her throat front and center so everyone would know she was taken. Claimed by alphas who truly cared for her, who would die for her, kill for her.

Enzo was still shaking his head as he pushed through the door leading inside, but I'd seen the smile he was trying his best to hide. The two of us had drunk far less than Ax, Issa, and Amir. At least I wouldn't be the only babysitter tonight.

Honestly, though, would I be able to reject Issa *or* Amir if one or both of them came onto me? I'd wanted Issa for months. And Amir's perfume was like a fucking siren's call to my dick, luring me in and tempting me every time we were together.

"Food," Ax said, carrying Issa straight to the kitchen before setting her on a counter and pulling away.

Her hands immediately darted forward and snagged my shirt, pulling me closer and wrapping her legs around my ass until my covered cock was lined up directly against her panties. Either she didn't realize her current position was flashing her lower half to the room or she didn't care. I knew I should have reminded her, being as I was currently the voice of reason, but it was hard to think straight with the heat of her core pressing against me as Amir leaned around me and kissed her deeply and passionately.

A purr burst to life from my chest at the sight of what had officially become the center of our pack, our sweet, beautiful beta and the tall, muscular, yet sexy as fuck omega.

Her fingers were still tangled in my shirt even as Amir practically devoured her mouth, his hands pushing into her hair and tilting her head to deepen the kiss further.

My hips began to rock against her of their own accord. My brain knew I should pull away, maybe throw a bucket of ice water on these two before they ended up fucking on the counter, but my hindbrain and my dick had other plans.

Amir pulled from Issa's mouth, lifted a hand to the back of my neck, and pulled me down until he could seal his lips over mine. And the whole time, my hips continued to gyrate against Issa as though I could telepathically will our clothing away and bury myself knot deep in her.

Fuck. No. I could never knot her. Her body wasn't born for an alpha's knot, and I'd rather cut my own throat than hurt my sweet girl.

But I could fuck her. And I could knot Amir.

I was supposed to be the voice of reason tonight, the sober one. But my alpha hindbrain decided then and there as Amir's sweet chocolate and strawberry essence coated my tongue and mixed with Issa's warm linen smell that I would have them both tonight. By morning, both would carry my alpha mark, both would be bonded to me, and Amir would officially be pack.

I just hoped when we all came down from our high – whether natural or alcohol induced – there would be no regrets.

A hand slid down my chest, my abs, to my hard cock, squeezing lightly before stroking me through my pants.

The hand was too small to be Amir's. My Issa was toying with me, touching me, and I feared I would blow my load before ever having her body wrapped around me.

This was another moment when I wondered whether I should pull away, if for no other reason than to suggest taking this little party to the bedroom. Or at least the couch.

But when the button then zipper on my slacks were undone and slim, warm fingers wrapped around my shaft, teasing the head and smoothing the precum beaded at the top, all logical thought was gone.

Rut. I was so close to fucking rut. I did not want my first time with either of them to be when I was out of my head, but the more Issa touched me and Amir kissed me as though trying to meld his soul with mine, I was quickly losing my fucking sanity.

My hips rocked, fucking myself into Issa's hand as Amir's fingers tangled in my hair, his tongue damned near claiming my mouth.

Alpha hormones warred with Amir's perfume. Enzo and Ax were somewhere nearby, watching this overt display of sexuality. And I didn't give a fuck. I didn't want this to stop. In fact, I wanted both Issa and Amir naked, wanted to taste them both, have them both on their hands and knees, presenting for me so I could take my time fucking into first one then the other.

Get your shit together.

Reluctantly, I pulled from Amir's kiss and gently pulled Issa's hand from my pants. "I will not have you for the first time on the kitchen counter."

The little vixen was drunker than I thought, because she actually leaned back on her hands and smiled up at me, watching me through her lashes. "I don't mind doing it on the counter."

"You might in the morning," I teased.

I didn't want to stop, but I also felt as though I was taking advantage of the beta and omega. Could they technically give consent in their condition?

"Living room," Enzo said, his voice deep and bordering on his alpha bark.

By the way Amir jerked, he'd felt that command deep in his bones.

I helped Issa off the counter and shook my head when she intentionally slid her body along mine, almost pulling my pants down with the move. And definitely making me even harder, something I wasn't aware was possible.

Amir laced his fingers through Issa's and they followed Enzo and Ax into the living room. The two vixens sat side by side on the couch, their lips kiss swollen, Issa's red lipstick smeared around Amir's mouth.

Lifting a hand, I wiped my fingertips across my mouth and came away with the same fire engine red. Damn. Why was that so fucking sexy?

Enzo sat on a coffee table directly across from the two while I leaned against the wall, zipping and buttoning my pants so I wasn't waving my hard cock around the room. It was obvious Enzo had a few things to say.

He was quiet a few seconds, but his lips twitched as he fought to hold back the smile at the way Amir and Issa giggled and snuggled against each other.

"Neither of you are capable of giving consent tonight," he announced. And fuck if it didn't feel like I deflated under those words.

Not my knot, though. That was still swollen and throbbing with the need for release.

An omega whine tore left Amir's chest as Issa crossed her arms and stuck out her bottom lip in the cutest fucking pout. I wanted to drag that lip between my teeth.

"I can consent just fine," she protested.

"Same," Amir said.

I huffed a laugh and coughed to cover it when Enzo shot me a glare.

The whole thing was just too damn funny. Amir had a few inches on her, yet they sat side by side like partners in crime while Ax sat in a chair across from them, his hand over his mouth as he hid a smile.

They were both horny. That was obvious. And I totally got it because I was pretty sure I could break through a concrete wall with my boner at this point.

But Enzo was right – if they were drunk, they couldn't fully consent. We all wanted her, wanted the same bond Ax now had with her, but she needed to be in her right mind before that could happen. They both did.

"I wasn't drunk at the bar when Amir agreed to be pack," she said, trying to find some point of attack that would work on the pack lead. And she wasn't wrong. She might have had a slight buzz at that point, but Amir had been sober.

Enzo dragged a hand down his face.

Amir leaned down and whispered into Issa's ear, causing her to giggle.

"What's so funny?" Ax asked as the two lunged to their feet, hands entwined, and ran for the stairs.

Issa skidded to a stop making Amir have to stop, as well, or risk pulling her off her feet.

"Since we're drunk and you aren't...we're going up to the nest," Issa said. And fuck...her defiant smirk made my dick twitch in my pants.

"Since you're worried about consent, we'll let you three decide whether you want to join in our drunken shenanigans."

And with that, they giggled again like teenagers and darted for the stairs that would lead them up to the omega quarters. To the nest. The pack bed that would fit all five of us comfortably.

"Nah. I'm joining them. I'll blame my inebriated state later," Ax said, pushing to his feet and eating up the space with his long legs.

"Idiot," Enzo muttered with a shake of his head.

He turned to me and cocked a brow.

Swiveling my head, I looked to the stairs, to my pack lead then shrugged. "Fuck it. If nothing else, I'll just watch and fuck my own hand. Win-win and I won't feel guilty later."

"Seriously?" Enzo called after me. "I thought you were supposed to be the commonsense of the pack."

"That was assigned against my will," I called back as I took the stairs two at a time.

That was bullshit. Enzo knew it as well as I did. I *was* the common-sense alpha of the pack. But that was before. Before Issa. Before Amir. Before I'd tasted Amir's lips while Issa stroked my cock.

CHAPTER 21

<u>Amir</u>

Enzo wasn't completely off base as far as how much Issa and I had to drink tonight. But it wasn't liquid courage spurring this moment. It was Issa. It was the alphas' pheromones swimming in the air and stirring my omega.

It was the sense of rightness that had washed over me when Issa had declared me pack.

Then adorably asked whether it was okay for her to do such a thing without speaking to me or her alphas.

Our alphas. They would be my alphas, hopefully before the night was over.

Ax had followed us upstairs and to the omega wing that would be mine when I officially moved in. I had made love to Issa with my mouth in this room once, but our scents were beginning to fade and it smelled too neutral, like some chemical cleaner that had been used before any of them knew I existed.

Did that mean they'd had someone else in this room before me? Had they courted other omegas? Fucked other omegas?

A possessive rage sizzled in my veins and sent my hormones on a rampage. Bite. Pack. Breed.

None of us had discussed our future as far as parenthood, but I was in no hurry. I wasn't even sure whether I wanted kids. Not that I didn't like them, I'd just never spent much time picturing myself pregnant or as a parent. Something else I could thank my parents for – they'd never made me feel as if my only role in life was to carry a pup for my future alphas.

That didn't mean I didn't want each of these alphas to sink their teeth into my shoulder, to knot me, to bond me to them and to their pack, to make me Issa's omega, their omega.

I had definitely spent more time with Issa than the alphas, but they worked a lot during the week. She and I spent a lot of time on the phone, FaceTiming, or texting for hours on end.

That was nothing compared to being with her, touching her, kissing her, having her in my arms.

Having her tight, wet pussy wrapped around my cock.

I was a few weeks away from my next heat. What I really wanted was to be settled here, to get my nest ready before that time came. I knew Enzo, Ax, and Cyrus would have zero problem with helping me through the fever and pain of my cycle. And there was no way I would want to go through that without my sweet beta present.

But things would have to be right or my omega wouldn't be settled.

Issa giggled the sweetest tinkling sound as Ax all but tackled the two of us to the cushioned floor of the nest. Just like the rest of the quarters, it was devoid of any scent but the lingering hints of Issa's warm linen and my sweet and fruity perfume.

I wanted it saturated with that sun dried sheet smell, copper wires, warm, damp wood, and spiced rum. I wanted the fabric soaked with our scents, our sweat, and our release. Then I wanted to roll around in it, to coat myself with their signatures, to wear them and their bites with pride for the world to know I was claimed by the most beautiful pack ever.

They weren't the first to court me, but they were the only ones who'd made me want to finally settle down. And I knew it had everything to do with the Italian beta kissing and nuzzling my neck while Ax worked at removing his clothes then started on Issa's.

Oh, hell no. I wanted to be naked, too. I wanted to feel their skin against mine. I wanted to finally feel Ax's knot locking us together.

Or Enzo's. Or Cyrus's. Or rather *and* Enzo's *and* Cyrus's, one after the other.

Fuck. The thought of finally being with not one but all three alphas while my beautiful Issa rode my cock made slick roll down my thighs.

Ax's nostrils flared and his pupils blew wide. A loud, rumbling purr burst from his chest.

"Fuck, you smell good," he said, pulling Issa's naked body closer to him while wrapping a hand around my neck to bring my face to his and slamming his lips against mine.

I was an omega, but I sure as fuck wasn't petite or dainty. And definitely not fragile. I didn't want any of them to treat me like glass. I wanted everything they could give me. I wanted Ax's lips wrapped around my cock while Issa straddled my face and used my tongue to get herself off. I wanted to drink down her release while shooting my cum down Ax's throat.

So many fantasies. So many possibilities.

As Issa lowered to her knees between Ax and I, copper tinged with frayed wires and damp wood filled the nest. Enzo and Cyrus hadn't stayed away. Even after Cyrus and Enzo tried to convince me and Issa we were too tipsy to consent, they couldn't stay away.

Ax's hand tangled in my long curls, tilting my head to deepen the kiss. When Issa's mouth closed over my cock and took me deep enough I felt the flared head bump the back of her throat, I moaned into Ax's mouth, practically leaning on him when my knees threatened to give out.

"You look so beautiful blowing your omega," Cyrus said from my right. He sounded as though he was kneeling.

I wanted to pull away to make sure everyone was naked, but Ax's kiss was hungry and desperate and was stealing not just my breath but all logical thought while Issa felt as though she was trying to suck my soul through the head of my dick.

"Fuck," I moaned against Ax's lips.

He pulled away with a moan, both of us lowering our heads as Issa took Ax's cock in her hand while bobbing her mouth on mine. Then she switched, her hand stroking me, her mouth wrapped around Ax's long, thick dick.

Enzo knelt beside her, pushing her hair over her shoulder. "Beta, I need to know this is you and not the liquor. None of us will forgive ourselves if we let this go too far and have you end up regretting everything in the morning."

Ax groaned in frustration when she pulled her mouth from him to look into the pack lead's eyes.

"I want this, alpha. I want to be yours. All of yours. I want us to be official. I've wanted this for so long but was too scared to say anything."

I knew she was terrified of being rejected. She'd felt as though they deserved more. And I knew it would take more than a couple weeks of my coaxing and a few months of the alphas doting on her for her to heal, but she was finally seeing her worth.

"And Amir agreed to it."

"I don't need to be courted. I'm yours if you'll have me." As long as Issa was in the picture. I would go anywhere this beautiful beta went. I wasn't above admitting I had fallen hard and fast for her. I had never been one to question my feelings or my instincts.

And every part of me down to my soul believed she and this pack were my home. They were mine.

Enzo searched Issa's face, then touched his fingers under her chin and turned her face toward him so he could press a soft, lingering kiss to her lips. When he pulled back, their smiles grew wider by the second.

And then the room exploded in perfume and hormones and pheromones as Cyrus urged me onto the nest's padding, Enzo removed his clothes, and Ax urged Issa onto my cock.

I hissed in a breath at the feel of her wet, tight heat wrapping around me, the heavy-lidded look she leveled on me, the way her full tits rose and fell with deep breaths.

I love you. I love you. I love you.

Those words constantly floated through my mind as I stared into her light brown eyes. I couldn't say them, not yet. This was a huge step. If the night went the way she and I wanted, both of us would be linked through all three alphas. We would be Issa and Amir Rivera. I would move my meager belongings into the omega nest.

And we would live happily ever after. Because my girl deserved no less.

For now, though, I wanted to be with my pack, to make love to my beta, to be knotted by my alphas.

My alphas. My beta. My pack.

Mine.

Issa's small warm hands rested on my chest as she leaned forward and began to ride me, slowly at first, her sweet smile barely pulling up the corners of her lips. I could smell the alcohol on her breath, but her eyes were focused even if her pupils were dilated.

Flattening a hand against her upper back, I urged her forward so I could taste her lips. There were hints of the shots and the martini, but there was also her warm, comforting taste along with the heady taste of Ax's signature that had transferred from his thick cock.

As our tongues danced and tasted each other, my knees were urged further apart. A finger gently tested my hole, smoothing slick around and making it easier for that same finger to slide inside me.

I had no idea who was touching me, not without pulling my mouth from Issa and craning my neck to look around. I didn't care. As long as I felt a knot before the night was over.

I'd never been a prude. I'd been with alphas, betas, and omegas since losing my virginity at seventeen. But nothing had ever compared to the feeling of an alpha's knot or a female locking around my cock.

Not until I'd felt Issa.

There was a small voice in the back of my head, something telling me to be leery, that everything was moving quickly, that I needed to shield myself from future pain.

But yeah, that voice was tiny in comparison to my omega hind-brain demanding I lock these four down immediately.

The finger disappeared, then warm strong thighs pressed against mine, opening my legs further until the blunt head of a cock pressed against my opening. I moaned as the cock slid into me slowly, pulling my mouth away and tossing my head back, the overload of pleasure from Issa riding my cock while one of the alphas took my ass nearly too much.

At this rate, I would blow my load too soon. And I wanted to enjoy every second of my first time with the whole pack.

When I opened my eyes, I spotted Enzo behind Issa, his head lowered, his eyes on where he was pumping into me slowly. A vein bulged on the side of his neck as though he was holding back. Any other time I might have told him to fuck me hard, fast, to give me everything he had. But I was practically doing algebra in my mind to keep myself from coming.

Not that I wouldn't immediately be ready for another round. And another. I would – could – never get tired of the way Issa felt wrapped around my cock. I could never get tired of her sweet, breathy moans, the lust drunk look in her eyes, the way she tasted on my tongue.

"Please tell me you're on something," I begged Issa as Enzo's pace picked up and rubbed all the right places inside me.

"I have an implant," she confirmed with a nod, silently giving me permission to paint her inner walls with my cum.

"Thank fuck," I groaned.

Ax leaned forward, his lips grazing Issa's ear as he whispered, "Can I take your ass while he fucks your pussy?"

Oh fuck. Oh shit. Any more pressure and I was goner. Just his words almost caused my balls to explode.

A siren's smile lit up her face as she nodded. I had no idea whether she'd ever taken a dick back there. Betas weren't built like omegas, weren't built to be bred over and over by alphas. It was some primal thing from our past when omegas were even rarer than they were today.

The fear she might get hurt actually helped ease those first tingles of an orgasm.

I watched, enraptured, as Ax threw a leg over both of mine until his ass was cradled in the space where my knees had been pushed open for Enzo. A moan escaped my lips when Ax smiled at me, reached down, and gathered some of my slick to lube our beta's back hole.

And just like that, those fucking tingles started at the base of my spine again.

"Tell me if it's too much," Ax whispered as he pressed soft kisses along her bare shoulders.

Her lips parted, a guttural noise left her throat, and then she fell forward, her breasts pressed against my chest.

I could see Enzo and Ax clearly now, could see Ax slowly pushing into Issa, could see Enzo's tight expression as he struggled for control over his own body.

Turning my head, I sought Cyrus. He sat a few feet away, his cock in his hand, his eyes roaming along every inch of the four of us.

"Plan to join us any time soon?" I asked then winked when he met my eyes.

Crawling closer, he leaned in and kissed me, his tongue slipping past the seam of my lips in a wet, licking kiss. His hand tangled in Issa's hair and pulled her head up so he could claim her mouth as well.

And then he settled on his knees, his cock bobbing between the two of us.

This was the first time we'd all fucked at the same time, but Issa and I apparently had the same idea. She instantly swallowed his length while I lifted my head and licked and sucked Cyrus's sac, alternating to teasing his swollen knot before returning to his balls, humming at the warm taste of him.

"Fuuuck," Cyrus groaned out, each of his hands resting on Issa's and my heads.

"Where do you want our marks, omega?" Enzo asked, the muscles in his jaw prominent as he clenched his teeth.

"I want everyone to see them," I said, then returned my attention to Cyrus's balls.

"Can I cum in your ass?" Enzo asked. His face was red, and those veins looked on the verge of exploding any second.

"Fill me, alpha. Fill me then come up here and make me yours."

My words set off a tidal wave. Enzo finished first with a growl, followed by Ax, his arm banding around Issa's chest as he sucked on the mark he'd left on her shoulder.

Cyrus gripped Issa's hair and stared into her eyes, waiting for her permission. She gripped his thighs and kept him from pulling away until he growled out his orgasm, filling her mouth and throat with his release.

Enzo carefully pulled from me, and I couldn't help the moan at the sensation of his cum and my slick trailing from my ass to soak into the padding below us. He hadn't knotted me, but I needed his mark more in this moment.

Once Ax pulled out of Issa, she was able to rise and fall on my cock, her head thrown back, back arched, breasts beautifully on display. I gripped her hips, urging her on, urging her to move faster. I wanted to feel her clenching around me as she fell apart before finding my own pleasure in her curvy body.

The alphas shuffled around on their knees, circling their beta and alpha.

"I need to mark you," Cyrus said to Issa, his voice growly and so full of need.

"Yes! Please!" she cried out, tilting her head back to give him access to her throat.

She'd told me she'd planned to ask at least one of them to cover the mark from her first alpha, and that was exactly where Ax's mark was, the skin pink but healing. It would be the most incredible silver crescents when fully healed.

By the end of the night, the two of us would wear necklaces of our alphas' marks, their bites. We would be bonded to them and each other.

Cyrus gently clasped her chin and pressed a kiss to her lips, her cheeks, then ran his mouth over her throat before opening his mouth and slowly clamping down directly in the center.

Issa cried out, her pussy clenching and fluttering, milking my cock the same time Enzo leaned over me and kissed me deeply, stealing my own sounds of pleasure before they could lift on the air.

He waited until my muscles were no longer taut, until I was no longer shooting streams of cum inside Issa before pulling back and lowering his mouth to my throat, his teeth instantly sinking into my flesh like a snake attacking its prey.

There was the faintest hint of a sting before so many sensations washed over me, through me, filling me with warmth and brightness. I needed Cyrus's mark. And Ax's. I needed to feel them and Issa.

As Enzo's tongue lapped at the blood seeping from the wound, my omega grew unsteady as the ridiculous sense of rejection squeezed my heart. Without a full bond, it felt as though they didn't want me. My logical side knew how stupid the thought was, but my hindbrain had fully taken over.

A whine tore from my chest even as Enzo tended to his bonding mark. He jerked away, his wide eyes finding mine.

"Did I hurt you?" He truly looked panicked as he searched my face.

"More." Damn it. This was the part that had always bothered me about my designation. I hated when my emotions hit that rollercoaster and refused to settle. And the only thing that would settle them now was a full bond.

Issa slowed and looked into my face. "More from me? A knot?"

Unable to force words to form on my tongue, I turned my head and craned my neck in silent invitation.

Ax chuckled a ridiculously sexy sound. "He wants more bites," he said as he lowered and peppered my chest with kisses, his tongue flicking out to tease one of my hard nipples. "Where do you want my mark, omega?"

A smile slowly stretched across my lips from both humor and a sense of rightness. Leave it to Ax to jump in feet first. Or rather head-first. I'd liked him from the start, liked the way he had all but cheered Issa on when he'd caught us in Cyrus's office, loved that he had been the first to climb over the wall that I'd simply bulldozed through.

"I want the world to see it," I said, lifting a hand from Issa's hip to push my fingers through his shoulder length hair as it framed his face.

He grinned, his expression bright and warm in the dim light of the thin lights around the edges of the nest.

The feeling of his teeth sinking into my throat, directly over my Adam's apple, sent another orgasm rippling through my body. I yelled with the intensity, my hips jerking up, shoving myself deeper into Issa as my dick twitched over and over, our combined release trailing from her to create the sexiest fucking puddle on my groin.

Instantly, I felt Issa bloom bright in my chest, felt her affection… her love. I could pretend that love was solely for her alphas. She'd told me she had been in love with them for a while.

But it was there, the love she felt for me.

My beta loved me. Issa fucking loved me.

CHAPTER 22

<u>Issa</u>

I giggled when Cyrus brushed past me, pressing a kiss to the top of my head as he hefted boxes through the house and up the stairs.

Today was move in day. As in, our omega was officially moving in.

The problem was he was only bringing his clothing since he really didn't have much in the way of furniture since he'd lived with his family. So, in true alpha fashion, Enzo, Ax, and Cyrus had sat Amir on the couch with a laptop and had him click through and order whatever he might need or want for his quarters and the nest.

Amir had only ordered a few things, declaring he needed to actually feel the fabric under his hands before he could commit to picking blankets, pillows, and such.

None of the guys would let me help carry the few boxes, as if the ten pounds was too heavy. That was fine. I'd plopped myself onto the huge pack bed centered against the wall in Amir's room and enjoyed watching the way they interacted with each other. It had only been two days since we'd all officially become pack, since all three alphas had marked me and Amir. And I was still floating on cloud nine.

To top off all my squishy feelings, I was scheduled to start training as a server at The Vault the following week and we had dinner planned with Amir's family. I was dying to meet the people who'd birthed and raised such an amazing person.

In less than a year, my life had gone from a nightmare to an absolute dream.

"We should invite my sister and her pack over for dinner soon," I announced as the four guys unpacked the boxes and put things away.

I had spent a bit of time living with Cora and her pack after finally getting away from Antonio, then had been invited to stay with Enzo, Ax, and Cyrus. My beautiful nephew had been born and I was absolutely crazy about him but hadn't seen in a few weeks.

What could I say? I'd been busy falling in love and getting bonded. I hadn't even mentioned to Cora I'd met and fallen for an omega or that I'd been bonded to Ax. And now, I had even more news to tell her.

The two of us hadn't been close growing up. I hadn't really been close with any of my siblings growing up. But that had been our parents' fault, not because we didn't get along.

I hadn't heard from or seen my brothers in over a year, but Cora and I had taken steps to mend the rift between us that had been caused by our alpha fathers reminding their beta children that we were lesser than their golden omega daughter.

Amir appeared to love his designation, loved being an omega. And had been teaching me *the ways of an omega*, as he called it. He was teaching me to go for what I wanted, to ask for what I wanted, to take what I wanted.

It was slow going, but at least it was working. I'd told Ax how I felt, had asked him to make love to me, had asked for his bite. Had Amir not given me the courage...

"Set it up and I'll buy the food," Ax said as he flattened one of the boxes to be set in the recycle bin.

With a squeal, I grabbed my phone, scooted until my back was against the headboard, and typed out a quick text to Cora, inviting her entire pack and my nephew for a laid-back cookout. No fancy restaurants. No fancy clothes. Just a few hours for her to meet and get to know my omega.

She already knew my alphas, being as Enzo was brother to her pack lead. But I was dying to introduce her to the sexy omega who was currently twisting his long, curly hair back into a messy bun, strands coming loose to frame his face no matter how hard he tried to manage it.

"What are you staring at?" he teased, stopping near the end of the bed then crawling toward me on his hands and knees.

"Now that's a sight," Ax muttered as he passed with more crushed boxes.

"You," I said when he settled between my thighs and rested his cheek on my stomach.

From the moment he'd pretended to be my boyfriend at The Vault, everything had felt so easy and natural with him, as easy as breathing.

His arms slid between me and the mattress, hugging me tightly as a sweet omega purr rumbled against me.

I couldn't resist the urge to run my fingers across his scalp, going as far as pulling the elastic away so I could feel the silky warmth of his curls against my fingers.

"That feels so good," he hummed, nuzzling his cheek against my stomach.

Cyrus stopped near the door to the nest, a minifridge in his arms, and smiled at me. It was one of those affectionate, wistful smiles that warmed my heart.

I could feel him through our bond. Each of the alphas were so different, yet I felt their love and affection through their individual threads every time they so much as glanced at me.

"We need to plan a shopping trip," Ax announced.

"How many plans are we making for the month?" Enzo asked as he stepped out of the walk-in closet and swung the door shut behind him. "We still have a job. We'll have to take a week off in a couple months; we can't start skipping out on work just because our pack is complete."

Amir and I sighed at the same time, then burst into giggles. My sweet omega brought out a more playful side of me, a flirtatious and romantic side that I'd either never realized existed or simply hadn't had the chance to acknowledge because of my former alpha. And my family. And...well, pretty much every asshole who'd been in my life before this pack.

Before I became beta to Pack Rivera. Before I became Issa Rivera.

"I didn't say we had to plan everything in one day, asshole," Ax grumbled.

And all I could do was smile. Life was...perfect. At least now it was. *Finally.*

I had a life I never could have dreamed was possible for me. I had a pack who truly cared for me and hadn't given a single fuck about my previous last name or who my fathers had been. They hadn't wanted me as their beta for the power or wealth that would, at one time, have come with bonding me.

"Can we have a pack cuddle?" I asked as my three alphas stopped and stared at me and Amir. "Like...for the rest of the day?"

Enzo growled. "We have to head to the club soon. But we shouldn't be out late. You two want to come hang out and listen to some music–"

"And watch me shake my ass," Ax said, cutting into Enzo's question.

"Or do you want to hang out here until we get back?"

"And have sex on every bed so the entire house smells like you." Ax said, again cutting into Enzo's question and earning a scowl from the pack lead.

Amir's head popped up and he looked at the alphas over his shoulder. "Option two. Hands down, option two."

He immediately slid further down my body, his fingers hooking in the sides of my leggings in an attempt to get me naked.

"I don't think they meant right now," I said with a giggle as his fingers dug into my ribs when I tried to keep my pants on. "And he said *all* the beds, not just the pack bed."

Had I smiled or laughed as much in my life as I had since meeting Amir? I knew I had smiled more in the past few months than I remembered ever smiling throughout my entire life. It had taken some time, but the three alphas felt as though they were removing bricks from my shoulder, one by one, while chiseling away at the ice that had frozen around my heart.

I wasn't sure there was more than a little frost remaining now that I could feel all of them down the invisible threads in my chest tying us together.

"By all means, don't stop on our account," Ax said, taking a few steps before launching himself onto the bed and grabbing one side of my leggings while Amir tugged on the other.

"We got to get going, idiot," Enzo said with a shake of his head. "Unless you want to get stuck at the club all night."

He dropped his forehead against my thigh and growled, a fake grumble that was more of a frustrated groan. "Fine."

Pushing onto his elbows, he kissed my hip, crawled forward to press a loud smack of a kiss against my lips, then rolled off the side of the bed, winking at me as he followed a smiling Cyrus and a grumpy Enzo through the door of the omega quarters.

My omega. My Amir.

There hadn't been an omega in my three person pack with Antonio. Hell, my fellow beta had split so early, I wasn't even sure how a full pack looked until I'd come here.

What I had seen of packs, the omega was always the top dog of the pack, the one who everyone revolved around. The beta was always just...there. Their scent and presence calmed the alphas due to their neutral status.

But not here. Not with this pack. Yeah, it was obvious the alphas were already protective of Amir and wanted to make him happy. But they'd chosen him for me, chosen a male omega for me. It had been my insistence that he become pack. It had been me who'd slept with him – many times – before any of my alphas touched him.

Merely the beta, yet all four men acted as though their lives revolved around *me*. It was a heady yet overwhelming reality.

"Do we have to start in the other rooms first?" Amir asked as he nipped and nibbled across my stomach and ribs, the soft touches making me squirm and squeal and giggle.

Something I'd noted early on was Amir's on switch remained *on* regardless of the situation. And that he came *a lot*.

Oh. And every inch of him tasted as sweet as his scent, including his release.

Everything about this beautiful man was addictive.

"I don't think there were any rules as to where to start or finish." And I was pretty sure Ax was kidding. Not one hundred percent sure, of course. It was hard to tell sometimes with my first official alpha.

Amir lunged from the end of the bed, dragging me with him. "I say we start on Ax's bed."

I squealed when he scooped me into his arms and sprinted from the room, down the stairs to the second level, then down the hall to the room that not only smelled heavily of Ax's heady spiced rum scent, but was covered in his dirty clothes, as though he'd simply let them fall wherever he happened to be standing when he'd changed clothes.

He tossed me onto Ax's unmade bed, and I couldn't resist the urge to roll over and bury my face in Ax's pillow, sucking deep breaths of his signature into my body. I wanted to go with Amir when they finally made the trip to Omega's Desires because I was determined to get some lotions with their scent. That way, I could wear them all day every day, smell them even when we weren't together.

"Stay right there," Amir said. His voice had gone all deep and husky and my pussy instantly grew wet. Or wet*ter*. It was hard not to be horny with the men in my life.

His fingers were warm as they hooked my leggings and tugged them the rest of the way down my legs until my ass was bared to him.

"Fuck, you're sexy." He kissed a path up my calves, the backs of my knees, licking and nipping at my thighs, before urging my legs apart.

The moment his tongue slid down the crack of my ass, teasing my back hole before sliding an arm under my waist to pull my hips up and attacking my pussy with earnest, a throaty moan tore from my chest.

I had to turn my head, resting my cheek on Ax's pillow, to keep from smothering myself as Amir ate me like a starved man and my cunt was a four-course meal.

"You taste so good," he murmured against my core, his breath warm, his lips soft and almost aggressive as he sucked my clit between his lips. "Lift that ass more for me," he said, his hands sliding below my hips and urging me onto my knees.

I was prepared for him to slide his cock into me. Instead, he rolled onto his back and pulled me so I was almost sitting on his face, then returned his attention to eating me, one finger teasing my back hole, another sliding into my pussy, as his tongue and lips sucked and licked and nipped at my clit.

"Amir. Holy shit," I cried out, sitting up fully and cupping my own tits, rolling my nipples between my fingers as my body began to tighten with the first tingles of orgasm.

Tossing my head back, I screamed as I imploded, coming on Amir's tongue as he lapped up my release, continuing to pump his fingers into my ass and pussy.

"I'm going to fuck you over and over," he said before returning his mouth to my pussy.

My breath whooshed from me when he wrapped his arm around my back and rolled us until his face was nestled between my thighs where he went right back to licking and sucking until he wrung another orgasm before the aftershocks from the first faded.

When he lifted his face, his chin and lips shimmered with my come and arousal. He didn't wipe it away, but he did lick his lips as though savoring my taste.

His cock was thick and hard as he slid into me in one hard thrust, his body lining along mine, the bulk of his weight held up on his elbows.

I could taste myself on his lips as he kissed me as though claiming me, devouring my mouth the way he'd devoured my cunt.

"I'm going to fuck you over and over on every bed in this house. Every surface. I'm going to make sure the alphas know what they were missing while they were gone. I'm going to make you come over and over until your legs shake and you can't keep your eyes open."

Wrapping my fingers in his hair, I forced him to look at me and stared into those hypnotic green eyes. "Promise?"

CHAPTER 23

<u>Cyrus</u>

My knee bounced under my desk as I tallied up last night's deposits and entered it into the appropriate spreadsheet before emailing it to Ax and Enzo. Ax was currently shaking his ass on stage, so he wouldn't get it until later.

I was mildly surprised he hadn't begged Amir and Issa to join us since he was performing tonight, but Issa would see plenty once she started Monday.

She had grown so much from that broken and battered woman who'd crashed into Bain's gate. I was so fucking proud of her, proud of her strength. She was learning to ask for exactly what she wanted, including me, us, our pack.

Checking in on her through our bond, I immediately slammed that shit down. Pure lust rushed through me, meaning she and Amir were more than likely doing as Ax had suggested and fucking on our beds. Or at least I hoped they were. As much as I would rather sleep every night with at least one of my pack in my arms, there was something unbelievably sexy about the thought of my sheets covered in slick and cum.

If they were too tired to fuck when I got home, I would either drag Ax in my bed or fuck my own hand while burying my face in my bed. One way or another, I was getting off tonight.

A few minutes later, my phone dinged on my desk.

Lifting it and bringing the screen to life, I noted it was a group text before opening it…and groaning.

Those little brats.

From the flooring, it looked like they were in the kitchen and the picture was from Amir's POV. The camera was pointed down at Issa who stared up into the camera, her lips wrapped around Amir's long, thick cock, and I could see a hint of a smile on Issa's plump lips.

Oh, fuck this.

Pushing from my desk, I yanked open my door and nearly slammed face first into Enzo. "You ready?" he asked, a muscle jumping in his jaw.

"Take it you saw the text?"

"That fucker better be done with his little routine or I'm leaving him here."

I wasn't sure which of the two I was more jealous of as I followed Enzo through the bar in search of our other packmate. I wanted so badly to have Issa's mouth around my cock again, to feel the flared head hitting the back of her throat. But I also wanted to taste Amir's sweetness on my tongue, to finally feel his ass clenching around my shaft until I filled him the way Enzo had.

The music turned over and I turned my head in time to see Ax running from backstage, his shirt still off, his wide eyes on his phone, before he found us and jerked his head toward the door.

"Where are your shoes?" I yelled over the music.

"I have more at home."

This was silly. We were all leaving the club we'd built from the ground up – with a loan from Enzo's brother – because our omega and beta had sent a naughty text.

Nah. Not silly. Completely rational. And I didn't give a fuck what anyone else thought.

We weren't in the corporate world and couldn't take the omega leave other companies might have offered. Therefore, we would take any and every chance we had to be with our omega. *And* our beta. At the same fucking time.

The time would come when we would *have* to take time off, when Amir went into heat and would require all three of us alphas to help him through. No doubt he'd demand Issa's presence – the man was as head over heels for her as much as we were.

But she didn't have a knot. She could ease him with orgasms, but his body, his biology required a knot to quell the dangerously high fevers and the pain that would wreck his abdomen for close to a week.

What a hardship. We would have to take off up to a week to fuck our omega nonstop. We would all be locked in the nest as our hind-brains took over and demanded we breed.

One of us needed to keep our heads during that time, to ensure everyone was eating and drinking enough. That typically fell on a beta, but I felt as though I could tell the future and knew Amir's omega would become unhinged without Issa in the room, even for the shortest amount of time.

Running barefoot ahead of us, Ax yelled to the bartender that we were taking off for the night and was almost floating as he tried to run across the blacktop without his feet touching the ground too much. I wished I had it on video; the idiot looked ridiculous.

Though I got it. He didn't want to take even the few minutes to tug on his shoes and shirt so we could head home.

We hadn't planned to stay long tonight, just putting in enough hours for Ax to try out some new choreography with a small number of his dance crew and finish up some paperwork and deal with other crap admin-wise.

This was still a little sooner than we'd originally intended.

Enzo climbed behind the wheel while I took shotgun, Ax in the backseat. No way would we let the idiot drive. He would break every speed limit and end up costing us more time by getting pulled over when he took the highway doing ninety.

"Faster," Ax said, leaning forward, his elbows on the backs of both of our seats.

"Sit back and put on your seatbelt," Enzo barked. He literally used his alpha bark on his fellow alpha packmate.

But it worked, even if Ax bit out a slew of curses and insults.

Twenty-two minutes later, Enzo pulled the SUV onto our street, the headlights bouncing across trees and bushes…

And caught on a black sedan parked along the end of our driveway.

It's brake lights glowed bright red, then the vehicle pulled away.

"Who the fuck is that?" Ax asked, leaning forward again, but this time, his safety belt kept him from scooting to the edge of his seat.

"Someone's probably lost," I said, squinting my eyes as the vehicle continued forward until it disappeared around the bend.

We lived in a fairly isolated area, so it wasn't uncommon for people to take a wrong turn and stop near our driveway, sometimes even pulling in a bit while they checked their directions. Yes. We had approached the drivers on more than one occasion, making sure none of Enzo's brother's enemies tracked us to get to Bain and his pack.

"Who cares? Go!" Ax said.

And yep. He'd already pulled his belt free and had a hand on the door, ready to burst from the backseat and sprint into the house the moment it was safe.

Or, knowing him, he might not even wait for Enzo to actually stop the damn vehicle before lunging from his seat.

I chuckled, my dick hard and ready, my knot already half inflated, as Enzo hit the gas and damn near left skid marks on the pavement as he made his way up the driveway, hitting the remote to send the garage door rumbling up so he could dart forward without taking the time to wait.

And just like I'd predicted, Ax pushed through his door before Enzo put the vehicle in park, running into the house and leaving the door wide open.

"Idiot," Enzo grumbled as he put the SUV in park and hit the button to kill the engine. I swore he called Ax that more than his fucking name. But it was always half-hearted and full of affection, at least to those of us who knew the two.

The moment my boots hit the concrete pad of the garage, my senses were overloaded with sun dried linen and chocolate covered strawberries. It poured through the open door and filled the space of the garage and would filter outside before the door rumbled closed behind us.

"Fuck," Enzo muttered, pocketing the fob and stomping inside with me hot on his heels.

At least I took the extra few seconds to make sure the garage door was closed and no one had attempted to follow us inside.

Moans floated on the air as I stepped into the mudroom, toeing off my shoes as I walked in without bothering to take the time to line them up neatly.

Those sounds were far too close for our two to be in one of the bedrooms. And the picture they'd sent had been from the kitchen.

Rounding the corner, I nearly slammed into Enzo's back as my socked feet slid on the tile.

They were still in the kitchen. On the fucking table. Or at least Issa was on the table, her back arched and pushing her breasts out, her legs spread wide as Amir buried his face between her thighs.

Her moans were soft and addictive and like a siren call, luring me forward.

Ax was already on the move, hopping on one foot as he struggled to pull his jeans off the other leg.

I wanted to dive in, to line myself behind Amir or kneel beside Issa's head and feed her my cock. But...

Fuck, they were beautiful together. Amir's long curly hair hung down his back, the muscles in his shoulders bunching as he held onto her thighs. Issa's hair fanned out on the table where we ate every meal together, her eyes closed, her full lips parted, her hands running along her stomach and breasts as our omega pleasured her.

All of this would be saved on the computer from the cameras in every room, but it was nothing compared to real life. Their scents, their sounds, the way they looked as though the rest of the world had ceased to exist.

Shooting a hand forward, I stopped Ax from diving for our omega and beta, then nodded my head at them when he shot me a disgruntled frown and growled a warning.

He turned his head and stared, then gradually relaxed in my hold.

All three of us stood there watching as Issa cried out her release. Amir continued to lap at her beautiful pussy, working her through the aftershocks, then pushed to his feet. He leaned over her, kissing a path up her stomach to her breasts, then finally claimed her mouth as his cock claimed her cunt.

The muscles in his firm ass bunched and loosened as he set a slow, sensual rhythm, his hand wrapping around the back of her neck to pull her to sitting, her ass hanging slightly off the edge of the table as he made love to her.

My knot was swollen, my cock engorged, but I couldn't move from my spot on the kitchen floor. My heart felt as though it would explode as Issa and Amir stared into each other's eyes, sharing breath, their bodies rocking together as her hands smoothed up his chest and over his shoulders.

They weren't fucking. They weren't putting on a show for their alphas.

Our omega and our beta were making love.

Dropping my guard, I let our bonds thrum to life in my chest and nearly stumbled. So much fucking love burst to life through the threads tying us all together, and it was coming from every direction, the love we all felt for Issa, the love she felt for all four of us, the love Amir felt for her.

My knees nearly buckled under the sensation.

We'd sought an omega to add to the pack, searching for the right person for Issa, someone who wouldn't make her feel as though she came in second place.

And we'd found an omega who worshipped our girl, who loved her as deeply as we did.

Our pack was complete. Our lives were complete. And it had everything to do with the two exchanging the softest whispers of their mutual adoration mere feet from where I stood.

CHAPTER 24

<u>Issa</u>

My nephew was currently balanced on my lap, his hands wrapped in my long hair, a slobbery smile on his lips as I talked to him in a high-pitched baby voice as his little head wobbled as he tried to hold it up.

Pietro was barely three months old and had the cutest fat rolls around his neck and I couldn't help but lean forward to kiss them, earning the cutest baby giggle ever. I pulled away wide-eyed and raised my brows at Cora. I'd had no idea they could laugh at such a young age. But what the hell did I know about babies?

Yet another reason me being a mother wasn't the greatest idea.

Amir was pressed against my right side, Cora sat on my left, our alphas surrounding us on all sides on the couch and chairs they'd pulled close.

"He's such a happy baby," I said. "Aren't you? You are such a happy baby."

His chubby little hands flapped in the air as his adorable baby smile widened as though confirming my statement.

"He loves his aunt. Aunty Issa…" Cora said to Pietro, leaning forward and taking one of his hands to press kisses along the back. "What about you guys? You planning on kids any time in the near future?"

Her eyes bounced between me and Amir, her brows raised.

A lump lodged itself in my throat and I had to cough to clear it. I had no desire to carry a child, but I wouldn't stand in the way if Amir and our alphas wanted children. I would love and cherish any son or daughter birthed by my beautiful omega.

"We haven't really talked about all that yet," Amir said, his eyes soft, his smile wistful as he watched me with my nephew. *Our* nephew?

I supposed since we were all officially mated, that made my family theirs. We'd all been somewhat connected already since Enzo was Cora's brother-in-law and all.

"I'm having fun getting to know my new pack. I think we'll hold off on that decision for a while," my omega said and gave me a sweet wink.

I smiled at Amir. I could have kissed him for saying that. Because that was exactly how I felt. I knew most packs added an omega solely to carry heirs for their family, even though betas were capable of getting pregnant, though not as easily. At least the packs I'd grown up around my whole life.

But that wasn't why my alphas had sought Amir. They'd finally admitted they decided on adding an omega for me, had waited until they found a male omega so I wouldn't feel as though any woman added would be my replacement. They knew I still held quite a bit of distrust and apprehension around other alphas.

Although we could have lived a happy life together, just the four of us, I was beyond happy that we had Amir. He made everything feel…

He made my heart feel so full. Made my life feel complete. Made it feel as though some weird hole I hadn't known existed in my heart had finally found its missing piece and I could feel it thumping like crazy as my pack's love and affection poured through our bond.

We all spent the next few hours talking and laughing, the guys grilled out on the patio, then fed Cora and me while insisting we relax and catch up. They even took over the care of Pietro when he got fussy and needed to go down for a nap.

No. Cora and I hadn't been close growing up. But we were no longer children, and our asshole fathers were no longer around to pit us against each other or make me feel as if I were less because of my designation.

Now, we were simply two sisters finally getting to know each other. Maybe someday, I could start to build a relationship with my brothers, as well.

"They're crazy about you," Cora said, leaning close to me to speak softly as the guys periodically checked on us while we chatted on the couch and they hung out in the kitchen, drinking beer, Cora's alphas getting a chance to get to know Amir. "And you look so happy."

A smile beamed on my face before I could stop it. "I am happy. Truly happy."

Her eyes lowered to the marks on my shoulder and throat, a wistful uptick of her lips preceding a soft sigh. "I knew Enzo and the guys were hot for you, but I could never have dreamed you all would...fuck, you make the perfect pack."

Even with the way we'd been raised, Cora had always had more of a rebellious streak. She would sneak out or demand our fathers' guards escort her so she could go dancing or shopping while I had always been more subdued. Sure, I enjoyed the same luxuries she had, but I'd never really been given the chance to spread my wings since I'd been shipped off to a pack after graduating high school.

"I have a job now, too," I said, my smile stretching into a wide grin when her brows shot up her forehead.

"Really?"

I nodded. "At The Vault. I'm a server three days a week. I just started last week and only worked a few hours each time. But Amir is determined to be there on the nights I work. Although I'm not sure how much of that has to do with being around me and how much is for the opportunity to see Ax dance."

She threw her head back and laughed. "I have to catch one of his shows one of these days. But we don't want to take advantage of our nanny."

Translation: She refused to allow someone else to raise her son the way our nannies had raised us. Our parents had been mostly hands off unless it came to consequences and punishments.

"You definitely need to come out soon. And make it a night I'm working so I can be your server. I'm not great at it, yet, but I'm still in training. And Cyrus said he'll teach me how to mix drinks so I can take some shifts behind the bar for when we're shorthanded or the club is packed."

"I think we should go to one of the strip clubs, too," Cora said a little loudly, winking at me before holding up a hand and counting down from five…

Four…

Three…

Two…

Before she'd folded down the first finger, Cohl rushed in and flopped onto the couch, his head in her lap, his face beaming up at her. "I'll go with you, but you have to sit on my lap while we watch the dancer shaking their tits."

My cheeks burned from the blush, but it was so cute that, not only had Cora known exactly how her announcement would go, but that Cohl was so enamored with my sister. I was surprised none of them had come into the room sooner. It had been almost twenty minutes since any of the alphas had made one excuse or another to enter, trailing a hand along one of our shoulders or pressing a kiss to the tops of our heads.

We were lucky women.

* * *

With promises to get together again soon, Cora and her pack loaded my adorable nephew into their extended SUV and headed home. That had been two days ago.

Now, I was in my personal bathroom applying makeup while Ax sat on the vanity and watched.

He'd done this exact thing for months, watching me get ready for the day or winding down for the night, before either of us had admitted how badly we'd wanted each other. All that time, I'd thought he saw me as simply another member of the pack, almost like a sister. He and the other two would fool around in one of their bedrooms while I tried not to listen too closely and struggled with the intense surges of jealousy and rejection.

"Is Amir coming again tonight?" I asked.

"He came twice already today," Ax teased.

Straightening, I raised one brow at him, even as my face burst into flames and my lower body warmed. Those two orgasms involved me and Ax taking turns with our omega while Cyrus and Enzo were out running errands before we all headed to work.

"Yes. He said he's coming out tonight."

Our omega had run home to visit with his parents for a bit, something about one of their goats having babies, or *kids* as I'd been informed. I'd been promised a trip to see the babies as soon as possible.

I wished he was here. As clingy as it made me feel, I hated when any of the pack weren't together, even if only for a few hours. And I wasn't even a damn omega.

Nope. I was simply a woman in love with four of the most amazing men to ever exist.

Applying another coat of mascara, I leaned back away from the mirror and checked my reflection.

"Fuck, you're beautiful," Ax said, but it was muttered, as though he was thinking out loud rather than paying me a compliment.

I smiled over at him and grabbed a bottle of perfume, spritzing it once in my cleavage before stepping closer and wedging myself between his knees.

"You make me feel beautiful." Even when I'd thought they didn't see me in that light, they'd made sure I felt pretty, forced me to at least try to see my own self-worth beyond what I had to offer an alpha.

I wasn't simply a beta or the daughter of the Alvarez alphas. I was Isabelle Rivera. I was strong and intelligent. And officially employed. I worked my butt off, even though I was still only scheduled for short shifts while I learned how to work the club. I was gaining independence, earning my own money, and was so close to being comfortable driving myself without an escort.

It wasn't the driving part that scared me – it was being alone in public around alphas, around people who always felt like a threat, whether imagined or not.

At the club, I had my pack, I had their employees who treated me like I was their friend, who kept an eye out for me when one of my alphas wasn't there to hawk-eye my every move.

I'd also chosen a new wardrobe specifically for my workdays, a way to feel like a different person. It might have sounded odd to someone else, that something as simple as new skirts and tops and a change in my makeup would give me a boost of self-esteem, but it worked for me.

Didn't hurt that I could feel my pack in my chest any time I took a peek down the threads, could feel how proud of me they were, how much they cared about me, could feel them right there with every step I took so I never felt alone.

An hour later, the four of us walked through the back employee entrance, the alphas stepping into their offices – including the one where Amir and I had first fucked – while I headed straight for the bar to grab my apron, clock in, and grab a tray from the stack.

It was early, but there were a few groups at some of the tables, others sitting on the stools at the bar. Aryn was tending bar tonight and was one of my favorites. She was so pretty and funny and was a freaking alpha. A *female* alpha. She and Amir tended to get quite a few stares due to their rarity.

Aryn was not only super sweet and funny, but also as tall as Amir and just as protective as the rest of my pack. We had formed a quick friendship and I found myself hoping she would find a pack of her own soon. I wanted her to be as happy as me. Hell, I was a big ol' bubble of joy these days and wanted the entire world to experience the rainbows and unicorns I swore I felt every day.

"Your sexy ass omega coming in tonight?" Aryn asked as I approached and turned my cheek for her to press a kiss.

I'd grown so much more comfortable with physical affection, so much so that I even looked forward to the gentle touches from Aryn and the other servers as they came or left. Hugs, brushes along my shoulders, pecks to the cheeks.

They were all careful to avoid leaving their scent on me, though. Being as all the servers were betas like me, I wasn't sure why them scent marking me would have been an issue, but I could understand why the alpha bouncers avoided transferring their signature to me, even my clothing.

Not Aryn. After kissing my cheek, she ran her chin over the top of my head, then lifted her phone and stared at the screen, waiting for the text we both knew was coming.

Just like the last few times I'd worked and Aryn touched me, all three alphas sent texts of various threats. Although both of us knew they were half-hearted. Aryn didn't want me romantically. I didn't want her. And my men would never hurt a woman, even a fellow alpha.

"Of course. Ax wants to show off yet another new routine," I said with a smile and a roll of my eyes.

"Yeah right. That omega's eyes follow you around the room. The only time they leave you is when your alpha is on stage, then..." She snapped her fingers. "Right back on his pretty little beta."

It might have been my imagination, but her last few words almost sounded sad. And I was right back to hoping she would find a pack, someone who would see how amazing she was and appreciate such a beautiful and strong woman.

My cheeks heated and I shrugged. "We're in love or whatever."

"No whatever to that one. I swear all five of you have been walking around with hearts in your eyes for weeks."

She shooed me from behind the bar and turned to a couple who'd walked up to the bar.

For the time, there were only two servers on the floor, but two others would arrive in an hour or so, right in time for the crowd that would pile in for their weekend plans and to catch Ax and the other strippers.

We're not strippers. It's a male dance review. I could hear Ax's voice in my head as I approached a table to check on them and smiled.

"You guys doing okay?" I asked.

Three sets of eyes lifted to me, scowls etched into their faces, faces that might have been handsome if they were to relax the muscles keeping their brows knitted together so tightly.

The man nearest me raised a brow when his attention zeroed in on my marks. "Your alphas haven't taught you how to approach a designation higher than yours?"

Old Issa tried to push to the forefront. My first instinct was to lower my eyes and apologize. They were right. They were alphas, top of the food chain. I was nothing but a beta.

But *new* Issa?

"You're not higher than me. And if you want to actually stay in the club owned by *my* pack, you'll show me more respect. So, let's try this again – you guys doing okay, or can I get you something else?"

One of the men smiled softly and nodded, respect shining in his pretty brown eyes. The first asshole made a scoffing sound in the back of his throat but asked for an old-fashioned – how apropos – while the others requested a bucket of beers.

"You got it," I said with an overly friendly smile.

I let it drop the moment I turned away from them and rolled my eyes.

But then…a genuine smile tugged at my lips. I had just stood up to three alphas. I hadn't backed down, hadn't let them treat me like trash.

I couldn't wait for Amir to get here so I could tell him. The first free moment I had, I planned to send a group text to my alphas to let them know I was officially a badass. I'd have to explain that later, but for now, that was exactly how I felt, like I could stand up to anyone without backing down.

Shoulders squared, I gave Aryn the order, the smile still on my face, and turned toward the door, just waiting for it to swing open and my omega to appear. I missed him. Only a few hours apart, and I missed him.

The tables continued to fill, the dance floor grew more and more crowded, and the music was turned up enough to create the right atmosphere. The lights were dim, but not so dark that I couldn't make my way around the room without tripping over my feet.

I had waited on the table of three alphas a couple more times, but that asshole hadn't made any more comments. He also wouldn't make eye contact with me, either. That was fine with me. He didn't like me, and I didn't like him.

I'd dressed to the nines, but I'd made sure to wear more comfortable shoes this time. The heels looked great and made me feel fierce, but damn...my feet throbbed and ached by the end of the night.

Which, of course, gave my pack an excuse to pamper me, soak with me in the tub, and rub my sore feet.

When the lights dimmed further and the beat changed, I turned toward the door, searching for Amir. He was going to miss Ax's show. I might have been on duty, but that never stopped me from ignoring thirsty customers to ogle my sexy ass alpha.

The beginning notes of *Save a Horse* by Big & Rich started, and I threw my head back and laughed. *Really?* Of all songs, that was what Ax had chosen for tonight?

Checking the door one more time, I leaned against the bar and focused my full attention on the stage, the empty tray tucked under my arm, and screamed at the top of my lungs when the spotlights lit up the stage with my alpha and four other dancers, all donning cowboy hats, ripped jeans, and white t-shirts.

The song might have been older, but it was fun, and I danced to the beat as Ax worked through choreography, rotating his hips, grabbing the back of his shirt and tugging it over his head, then throwing it into the crowd of excited men and women.

I wasn't jealous. Even when two women fought over Ax's shirt, subsequently ruining it when it was ripped in two between them, I wasn't jealous. Because he was mine.

His eyes found me, and his smile grew blinding, his hand smoothing down his pec, down his stomach, to cup his junk as he swiveled his hips in a promise of what was to come later.

Arms circled around my waist, and I tensed for the briefest moment before I was surrounded by Amir's sweet signature. It didn't matter whether he wore scent blockers or how hard the filtration system worked – Amir's essence was powerful and delicious and made me fucking crazy.

Turning my head, I smiled at him and tilted my face up so he could kiss me. "Just in time," I yelled over the music.

Amir's hips swayed against mine, his cock hard against my ass. His chin rested on the top of my head as we watched one of our alphas work through the rest of his routine before pointing at us, then raising a hand to his lips and blowing us a kiss.

I couldn't help myself – I returned the gesture. All four of my men were just too damn irresistible.

"It is literally taking everything in me not to drag you to one of our alphas' offices, bend you over, and fuck you senseless," Amir muttered in my ear, sending butterflies to my stomach and heat low in my belly. If I were an omega, my panties would have become instantly damp with slick from his words, the sweet heat from his breath, and his cock pushed against my ass.

"You're going to keep me distracted all night, aren't you?" I asked, turning in his arms and tilting my head back for another kiss. "Aryn is tending bar. Go cop a squat and I'll visit when I can."

I pressed another quick kiss to his lips, then smiled over his shoulder at Cyrus as he approached. "Alpha incoming," I teased with a smile.

Tray still tucked under my arm, I hurried to check on the tables I'd ignored during Ax's performance. Everyone smiled and either put in another order or waved me off, saying they were fine for now.

Everyone except that first table of the night with the asshole alpha.

"Do you get paid to make out?" he asked, before turning his head to look at me over his shoulder.

"Well, being as that was my omega and my alphas own this place, I'm going to go ahead and say yes, I do get paid to make out. Would you like me to close out your tab?" Nope. Didn't ask if he wanted anything else. Because I wanted this jackwad out of here.

"Can we get another bucket?" one of his friends asked with a small but friendly smile.

Damn.

"Absolutely. Anything else for you, boys?" And yes, I had intentionally referred to the three alphas as boys on purpose.

Something had come over me tonight. I'd started feeling like a new person during my time with the pack, even more so after Amir had joined us. But this asshole was bringing out a feisty side I hadn't known existed.

A rumbling growl trickled over the music as the asshole alpha turned and glared at me while his buddies grinned and chuckled. They seemed…nicer. Why would they hang around such a jerk?

Maybe he was their boss. Or family member. Of all people, I knew how shitty one's family could be.

With a forced smile, I turned my back on the trio and headed for the bar, letting that smile drop as quickly as I had last time. I'd really hoped they were done for the night. They'd been here a couple hours and I was tired of dealing with the alphahole.

"You good?" Aryn asked me as I sidled to the bar beside Amir.

Generally, I would have gone to the end where the rest of the servers waited for their orders, but I needed a hit of my omega. And yeah, I was an addict and Amir was my own personal drug.

"Yep. Just ready for that table to leave. Another bucket," I answered, turning my cheek when Amir nuzzled against me.

"You're allowed to refuse service. Pretty sure the owners of this place would love to kick someone out," he said, his lips brushing along my jaw.

And just like that, my foul mood was gone.

"As long as they're paying customers, there's no reason to boot them. Yet."

I didn't bother telling either Amir or Aryn why I wanted them to go. No reason to get everyone pissy over one person out of two hundred.

A squeal left my lips as Amir swatted my ass, then a smile plastered itself on my lips. They were all here. All four of my men were under one roof. Our alphas and I were working, but Amir had still come to hang out until we could leave for the night. Although I would probably head home with Amir after my shift instead of waiting for our alphas to finish up their paperwork and closing duties.

Carrying the bucket by the handle, I lifted my arm and hoisted it onto the table occupied by the alphaholes. Okay, only one alphahole, but still. I wished they would finish up their night and leave. They hadn't watched the show, weren't dancing, and I hadn't noticed them talking to anyone else. So, if they were simply having some kind of meeting or reuniting or whatever, they could easily go elsewhere.

I kept my eyes on the two who'd been friendly, hoping it wasn't overly obvious I was intentionally ignoring the jerk who seemed to enjoy insulting me and felt as though my designation made me inferior to him.

There was absolutely a time I would have agreed. But three alphas and an omega taught me that shit meant nothing. Those four men treated me as though I was their queen, royalty, doted on me and cherished me as though *I* was their omega.

As I turned to go check on my other tables, a hand clamped around my wrist, pulling me to a stop.

My eyes dropped to the hand and trailed up the arm to find the alphahole glaring a hole through my damn head. As in, if he could have shot daggers from his eyes, I would have bled out right there on the club floor.

"Please don't touch me," I said, forcing my voice to remain steady and loud enough for him to hear it over the music.

I was growing, healing from my past. But alphas still made me a little nervous.

Your alphas are here. Your omega is here. The staff will see if anyone tries to hurt you.

I repeated those thoughts over and over as I tugged at my arm, trying to pull free.

"This is the second time we've had to wait for our drinks while you flirted with that omega," he said, his fingers tightening rather than loosening.

"You waited because the bartender was waiting on other patrons and had to actually fill the bucket," I said.

"How about when you took time to be a slut while the strippers were dancing?"

My wrist ached from his hold, his fingertips digging in hard enough I feared there would be bruises.

"Let me go," I said louder, tugging.

"You're going to get us kicked out," one of his buddies said. Except he was grinning and watching rather than actually stepping in to help.

Opening my mouth to issue a final warning before flagging down one of the bouncers, I was jerked away from the alpha so hard I stumbled into a table nearby...

And then chaos exploded all around me.

Fuck.

CHAPTER 25

<u>Ax</u>

I swore every time I caught my beta and omega watching one of my shows, I ended up with perma-wood. As in, I needed to fuck one of my sweethearts as soon as possible. Would Issa be up for a quickie in the office?

Or maybe Amir since our beta was technically on the clock.

After drying off the sweat and changing into my usual slacks and button up I wore when acting as a club owner instead of a performer, I shoved my feet into my shoes and headed out of my personal office to check on things.

Translation – to check on my beta and omega.

Issa had quickly formed a bond with Aryn, and I knew the female alpha would keep an eye on her, as well as the rest of our trusted crew, when she was here.

I'd hated to betray her confidence, but I wanted as many eyes on her as possible. Therefore, I'd made sure the bouncers, bartenders, and even her fellow servers knew of her aversion to alphas, that she was nervous around them, and to watch over her when one of her three alphas weren't on the floor.

Not that I tended to speak for my packmates, but I knew Enzo and Cyrus wished they could be on the floor when she worked as much as I did. But running a bar went beyond simply making sure there was liquor and IDs were checked at the door. There was a shit load of paperwork, security, making sure the filtration systems were running nonstop, and so much more.

As much as I'd loved this club since the day we opened it, I'd started to resent it when we were away from our girl. But she was here now. She worked three days a week and Amir always made sure to come in when she worked. *Win-win, baby.*

Nodding at a bouncer as I crossed through the hallway, I stepped into the main area and did a quick scan. The place was hopping tonight, packed to the gills. I could practically hear the cash register clanging over the music.

The bar was packed two people deep, the floor was full of couples and packs, the tables were all filled. Amir sat at the bar, partially turned toward the bar as he lifted his drink.

Where was Issa?

Craning my neck, I checked over each of the servers, looking for long, dark hair and the most beautiful face I'd ever seen in my life.

And zeroed in a cocksucker's hand wrapped around my beta's arm. By the pained look on her face, that mother fucker was hurting her.

Protests rose as I bulldozed through the crowd, not paying a lick of attention as to who I was shoving out of the way as I made my way to the table of three alphas and Issa.

One of the bouncers caught sight of my charge and turned his attention, then joined me halfway to where the table sat close to the front wall.

Wrapping one arm around her waist, I lifted her from the ground the same time I latched onto the fucker's thumb and bent until he had no choice but to release her or risk a broken fucking hand.

I should have tended to Issa. I should have taken her to safety before dealing with this asshole, before kicking him out and barring him for life.

But I didn't do any of those things.

The second I saw the bouncer pull Issa away from the corner of my eye, I grabbed the alpha by the throat and lifted him out of his seat until his feet barely touched the floor.

"You fucking touched *my beta?*" I roared out, my voice growing louder than the music.

His two buddies shot to their feet and immediately dove for me, one from my right, the other circling to wrap an arm around my throat.

They might as well have been a breeze coasting across my skin for all the good they did. My rage had sent my alpha into full rut. This mother fucker needed to die.

Tossing him to the ground, I followed him down, my fists flying and slamming against his face over and over as an arm squeezed around my throat and pulled, trying to disengage me from the alpha whose face was quickly becoming covered with blood as his bones crunched under my knuckles.

"Ax!" someone bellowed, but I could barely hear anything over the thumping of my heart or the blood rushing in my ears. My body vibrated with rage, with bloodlust, with the urge to punish and inflict pain.

To kill.

I had never in my life felt this insane need to spill blood. I had never felt an urge to end someone's life as strongly as I did now.

I hadn't grown up like Enzo and his brother, had never had any interactions with violent criminals.

Didn't matter. All I could see as I continued to throttle this piece of shit was his hand clenched around Issa's wrist as she tugged and struggled to get out of his grip.

We'd promised to protect her. Had promised we would never allow another alpha to hurt her. And none of us had been there when he'd touched her.

"Fuck! Ax, stop!" A familiar voice. An alpha bark. But it did nothing to stop me, didn't so much as brush through my nerve endings as nothing more than a suggestion.

More arms wrapped around my shoulders, my arms, even my torso and I was lifted from the ground, my hand still wrapped in the alpha's shirt until it ripped under my grip.

A constant growl mixed with my curses and struggles to get back to the asshole, even as I was dragged through the crowd and literally thrown into one of the offices.

As I lunged forward, intent on getting back to pummeling the fucker to death, Cyrus, Enzo, and even Amir stepped in my way, using their bodies as a wall to keep me from exiting.

"Stop! Now!" Enzo barked. But just like before, his command merely brushed over my skin.

My joints and muscle were taut, my brain was on a single track, and my vision was tinted with red. Breaths sawed in and out of my lungs as I glared at the three men blocking me from punishing someone who dared to touch my girl, my beta, the person who held my heart in her tiny fucking hands.

My omega was here. I needed to calm down. My rational, logical side kept trying to push forward, to take control. Amir wasn't small, but he was still my omega. I couldn't risk hurting him.

The door behind them opened and I tensed, prepared to lunge at anyone else who came near my pack.

Hands shoved at shoulders until Issa's worried face appeared through the space between the bodies.

I didn't think. I just reacted.

Lunging for her, I swept her into my arms, hugging her tightly to me as I lifted her off the ground and slammed my mouth over hers. Turning, I set her on the desktop, kissing her until I had to pull away to take a full breath, then lifted her arm to inspect it for any damages.

Her skin was dark pink, slightly swollen, and would absolutely be bruised within a few hours.

A fresh wave of rage lit my blood on fire.

When I turned to rush back into the club, Issa wrapped her legs around my waist and locked her feet, keeping me pressed against her body.

"Stay with me," she said so softly, her voice forcing my alpha to obey, the force of those words stronger than Enzo's bark.

Turning in her hold, I cupped her face in my hands and stared down into her face. "Did he hurt you?"

"I'm okay," she breathed out, her arms snaking around my neck and pulling me down so she could press her lips to mine. "I'm okay."

She wasn't okay. Someone had touched her. Hurt her. Her wrist would bruise from that cocksucker. And I'd been stopped from doling out the punishment he fucking deserved.

The growl still rumbled from my chest, increasing in volume as her soft, warm tongue teased the seam of my lips then danced with mine when I opened for her.

Then I lost control in a completely different way.

My hands shook as I yanked her shirt up, only separating from her lips long enough to pull it over her head before reclaiming her lips. Her fingers struggled with my button and zipper of my slacks as I tugged her pants over her hips.

The moment my cock was free, I pushed her back onto the desk, lifted her knees over my elbows, and slammed into her. Her cry lifted on the air, but I swallowed it, keeping it all to myself.

Music and sound grew louder, then was cut off again as the office door was opened and closed. A possessive growl lifted louder at the thought someone had dared to enter the office while my beta was so vulnerable, but Issa's hands smoothed down my face, over the back of my neck, down my shoulders until all I knew was her, my beautiful girl, her touch and the way her cunt strangled my cock.

"He hurt you," I growled against her lips. "I'm supposed to protect you."

My chest ached, the pain riding shotgun beside the burning anger deep in my heart.

Her hands cupped my face and forced me to look into her eyes as I continued to pump inside of her at a bruising, toe curling pace.

"You did protect me, alpha. I'm okay."

Fuck. I wanted to knot my beta so badly. I wanted to lock us together, to paint her inner walls with my cum, to fill her belly with my pups.

All things that couldn't happen.

Not *all*. I could still fill her with my release, leave my scent all over her body, claim her in every way possible.

She carried my mark. And she would carry my scent and seed for the rest of the night. I wanted it spilling from her, spilling down her thighs the moment she stood up. I wanted any piece of shit alpha who dared to even contemplate touching my girl to know death would follow the moment they so much as laid a finger on her.

CHAPTER 26

<u>Enzo</u>

This was a fucking mess. While fights had happened since we'd opened the club, they were rare.

And not once had any of us actually been the cause of any of those fights.

I couldn't fully blame Ax for the current situation or the fact that not only the police, but an ambulance had been called. The asshole alpha had had no right to lay his hands on one of our employees.

And not just any employee – our fucking beta.

I'd seen her wrist when Ax had inspected it, had seen how hard he'd gripped her. She would have yet another bruise by yet another cock sucking mother fucker who thought he was top dog, who thought his designation gave him the right to play by his own rules.

Not fully blaming Ax for beating the piss out of him, but this wasn't a good look for him or us. He'd beat the dude unconscious and continued to pummel him, even with the guy's buddies doing every-thing in their power to pull Ax away.

He'd looked like a man possessed when I'd finally gotten through the gawking crowd. I'd never seen him look so unhinged, so fully out of control of his alpha. It had taken me, Cyrus, one of our bouncers, and even Amir to finally get him away from the prone alpha. Then the three of us had stood in front of the door to keep him from rushing back out to…

What? What would Ax have done had we not intervened?

Stupid question. As completely lost to his alpha as he'd been, I had no doubt Ax would have ended up beating someone to death right there in the middle of the club with hundreds of fucking witnesses.

Now I had to find a way to keep the cops from arresting my packmate. Especially since I knew he would be balls deep inside of Issa as she did her best to bring him back down. If a single person outside of the pack stepped through that office door, he would go insane. The fucker was in rut.

He'd better not attempt to knot Issa. Her beta body wasn't built for that. Had this been a different situation, I might have suggested our omega help settle him, but he needed Issa to reassure him she was okay.

How had that beautiful girl wrapped us all so tightly around her finger?

Stupid fucking question. Not only was she physically beautiful, she was beautiful inside, too. Funny. Witty. Smart. And so fucking strong.

Something like what had happened tonight would have sent her into a tailspin in the past. She would have retreated back into her shell, hidden away, maybe even refused to leave the house again for a while. Instead, she'd made her way to the office and pushed through our bodies to make sure her alpha was okay, to reassure him instead of the other way around.

Cyrus stood just outside the main doors speaking with the police while Amir and I cleaned up the broken glass, and righted tables and chairs. "You don't have to help," I told him.

We'd assured him we weren't assholes, that we weren't power hungry or violent. Issa had assured him we weren't like a lot of other packs out there. And then he'd been witness to Ax breaking a man's face with his bare fists.

"I need to do something."

I glanced in his direction then did a double take. That wasn't fear or even anger on his face. It was something else.

"What? What's wrong?"

He pushed his hand through his long curls, then pulled an elastic from his pocket to tie his thick locks into a messy bun at the base of his neck.

"I should have been there. I should have been watching her closer."

Leaning the broom and dustpan against the table, I turned and gripped Amir by his shoulders, forcing him to look up at me. He was tall for an omega, but still quite a few inches shorter than me.

"It's not your job to protect her, Amir. That's our job. If anyone failed her, it was us."

His head wagged slowly side to side. "I turned away for a minute. I was just asking for another drink. By the time I looked back…"

Softly shaking him by his shoulders, I bent lower so we were eye to eye. "Your job is to make her happy. To love her. You did not fucking fail her."

And, as an omega – even one who was closer to an alpha's size – he was at risk, as well. A male omega was as rare as a female alpha. And there just happened to be one of both in the club at this very moment.

Aryn made her way over, her head turned toward the doors until she was close enough. "They going to arrest him? I'll be a fucking witness. That douche has been giving her trouble all night."

My brows slammed together. "Why the fuck didn't you kick him out?"

Her shoulders rose and fell. She was about an inch taller than Amir, but not as muscular or broad. "She didn't tell me until after. I knew something was up, but she said it was fine. I think he'd just made some shitty comments and she was doing her best to blow them off."

Because she was either trying to prove to herself or to us she could handle alphas.

"Is she okay?" Aryn asked. "Is Ax okay?"

"They're alright. They're in Cyrus's office."

Cyrus whistled, waving me toward him where he spoke with the police.

"I'll finish this," Amir said.

"Not your job, omega," I said, pressing my lips to his before walking away.

But when I looked back, he had gone right back to cleaning up as one of the servers rolled a mop bucket to the mess. To clean up the beer and spilled blood.

What a fucking mess.

"They want Issa to make a statement," Cyrus said with a raised brow.

Glancing over my shoulder toward the closed office door, I turned back to the police officer with his hands resting on his belt.

"She's with one of her alphas right now. She needed to be calmed down after that asshole assaulted her."

"His buddies are telling a different story."

The cop was a beta, and his tone sounded as though he was leaning more toward Issa's side than the alphas.

"Let me guess – they were attacked unprovoked? Our beta already has bruising and swelling where that fucker grabbed her."

The officer pulled a notebook from his breast pocket and started jotting down notes. "Had anything else transpired before?"

"I don't know the details, but she'd told our bartender he was verbally accosting her."

"Accosting her how?"

"I don't know the full details. I was in my office when everything was happening." Instead of out here where I could keep an eye on her.

Mother...fucker. I had supported her decision to get a job and had been overjoyed that she wanted to work for us. In my mind, it would have been easier to keep her safe if she was under the same roof as her three alphas.

And we'd fucking failed her.

We had plenty of security in this place, though. Issa could have simply said something to one of the bouncers or even Aryn and the alpha would have been booted out the door.

She was trying to be strong, trying to prove she could handle this job and being around alphas.

And…she'd done exactly that. Yeah, the fucker had put his hands on her, but she hadn't been seriously injured. I wouldn't know the full story until I had some time to talk to her, but I was proud of her. Pissed at myself and my staff, but proud as fuck of our girl.

"Would it be possible to bring her out to speak to me? Or could I–"

"No," Cyrus and I said at the same time when the officer started to ask whether he could step into the office.

Beta or not, a strange man in the room with Issa when Ax was so out of control would be…well, our packmate would definitely end up in the clink.

"Could we bring her by the station later tonight or in the morning?" Cyrus, ever the diplomat, asked, looking between me and the officer while rubbing the back of his neck.

The policeman looked between the two of us and the reason behind our protests seemed to sink in because his brows raised and he nodded.

"Could someone take pictures of her injuries tonight while they're fresh?"

Warm linen and chocolate covered strawberries lifted on the breeze a second before Issa and Amir stepped outside and stopped beside me. For some reason, I didn't like the two of them so exposed out here and pushed them both until they were between Cyrus and myself.

Stupid, being as there were enough officers here to ensure their safety. But my alpha was barely hanging on by a thread after tonight's incident.

"I'm Isabelle Rivera," she said, offering the officer her hand, and it wasn't lost on me that she'd intentionally offered the hand with her bruised wrist.

The officer's eyes scanned her, not a slow perusal, but rather looking for injuries. "Other than the obvious bruising on your wrist, did the alpha cause any other injuries?"

"No. Because my alpha stopped him before he could go any further. I have no doubt he would have–" She cut herself off and blinked rapidly as her eyes grew glassy with unshed tears.

Mother fucker.

Rage started to boil fresh in my veins. I was the fucking pack lead. I needed to keep my shit together or I could end up making the situation far worse than it already was.

"The victim's friends–"

"*She's* the victim," Amir said, his arm wrapped tightly around her shoulders.

The officer nodded. "His friends said he was attacked unprovoked."

"Good thing the entire club is covered by cameras," Cyrus said, eternally calm.

"He was making comments all night. Berating me. Degrading me because of my designation," Issa said, her chin lifted as she continued to blink away those tears.

The officer's shoulders straightened, and I could have sworn he bristled at her words. Because...*he* was a beta, as well. He would know the sting of having someone treat him as though he was less simply because of how he'd presented.

Shoving the notebook back into his pocket, he hooked his hands in his belt again. "Do you want to press charges, Beta Rivera?"

Hearing the use of my last name attached to my beautiful girl made my alpha sit up and pay attention.

Along with my dick.

"No. I just want him out of here."

"He's barred," I growled. "Along with his buddies. I want them trespassed."

Cyrus glanced at me but didn't argue. I wasn't sure whether that look was approving or disapproving, but I didn't give a fuck. There wasn't a doubt in my mind they would mistreat Issa again the first moment they had. And even if she wasn't here, they were obviously not the type of patrons we wanted in our club.

"You got it." The officer turned his attention to Issa. "Do you need medical attention?"

She shook her head, leaning heavily against Amir. "No. I think I'm okay."

I would have preferred she at least let a medic check her out but knew my girl wouldn't want the extra attention. And bruising would heal. She looked as though she had full use of her arm, so nothing was broken.

Amir tensed, and his perfume lifted on the air, but he didn't say anything, just kept Issa hugged tightly to his side.

Turning my attention to my beta and omega, I frowned at the tension not just in Amir's body language, but in his face, as well. His brows were pinched together, and his eyes looked a little unfocused.

We should have a few more weeks before his heat. But stress could and did often bring on the cycle sooner. Looked like we would have to spend the next few days making sure his nest was ready and perfect before we were all locked away for up to a week.

CHAPTER 27

<u>Issa</u>

The entire pack had squeezed into the pack bed in the omega quarters when we got home. Where most packs, most alphas would have been wrapped around their omega, all four men had been wrapped around me, all finding ways to touch me as though unable to bear being so much as a few inches away.

Yeah, that night had sucked. At least the part where the alpha had treated me like shit, my alpha beating him to a pulp, then the cops showing up.

But my time with Ax in the office, my time calming his alpha, then the hour all five of us spent touching and kissing and making love once we got home was nothing short of perfection.

It had been three days since all that had transpired, and we were planning a pack outing to a local store designed for omega needs. Omega's Desires carried practically anything that could be imagined, and what wasn't on the shelves could be ordered and delivered directly to our house within a day or two.

The nest in Amir's quarters had a cushioned floor and walls along with some bland, neutral pillows, but it would need more. At least we had made use of the room on more than a few occasions and covered it with our scents instead of that chemical scent blocker that had covered every inch before.

Amir was trying his best to hide it, but he was definitely in preheat. He'd already been damned near insatiable before, but now, it felt as though he was constantly rubbing up against one of us, luring one of us for a quickie or a blowjob, or simply dragging me to the couch to straddle him whether I was clothed or not.

Had someone told me last year that I would be in a constant state of arousal, I would have laughed in their face. Especially if they'd told me I would be so comfortable around and turned on by three alphas while completely obsessed with an omega.

But here I was, tucked under Ax's arm as Enzo pushed the cart with Cyrus helping Amir pick out various colors and textures of pillows and blankets for his nest before his heat came crashing in and his omega went crazy when his space wasn't right.

Amir's beautiful face was taut, his pupils dilated, and sweat dampened the rogue curls that had come loose from the bun at the nape of his neck.

Slipping out from under Ax's arm, I sidled up beside my omega and nuzzled against his chest.

"You okay?" I whispered. "We can go home and shop online."

He shook his head and rubbed his chin against my head then nuzzled against my cheek, a rusty, broken purr rumbling from his chest. "I still have some time."

His perfume had pushed past the scent blockers and even the filtration system working overtime in the store since omegas didn't tend to appreciate other omegas' scents. *Especially* when their pack was present.

Amir continued to scent mark me as I wrapped my arms around his back and hugged him tightly. I could feel his cock hard against my stomach and could scent his slick. He was much closer than he was letting on.

My beautiful omega was so damn strong.

The cart Enzo pushed was full and items occasionally tilted over the side, causing one of the alphas to have to dart forward to catch a pillow or rolled up blanket before it could fall and hit the floor.

"Heat gifts," Cyrus muttered to himself, completely unaware that his omega was struggling behind him.

"We can deal with that later. Let's get Amir home," I said, tilting my head back to look into my omega's face.

His pupils were blown, his cheeks were flushed a dark pink, and I swore I could feel his body temperature growing by the second where we were pressed together.

Cyrus turned to glance at us over his shoulder then did a quick double take. "Are you in pain?"

If Amir was cramping, he hadn't made a single whimper or touched his abdomen. But his fever was definitely kicking in and his pheromones were strong, his scent coating my tongue and nestling its way into my pores.

"I'm fine," Amir said, his voice deeper, more guttural, but not in that sexy way he sounded when he was taking me hard and fast.

"Is there somewhere we can ease him?" Cyrus asked, leaning to the side to look down an aisle, though I wasn't sure whether he was looking for a pack room or a sales associate.

"I've got a couple more days," Amir said, the rusty purr broken and stuttering as he held me tight and continued to rub his scent gland along my cheek and head.

"I think you're down to a few hours," I said, tilting my chin back to look into his face again.

His warm, light brown skin looked pale, sweat was beading along his forehead, and his pupils were blown so wide the green of his irises were nearly invisible.

"Let's finish up and get him home," Enzo said, pushing the cart toward the registers while attempting to juggle the items that kept trying to fall over the sides.

Amir didn't loosen his hold as we all followed our pack lead to the front of the store, but I guided our omega through the front doors and to the waiting SUV with Ax on our heels. The alarm beeped and the doors unlocked before we reached the vehicle as Ax hit the fob and gave us entry instead of making us wait for the whole pack to join us.

Amir could pretend he was fine all he wanted, but his appearance and tight, jerky movements said otherwise.

The moment we were enclosed behind the confines of the SUV, Amir leaned forward, an arm wrapping around his middle as a pained whimper tore from his throat.

"Oh my gosh, sweetheart. I could have eased you in a backroom or something," I said, running my hand through his hair to push it away from his face. "Can I help?"

"Do you need some water or something?" Ax asked as he climbed in on the other side of our omega.

This was a change. The guys always demanded I stay between them, as though they all wanted to protect me with their own bodies. But our beautiful omega needed us.

I didn't have the proper equipment to help chase away the worst of his heat symptoms, would end up being the one to ensure everyone was eating and drinking enough to avoid dehydration. But there was no way he would let me stay away for long. Nor did I want to. I was so fucking crazy in love with our omega.

With all of them. And I really needed to start saying it more often. Or, you know, at all. I'd really only told Ax how I felt, but I'd meant that about all of them, even if they hadn't heard me that day. Though I was sure they had either watched us on the cameras or at least watched the playback.

Yep. I was bonded to a bunch of perverts, and it was endearing.

"I'm fine," Amir said, forcing a smile at me that looked more like a grimace, even as another whimper tore from his throat.

"We're alone in here. Let us help you," Ax said.

But Amir's eyes were on me, boring into mine, and for a brief moment, it felt as though he wasn't actually seeing me, as though, for a second, he was lost to his hindbrain before we'd gotten him home.

He didn't have days. And I was beginning to think he didn't have hours left, either. Our last two alphas needed to hurry up so we could get Amir home, get the nest ready, and get him settled. We still needed to make sure the new items didn't carry the scents of any other omegas who might have touched the pillows or blankets while shopping, had to stock the minifridge with bottles of water, had to make sure there were plenty of easy to eat options for the next few days...

And now I felt a bit like a failure of a beta. It was generally our job to make sure our pack was stable and healthy when they lost themselves to their baser sides. And I'd been so distracted by my job and our new relationship that I'd let time pass by entirely too quickly.

Then again, we'd thought we had a few more weeks.

We all believed the incident at the club with the asshole alpha had messed with Amir's biology, the stress sending his body into overdrive with his need to protect me.

Which, of course, was silly. *He* was the omega. I was just the beta. *He* was the one who was to be protected at all times.

Cyrus and Enzo hurried through the front doors, their arms loaded with bags, before Amir could answer Ax. He was still staring at me, his lips parted as his breath came in pants, but he looked dazed.

After the bags were secured in the hatchback, Enzo climbed behind the wheel while Cyrus took the passenger seat, turning his upper body to look back at us. "You doing okay, omega?"

But Amir continued to stare at me, his blinks coming slowly, the softest whine lifting on the air barely louder than his pants.

"I think we need to hurry," I said, frowning up at Amir.

The longer he stared, the longer he went without responding, the more worried I was growing. I was beginning to sweat where our bodies touched, his fever so high I felt it through our clothes.

"Omega?" Cyrus said, a deep crease forming between his brows.

"Amir," Enzo barked, checking the rearview mirror as he split his attention between us and the road.

Our pack lead's bark broke through whatever trance Amir was in and he slowly – and eerily – turned his head toward the front of the vehicle.

And then a heart wrenching whine tore from his throat and he wrapped both arms around his middle as the first major wave of cramping clenched his insides.

"Oh baby," I cried out as tears welled in my eyes. Releasing my seatbelt, I immediately climbed onto his lap and threw my legs on either side of his hips. "Let me help. I know it won't be as good as a knot, but I hate seeing you…like this."

I cupped his face in my hands and pressed kisses to his forehead, cheeks, and nose, before slanting my mouth over his and sighing when his arms wrapped around my back and hugged me tightly. Almost immediately, his hips began to rise under me, gyrating and grinding his erection against my covered core.

Damn it. Why hadn't I worn a dress or skirt today? I could have easily lifted the hem and pushed my underwear to the side for better access.

His perfume practically exploded from him, stirring the alphas until their growls rumbled nonstop throughout the cab. Their scents rose as their hormones urged them to rut their omega. We were no less than thirty minutes from home and there was only so much room in the SUV, even if we were to put all the seats down.

Amir's lips tore from my mine and nipped at my throat as he continued to hold me tightly against his chest, his hips thrusting up over and over as though stimulating himself or trying to tear through our clothes.

"Ax. Help me," I said, trying to pull away to undo and remove my pants enough to give Amir a little relief.

Strong, deft fingers undid my pants then dragged them over my hips, even helping me lift to get them low enough for Amir to have access to my pussy. I assumed Ax was the one to also release Amir's cock from his pants and hold him steady for me to lower onto his shaft since Amir refused to release his grip on me even the slightest.

As I lowered onto him, his girth stretched me and pulled a breathy moan from my throat.

My gentle, sweet omega didn't give me any time to adjust to the intrusion before he began to thrust up into me. His lips were parted as a nearly constant whine lifted on the air with his perfume and his pupils fully engulfed the green of his beautiful eyes until they appeared almost black.

This wasn't preheat. We absolutely did not have days or even hours.

My beautiful Amir was in heat, and we were trapped inside this SUV until we could get him home, in his nest, and knotted by one of our alphas.

CHAPTER 28

<u>Amir</u>

Even as Enzo pulled the SUV into the garage and opened the back door, I refused to release Issa, refused to allow anyone to pull her from my cock. My slick dampened my jeans and my cum rolled from her and pooled on my lap after orgasming twice already in the thirty-minute drive from the omega store to our home.

Those two orgasms had taken the edge off the worst of the pain, but it was still there. And her soft, warm body against mine gave me some comfort.

Sweat beaded along her hairline, and I feared it was from my fever cooking her. Yet I still refused to let her go. It felt as though the moment she was no longer in my arms the worst of the symptoms would crash into me and sweep me under.

My cycles weren't exactly fun in the past, but this one was grabbing me by the throat.

And kicking me in the balls.

While tearing through my fucking uterus.

Yep. Male omegas were rare. And we were blessed with the chance to carry children. But honestly, this part sucked balls. And not in the sexy kind of way, either.

Issa's pants were pulled down at an awkward angle, so I either had to release her and walk through the door without her cunt wrapped around my cock or beg someone to tear those fucking jeans away from her body so she could wrap her legs around my waist. And yeah. I had every intention of taking her against every surface possible until we made it to the nest.

But the sooner I released her, the sooner we could all get to the nest, the sooner one of my alphas could knot me and chase away the cramping and fever before it got a full stranglehold on me.

Reluctantly, I lifted her off my cock and helped her pull her pants up her hips enough that she could walk without tripping over herself. At least I hadn't fully lost my mind to my hindbrain and had enough forethought to avoid letting my beta get hurt.

Though I wasn't sure how much longer the coherency would last.

The second she could walk without getting caught up in the hem of her jeans, I wrapped my hand around hers and began to rush through the garage and into the house, Enzo ahead of us, Ax and Cyrus following right behind.

Bags rustled as we hurried through the house, up the stairs, and to the omega quarters.

It wasn't right. None of it was right. I wanted time for my pack to leave their scents on all the new stuff before bringing it into my nest. I hadn't even had enough time to arrange everything the way my omega needed.

Issa tugged free from my hand and veered off toward the refrigerator and a whine immediately tore from my chest before I could stop it.

Everyone froze in their tracks, hefty levels of alpha hormones exploding into the air.

"I'm just getting water. Go get ready, set everything the way you want it, and I'll be there before you're done."

The whine still filled the air, but it was softer. Stupid omega hormones. My logical side knew what she was doing, but my omega side feared she was rejecting me when I needed her.

"Come on, omega. Let's get you ready," Cyrus, the ever calm and steady alpha, said, wrapping his free arm around my shoulders and urging me toward the stairs.

His warm, rain dampened wood scent wrapped around me like a blanket, and I rubbed my cheek against his chest and shoulder as we made our way down the hall.

Enzo stepped in ahead of us, both hands clutched around the handles of several bags. He pulled open the door to the nest and flipped on the dim lights that hung overhead. A lot of omegas preferred something simple like fairy lights or even candles. My omega leaned toward the exposed Edison bulbs, aiding me to see my pack clearly without assaulting my overly sensitive eyes.

Everything felt sensitive. My skin was tight and itchy, and my clothes felt like sandpaper against my flesh with every step. I was both hot and freezing cold as my fever rose and rose until my heart raced and my vision blurred.

Sounds escaped my mouth as I yanked the bags from my alphas' hands and began to arrange the pillows and blankets around the room.

But they smelled wrong. It all smelled wrong.

Not right.

As though anticipating my needs, Enzo, Ax, and Cyrus darted forward, stripped naked, and began to lift the new items and rub them against their scent glands before setting them exactly where I'd arranged them.

But it still wasn't right. Something was missing. Some*one* was missing.

"Issa," I said. Or rather whined. Her name came out on a whimper even as my alphas carefully and gently began to remove my clothing and guided me to the cushioned floor.

"She's coming, omega," Cyrus cooed, smoothing his hands over my hair. "Fuck, you're burning up."

Enzo left the room, and my stupid fucking omega began to whine at the sense of abandonment. Two of my packmates were now missing.

Enzo left me. My pack lead left me.

"Shh. He's coming back. We're all here."

"Should we ease him?" Ax asked, stroking his hand along my chest, down to my cock where he gave a soft, gentle stroke, then back up.

Not enough. Damn it. I needed more. I needed…

I couldn't even finish that sentence. I needed knots. I needed my alphas. I needed my beta.

I needed a release and I needed to be bred.

When the lust haze faded and my heat passed, I would be thankful I was on birth control.

But my omega wanted my alphas to fill me with their cum, to fill me with their pups, to breed me until my body couldn't take any more.

Enzo hurried back into the room carrying a few towels and a wet washcloth that he pressed to my forehead.

"Should we put him in the bath?" Cyrus asked.

"No," I murmured. "Knot. Please."

"Fuck," Ax growled a moment before he urged my knees apart and tested my entrance with his finger. "So slick. So warm and tight," he said in a guttural voice before lining the head of his cock to my ass and slowly pushing forward.

The feeling of him deep inside of me eased some of the painful cramping, but I needed his knot, I needed the heat of his release painting my inner walls.

I needed my beta.

"Issa," I cried out as tears burned the backs of my eyes then spilled over my temples to soak into my hair and the pillow under my head.

"I'm here," she said, breathing heavily as she dropped the armful of water bottles and lowered to my side. "I'm here, baby."

With Ax slowly thrusting into me, his knot pressing against my opening each time, and Issa lowering her lips to mine, my omega began to settle. At least the sense of rejection began to settle.

But the rest…

The five of us had a few days before we would finally get any rest. And were I not in pain and feeling as though I was being burned alive from the inside out, I might have celebrated the fact I would be fucked by my pack over and over for days on end.

"Naked. Please," I begged Issa as she took over for Enzo and pressed the cool cloth to my forehead and cheeks. "I need you."

Cyrus helped her undress quickly, then held her hand to keep her steady as she threw a leg over my hips and lowered onto my cock, her core so tight, so warm and wet around me.

"Holy fuck, that's hot," Ax said as Issa began to ride me. His thrusts grew faster, harder, more desperate. "I'm going to knot you, omega. I want to hear you cum and fill our beta while I fill this tight little ass."

He sure as hell didn't need to tell me twice. Between having Ax's thick cock stimulating my prostate and my beta's cunt swallowing my dick...my body tightened to the point of pain before an orgasm ripped through me, filling Issa with jet after jet of my hot cum, my ass spasming around Ax's cock.

"Fuuuck," he growled out before gripping my thighs in a bruising hold and pushed forward until his knot worked past the tight ring of muscles and locked us together, his release feeling as though someone had doused me with ice water to put out the flames licking at my nerve endings.

Cyrus pressed his soft lips to my forehead. "You're so perfect, omega. Look how good you make your beta feel. Look how good you're taking your alpha."

Another whimper tore from my chest, but this one at least wasn't from pain. For a pack who'd never had an omega in their life, they sure as hell knew exactly what I needed when I needed it.

CHAPTER 29

Issa

e hadn't even gotten through the first day of Amir's heat, and already, I was exhausted. Omegas tended to demand their alphas during this time. They needed an alpha's knot to ease the terrible symptoms of their cycle.

Not our omega. He refused to let me out of his sight for even a few moments. Any time I so much as ran to the bathroom to relieve my bladder or bring in clean towels, Amir's omega would go nuts, a long, keening whine tearing through the air nonstop until I was back in sight.

It wasn't until he'd fallen asleep with Cyrus's knot locking them together that I was able to retrieve more water bottles and some fruit. I'd had to cut up apples, strawberries, and wash blueberries before putting them all in a big bowl, then grabbed a box of protein bars before sprinting through the house and back to the nest.

For now, he was still asleep. I'd dozed in and out between waves, but now, I was having a hard time getting any rest. I kept wondering whether it was partially my fault that his heat had come early.

Of course, it would have eventually hit him, but we should have had a little more time. It felt as though it was after the night that asshole had grabbed my wrist – then gotten his ass kicked by Ax – that Amir had begun to show the first signs and symptoms of his cycle.

He would never blame me. None of them would.

That didn't stop me from blaming myself.

Maybe it had been a bad idea to go to work, especially at a place filled with drunk alphas.

But…why the hell should I have to hide away? Why should I have to shape my life around those who didn't know how to control their emotions or conduct themselves with class and maturity?

Chocolate and strawberries grew stronger in the air as a soft whimpering came from Amir. His eyes were closed, and his breathing was slow and even, but his brows were puckered and his face looked taut like he was in pain, even while he slept.

I hated this for him. I knew there was absolutely nothing I could do to make it go away, not permanently, but I still hated that he had to go through this a few times a year. After watching how my sister had been treated our whole lives, I'd never had any desire to be an omega and was thankful I'd presented as a beta. But I would take Amir's place in a heartbeat if it meant I could spare him the pain.

"You should get some sleep," Cyrus whispered to me from where he was wrapped around Amir.

His knot would have deflated, but I couldn't see whether he'd pulled free from our omega. The waves had woken Amir a few times each hour, the longest period of sleep only lasting around thirty minutes since we'd gotten home yesterday evening.

Not even twenty-four hours, and I was positive none of us had gotten more than a few hours of sleep in that time. As in, maybe an *accumulation* of three or four total.

The alphas had put in the most work physically, but Amir still required me to at least be in his line of sight if not physically touching him.

Or sucking him.

Or fucking him.

Carefully extricating myself from the tangle of limbs, I crawled closer to Cyrus to avoid waking Amir. The longer he slept, the more rest our alphas could get. And the more rest *I* could get, if I could ever fall back to sleep.

"I'm going to run downstairs and get more water and food. Maybe take a quick shower."

"Better hurry," he said with a silent chuckle that shook his body.

Because, yeah, my sweet Amir became unhinged if even one of us wasn't in the room when each wave hit. Didn't matter if all three alphas were servicing him, fucking him, knotting him. If he turned his head and couldn't see me, a heartbreaking keening whine would lift into the air and tears would fill his pretty green eyes.

Pressing a quick peck to Cyrus's lips, I shuffled from the room as quickly and quietly as possible, stopping in the shower first. I wouldn't have time to shave or even wash my hair, but I needed to wash away the sweat, slick, and cum that coated my skin.

After I'd dried, I skipped pulling on clothes since I'd have to remove them as soon as I stepped back into the nest, anyway, and jogged downstairs to load up my arms with water bottles and grabbed a few bags of chips, pretzels, and an unopened roll of cookies. Not exactly the epitome of nutrition, but everyone needed the calories to keep their energy up.

I hadn't been out of the room for more than fifteen minutes, but Amir was awake, that whine filling the space, his sweet perfume carrying a bitter hint to it as the alphas struggled to reassure him I was still here, that I'd only stepped out for a minute, promising him I would come back. Promising him that I hadn't rejected him. Promising him that I hadn't abandoned him.

Dropping everything beside the door, I hurried to Amir, rushing into his open arms and burying my face in his neck when he closed his muscular arms around my back.

"I'm sorry, *habibi*," I said, using his nickname for me and hoping I wasn't using it incorrectly. "I just got some food and water for us. I'm here. I would never leave you."

Leaning back, I cupped his now stubbled cheeks in my hands and stared into his eyes. "You know I love you, omega. I'm here. I will *never* leave you. I couldn't."

The whine finally faded out, but a tear escaped over his bottom lash and trailed down his left cheek.

I kissed it away before pressing my lips to his, tasting the saltiness of his tear mixed with the sweetness of his mouth.

Another arm wrapped around my waist and lifted me. Amir's cock was held steady by one of our alphas, then I was lowered slowly onto my omega, a moan pulling from our throats as I settled fully on him.

"You two are so beautiful together," Cyrus muttered into my ear as he pressed kisses to my cheek and shoulder as his fingers gently stroked along the mark he left on my throat.

Amir's fingers tightened in my hair and held me steady as he claimed my mouth, devoured my mouth in a desperate and hungry kiss. He was reassuring himself and his omega that his beta was still here, that his pack was whole.

That I hadn't abandoned him.

Never. I could never willingly walk away from Amir. I could never walk away from any of them. It would be easier to rip my heart from my damn chest.

Actually, that was exactly how it would feel if I were to lose a single one of these men, as though someone had torn open my chest and yanked the organ from its cavity.

A moan sounded from somewhere to my right. I desperately wanted to turn my head, see which of my alphas were pleasuring themselves – or each other – to the sight of Amir and I making love.

And that was exactly what we were doing. It didn't matter that this because of his biology, or that he needed the release to help with the cramping or heat. I would make love to my omega every day for the rest of my life if I had a choice in the matter.

Amir's arms tightened around me as his kiss grew frantic, his hips thrusting up into me harder, faster.

I squealed when he lunged forward, laying me on my back as he pumped into me, his cock stretching and filling me until it felt as though I was moaning nonstop.

"Can I take you while you fuck our beta?" Enzo asked Amir.

"Please, alpha. Knot. Please." Amir's eyes were unfocused, his pupils fully dilated until there was only a sliver of the seafoam green of his irises. His hindbrain had completely taken over and this wave of his heat had washed away any other thought but the need to breed.

We were both on birth control, but even I felt the need to see my alphas fill him with their seed in hopes of one day seeing his belly rounded with our first child.

And it would absolutely be *ours*. He might carry and birth a child since I wasn't sure I ever wanted to experience pregnancy, but I would be more than proud to be a mother to any children from our omega.

Enzo positioned himself behind Amir and I knew the moment he entered him from the guttural moan that escaped both men and how deeply Amir's cock was pushed inside me.

Ax gripped my thighs and opened me wider until my knees were nearly touching my chest, giving Amir more room to move.

Amir began to fuck into me, which pushed him back against Enzo. He was taking us both at the same time as Enzo moaned and grunted and the first tingles of an orgasm tightened the muscles in my lower belly and ran up my spine.

"You're taking your alpha so well," Cyrus cooed to Amir, pushing his hair from his face and running his lips over the marks they'd all three left on him, almost exactly in the same placement as my own marks.

Ax knelt beside my head, his cock fisted in his hand. He didn't need to say a word. I immediately opened my mouth, maintaining eye contact as he moved closer and fed me his length until the head hit the back of my throat and activated my gag reflex.

But I didn't want him to stop.

I wasn't sure what it said about me that I loved when Ax lost control of himself, when he fucked into my mouth until tears welled in my eyes.

Between the absolute bliss and carnal need in his eyes, the pleased growl rumbling through him, the moans and grunts from Enzo and Amir...

I imploded. My eyes rolled closed, and I moaned around Ax as little explosions rocketed through me, tightening my abdomen muscles and sending fireworks and stars dancing behind my closed lids.

Amir's moans grew louder, and he pumped into me harder, faster, pushing me further into the mattress. He grunted and his cock danced and jerked in my pussy as he filled me so full his cum ran down the seam of my ass to soak into the cushion below me.

But he didn't stop. He kept thrusting into me, pushing himself back against Enzo to take his alpha deeper.

My omega's arms gave out, and he collapsed on top of me, his weight only held up on his elbows, his hips still snapping forward while Enzo fucked into him from behind.

"I'm coming," Enzo growled out, the sound tickling something inside me and awakening a fresh wave of need.

"I'm going to come down your throat," Ax said.

And my body tightened again, milking Amir's cock inside me, sending him spiraling into another orgasm.

He was the first omega I'd ever been with and had had no idea how much spilled from them during their release. I could practically taste it on the air mixed with the spicy sweetness of Ax as he shouted, his hand tightening in the hair at the top of my head and shot his load into my mouth and down my throat.

Amir's body was pushed into me hard as Enzo thrust forward, knotting our omega, before rutting into him in shallow thrusts, his own sounds of pleasure added to the three of ours as he came inside Amir.

When Amir's arms gave out, he crushed me under his weight, and I struggled to pull in a deep breath.

Ax pulled from my mouth and arms snaked under mine and began to tug.

"Your beta can't breathe, omega," Cyrus said. Even during our omega's heat, my sweet alpha kept his head, remained lucid enough to protect me.

As much as I wanted a gulp of oxygen, I had to bite the inside of my cheek when Amir lifted enough to pull from my core and allow Cyrus to pull me out from under him.

Enzo rolled the two of them to their sides while they waited for his knot to deflate. With Amir's own release trailing down my thighs, I shifted my position to get a better look at where the two were connected and felt my heart swell with so much love, so much affection.

This…this was perfection. This moment, these men, this pack.

I finally had the life of my dreams, even if my muscles and joints were sore and I was growing exhausted.

And we still had a few more days to go before any of us would be able to rest.

CHAPTER 30

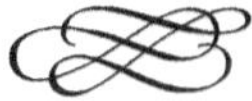

<u>Enzo</u>

I rested against the side of the garden tub, Amir's back against my chest and his head laid on my shoulder. Cyrus was currently rubbing our omega's feet while Ax held Issa straddled around his lap, her cheek on his shoulder, his arms locked around her waist.

When my brother had made the decision to kidnap the omega princess of Pack Alvarez, I'd thought he was fucking crazy. Not only was he poking a hornet's nest, but having an omega in your home, in your pack, changed everything. It didn't matter how often he'd tried to convince me – or himself – that it had been nothing more than business, that the four of them had had no desire to add an omega to their pack, I'd known better. I'd watched as each of them had fallen in love with Issa's youngest – and only – sister.

Bain's life might have changed because of that one choice, the decision to kidnap the only omega child of the elder – and now *dead* – Alvarez alphas, but my life had been irrevocably altered, as well.

Because their bond with Corazon had brought Isabelle into our lives, even if it wasn't the greatest start of our relationship.

I'd felt a shift in my chest, in my very being at the first sight of her. We'd all convinced her to stay with us until she could get back on her feet, build a life away from that piece of shit alpha who'd disappeared at the first sign of danger, and to let us keep her safe.

Little did any of us know how profoundly her mere presence would alter everything we thought we knew about life, about ourselves, about our pack.

An omega was often the heart of any pack, the center of which every member gravitated toward…except our pack.

Issa was our heart. Issa was our center. Even when one of us had been knot deep inside Amir during his cycle, he'd whined and keened and begged for Issa if she so much as stepped into the bathroom to relieve her bladder.

Tilting my chin down, I smiled at the slack expression on Amir's face, his eyes closed, his chest rising and falling in a steady rhythm. He'd fallen asleep in the warm bubble bath. We'd all piled into the shower first to rid ourselves of days' worth of cum, slick, sweat, and general body oils, but then had promptly climbed into the tub to let our muscles and joints soak in the heat and steam.

Five days. We'd been locked in that nest for five fucking days. All of us were fairly dehydrated and hadn't actually had a full meal since the morning before we'd headed for supplies for the nest. Issa had made sure to keep the room stocked with bottled water and snacks, forcing all of us to eat between cycles, holding water bottles to Amir's lips even when he was lost to his hindbrain and being knotted.

If it weren't for our sweet beta…

Fuck, she was amazing. Perfect. How anyone could have ever looked at her and seen anything other was a complete and utter mystery to me. How any fucker could look into her beautiful honey brown eyes and intentionally hurt her…that shit sent rage singeing through my veins.

Cyrus and Ax both frowned in my direction as my scent took on that bitter, burned wire smell.

I had to keep my shit in check. There was no reason to dwell on the past. I couldn't change it for her.

But I would absolutely beat the ever-living fuck out of Antonio if we ever saw him again.

Dude was smart – he'd taken off and stayed off the radar since Issa had shown up at Enzo's pack's estate. Almost like he'd known she was officially under our protection.

Or maybe he knew Enzo's pack planned to end the lives of Cora's and Issa's fathers, therefore, there was no longer any reason to stay tied to the beta.

Rubbing my cheek against Amir's temple, I stared at Issa's long dark hair hanging in wet tendrils down her back. Either she was asleep, as well, or just seriously comfortable, because the only movement I'd seen from her in the last ten minutes was the soft rise and fall from her deep breaths.

"Grocery delivery or junk food?" Cyrus asked as he gently moved away from Amir, barely disturbing the bubbles, and leaned against Ax's side. His eyes lowered to Issa's face and a soft smile tugged up his lips.

"I love you," she whispered, and Cyrus's eyes widened the slightest bit before his soft smile grew into a full-blown grin.

"I love you, too," he whispered back, shifting over a little to press a kiss to her temple before rubbing the underside of his chin along her face to leave his scent.

"Junk food," she muttered a little louder. "But ask Amir. He might need something– "

"Junk food," Amir said, his voice little more than a hoarse croak from all the whimpering, whining, begging, and screaming. "Soda. Some sweets."

My chest shook as I chuckled, then wrapped my arms around his chest and nuzzled his cheek and throat before pressing a kiss to the mark I'd left on the side of his throat, earning a shiver from my sexy omega.

His nipples pebbled where they peeked out just above the water line, the dark, sienna buds making my mouth water with the urge to flick them with my tongue and nibble them with my teeth.

No matter how hard I fought it, and even after exhausting ourselves over the past few days, my dick instantly hardened and twitched against his back.

His wet curls trailed over my chest as he turned his head to look into my face. "I'm trying to relax and you're tempting me with more cock. I thought *I* was the one who was supposed to be sex crazed this week."

Issa turned her head and smiled at us over her shoulder. "I thought Amir was supposed to be for me," she teased.

"Oh, *habibi*. I have more than enough love to go around."

Love. There wasn't a single doubt in my mind our omega was completely in love with our beta. I could feel it through our bond. But I could also feel how deeply his feelings were growing for each of his alphas, as well.

Issa had taken months to finally tell Ax how she felt about him, then Cyrus. She hadn't told me, yet. Not verbally.

But I could feel it. I could feel her as though our hearts beat to the same rhythm. She loved me and I would be patient and give her as much time as she needed to voice the words.

"You seriously just made it sound like we got you a puppy instead of a delicious omega," Ax said.

"Thanks, big guy," Amir teased. "There was talk of food?"

I held back a frustrated sigh because I was hoping he'd been dropping a hint about me putting my still achingly hard dick to use.

He was sore. We all were. And had it not been for Issa, we all might have been dangerously dehydrated. Even with the bottled water and snacks, I was sure we had all dropped a few pounds over the last few days.

As though confirming my suspicion, Amir's stomach grumbled a protest at being empty for so long.

With a chuckle, I jerked my chin for Cyrus to take my place.

"I can order it," he said, but was already moving through the water to drag Amir between his knees and against his chest.

Once Amir was no longer wedged between my legs, I pushed to my feet and carefully stepped out of the massive garden tub.

Whistles, catcalls, and a sweet, tinkling giggle echoed off the tile. I couldn't help myself – I wiggled my ass at them as I grabbed a towel and dried off before wrapping it around my waist, taking a move from Ax's playbook.

Fuck, I was a lucky man. Two of the best friends an alpha could have, the most beautiful beta, and a loving, kind, and eccentric omega. If I could bottle the feeling in my chest and sell it, I would be the richest fucking alpha on the planet.

Who the fuck was I kidding? I might not be the richest in monetary measures, but I sure as fuck had everything I could have ever dreamed of or ever wanted.

Digging through the pillows and blankets spread throughout the nest, I finally found my pants and pulled out my phone.

"Any requests?" I yelled from the bedroom as I stepped out of the nest.

"Chinese," Amir, Ax, and Issa called back at the same time, then Amir and Issa broke into giggles.

Ax, Cyrus, and I might not have been actively seeking an omega or even a beta before Issa, but seeking and approaching Amir was hands down one of our best decisions to date. Because he made her happy. He made us happy.

As sappy as it sounded, Amir completed our little family.

CHAPTER 31

Issa

We had all opted to take an additional two days off from the bar. Not only were we sore, but Amir's parents were adamant they finally meet his new pack.

Enzo had tried to convince Amir to invite them to the pack house so he could ensure our in-laws their son was safe and protected as well as living in the lap of luxury.

Athena Khalid demanded Amir either give the pack lead the phone or put her on speaker, then promptly told him to stop being ridiculous, that she couldn't *not* cook for her new sons-in-law and daughter-in-law, then planned the day and time.

So, now I was on pins and needles, constantly smoothing down my dress and checking my hair as Cyrus drove us to that adorable house where we'd found Amir wearing a sun dress while working on his muscle car that I was informed was a vintage Thunderbird. And that it would be brought to the house soon so Amir could go back to restoring it.

A smile tugged at the corners of my lips as I turned my attention to Amir and wondered if he would end up in one of my sundresses while tooling away at the engine. Highly doubtful; no way could he fit in my clothes without playing the Hulk and ripping it at the seams every time he moved.

"What are you smiling about?" he asked.

His hand was wrapped around my right one while Ax had his arm draped around my shoulders from the left. I was surrounded on all sides by the greatest – and only – loves of my life. I never for a second would have believed I could love someone so much, and sure as hell never would have believed I could not only trust alphas but feel so deeply for them.

"I was thinking about that first time we went to your house, your parents' house. You were wearing a dress while working on that car."

"It wasn't *just a car*. It was a vintage 1963–"

"Thunderbird. Yes, I remember," I teased Ax, playfully elbowing him in the ribs.

"It was sexy as fuck," Ax muttered.

It was. And not because he was wearing a dress, but it was so…

It was like he was so comfortable in his own skin he didn't feel the need to don fancy clothes or behave in a certain manner. He'd just made sure he wasn't naked and worked at rebuilding the engine to his dream vehicle. He'd been covered in grease and sweat and smelled like heaven.

After smoothing my skirt and hair for the hundredth time, Amir squeezed my hand and pulled it to his lips. "Relax. They're going to love all of you. My parents are super chill and laid back. But I do need to warn you…my mom more than likely cooked a full ass feast and will pester the shit out of you about not eating enough. Don't let it get to you. She's always trying to feed people." He shrugged and smiled. "Probably the most stereotypically Greek thing about her."

Too soon, Cyrus pulled the SUV down the same long driveway and parked along the row of trucks and a single minivan.

Three young girls came pouring from the front door, smiles bright on their tanned faces, squeals of excitement lifting on the air even before we'd opened the doors to step out.

"Amir!" the smallest one with hair darker than Amir's screamed, lunging into his open arms the moment she was close enough.

"My little monster," he said so affectionately, lifting her from her feet and swinging her in a circle.

A smile stretched across my face the same time a touch of jealousy pierced my heart. Cora and I were finally building a sisterly relationship, but I had never seen such a beautiful display of love within a family.

"Mama! Babas! They're here!" a girl who didn't look much older than the one now clinging to Amir called out.

"This little monster is Annalise. The little hellraiser there is Amini," he said about the second girl. "And Alysia is the oldest girl but still a brat."

She stuck her tongue out at him, but then approached me. I moved to offer my hand, but then stiffened when she immediately wrapped her arms around my neck for a hug. She looked to be somewhere around fourteen or fifteen and wasn't much shorter than myself.

"My baby is finally home," a beautiful woman called from the porch before descending the three steps and hurrying to where we all stood. Even my alphas looked as though they weren't sure how to act.

Enzo, Ax, and Cyrus might not have been raised with a stuffy as fuck family like my own, but it appeared as though they weren't used to so much love in one place. This family truly cared about each other.

Amir set little Annalise on her feet then hugged his mom tightly, lifting her from her feet and earning a slap on the shoulder. "Put me down. You're not too big for me to put over my knee."

"Leave the boy alone," a man who looked almost like Amir's twin – minus the long hair – said as he approached. He extended a hand first to Enzo before moving on to our other two alphas. "I'm Ghazi Khalid. My omega Athena." Another man stepped out, his hair salt and pepper in color and cut short. "This is our packmate Myer."

"Enzo. That's Ax and Cyrus." Each alpha shook Amir's fathers' hands. Though it was more than obvious Ghazi was the biological father of Amir and his youngest sister where the other two heavily resembled their mother.

"This is our beautiful beta, Issa," Amir said, wrapping an arm around me and beaming as though showing off the most precious diamond.

There was the briefest moment of silence where the family stared at me, then the air exploded with excitement and chatter.

"*Abnati!*" Ghazi exclaimed as he pulled me into his arms, then pulled back to press a kiss to each of my cheeks.

Athena was next, practically yanking me away from her alpha and hugging me so tightly it was hard to breathe. I could totally see where Amir got his affectionate tendencies. "I am so damn excited to meet you. Come on inside. I made lunch."

"Told you," Amir muttered in my ear as his mom led me inside with an arm around my shoulders.

The alphas lingered back while the three girls followed me, their mother, and their brother, firing off questions and speaking at the same time until I was both overwhelmed and nearly exploding with happiness.

This was how a family should behave. This was how people reacted to those they loved. I had only just met these people, yet I felt more cherished by them than I had my entire life with my family pack.

"Do you love my brother?"

"Are you going to have a ceremony? Can I help plan it?"

"You're so pretty. How come you're not an omega?"

"Girls! You're overwhelming her. And I told you, Annalise – we don't pick our designations. And betas are just as amazing and beautiful as omegas or alphas."

Amir's sisters were still a little too young to present, but I loved that their parents were already setting them up for success by not making them feel as though they would be a failure if they were a beta. Something I'd never experienced.

"We're not having a ceremony," Amir answered as we stepped through the cozy living room and was guided straight to a fairly large dining room with enough chairs to fit the whole family plus company.

"Why not?" Annalise and Amini whined at the same time, then startled giggling.

This was how a home was supposed to sound, how it was supposed to feel. Their absolute commitment and adoration to and for each other was palpable in the air and evident in all the framed family pictures and obvious child art. There were literal child paintings of crooked houses complete with the sun in the corner framed and hanging on the walls as though they were displaying a Renoir or Picasso.

Instant peace washed over me, chasing away the earlier jealousy as I was led to the kitchen and was instantly swept away by the scents of home cooking.

Sure, we cooked for each other at home now, but growing up, it was the nannies or the housekeepers who would provide the meals and it never smelled so much like...like a homecoming.

That was the only way to describe it, as though Athena had found a way to literally infuse her food with love before serving it to her alphas and her children.

"Your home is so beautiful," I said as I let my eyes roam the space, the children's art, the backpack hanging over the back of one of the chairs, the laptop sitting on an end table, even the pillows and throws that weren't perfectly folded and arranged to make the house look like a museum.

"I would say sorry about the mess, but we live in a perpetual mess," Athena said with a chuckle. "Now," she started, guiding me to a chair as she went back to work in the kitchen, "tell me everything."

I looked around for Amir – or anyone – to save me from this line of questioning. I was a little worried about how my omega's family would react to the fact I'd had a previous alpha and had walked away, or that my family had been one of the most notorious crime families in the area.

Or that my sister was bonded to a pack of criminals.

"Um..."

"You're so pretty," little Annalise said, saving me for a moment.

"Are you the one who named Princess Fancy Pants?"

She giggled and tilted her head to the side like I'd embarrassed her, or maybe she was excited that I was actually talking to her.

"Yes," she said with that same sweet giggle.

"How come you guys aren't having a bonding ceremony?" Amini asked.

I had hoped to be saved from another line of quickfire questioning, but now, Athena was turned around watching me, a ladle in her hand.

My heart began to thump a little faster as I wondered how much to actually tell Amir's family. I hadn't been coached on what to say or not to say. I didn't want his family to forbid him to be with us or to dislike us because of my past.

"She already had a ceremony and her alpha was an asshole," Amir said as he entered the room, scooping Annalise up and tossing her over his shoulder like a sack of potatoes.

She squealed and giggled, kicking her little feet.

Amini and Athena were both looking between me and Amir and I waited for the judgment.

But Athena nodded and pursed her lips. "He hurt you," she said before turning back to the stove.

It wasn't a question. She'd simply stated it.

But when she turned off the stove and faced me again, there was anger in her dark eyes.

"Is he still breathing?"

"*Mama!*" Amir said with a shake of his head. "Could we at least eat before you start with your Greek anger?"

"You think it's going to be any better with your Arab father?"

My attention bounced back and forth between them, unsure of exactly what either of them meant? Did this mean his father had a temper? Would I be peppered with even more questions? Surely, they wouldn't want to discuss things like violence and abuse in front of the young girls.

"Girls, set the table," Athena said.

Amir set Annalise on her feet and the girls instantly got to work, pulling plates and utensils from cabinets and laying them out on the table.

"Can I help with anything?" I asked as I pushed to my feet.

"Absolutely not," Athena said, pointing at me with a spatula as Amir looped an arm around my waist and tugged me onto his lap.

I turned wide eyes on him when he nuzzled his cheek against mine.

"Amir," I whispered through clenched teeth.

But Athena merely smiled in our direction as she began carrying dish over overfilled dish to the table and set them on potholders and trivets.

Heavy steps echoed through the house as the alphas finally joined us in the dining room that was just off the kitchen. The entire house was mostly an open floor plan, yet still felt cozy.

"What is Antonio's last name?" Ghazi asked as he stormed into the dining room.

And there went my damn heart, thundering like crazy behind my ribs as Amir kept me hugged tightly to his chest.

Turning wide eyes on my alphas, I raised my brows in a silent *what the fuck* before turning back to my new father-in-law. Myer was right behind him, his arms crossed over his broad chest, his brows pinched together causing a deep groove between them.

"Baba, maybe not right before we eat. Or…you know…ever," Amir said as he continued to nuzzle his cheek against mine, the side of my neck, and my shoulder.

"If someone hurt *abnati*, they will be punished."

That was the second time he'd referred to me in that way and I assumed it was a term of endearment the way Amir called me *habibi*.

"Not now, alpha. We're all going to sit down and eat and get to know our new children," Athena said, grabbing both of her alphas' arms and guiding them to the table as though they were two more of her sons.

It wasn't lost on me the way their muscles relaxed and their expressions softened under her touch.

"We *will* talk later, *abnati*. You're family now." His accent was slight but still obvious and his tone held no room for argument.

What had my alphas told these two alphas? More importantly, why had they told them anything about my past? I didn't want them to hate me because of my family. I was nothing like them. In fact, even without having a relationship with my beta brothers, I knew they were nothing like my fathers, either.

Eventually, I wanted to reach out to them and build a relationship the way I was with Cora. We had all endured the same bullshit from our parents, had all been forced into packs against our will, had all had our futures planned for us.

Everyone took their seats, and I tilted my head and smiled when Athena was situated at the head of the table. Not Ghazi. Not Myer. Her alphas were putting their omega ahead of themselves.

No wonder Amir was so damn sweet; he'd been raised by loving parents.

"We'll host a bonding ceremony for you," Ghazi said between bites, his tone conversational yet left zero space for argument.

"She doesn't want–"

"She didn't want her previous alpha. This pack loves her. She deserves to be a princess. And I want to see my oldest pledge himself to his pack." Ghazi nodded and no one made another protest. It was like that simple gesture was a signal that the subject was no longer on the table.

The table erupted into conversation, Amir's family filling him in on what he'd missed around their little hobby farm, while everyone fired questions at me, Ax, Cyrus, and Enzo. They wanted to know about the club and even asked questions about Ax's dancing.

"But if you're classically trained, why strip?" Athena asked.

And a grin stretched across my face at how red Ax's cheeks grew over her question.

"I don't strip. I *dance*. And there aren't many opportunities for a classically trained alpha. My family believed I would present as a beta or omega, hence the ballet and lyrical training."

"I would love to see you dance someday. The ballet, not the...

other," Ghazi said, dropping his eyes to his plate as his own cheeks darkened a bit with a blush.

Athena met my eyes and winked with a smile. She was enjoying seeing her alphas uncomfortable as much as I was.

The evening continued on that way, just easy conversation, laughter, teasing, and so much love. When it was time to say our goodbyes, I easily promised to visit soon, and they all promised to come to our house.

Within a span of a few hours, I had gained a big, loud, affectionate family who'd easily accepted me and my alphas as their son's pack.

And I'd learned what Ghazi kept calling me, what *abnati* meant – the alpha was calling me his daughter.

CHAPTER 32

<u>Ax</u>

$\mathcal{I}$t had been a week since we'd met Amir's family and us three alphas had received daily phone calls from his mom and his fathers. They were loving people, similar to my own, complete with the little sisters, though mine were all grown up now.

Only a few hours with Issa and she'd managed to wrap them around her finger the way she had with us.

It had been Enzo's idea to let them in on her past to avoid anything delicate being brought up at the dinner table. I'd had no idea the Syrian alpha would rush inside and demand to know her former alpha's whereabouts. Not that I blamed him.

In fact, he'd earned my utmost respect that day.

The three of us had done some research on Amir's family – we already knew Ghazi's family had come to the states as refugees a while ago, but it turned out both Ghazi and Myer had met when they were teens and gotten into some trouble. Not only were they fully aware of who Issa's family pack was, but they'd had interactions with them before bonding with Athena then having Amir.

Parenthood had put them on different – and legal – paths. They still had connections but were real estate investors now. Though I had a feeling neither of them would have a single issue fucking someone up for hurting any member of their family, and that now extended to Issa.

We had returned to the bar the day after and the four of us had worked four consecutive days before finally taking a day off. Issa was originally only supposed to work three days a week, but she seemed to enjoy making her own money since she hadn't been allowed that small act her entire life.

And none of us would ever stop her from doing something she enjoyed.

While the rest of the pack huddled on the couch binging a new show, I was downstairs in our home gym/dance studio trying out some new choreography. The music thumped through the space and urged my body to move.

But I missed ballet. I missed fully expressing myself through lyrical.

Someday. Someday I would find a way to use my formal training for something other than entertaining a screaming crowd.

Grabbing a towel from the rack, I rubbed it across my face and down my chest. My hair was pulled back in a bun, but tendrils had escaped around my face and was sticking to the sweat.

The song faded out and rolled into the next on my playlist.

"You know what? Fuck it."

Stomping to my phone, I scrolled through until I found something that called to me and hit play. Luckily, I was only wearing a pair of basketball shorts so my movements wouldn't be too constricted.

River by Bishop started, the beginning beats sending a tingle down my spine as though my body knew exactly what was coming.

Note by note, I let my arms swing, my legs kick, my body becoming part of the music instead of merely dancing to structured and planned out moves. I leapt in the air, landing to roll on the ground before pushing back up. I incorporated a little ballet and a little hip hop into the dance, making it my own.

By the time the song began to fade out, my lungs were on fire, my heart raced, and sweat glistened on every inch of my body.

Bending forward, I propped my hands on my knees as I sucked in gulps of air until the sweetness of chocolates and strawberries landed on my tongue and filled my senses.

Amir was standing at the base of the stairs watching me with nothing short of awe on his beautiful face. His green eyes looked darker from his dilated pupils and his lips were parted.

"Wow," he breathed out barely above a whisper. "That was… wow."

A smile pulled up one corner of my mouth. "Thanks."

"Seriously. Just…wow." He crossed the room and grabbed a towel before coming to sit beside me, holding it out to me. "I would offer to lick every drop of sweat from your body after that, but you look like you need a break."

The mere mention of his tongue on my body created an instant tent in my shorts as my cock stood at attention.

"There has to be somewhere you can dance like that. I mean, even at the club. You have so much damn talent."

His compliments and gushing actually made my cheeks hot as I grew a little uncomfortable with his praises. Not that I didn't know I could dance. But he was laying it on thick and talking about licking away my sweat and looking all sexy as fuck with his thick, long curls and those black lashes framing his light eyes.

Raising a hand, I pushed my fingers through the curls, reveling in their silky warmth. "I'm in love with you," I blurted out before my brain had a chance to catch up to my mouth.

I froze, my hand still in his hair, and stared down into his eyes, waiting to see how he would react or what he would say.

A rush of warmth flooded my chest from the invisible thread through our bond and he lunged at me, his lips crashing onto mine and nearly knocking me backward.

The kiss turned messy, teeth bumping, tongues dancing, until I wrapped an arm around his waist and tugged him closer then urged his legs around my hips.

He began to grind against me, rubbing his hard cock against mine until my knot swelled to life and the urge to take him right here in the middle of the gym was damned near overwhelming. I couldn't think past the need to feel him wrapped around me, couldn't sense anything but the feeling of his legs hooked around my back, his arms around my neck, the taste of his mouth drowning me in sweetness.

A needy whimper worked up his throat. I swallowed it, keeping it all to myself.

Reaching between us, I struggled to remove his pants, before returning him back to his feet. He had to pull away and tugged his shirt over his head as I pushed his pants down far enough he could kick out of them.

We both dropped to our knees as lust and need overcame us, stealing all other thoughts.

I leaned back when his hands gripped the waist of my shorts and tugged it down, his long warm fingers wrapping around my shaft and giving it a squeeze before tugging on it a few times.

My head dropped back between my shoulders as he continued to stroke me, then lowered his head and wrapped his lips around me, his mouth so soft, so fucking warm.

He'd gotten me so revved with his comment about licking me I wasn't sure how long I would last if he kept blowing me. And I needed to feel his ass clenching around me, needed to feel his hot cum hitting my chest and stomach as he blew his load.

Tightening my fingers in his hair, I yanked his head up, pulling his mouth from my cock with a pop.

He licked his lips as he looked up at me with a questioning frown.

"As much as I'd love to shoot my wad down your throat, I need to feel your ass strangling my cock."

His smile was slow and seductive and made my dick twitch.

My omega might not be a professional dancer, but he sure as fuck moved like one as he straddled my hips, pushing me so I was on my ass instead of my knees, and moved forward until he hovered over the head of my achingly hard dick, his hand firm as he held me in place while he sank onto me, slowly taking my whole length until he was seated, my knot pushed against his tight ring.

"Fuck," I ground out through clenched teeth. I had to hug him against my chest to keep him from moving for a few seconds as the tingles started in my spine already.

Not yet. *Not fucking yet.* I wanted to enjoy this and, yeah, an orgasm was always amazing, but I wanted to feel his inner walls sliding against my cock, feel him squeezing me as he found his own release.

His slick coated my knot the longer I held him there, and his scent amplified to the point of making me dizzy.

"Alpha. Please," he whined, nuzzling against my throat as though to scent mark himself with my signature.

That fucking whine. An omega whine was the undoing of any alpha. And it was no different for me.

With my arms still locked around his waist, I lifted him as I drew back my hips, then tugged him down as I thrust forward. Over and over, my knot bumping against his tight hole.

His hair tickled my cheek and shoulder when he leaned forward and nibbled at my throat, his lips and tongue working along the skin until he took my earlobe between his teeth.

A growl burst from my chest as the first tingle started at the base of my spine and drew up my balls.

"I need to knot you," I growled out.

"Yes. Please, yes, alpha," he cried out, rising and falling fast, meeting me thrust for thrust as he started working himself around my knot.

It was just a tease at first, his body opening enough for the base of my knot to breach before he'd rise up again.

And then the world shattered around me and I nearly went blind on his next rise, slamming down on me hard, taking my knot in one go and milking my body of every drop of cum.

Amir's head dropped back, his arms locked around my neck, and hot jets hit my abs, my chest, even my throat as my knot and cock stimulated the perfect place and sent him freefalling over the cliff with me, my name floating from his lips and echoing off the walls like a well composed symphony.

When he fell forward and dropped his forehead on my shoulder, I hugged him tightly against my body, his release smearing between us, and pressed my lips to the marks on his throat from the three of us.

His shiver was too fucking cute.

"I'm in love with you, too," he muttered, his voice sounding tired yet satisfied.

My smile stretched into a grin, and I hugged him tighter, burying my face in the crook of his throat.

There was an explosion of emotions in my chest and, when I examined it closer, I realized it wasn't just from me and Amir. Issa was there, too. I could literally feel her joy through our bond.

There was no way she'd heard us speaking – though the whole house had more than likely heard us fucking – but had felt the moment we'd allowed our hearts to engulf the other, the moment our souls became as entwined to each other as they were to Issa.

It was no secret how I felt about my first two packmates. And all three of us had fallen for Issa pretty much the first time we'd heard her voice and caught her sun-dried linen scent.

But me, Enzo, and Cyrus didn't exactly go around declaring our feelings to each other. Had either of them told Amir how they felt? I could feel them through the bond with both Amir and Issa and knew they adored him.

Then again, I'd always believed actions were so much more powerful than words. Whether none of them ever told me how they felt, I could sense it through our bond and see it in the way they treated me and each other.

We were a family. I had not only my two alpha packmates, but a gorgeous beta and a sexy, funny, loyal omega now, as well.

Yep. My life was fucking amazing.

CHAPTER 33

<u>Issa</u>

I loved my job. I really did. But I loved being home with my pack more.

The week we'd been together during Amir's heat, then the extra time we'd taken off to meet our omega's family had been a dream. We'd spent so much time snuggling in puppy piles, making love, and talking.

And now, four of us were back at work while Amir took up his post at the bar while he stole any and every chance to touch or kiss me and waited for our alpha to appear on stage.

I'd not only heard the two of them making love last night, but Amir had told me all about watching Ax dance, watching his body flow like water.

I'd seen our alpha dance, but I was dying to see him show us his ballet skills. Being as the three alphas owned this club, I saw no reason he couldn't give us a show before or after hours before the patrons began to file in.

So far, our requests had gone unfulfilled. We had time, though. We had the rest of our lives.

Smiling at Amir as I passed, I felt a surge of affection glow in my chest, the sensation lighting up the thread tying me to Amir.

I'd felt the moment Amir and Ax had finally admitted how deeply their feelings ran for each other. It was like every single day, these four men showed me how absolutely beautiful life could be, how not all alphas were abusive assholes, that omegas weren't all seen as nothing more than breeders or felt as though they were better than other designations.

Amir behaved as though he loved being an omega. My sister had always seemed to resent it. Although that had had a lot to do with the way our parents had treated her and the rest of us.

Within a span of less than a year, I'd realized how happy a person truly could be. And I owed it all to Enzo, Ax, Cyrus, and Amir. Not only because they'd protected me and given me a place to stay – and a pack – but because they'd given me the space and support to find my own strength, to find my voice, to carve out a place of my own in this world.

The Vault was filling up quickly being as it was a Saturday evening and Cyrus had announced on the club's social media page that the male dance review had a whole new set. I'd heard music thumping from the basement, but the song had changed several times so I had no idea what music they would be dancing to. And I'd stopped peeking when Ax was working on new choreography so I would be as surprised as the rest of the patrons here.

I was growing more comfortable around alphas, especially since my three *and* my omega always kept an eye on me while I worked, but I was happy a majority of the crowd tonight consisted of betas.

While there had only been one incident since I'd worked here – and it had been started because of me – I was still always leery of drunk, power-hungry alphas.

"Here you go," I said as I set down a variety of mixed drinks for a table of beautiful, giggling beta women, one of them donning a veil and a sash that said Bride to Be in gold letters.

A bachelorette party. And, yeah, this club was pretty popular in the area, but I was pretty sure they were here to watch the dancers, including my sexy as sin alpha.

I supposed others would be jealous that so many people ogled one of the loves of their life – and I hadn't actually asked Amir how it made him feel – but I was proud Ax was mine, that, no matter how much he grinned and gyrated his hips to screaming men and women, he would be coming home to Amir and me.

It was us that he loved.

"What time do the guys start?" one of the women asked, her question followed by cheers and more giggles.

"Uh," I glanced back at the clock hanging over the bar. "In about twenty minutes."

"Have you seen the show yet?"

"The new one or the guys in general?" I asked.

"All of it. Are they…" She glanced toward her friends. "Are any of them single?"

Even that question didn't send the green fog of jealousy slithering through my stomach. For the first time in my life, I felt secure of my place in someone's life and their heart.

"I think a few of them are, but I'm not sure."

The bride lifted her phone and turned it toward me, pointing out Ax. I tried to hide my grin but failed miserably.

"This one. Alpha Ax."

"Sorry, ladies," I said, lifting my chin and pointing to the mark he'd left to cover Antonio's.

"OMG, girl! You are lucky as hell," the bride said to nods from every woman at the table.

"He's one of three. They own this place. And that sexy omega there," I said, pointing toward Amir, who winked when he caught us all staring, "is mine, too."

"Damn, girl. You *must* teach us your ways," one of the women said before raising her hand for a high five.

Which, of course, I returned because yeah…I was definitely lucky as hell.

"Since when does a beta claim an omega?"

That voice. It was the same one from my nightmares.

I couldn't move. Couldn't turn to look. I could hardly fucking breathe.

A hand gently wrapped around my bicep and turned me until I was staring into a man's chest.

An alpha's chest.

Antonio's chest.

I didn't have to look into his face to know. I would recognize his voice and his wet newspaper smell anywhere.

Fingers dipped under my chin and gently raised my face until I was forced to either look up at him or make a scene. And being as I'd already been the cause of one fight that resulted in the police showing up at my alphas' club, I didn't want to have a repeat performance.

"You look amazing," he said, his voice deceivingly tender, as though he gave a single shit about me.

Why was he here?

I had zero to offer him now that my parents were dead and any amount of money or power was gone with them. Not that I would have ever been a cash cow.

Cora had been the golden ticket, the one alphas fell over themselves to claim, the one my fathers had made a deal with another powerful family in exchange for her place in their pack.

"Excuse me," I said, pulling my face away from his hand and turning my back on him, hurrying through the crowd while struggling not to return to the old Issa, the one who would curl in on herself, lower her eyes to the ground in submission, and allow a fucker like Antonio to make me feel inferior.

Inhaling deeply, I blew the breath through pursed lips, then smiled at Amir when he frowned and tilted his head in his little silent way of asking if I was okay.

No way would I tell him who had found me, who was currently in the middle of the club. He wouldn't waste a second to confront him and that was the last thing I wanted.

I would simply finish up the night, ignore him as much as possible, and hope he got the message that he wasn't welcome here and I had a new pack, one that didn't involve him. The asshole had held a knife to my sister's throat when she'd allowed her alphas to claim her.

No matter how nice he tried to pretend he was in front of that table of betas, I knew the real Antonio.

Memories assaulted my senses, the names, the curses, the physical, emotional, and mental abuse. Most of my time with him was a haze since he'd kept me sedated and pliant, but those memories were still as vivid as if everything had happened yesterday.

No. I was happy now. I was stronger than the woman who'd allowed him to treat me that way. I would not allow him to take away my peace.

Stepping between Amir's spread knees, I pressed a soft, but passionate kiss to his lips then turned and went back to checking on my tables and taking orders.

There were a few of us waiting tables tonight, so I'd hoped Antonio found himself in one of their sections.

When I wandered over to a table with a mixture of alphas, betas, and two omegas, I spotted my former alpha from the corner of my eye…and the asshole was absolutely sitting in my section.

How long had he been here? Couldn't have been long or I would have noted a new patron and would have taken their order. So that meant he'd watched me, waited to see where I was working, then took up space there.

I was shocked he'd been able to find an empty table, even the four-seater high top. Tables were valuable and rare real estate on the weekends.

I should have alerted my alphas to his presence. At least let them know in case there were any issues.

No. I could do this. I would remain professional, do my job, and treat him like any other asshole I'd waited on in my short stint as a server at The Vault.

Squaring my shoulders and lifting my chin, I made my way to his table, keeping my eyes on him the entire way, and stopped with my tray under my arm. "What can I get for you?"

He didn't speak for a few seconds, merely studied my face as though looking for a difference or seeing me for the first time.

"If you're just here for the show, I'll bring you a glass of water." I turned to check on my other tables, but his hand wrapped around my arm again. Turning just my head, I glared at him.

"That's the second time you've put your hands on me. I would suggest keeping them to yourself."

A smirk pulled up one corner of his mouth and his body shook slightly with a chuckle. "Look who learned to speak up for herself."

I tugged my arm from his grip, keeping it casual so as not to garner attention from my coworkers or pack, and returned his smirk.

"Easy to do when my alphas aren't drugging me to keep me silent. Last chance – do you want something to drink or not?"

"Vodka martini," he said, his smirk gone and something dark and slightly sinister flashing through his eyes.

Putting on the most saccharine smile possible, I nodded. "Got it. Be back in a few."

And then I hurried through the crowd, smiling at the bachelorette party, who had all turned their chairs toward the stage in anticipation for the show that would be starting soon.

I let the smile drop but blew a kiss at Amir, who was watching me closely. I could put on the best act in the world, but he would feel my apprehension and anxiety through our bond. Which meant our alphas would feel it, too, if they were paying attention.

His eyes left my face and looked in the direction where Antonio was sitting. He had never met the alpha, had never seen a picture of him. But he would have felt my spiking nerves and might have even seen Antonio grabbing my arm.

While I had no intention of telling him or my alphas that my former alpha was here right now, I would absolutely tell them after he left or when we got home, and fully expected a whole lot of lecturing.

I didn't want to be the reason The Vault got a bad reputation, didn't want to be the reason for yet another brawl to break out. I wanted to be seen as simply another employee as long as I was on the clock.

Aryn turned and raised her brows at me, then lowered them until there was a fairly deep groove marring her beautiful face. "What's going on?"

"Nothing. Need a vodka martini," I answered, trying to keep my voice and expression as neutral as possible.

She jerked her head toward the door that would flip open and allow me to step behind the bar, then pulled me close. Bending her knees, she looked into my eyes and narrowed her own. "Something's up."

"It's fine. Just…tired. That's all," I lied. And I'd always been terrible at lying.

She didn't back off. Instead, she rested her warm hands on my shoulders. "Someone fucking with you?"

"Not yet. But hey, the night is young," I said, hoping my smile didn't look like a grimace.

It was another few seconds before she straightened and stepped away to make the cocktail.

Setting it on my tray, she put her hand on my arm before I could walk away. "Say the word. If someone ever makes you uncomfortable, we'll either have one of the other servers take the table or have them tossed out on their ass."

"Thanks, Mom," I teased.

Her nose scrunched up. "That makes me feel dirty. You're far too hot and I'm far too young to be your mother." Then she did as she'd done on several occasions and marked me with the scent gland on her wrist.

That was a huge faux pas being as I had a pack and was claimed by not only three alphas but her bosses. But Aryn didn't do it because she was laying claim or trying to steal me away. It felt more like a big sister protecting me or like a best friend watching out for me and letting other alphas know someone was watching over me.

"You're such a cock tease," I heard Amir tease the alpha bartender as I carried Antonio's drink to his table.

If I got my way, he would drink this one and hit the street. Because

I wasn't sure how long I could keep up this act or keep my pack from knowing how seeing him shook me to my core.

Staying on the opposite side of the table so as to avoid being within grabbing distance again, I set his drink on the table and forced another sickeningly sweet smile. "Anything else I can get you? Your check?"

The smirk was gone. Any hint of softness had completely vanished from his face. As he slapped his card on the table, he lifted his drink. "Nah. Think I'll start a tab."

Asshole.

The lights on the dance floor dimmed while the spotlight lit up the stage.

"Oh, look. One of my alphas is about to go on stage," I said loud enough for him to hear, then skipped away to nudge and wink at the bachelorette party and join my omega to watch Ax's new performance.

If Antonio thought I would let him break me again, he was in for a surprise.

Or rather *four* surprises.

I wouldn't say anything about his presence unless absolutely necessary, but it felt good that all I had to do was say a single word to Aryn or Amir or one of my alphas and he would be carried out and tossed onto the sidewalk like a bag of trash.

This time, the smile that stretched my lips was genuine and right on time as *River* by Bishop started, the same song he'd played when Amir had watched him dance then the two had exchanged the three most beautiful words in the world. It was the song he'd danced to the night they'd admitted they were in love with each other.

Fuck Antonio.

I had a new life, a new pack, and men who loved me.

He...

Antonio was *nothing*.

CHAPTER 34

<u>Cyrus</u>

As soon as I heard the music fade out then a separate beat begin, I hurried from my office to find my beta and omega to join them for the show. I'd seen Ax dance more times than I could count, but I loved the looks on Issa's and Amir's faces as well as their increased scents when they watched one of their alphas shake his ass and rip off his shirt.

"Perfect timing," Amir said, lifting his head for a kiss when I bent forward.

Issa was nestled between his knees. I knew we should probably tell her she still needed to wait tables while Ax was performing, but she wasn't the only server in the room who froze to watch the show. Nearly every single person was zeroed in on the stage as first one dancer then another came out, the routine a little different than usual.

Oh, they still made sure the crowd got rowdy, still circled their hips, but it looked as though Ax was utilizing the skills of each individual dancer for this one.

Finally, Ax came out on stage. Or rather leapt out on stage, his legs spread into splits, the move uninhibited by the short ass shorts he was wearing, the outline of his junk prominent against the material.

"Holy shit!" Amir said before putting his fingers to his lips and whistling.

Issa winced and elbowed him playfully in his stomach, but she was grinning just as wildly.

My eyes scanned the crowd, my own smile widening at the reaction of our patrons. They always tended to go wild for the dance review, but seeing an alpha's cock, balls, and knot on display like this was abnormal for our club.

Oddly enough, though, even as prominent his lower half was in those shorts, it didn't look vulgar.

As I continued to look over the crowd, watching for anyone who might need a drink or refill of some form while all my servers were ogling the dancers, my eyes fell upon someone staring directly at Issa. Not the stage. Not the show. Not even the gorgeous omega at her back.

He was staring at my beta.

As the lights flashed, a beam ghosted over his face, and I realized I recognized him from a day we'd gone out with Enzo's brother's pack and their omega.

Issa's fucking former alpha.

Before I could take a step forward, Issa's hand landed on my arm. Turning my head down to her, she shook her head at me with a crease between her brows. Amir was unaware of the tension in the air, his eyes locked on Ax as he danced across the stage.

The rest of the place was completely unaware there was a dead man sitting among them.

Clenching my teeth, I swallowed back the growl that swelled in my chest and did my best to control my hormones. But when Amir's head whipped in my direction, I knew he'd caught the change in my scent.

I smiled at him, hoping it looked genuine, then turned and pretended to watch Ax. When Issa was no longer watching my every move, I pulled my phone from my back pocket and shot a text to Enzo.

Antonio is here.

Are you fucking kidding me?

In the bar. In Issa's section.

No more bubbles danced across the screen, and when I saw his head towering over the mostly beta crowd and storming in our direction, I gave him a shake of my head in hopes of getting him to reel in his rage before he got close enough to our beta and omega. Anything that happened needed to happen away from them and without witnesses.

But one way or another, that mother fucker would pay for how he'd treated Issa in the past then daring to breathe the same fucking air as her now.

His pace slowed and he was no longer shoving people out of his way, but his brows were furrowed so deeply a shadow was cast over his eyes that bounced between me and Issa.

As soon as he was close enough, he leaned and muttered, "Where?" so Issa wouldn't overhear him.

I leaned in and told him the section and table number, his burnt wire scent telling me the exact moment he caught sight of the cocksucker who'd drugged and abused our beta.

None of us gave two shits that she was technically bonded to him at the time or that we didn't know she even existed. We knew now, we knew what he'd put her through, and the fact he was here was more than enough to dole out a little back-alley punishment.

"Let your brother know. I'm sure he'd want in on this, too," I said, leaning away from Issa.

But the way she kept glancing at us with a worried frown on her face showed she knew exactly what – or rather who – we were discussing.

Enzo leaned against the bar and turned his body away slightly, blocking Issa's view from his phone as he shot a text to his brother and the head of a criminal empire. Not only was Issa his sister-in-law, but this cocksucker had threatened their omega. Seven alphas out for blood against one piece of shit who was currently glaring at my beta.

Or was he glaring at Amir?

Either away, the urge to cross the bar and pluck his eyeballs from his skull was not only strong but surprising. I was the voice of reason. I was the calm alpha. I was the one who kept the other two from sinking into rut or bloodlust.

But in this moment, I was struggling to keep my alpha instincts at bay, to refrain from storming across the room and putting Antonio down like a rabid animal.

Nah. That would be entirely too easy of a death for him. That mother fucker deserved pain. Lots and lots of pain.

Glancing up, I realized Ax's eyes had found us and his usual flirty smile was forced as he worked through the last of the song.

Well, shit. I was having a hard enough time controlling my own instincts while hiding from our omega there was a threat in the building. But if Ax caught wind of Antonio's presence, there might be no stopping him.

"We should send Issa and Amir home," I muttered to Enzo.

He nodded once and stepped away, heading to the bouncer at the door. He then moved to each of our security spread throughout the room. Problem was, he didn't exactly tell me his plan, whether he was telling them to keep an eye on Antonio, to keep an eye on Issa and Amir, to kick the asshole out…

The moment the song ended, and Ax stepped out of the spotlight, I smiled at Amir and guided Issa toward the end of the bar where the servers waited for their drinks. "Get your stuff and head home with Amir."

Her brows slammed together, and she looked over her shoulder, searching until she found Enzo stalking toward us, his anger evident on his face and in every step through the club.

When she swung her head toward me, her eyes were wide, her bottom lip trembled, and her warm, summer scent carried a bitter edge to it.

"You can't…I've already caused problems here once. If you guys… you can't…"

Gripping her by her shoulders, I pulled her close and rubbed my chin over the top of her head, letting a purr rumble from my chest. An alpha's purr worked best on omegas, but it always seemed to comfort her when her anxiety kicked into overdrive.

And this was absolutely one of those moments. The man who had made her life hell for years was in the same fucking room as her. And since she'd been brought up by fuckhead alphas, she truly believed the fight that had occurred between Ax and the alpha who'd insulted and manhandled her was her fault.

Because alphas were king dick and all that.

Fucking assholes.

My calm exterior was completely at odds with the rage burning through my insides. I was doing my best to keep the bond locked down so she and Amir wouldn't feel it. If Amir's omega reacted, any alpha in the club might react to him. And that would result in a lot of dead fuckers if they dared touch any member of my pack, my family.

"I'm not going anywhere," she said, crossing her arms over her chest and jutting her chin forward.

Her attention caught on something over my shoulder and her eyes widened.

"Ax! Stop!" she screamed.

Fuck!

So much for handling this quietly.

CHAPTER 35

<u>Issa</u>

o. This could not happen. Not again. Not because of me. And not with a club full of patrons.

"Ax!" I screamed, chasing after him only to be pulled back by Cyrus. His hand around my arm was too tight to pull free.

I was shoved toward Amir, who was now on his feet and watching Ax with a look of both concern and anger on his face. My omega was far from small and was as protective of me as our alphas were of the two of us.

But he was still a fucking omega, still at risk, still a hot commodity to assholes like Antonio.

"Get her out of here," Cyrus barked. Amir stiffened against me under the alpha command.

"Hell no!" I yelled over the increasing noise.

It was hard to see past the throng of bodies that was now circling what I knew was a fight right there between the tables. The women from the bachelorette party had vacated their table and were huddled against the wall together, their eyes wide as they watched what was hidden from me.

"Damn it, Amir! Let me go!"

But my omega's arms stayed banded around me until I was lifted from the ground and carried around the bar and thrust toward Aryn.

"Keep her back here," he said, turning and rushing toward the bodies that surged and receded like a wave.

"Amir!" I screamed at the top of my lungs as pure, unadulterated panic squeezed my heart and stole my breath. I focused on the threads to my alphas and my omega, but they'd all shut them down so tightly I could barely even detect their presence, let alone their emotions.

"Let me go!" I screamed, thrashing against Aryn's hold. She was as tall and strong as Amir.

Another security guard joined us, blocking me from stepping through the opened swing door that would lead onto the floor.

If they thought that would stop me from getting to my pack, to ensuring they were safe, alive, in one piece, then they hadn't been paying close enough attention.

Remorse hit me the same time I lifted my foot and stomped on Aryn's instep and wriggled from her hold when she grunted and loosened her arms as the pain rocked up her leg.

The moment I was free from her grasp, I climbed onto the bar and scrambled over top, shoving patrons who'd pressed themselves against it to get away from the growing melee.

Others had joined the fight. Beer bottles and chairs flew through the air.

What the hell would I do when I got to the center? Not like I could take on an alpha. And even if I had a weapon, I couldn't brandish it when the club was packed nearly to capacity.

The crowd was packed tight, those who hadn't rushed away from the violence acting as some kind of voyeurs. I shoved and pinched and even punched people, trying my damnedest to get through to no fucking avail.

And then I was lifted off my feet again, wrenching a frustrated and fear filled screech from my throat.

Frayed wires and copper filled my nostrils. Enzo. He wasn't in the middle of all this.

How the hell did he not get pulled into the fight? Why the fuck wasn't he in there protecting Amir?

"Amir's in there!" I screamed over the cacophony of sound as my stomach lurched, though I wasn't sure whether the nausea was from Enzo's shoulder hitting my stomach with every step or the fear of losing one or more of my packmates.

Enzo practically threw me at Aryn and the other guard, jabbing a finger in their direction.

"Do not let my beta out here again!" The two were also alphas, but there was so much power behind Enzo's words I felt my own muscles stiffen with the need to obey.

"Wait!" I screamed as the security guard wrapped an arm around my waist and kept me from following him.

Aryn stepped into my line of view, bending her knees so we were eye to eye. "Beta, I need you to chill the fuck out for a minute. Your alphas aren't stupid. They'll be fine."

"Amir!" I screamed, the sound strangled and hoarse, tears blurring her face that was still only inches from mine.

"He's a big guy. He's not a dainty omega. He'll be fine. Your alphas will get him out safely."

She had no idea what caused this fight, why my beautiful Ax had decided to rush headlong into a fight with my former alpha. I wasn't even sure Amir knew what was going on or who he was fighting, only that his alphas were in the middle of a vortex of violence.

As Enzo's big body moved further away, I realized his shirt was ripped and blood trickled down his neck as though he'd been hit over the head. He'd been in the middle of that and had extricated himself to carry me away.

But he had to get Amir away. Not only were omegas rare but he was a fucking male omega. Any sicko would try to take him away from me, away from us. They could hurt him. Steal him. And I would never see him again.

They might as well rip open my chest and remove my heart.

Eventually, red and blue lights flashed through the windows. Someone had called the police, though I wasn't sure whether it was a patron or an employee. And as much as I knew my alphas didn't want attention on their club, I was more than thankful for the presence of law enforcement as people began to scramble away until there was only a small pile of bodies swinging fists and kicking someone who was on the ground.

Please don't let that be one of my loves. Please don't let one of my pack-mates be on the ground.

But then long, curly hair began to make it through the crowd, Enzo's arm around Amir's shoulders as he was guided toward the hallway where the offices were located.

"Let go!" I screamed at the guard.

Only when Enzo nodded did the alpha guard release his ironclad hold on me so I could rush toward Amir and Enzo. Both were bloody, both sported bruising on their faces, both had tears in their clothes.

"The office. Now. If I see either of your faces before one of us come to get you..." I had never heard my alpha's voice so deep, so growly, so fucking deadly.

He was pissed. And I had a feeling some of that anger was for Amir and me since we'd both attempted to put ourselves in harm's way, though I'd failed tremendously.

Wrapping my hand around Amir's, I pulled him toward the office, punched in the security code, then dragged him inside behind me.

Those stupid tears had begun to fall over my lashes before I'd spotted my omega and one of my alphas.

But now, looking at the cut near Amir's hairline, the split lip, and the bruising over his right cheek and left eye, they began to fall in big drops down my cheeks to drip from my chin.

It took me a few minutes of rifling around before I found the first aid kit Cyrus stashed in his office. All the offices had one as did the kitchen for any injuries the employees or patrons might need tended to while here.

Unfortunately, it was rudimentary at best. All I could do for now was clean up the blood, apply a little antibiotic cream, and some butterfly bandages. But I definitely wanted him checked for a concussion or the possible need for stitches.

"Take off your shirt," I squeezed out through the lump in my throat.

A whimper filled the air along with a bitter tang to his usual sweet scent. I could only hold his eyes for a second at a time as anger and panic continued to hammer at my heart.

That was too damn close. I'd come too damn close to losing him. And I still had no idea whether Cyrus and Ax were okay, especially since Ax had let his alpha instincts override his logical brain and charged at Antonio as though ready to slaughter him right there at the high-top table.

The front of Amir's shirt was ripped open, exposing an expanse of his beautifully chiseled chest. When he yanked it the rest of the way instead of taking his time to loop the remaining buttons through the holes and let the ruined fabric fall down his arms, I slapped a hand over my mouth to cover the gasp. Or maybe to hold back the sob clogging my throat.

Bruises covered his warm brown skin, several looking like the perfect outline of shoes. He had been one of the people on the ground who'd been kicked while I'd been forced to huddle behind the bar and watch.

"What the hell were you thinking?" I gritted out as I forced him to turn to the side so I could check his back, as well.

"Why were they fighting?" he asked, his voice low enough it almost sounded like an alpha.

"We'll talk about it when we get home," I said.

His hands were firm and not quite gentle as they wrapped around my biceps. "What the fuck is going on? Is someone trying to hurt you?"

Fresh tears welled in my eyes as I stared into his face now marred with injuries...because of *me*. Someone from my past had sauntered right into my alphas' club and had caused what was nothing short of a full-on bar brawl.

His grip loosened and he lifted his hands to my face, cupping my cheeks and tilting my head so I was forced to either close my eyes or look him in his beautiful green eyes.

The bond to him was open now and I could feel his anger and concern warring and vibrating down the thread connecting his heart to mine.

Amir's lips were soft and warm as he kissed away my tears, but I was more concerned with the injuries covering him literally from head to toe.

"Did anyone hit your head? We need to make sure a paramedic checks you out."

"I'm fine," he said, his hands still gently holding my face.

"No, you're not. You look like someone used you as a punching bag."

The door banged open so hard the knob got lodged in the plaster and kept the door open.

Ax stormed in, his eyes wild, his hair a chaotic mess, the elastic barely hanging onto the ends of his shoulder length hair.

"Do not go into rut in here," Enzo ordered as he followed Ax in. "I want you both checked out by the medics."

"I wasn't hurt. I didn't get anywhere near the fight."

"You sure as fuck did," Enzo said, his dark brows puckered, a growl rumbling nonstop from his chest.

"I sure as fuck *didn't*. I couldn't get through the crowd and then you carried me away like some kind of caveman," I bit back.

His brows were still pinched together, but his face softened the slightest bit.

Ax ran his hands over my face, my head, down my arms and back before turning to Amir and doing the exact same thing. His growl was damn near bone rattling, growing in intensity with every bruise and cut he found on our omega's body.

"Where is he?" I asked Enzo since Ax looked too close to snapping at any second.

His eyes darted to Ax then back to me before he shook his head in the smallest movement. I felt unease down the thread between us, so I opted to table that question for when everyone was calmed down and

I was sure my pack was whole and hadn't endured anything more than superficial wounds.

At least my alphas *and* my omega had increased healing. Had I been hurt it would have taken longer to get over any split lips or bruising. But the four men in my life would be good as new within a few days.

Enzo pulled his phone free and glanced at the screen before wrapping his hand around mine. "Outside. The medics are waiting for us."

Ax pressed his lips to Amir's in what could only be described as desperate and claiming before pulling free and repeating the action with me. He was reassuring himself, confirming the two of us were okay, confirming we were safe and in one piece.

He threw an arm around Amir and grabbed my free hand before filing out of the office and through the club.

The staff were currently doing their best to clean up the mess from the fight while policemen took statements. A few people were handcuffed and sitting on the sidewalk out front...

But no Antonio. Maybe I'd get lucky, and he had already been taken away by the cops or in an ambulance.

CHAPTER 36

<u>Enzo</u>

The paramedics had given my pack a green light to head home, but we were instructed to keep an eye on each other. Just in case.

I didn't like the warning hanging in the air like that.

We'd been able to keep Issa safely away, but Amir had run headfirst into danger without knowing what the fuck was going on. And all because he'd been worried about his alphas.

"It's our fucking job to protect *you two*, not the other way around," I barked out as I paced the living room.

We'd all showered and changed, but I'd demanded the pack meet in the living room when everyone was done and had to use my bark on Ax to keep him from stripping our omega and beta naked and knotting either or both of them as his hindbrain began to take over. His alpha instincts were on high. His pupils were still blown, his scent still all wrong, and his thread in the bond completely unsteady.

"I'm not some fragile fucking flower, alpha. My pack was in trouble. You think I could sit by and do nothing? Would you?"

"You were supposed to watch over Issa to keep her away from–" I cut myself off, earning a glare from Amir so sharp it could cut.

"Who the fuck was in there?"

Had I not known better, I might have thought Amir was an alpha with the way he was more than ready to protect his pack and the rusty growl that wrapped around his words.

"My former alpha," Issa said.

She'd situated herself against the side of the couch, her arms around her shins, her chin propped on top of her knees.

She looked so fucking small, so fragile like that. Memories of the day she'd crashed her car into my brother's gate in her rush to warn her sister and their pack of her family's plans sent a red haze across my vision.

She'd looked worse than the four of us combined. Her eyes had been nearly swollen closed, her bruising as well as the cuts from Antonio's fists had taken weeks to heal. Her heart and mind were still in the process of healing.

Amir turned his head and stared at her, that rusty growl turning to a whine. But it wasn't a sound of need or lust.

It was a sound of pain for Issa.

"Tell me someone beat him to a pulp," he muttered while still staring at our beta.

I personally hadn't even seen him. I'd been too busy trying to break up the fight and get my omega to safety. Then I'd caught the scent and sight of Issa's thin body trying to push through the crowd watching like high school punks enjoying a house party fight.

The growl that had yet to cease from rumbling from my chest grew louder as the memory of seeing Amir being kicked as he tried to get back on his feet turned my fucking stomach.

I could have lost my omega. I could have lost my beta. I could have lost my fucking pack because–

"You need to get your fucking anger under control," I growled, turning and jabbing a finger in Ax's direction.

I was the only one on my feet, pacing the living room as I berated three of my packmates like a father upbraiding his kids. Cyrus had attempted to keep the peace but ended up in the foray when he tried to catch Ax before he could do something stupid.

Like punching Antonio and knocking him off his barstool. From what I'd seen, it had only taken moments for those who thrived on chaos to use their one-on-one fight as a reason to become anarchists.

Our club was not known for fights or violence. We offered safety for betas and even omegas to enjoy themselves without alphaholes ruining everyone's night. We offered a top-notch show with a male dance review and were a highly popular spot.

After tonight, I couldn't help but worry about our reputation.

Oh, and the fact I was more than likely only moments away from pissing off my beta.

"You're done at the club until further notice. Neither of you will be there until we track down Antonio and end the threat."

"What?!" Issa blurted, lunging to her feet and out of Amir's hold. "You said I could work."

"And I hold to that. But that was before that fucker decided to stalk you like a fucking...."

"Stalker?" Cyrus offered.

I turned a glare on him, but he simply shrugged.

"How long will that take? We didn't even know he was still around. I worked all that time with no issue."

"Until last night. You didn't even bother telling any of us he was there," I said, gesturing to Ax, Cyrus, and myself. I understood why she hadn't told Amir, but she should have at least either told our security or one of us.

"Because I didn't want *that* to happen," she said, throwing her arms wide as though to indicate what had happened tonight. "I was going to tell you if he caused me any problems or after he left. Not when our omega was there. Not when the place was packed."

"I can take care of my-fucking-self," Amir grumbled.

He reached forward and tugged Issa down onto his lap, wrapping his arms around her waist and nuzzling his cheek against hers, his chin along her shoulder, scent marking her for his own comfort.

"Both of you are out of the club until further notice. My brother is going to send someone over to watch over the house while we're at work." My muscles were taut, and my alpha wanted…something. Retribution. Confirmation that my pack was whole.

Blood.

Revenge.

Issa's mouth opened as her brows slammed together, but I held up my hand.

"Not open for negotiation. And it's only temporary. The second this Antonio bullshit is settled you can work as many fucking hours at the club as you want. And you," I said, turning my attention to Amir, "can go back to watching her every move while she's there."

"Or you could both stay here permanently so we know you're safe when we're working," Ax grumbled. His voice was deep, growly, and his scent was all wrong, the usually sweet, spiced rum signature smelling more like stale or cheap liquor with his rage.

"Do we really need a babysitter? The two of us could hang out at my family's house. Or I could have my dad send someone over," Amir offered, somewhat confirming my suspicions of how far his fathers' influence reached.

I glanced at Cyrus. His brows were raised, and he looked calm, but his scent was a little off, too.

As alphas, it was our job to protect our omega, to protect our beta. The former dove straight into the fight and gotten hurt and the latter had tried her best to get to the brawl. She could have been so easily hurt. We'd lost sight of Antonio, meaning he could have easily absconded with our girl before we had a clue she was gone.

"I don't see why not. It'd be another set of eyes. Whether they go to his parents' house or they send backup to Enzo's men, we could get through our shifts without the distraction of constantly checking through the bonds or watching the cameras."

It wasn't a secret the entire place was wired with cameras and alarms. Not like we had anything to hide from each other. But all our security measures had been upped when Issa had agreed to stay with us.

"If you're going to your parents, let us know before you leave. I want someone with you when you go."

"So we *will* have a babysitter," Amir grumbled.

Crossing my arms over my chest, I looked down at our omega. "Would you rather risk the two of you being taken where we can't find you? I have no doubt Antonio will do far worse to Issa than he had in the past. Could you live with that?"

Growls erupted and bitter scents exploded into the air at my statement. I didn't care how much it pissed off or scared the pack, as long as it got through Amir's and Issa's thick as fuck skulls.

Amir's arms tightened around Issa as an omega whine lifted on the air. Which, of course, set off all three alphas. The growls grew louder as though a threat was in the house, right there in the living room.

"I'll contact my brother's pack in the morning. Amir, talk to your fathers, see if they're okay with the two of you either hanging out there while we're at work, or if they have anyone they want to send as backup. For now, the two of you aren't to leave this house without one of us or another guard. I will not risk your safety because you're both stubborn."

My lips twisted when their brows slammed together in unison and they both looked as though they were pouting.

We'd hoped bringing in an omega would help Issa heal. We'd hoped she would get along with a male omega instead of making her place feel threatened by adding a female omega.

Instead, we'd bonded a missing piece of her heart, a piece that only Amir could fill.

"Pack bed?" Amir asked hopefully, though his brows were still pinched together.

"Pack bed. To *sleep*," I said, turning a pointed look at Ax.

It wasn't that I wasn't amenable to feeling Issa or Amir – or both – under my hands or mouth or wrapped around my cock, but my pack-mate looked as though he could lose control over his rational side. And I refused to risk him hurting either our omega or beta. Ax could lose himself to rut and attempt to knot our beta, and I would never allow anyone to cause her any pain if I had any control over the situation.

Ax's pupils were blown, and his growl continued to rattle forth, though it was quiet even as his top lip pulled up in a snarl.

I had a feeling we would need to put him on the outside of the puppy pile to keep him from rutting into either Issa or Amir the first second we were all in bed.

CHAPTER 37

<u>Amir</u>

*I*t had been a week since that fucker had shown up at the club. A week since he'd stalked my beautiful beta to her place of employment.

A week since the place had erupted into chaos and violence when Ax acted without thinking and charged through the crowd to put the son of a bitch on his ass.

I hadn't even known what was going on or why my alphas were fighting. All I'd known was they were in the crowd who were throwing fists, chairs, and beer bottles and there wasn't a chance in hell I would sit by and watch them get hurt.

While I enjoyed some of the finer aspects of being an omega, like the attention from alphas and betas, even the constantly raging libido – and the gifts we often received from packs courting us – I wasn't fragile or small like our beta.

And that sure as fuck wasn't my first fight nor would it be my last.

I was still mildly embarrassed I'd ended up on the ground getting kicked, but it wasn't like I'd been knocked down. I'd taken down a cock sucker who'd attempted to sucker punch Cyrus when the sweet alpha was doing his best to break up the brawl and restore peace.

Poor Issa had felt dejected when she'd admitted to me what had started the fight, why the four of us guys had gotten hurt, and why she and I were no longer allowed at the club or allowed to leave without at least one of our alphas.

Oh, and the extra manpower now walking the property as though the freaking president was holed up in here.

But I didn't blame her for shit. Neither did the alphas. No matter how many times they actually said the words aloud, I could feel them through our bond, and I knew Issa could, as well.

And the whole not working thing was only temporary. Just until Enzo's brother and his pack were able to track down Issa's former alpha.

Apparently, they had a bone to pick with the mother fucker, too. I didn't care if they got their pound of flesh, as long as they didn't steal all the fun from us.

At the moment, we were stretched out on the deep couch, my arms wrapped around her, the top of her head under my chin as we watched yet another black and white film. I knew my girl liked action, but apparently, the older movies were her comfort flicks. She tended to gravitate toward shows like *Andy Griffith Show*, *I Love Lucy*, and reruns of sitcoms from the eighties like *Golden Girls* when her anxiety was high.

Even if I hadn't caught on to her habit, her scent would give her away every time. Hers was warm and comforting like Cyrus's. But when she was afraid or anxious, that sun-dried linen scent took on a burnt or bitter note.

Right now, my sweetheart was angry. And growing bored.

I didn't blame her. I wasn't exactly used to sitting around the house all day or having to have armed guards when leaving the house. But I'd also been raised by two men who had worked for terrifying organizations before they'd found my mom and settled down.

Those two men in question had sent their own guard after I'd told them what had transpired at the club and all about Antonio. I wouldn't be surprised if they had someone of their own out there searching for him for daring to touch their son or his pack.

There were always ways to distract her from the fact our alphas wouldn't be home for a few hours.

Raising slightly, I glanced down at her face to make sure she was still awake. She tended to fall asleep while waiting for Ax, Cyrus, and Enzo to return from the club. And refused to go to bed unless I went with her.

Not that she ever had to ask more than once.

I wanted nothing more than to be surrounded by my whole pack as often as possible, to be buried in Issa's wet, tight cunt, to have one of my alphas knotting me every moment of every day if that was ever possible.

Her eyes were glued to the screen, her hands folded under cheek. She looked like a freaking angel when she was fully relaxed.

And now, I had every intention of making her cheeks flush, her skin coat with sweat, and covering her in my scent in every way possible.

With my hand resting on her belly, I let it travel south until it dipped below the waist band of the sleep shorts she'd changed into after her shower an hour ago. She tensed when my fingers glided through her folds then gasped lightly when I so softly toyed with her clit.

Applying a little more pressure, I made slow circles against the sensitive bundle of nerves, lowering my face to run my lips and tongue along the marks left by our alphas before pulling her earlobe between my lips and sucking it lightly before nipping it with my teeth.

"I have an idea," I murmured, my lips grazing the shell of her ear.

She hummed then said, "As long as it involves what you're doing now, I'm in."

A chuckle shook me as she groaned in frustration when I pulled my hand from her pants. "Since the alphas want to leave us home alone all the time, how about we go fuck on their beds and coat their sheets and blankets in our scents?"

She rolled onto her back enough to look into my eyes. "You've seen Ax's room. I'm pretty sure he hasn't cleaned it or changed the sheets since I moved in."

My nose curled. "Okay, so I'll take you against the wall in his room. Or the dresser. Or on the floor."

"Definitely not the floor. But the other two are definitely viable options."

Matching smiles stretched on our faces then she rolled from the couch and started sprinting through the house with me right on her heels. I hadn't bothered with a shirt after my shower, but we shed our clothes as we made our way through the living room, up the stairs, and crashed through Enzo's door first.

I lunged at her the moment she was close enough to the bed and lowered myself over her body, gripping my raging hard boner and positioning against her wet opening as she spread her thighs for me.

Our moans were in unison as I fully sheathed myself inside her, hooking one of her knees over the crook of my elbow to open her more fully for me. I wanted to be deep inside of her, to stretch her and fill her. I planned to come inside her on every bed, in every room, to cover this entire house with our scents until our alphas were driven nearly to rut.

And no. That thought didn't scare me in the least.

I wasn't sure I would ever get enough of my pack, my alphas and my beta, of feeling them in me or wrapped around me, their mouths and hands and cocks and Issa's pussy bringing me levels of pleasure that should be illegal.

"Fuck, you feel amazing," I said around a satisfied purr as I thrust my hips over and over, losing myself in her tight, wet heat.

"I love you. I love you. I love you," she panted out over and over like a mantra. Or a prayer.

I could listen to her saying those words every day for the rest of my fucking life. They were a balm to the soul, the very blood in my veins, the beat of my heart. And a whole lot of other poetic, sappy shit that I couldn't begin to conjure when my balls tightened, and the first tingles of release rippled up my spine.

Burying my face in the crook of her neck, I opened my mouth and latched onto her skin, just hard enough to leave imprints without breaking the skin. Not that my bite would change our bond.

But my body was acting on impulse and instinct.

A low groan tore from my throat as cum exploded from the tip of my dick and painted her inner walls, pulsing over and over until it seeped from her to pool on Enzo's bed.

As the aftershocks began to fade, something hit me. Jerking my head up, I frowned down into her face.

"You didn't come," I said rather than I asked.

She smiled softly. "I did. It was a small sneaker."

I couldn't help the laugh that huffed from my chest. "Mind explaining that one?"

"It crept up on me without the buildup or preamble. But it wasn't one of those mind-melting, toe-curling, earth-shattering ones. Enough to take the edge off."

"Oh, fuck no," I said, grabbing her thighs and forcing her legs around my hips so I could lift her from the bed while keeping my cock buried inside her.

She was going to have one of those mind-melting, toe-curling, earth-shattering orgasms immediately. And I didn't give a fuck how long I had to lick, suck, or fuck her to make that happen.

* * *

BY THE TIME the alphas returned home, we were coated in sweat and cum and slick, panting as we laid sprawled out on the kitchen floor similar to the last time we'd enjoyed the day together while the alphas were away.

We had literally fucked in every single room, on every bed except Ax's. I did as I said I would and bent her over his dresser while taking her from behind. The view in the mirror was by far the most erotic and sexiest thing I'd ever seen.

"So...you guys had fun," Cyrus said as he entered ahead of the other two. His nostrils flared and his alpha hormones practically exploded from him.

This might be one of the very few times in my life I would have to turn down any advances from one of the four loves of my life. And yeah, I was so crazy in love with all four of them, regardless of who I'd told and when.

"We left you presents in your rooms," Issa said with a drunken smile. She barely rolled her head to the side to watch Enzo and Ax enter from the garage.

Ax's eyes went wide, his brows popped up his forehead, then he was jogging for us and jumped in the air before catching himself as though doing one of those sexy as sin moves on stage. His nose ran from my crotch to my lips before he kissed me deeply, then did the same to Issa, though he stopped a second to lap at her cunt before making his way to her mouth.

"What kind of presents?" he asked, a purr wrapped around his words.

Enzo reached down and pulled him off Issa by a hand wrapped in the back of his shirt.

"We fucked on your beds," she said with the sexiest fucking giggle.

"Well, we fucked and sucked and licked and–"

Ax sprinted away before I could finish my sentence, his feet thundering up the stairs, though I had a feeling he was taking them two at a time.

"Holy shit," Ax called out.

"What did you two do?" Enzo asked, his thick arms crossed over his chest, but an affectionate smile graced that ruggedly beautiful face.

"I told you. We left you presents."

Thundering steps heralded Ax's return. "They came all over my room."

"Not all over your room. Just by the dresser," Issa said with another giggle.

She seriously looked and sounded drunk from all the orgasms I'd forced from her petite body. And there had been no more of those pesky small sneakers.

Nope. I'd made damn sure she had several mind-melting, toe-curling, earth-shattering orgasms before we'd ended up in a boneless sprawl of limbs on the floor.

"We figured since you three decided we were on lockdown, we'd make sure you remembered how important it was for you to return home as soon as possible every night." I folded my arms under my head, using what little energy I had left.

"We already come home to you as soon as possible," Cyrus said.

Enzo bent at the knees and scooped Issa into his arms to carry her to the pack bed in my room since that was where we tended to congregate most often.

When Cyrus lowered his hand and offered me help to my feet, Ax lowered and tossed me over his shoulder like a damn firefighter carrying me from a burning house.

His broad back and tight ass were in perfect view as I chuckled the entire way up the stairs and down the hall.

"I love you, but I don't think I can go another round tonight." Though my dick was already awakening against Ax's firm chest.

"Don't worry. You can lie like a log while I suck and fuck you both until I look as lust drunk as the two of you." Ax smacked my bare ass, a punctuation to his sentence or maybe a promise of what was to come as I lifted my head to watch Cyrus swing the door closed to my room.

Just because I didn't think I could physically move didn't mean I wasn't down for another round of pleasure.

Who was I to deny my alphas anything?

CHAPTER 38

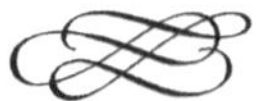

<u>Issa</u>

*A*x had made good on his promise to let Amir and me lay back while he tended to us in the most delicious way possible. He'd licked or sucked us, then fucked each of us through yet another orgasm before shooting his release across our bodies then rubbing it in like his own private line of skin moisturizer.

And as amazing as that day had been, I was back to being bored as yet another week passed where I wasn't allowed to return to work. No matter how hard I tried, I couldn't keep all those voices from my past from echoing in my head, reminding me I was nothing, that my alphas controlled every aspect of my life, that my every action, every decision, and my future was in their hands.

I knew it wasn't true. Of course I did. But that didn't keep my mother's and fathers' voices from chattering in my head like a herd of demons.

"It's temporary," Amir said to me for the millionth time since that night Enzo had laid down the law and ordered the two of us to stick around the house with the guards watching over us.

"I know."

"So why do you look so damn...defeated?"

I dropped my head against the cushion and pulled my feet from where they'd been resting on his lap. He didn't like that and dragged them right back, wrapping his hands around my ankles to keep them in place.

"I'm bored," I lied. Or *half* lied. Because I *was* bored. "Can we go to your parents' house and ride the horses? If they're rideable." I chewed on my bottom lip. "Is that the right phrasing? It sounded weird when I said it."

He chuckled and stretched until he could reach my lips, pressing a kiss to them. "Yes. That's the right word. And as long as the guards are willing to escort us, we can absolutely go ride Princess Fancy Pants and Pearl. I'm sure my mom would love to see you again."

It was the middle of the day in the middle of the week, so his sisters would be in school. Although we could always stick around for a while to visit with them, too. After growing up nearly resenting my only sister, it was nice to be able to form bonds with the girls.

"Should you call her first? Make sure it's okay?" Because he officially lived here now. Surely, his parents would want to know if one of their adult children planned to pop by their house.

"Seriously? No, I don't need to call and ask if I can visit my horse or my mom. She'll be fucking thrilled."

Excitement at the prospect of leaving the house for something other than eating dinner with my pack bubbled up in my chest. "Oh my gosh! I'm calling Enzo to make sure it's okay. Will you check with the guards to see if they'll take us?"

"I know my fathers' man will. I'll ask Bain's guy, too."

He pushed to his feet to go talk to the guards at the front and back doors, and I hit Enzo's number on my phone.

"You okay?" he asked as a greeting.

"Amir and I want to go horseback riding at his family's house. He's asking the guards now. Is that okay?"

"Sweetheart, you don't have to ask to leave the house as long as one of the guards go with you. We're not trying to keep you on lockdown or some shit. Just trying to keep you safe until we find Antonio."

"I know." But those voices in my head sometimes were louder than my alphas'.

"I can feel that, you know," he said, his tone softer. "Stop doubting us, beta. We love you and want you to be safe. That's it. When this shit is over and Antonio is no longer breathing the same air as you, you're free to return to the club or work wherever the hell you want. But we can't risk losing you. Either of you."

"I love you, too," I sighed over the line, those squishy, warm tendrils slithering down the thread of our bond.

"That's better," he said, and I could picture him rubbing the heel of his hand against the middle of his chest as he often did when a rush of emotions came from me or Amir. I wasn't sure whether it was still an unfamiliar feeling or if he simply enjoyed having our souls so entwined; he could feel us with him no matter how much distance was between us. "Text me when you get to his mom's, when you're leaving, and when you get back home."

I sighed and dropped my head against the cushion again.

"Sweetheart, it's temporary."

"I know. That's what Amir keeps saying."

"Because it is. You know the three of us would never force anything on you."

Of course, they wouldn't. They'd all hidden their feelings from me, their desire to bond me as their beta because they were waiting for me to make the first move, to indicate when I was ready for more than the easy friendship we'd built over the first few months.

"Have fun. Please be careful. Keep us updated. Love you, beautiful," he said, his deep voice so warm and delicious.

"I love you, too. And thank you."

It was his turn to sigh. "Why does this feel like we've taken several steps back? You don't have to thank me for anything, especially something as simple as enjoying the day with our omega."

A smile tugged at my lips, and I sent a rush of affection down the bond.

"Damn, I love that."

I ended the call before we could get into another round of *I love you* and reassurances from my alpha. Because, as much as the current situation sucked, I knew everyone was right – this was temporary.

I would just have to be patient and then I could return to the club, Amir and I could leave the house without an armed escort, and the five of us would go back to living happily ever after.

* * *

AMIR'S MOM had been overjoyed when she spotted us climbing out the back of the SUV. She'd even made the guards come into the house to eat while Amir and I climbed onto the backs of the horses.

He had demanded I ride Pearl, warning me that Princess Fancy Pants was spoiled and could be rank at times. And yeah, I had totally had to ask what the hell he'd meant by the horse being rank. Apparently, horse lovers used that term and the rest of us were left clueless.

We were currently sitting on the backs of the mares as they casually walked through a heavily wooded path. It was obvious by how worn it was that this path had been used hundreds of times. But I loved looking up and around, watching birds and other critters go from limb to limb or forage along the forest floor for a meal.

"It's so beautiful out here," I said quietly as though I might ruin the moment if I spoke any louder.

"Wait until you see my favorite spot," he said, nudging his heels into his horse's ribs and taking off at a faster clip.

"Wait! How do I make mine go fas—" I didn't get the question out of my mouth before Pearl took off after Princess Fancy Pants and I clung to her like a spider monkey.

Luckily, Amir had taken some time to teach me how to hang on with my thighs, so I wasn't holding onto the saddle horn for dear life the entire time.

But the speed still scared the crap out of me as my hair blew behind me and I had to duck to avoid hitting a few low hanging branches.

A scream tore from my lips, but I couldn't stop smiling and giggling. It was terrifying but so freaking thrilling at the same time.

Amir slowed until our horses were running side by side. "You doing okay?"

"This is amazing!" I said through laughter.

Tears were streaming down my face, and I wasn't sure whether it was from the wind in my eyes, the adrenaline rush, or just sheer joy.

His megawatt smile beamed at me, sending butterflies fluttering through my stomach and making my heart thump like crazy.

Though the increased heartrate could have also been from the fact I was on a huge beast and running through a forest like some kind of fairy tale princess.

When Amir reached over and grabbed the reign from my hands, he helped steer Pearl down a small embankment. I was terrified I was going to go flying over the horse's head or tumble over the side, but Amir was there. He wouldn't let anything happen to me.

And the fact I felt that with such certainty sent a fresh wave of love and trust rushing through my system until it felt as though the whole world was cast in rainbows and shades of rose.

Eventually, Amir slowed our horses as we entered a clearing complete with a babbling creek.

"Oh my gosh," I breathed out as my eyes went wide.

I was seriously inserted smack dab in the middle of a fairy tale, and my beautiful prince was watching me with the most heartwarming smile.

He stopped both horses and climbed off the top of Princess Fancy Pants before offering his hand and grabbing me by the hips to lower me to the ground after I threw one of my legs over the side of the saddle.

"What do you think?" he asked, his warm voice quiet as he guided me to the side of the creek.

The water was crystal clear, and every once in a while, I'd see a tiny fish or turtle swim past.

"It's perfect. This whole day has been perfect."

For a few hours, we got to pretend we lived a normal life, that I didn't have a former alpha out there intent on making my life a nightmare, that there weren't guards waiting for us to return so they could escort us back to the pack house.

Amir disappeared from my periphery, but I couldn't stop gawking at the spring, the trees that swayed in the wind across the way, then tilting my head back to watch as a hawk circled overhead, its shadow following its path on the ground.

"I love it here," I said, turning to find Amir on one knee, a black, velvet box in his outstretched hand. "What are you doing?"

"I know this isn't the norm, and I know you don't want a bonding ceremony. But I want you to be mine in every possible way. The alphas were able to mark you, to leave physical evidence of their connection to you, and I want nothing more than to be represented, as well."

"What..." Words refused to leave my mouth.

"Will you marry me, Issa?"

"I...we could just get matching tattoos." *Really, Issa? That's the first thing out of your mouth?*

His smile faltered and uncertainty flashed through his eyes and over his face.

"Oh. Yeah...um..."

"Wait. That's not what I meant to say. It...I...I'm ruining this. I'm ruining the moment." Tears welled for a whole new reason. "Of course, I'll marry you," I said as his face blurred through the moisture welling in my eyes before rolling over my lashes and down my cheeks.

"Yeah?" he asked, that smile stretching again.

"Yes. Absolutely yes." My voice was breathless but the grin on my face reassured him.

He lunged to his feet, wrapped his arms around my waist, and lifted me from my feet, swinging me in a circle as I cried happy tears on his shoulder.

"Shit. Wait," he said, setting me back on my feet and pulling the ring from the box. "I almost forgot."

New tears formed at the first sight of the ring. Instead of a single diamond ring on a gold band, he'd chosen a ring with various colored stones that topped a rose gold colored band.

"I got a gem to represent each of our birth stones. Well, not yours, but mine, Ax's, Cyrus's, and Enzo's."

"It's perfect." I hiccupped as he slid the ring on my left fourth finger, then lifted my hand to feather a kiss to the back.

I'd thought the day had been perfect as we'd lazily ridden down the trail. Then it grew even more perfect when he showed me this idealistic setting.

Now, as I stared down at the ring representing the four greatest loves of my life, I realized this moment would be the moment that would forever be the best day of my life.

At least until the actual wedding day.

CHAPTER 39

<u>Enzo</u>

Amir had told us of his plans to propose to Issa, but we'd had no idea exactly when that would happen, whether he would be content doing it lowkey while they were locked away at home or if he would wait until the five of us were out to dinner.

But I had a feeling it would be while they were out on the horses. What better time to do something so romantic than when the two were alone and not being shadowed?

Sure, I was mildly jealous he was the one she would marry, but she was bonded to the three of us alphas. She carried our marks, completed the threads between the five of us. This was the only way the two of them could have their own public display of claim over each other.

The fact he'd chosen to represent me, Ax, and Cyrus on the ring, as well, cemented the fact we'd chosen the perfect omega for our pack.

And not just for Issa but us alphas, too.

"Did you hear a word I just said?" my brother growled over the phone.

"Yeah. Something about your men having a lead."

A frustrated sigh from Bain sounded like static over the line. "I'll take that as a no. My men have nothing. Not a whiff of Antonio's knockoff cologne, no hits from his bank accounts, and if the fucker has any social medias or a cell phone, my hackers have found nothing."

My brother had built quite the empire and had managed to take over two other businesses after killing Issa's and her sister's fathers as well as the cocksuckers who'd wanted to bond his omega as some kind of arranged deal. They had killed off those who weren't loyal, but other than that, shit had gone pretty smooth.

He'd also inherited a few more hackers in the takeover, something that we'd hoped would aid in tracking Antonio's whereabouts before he made another appearance. My girl was tired of being locked up in the house, tired of losing her recently earned freedom, tired of having to have armed guards any time she wanted to step off the property for something as simple as grocery shopping or lunch with our omega.

"Fuck," I gritted out, finally homing in on the conversation instead of letting my mind wander to what my beta and omega were doing at this very moment.

From the rush of love and lust, I assumed they were currently a tangle of arms and legs – as usual – but had no idea whether they'd returned home yet.

I'd asked Issa to text me the moment they got to Amir's parents' house, which she did, but also asked her to let me know when they left and when they returned home.

Being as the guards also let me know when they'd pulled into the driveway of Pack Khalid, I hoped they would do the same when they returned home in case Issa was too distracted by our omega to let me know they were safely back home.

"Now you're listening."

"How the fuck is that mother fucker staying so far under the radar?"

He'd been ballsy enough to attempt to threaten Cora when all of us had been separated by nothing more than a wall. Yet he was hiding now?

"We'll find him," Bain tried to reassure me.

"Are you keeping Cora on lockdown, too?"

A growl rumbled over the line. "Fuck yes. But I don't let her leave the house without guards, anyway. Too many enemies would love to use my omega against me, against us."

"Good point." Propping my feet up on the desk, I tilted my head against the seat rest until I was staring at the ceiling. "My girl is getting…depressed. She wants to go back to work."

"Not a good idea," Bain said.

"Yeah, I know. Our omega's fathers sent over one of their guys, too."

Bain went quiet for a second then huffed a laugh. "I'm surprised Ghazi Khalid didn't send over a full army to protect his son."

Of course, my brother would have done some research on Amir's family. Since Issa and Cora were rebuilding – or finally building – a relationship, he wanted to make sure his omega and son were safe anytime they visited our house.

"We'll keep digging. I'll find that motherfucker—"

"You get him after we get our pound of flesh," I said, interrupting my big brother.

He chuckled, the sound deep and dark. "I'll try to keep Cohl in check, but I can't promise anything."

And then he ended the call.

Shit. I'd hoped Bain had at least found a way to put a tracker on Antonio or had figured out a way to keep an eye on his movements. I wanted to know where he was and what he was doing at all times. I wanted to know whether he'd planned on fucking with my girl any further or if Ax going all berserker on him in the crowded bar had been enough to scare him off.

Pulling up the cameras at home, I checked through the feeds to find an empty house. Then I shot off a text to the guard my brother had sent and received a confirmation they were still at Pack Khalid's and were currently celebrating the engagement of our beta and omega.

I smiled as I pictured the way Amir's beautiful and outwardly loving mom would be shoving food at them and begging to be part of the planning.

We didn't need any financial help, but I was sure Issa would love to have an actual mother figure who'd gush over her, help her choose a gown, flowers, and all the other shit that came with a bonding ceremony.

Not a bonding ceremony – a *wedding*. They would have a wedding as though they were two betas who'd fallen in love and wanted to be legally bound.

Tossing my phone back onto my desk, I focused on my computer, running through the open spreadsheets.

Or I tried to focus.

It was virtually impossible to disappear anymore, especially in the states. It was absolutely impossible to disappear from my brother's reach.

Yet Antonio had done exactly that. He was a fucking ghost. More like a demon biding his time until he could terrorize Issa again.

As I stared at the computer screen without actually seeing the numbers, my phone dinged with an incoming message.

HEADING HOME.

ATTACHED WAS a picture of Amir and Issa snuggled in the back seat, wearing matching grins, with Issa's left hand held up and showcasing the ring we'd all already seen.

A few minutes later, Ax and Cyrus stepped into my office, smiles on their faces. "You get it, too?" Cyrus asked.

I turned my phone to show the picture.

"I was wondering when he'd finally go through with it," Cyrus said.

"You think he was nervous? No way she would have said no," Ax said.

I shook my head. "Nah. He's a romantic at heart. A true omega. He wanted it to be perfect for Issa."

Ax and Cyrus lowered into the chairs across from me and all three of us stared down at our phones.

"We're a strange pack," Ax muttered.

"How so?" Cyrus asked, still staring at the picture with a sappy smile on his face.

"Took us forever to bond with Issa. She claimed the omega before we did. She fucked him before us. Didn't really court Amir. And now, we're skipping a bonding ceremony with either our omega or our beta and the two of them are getting married." He lifted his eyes from the screen. "Think he'll let us at least be groomsmen? I look hot in a tux."

I shook my head as Cyrus rolled his eyes.

"We'll do exactly whatever the two of them ask us to do, even if that means sitting in the front row and watching them at the altar," I declared.

Although...yeah, I really did want to stand up there with them. I wanted to walk her down the aisle with her other two alphas and stand proudly while she and Amir swore their hearts and souls to each other in front of witnesses.

Not sure how many witnesses there would be, though.

Unlike her now deceased fathers, we didn't give a shit about appearances or prestige, nor did my brother or his pack.

Didn't matter. Didn't matter if it was only the five of us and someone to officiate. We would put together the wedding of her dreams, no matter how simple or extravagant she wanted.

"Dude," Ax said, leaning back in his chair and spreading his knees wide as he adjusted his obvious boner. "I just had a thought...Amir is going to look smoking hot in a tux. Issa will probably wear some sexy ass lingerie under her dress. And we'll have to wait until after the fucking ceremony to get them home."

And once again, Cyrus rolled his eyes while I shook my head at our horndog packmate.

CHAPTER 40

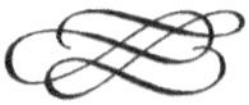

Issa

My eyes flitted from Amir to Athena, then back to my omega again.

Everyone was excited about the wedding. Overly excited. Yet I…

I was a bundle of nerves.

We'd set a date for a year from now in hopes of the whole Antonio thing finally being over. Either way, Bain had offered as many guards as we wanted to watch over us to make sure we didn't end up like an episode of *Game of Thrones*.

"What about something like this?" Athena asked, turning the laptop toward me.

"Mom! Seriously?" Amir admonished his mom with the biggest smile on his face.

The gown on the screen was poofy and white and covered in lace.

"I don't think I can pull something like that off," I said instead of telling her I'd rather not look like a giant cupcake on my wedding day.

"We're trying for lowkey, Mom. That is more like a Greek travesty."

"What's wrong with a Greek wedding?" Athena said, pushing Amir's shoulder.

"Issa isn't Greek."

"But you are."

"Ah, but only half."

"Oh! I know! What if we mix Greek and Syrian for the ceremony?! Think of the food I could make."

A dull throb began behind my eyes as she rambled on. I'd been overjoyed that I would have some form of a mother to help with all of this, but she was…a lot!

Amir's hand landed on my thigh and squeezed gently. I turned my eyes to my omega's face and forced a smile.

His gaze bounced between my eyes a second before he nodded as though he'd read my mind and come to the same conclusion.

"Reel it in, Mom. Too much. My girl isn't used to…all this." His arms went wide.

"All of what? I mean, I know you didn't want a ceremony…oh, man. Am I being way overly excited? I'm sorry. It's just…my first child's ceremony. Wedding. Whatever. And you're so perfect for him and I want the whole day to be perfect for your whole pack."

"I'm not used to having a mom," I admitted softly, trying to keep my expression neutral instead of letting the mixture of heartache and gratitude fill my face.

There was a beat of silence. Then another. The longer it stretched on with Athena staring at me, the more uncomfortable I grew.

This was why I hated telling new people about my past. I hated the look of pity that always appeared on their faces no matter how hard they tried to cover it.

Tears welled in Athena's eyes, and she lunged to her feet, rounding the table and kneeling at my feet.

Confusion pulled my brows down as I stared into her watery eyes.

"You do now, Kóri. I am your mother. *You* are *my* daughter. You are as much my daughter as Annalise, Amini, or Alysia."

Damn it. Now my eyes were blurred with unshed tears. "Th– " My voice caught as a sob threatened to steal my breath. "Thank you."

"Now…" She leaned forward and pressed a kiss to my cheek before pushing to her feet. "I know I'm a lot to take in all at once. So you've got to use your voice, Kóri. You won't hurt my feelings or offend me."

"She's used to four kids reminding her to chill out on a daily basis," Amir said from my right.

"I want to make your wedding day absolutely perfect, but perfect for *you two*, not my vision. You tell me what you want, what part you want me to play, and I promise I will do my best to keep from squealing at every decision or inserting my opinion too much. But again, you say the word and I'll back off. No hard feelings."

A rogue tear trailed over my lashes, but Amir caught it with his thumb, leaning forward to press a soft but lingering kiss to my lips. "Good now?"

After a deep inhale, I gave him a wobbly smile. "Yeah. I'm good now."

We all relaxed, and it felt as though the room took a collective cleansing breath. "Now," Athena started. "Tell me what you're thinking. Are you two wanting something small, casual, and intimate? Extravagant with hundreds of guests?"

I barked out a laugh. "I don't think I even know a dozen people anymore. At least not that I would want to be there for the best day of my life."

A rush of love and affection flooded my chest as it trickled down the bond from Amir.

I smiled when he nuzzled his cheek against mine, his strawberry and chocolate scent covering me and floating around me in a sweet cloud.

"Okay," I said, getting serious, or at least trying to with Amir rubbing his cheek along mine, along my shoulder, and running his hand up and down my spine. "Small. Simple and elegant. And intimate. Does that help?"

Athena clapped her hands then rubbed them together. "Absolutely. Have you thought about what kind of dress you would want?"

"Not really. I know I don't want anything frilly or a big, ridiculous train."

My poor sister had been stuffed into so much lace and taffeta and had been forced to wear a veil that covered her face on the day of her – thankfully – failed bonding ceremony.

That dress had been ruined by the blood of the guards who'd been escorting her, but her kidnapping had ended up being a blessing in disguise as she was now madly in love with her pack, had a beautiful baby boy, and was so damn happy.

"We've got some time to go shopping and make sure you get exactly what you want. As far as a venue...I haven't been to your house yet, but we'd be more than happy to host something here," she offered.

The field near the creek where Amir had proposed flashed through my mind, but I wasn't sure how willing the few guests we might have would be to either find a horse to ride to the area or traipse through the woods for over an hour to get there. It might have been my wedding I was planning, but I didn't want to put anyone out.

"We have a pretty big yard. You'll have to bring the girls over to swim when it gets warmer," Amir offered, saving me from having to decide then and there.

The next few hours went about the same, with Athena offering suggestions and me either vetoing them or agreeing. Amir was silent, even when I asked for his input. According to him, he would wear a dinosaur costume if it made me happy.

I would have felt awful for the guards who were stuck with us all day, but Athena kept their bellies full, and they spent their time in front of the TV when they weren't communicating with our alphas or checking the perimeter as though some threat might wander onto the property.

"We should get going," Amir said, standing and stretching.

"Your sisters, dad, and baba will be disappointed they missed you," Athena said, hugging first Amir then me as we stood at the door, our guards already at the SUV and waiting patiently.

"We'll be back soon. From what I saw online, there's a lot to wedding or bonding ceremony planning."

I tilted my head back and raised my brows. "You were researching wedding planning?"

"I'm an omega. Just because I'm a man doesn't mean I don't still want all the pretty, frilly shit, too."

The smile that lit up my face was both from his words and the image of him working on his muscle car in one of his mom's sundresses that first time we came here for a day date.

As we approached the SUV, both guards were on high alert as one searched the area and the other opened the back door for us.

"I really don't think anyone is hiding in the bushes or in the horse pasture waiting for us," I teased.

There wasn't a doubt in my mind that Ghazi and Myer were more than capable of protecting their family. If the burly, dark-skinned guard they'd sent as backup to watch over me and Amir was anything to go by, those two had some connections.

"Do we have to go straight home?" I asked, leaning forward a little to address our current babysitters.

The only time I saw someone new was the evening switch over. The four men assigned to shadow me and Amir were working seven days a week, but at least they switched shifts so they could get some rest.

I thought it was a little silly for them to be there when our three alphas were home. I highly doubted Enzo, Cyrus, and especially Ax would let anyone get close enough to the two of us when they were home.

"Your alphas don't want you at the club," Abdel, one of our day guards, answered with his thickly accented deep voice. Even if he hadn't been assigned to us, I would have assumed simply by his demeanor and voice he was some kind of badass.

But he was also sweet. I'd caught him interacting with Amir's sisters once and had seen how gentle he was with the animals on Athena's little hobby farm.

My eyes rolled of their own freaking accord. "Fine. But can we do something else? Anything else?"

We hadn't been on lock down that long, but now that I was finally getting over my fear of being in public and around alphas, I had grown tired of being cooped up in the house and had developed a mild case of cabin fever.

Sure, we had just spent hours with Amir's mom, but I wasn't quite ready to go home and plop down in front of the television until the two of us either fell asleep or our alphas finally returned home.

"What do you have in mind, *fiancée*?" Amir asked, nuzzling my neck and nipping one of the marks left by our alphas.

A full body shudder rippled through me, and I almost changed my mind. Going home suddenly didn't sound so bad. It would mean we would be alone… and naked.

"I was…thinking…Okay, you have to stop. I can't think straight when you're doing that," I said through a breathy giggle.

He left one more kiss on my neck and pulled away.

"I've never gotten my nails done," I was finally able to blurt out. "I want to get a manicure. But none of those super long nails."

Amir's brows drew down. "How the hell have you never gotten your nails done? I thought your family was all about appearances."

"They were. But dramatic nails were considered trashy. So, I just… kept them short and didn't bother with polish."

"Okay, we're totally getting you something wild and colorful. And we're getting pedicures, too."

"You'll have to tell me where to go," the guard driving, Oscar, said, glancing at me through the rearview mirror.

Amir rattled off the name of a salon and the street where it was located. I wasn't the least bit surprised being as my beautiful omega was unrepentantly and effortlessly glamourous from his impeccable and unique clothing style to his always perfect long, curly hair.

The nail place was only about ten or fifteen minutes from Amir's parents' and, luckily for us, there wasn't a line. In fact, there were only a few omegas and betas in the place. And not a single alpha.

Or there wasn't until Abdel entered behind us and took up sentry at the door while Oscar stayed on the sidewalk. They both stood with their backs ramrod straight and their hands folded in front of them. I knew there were guns hidden under their clothes, but at least they weren't donning the big rifles strapped over their chests like they did at home.

As much as I hated why I had so much time to hang out with Athena or spend time doing something so frivolous as getting a manicure and pedicure, this day was damn near perfect.

Maybe learning the ways of the omega – as Amir called it – wasn't so bad after all.

CHAPTER 41

<u>Ax</u>

*J*ssa giggled and tried to get away as I held her ankle in my hands and took my time sucking her toes into my mouth.

I couldn't fucking help myself. When we'd finally stumbled through the door after work, we'd followed Amir's perfume through the house and found our omega and beta putting on the most delicious display. She'd been straddling his face while sucking his cock, her hair creating a curtain so only their movements were visible while Amir's cock and her cunt were hidden.

At least they were until the three of us barged in, ripped off our clothes, and joined in.

Now, we were all lying on the pack bed snuggling, the TV playing lightly in the background in the omega wing.

Enzo, Cyrus, and I decided to take off a few hours early since the bar was a little slow tonight, pushing our Harleys just over the speed limit to return to the pack house. Aryn and the rest of the staff were more than capable of handling things and shutting down for the night. And we all had our phones if anything arose.

I was at the foot of the bed, admiring her eccentric nail design while worshipping her dainty little toes. And by worshipping, I meant I was alternating between admiring, kissing, and sucking on her little toes. How had I never noticed how adorable her feet were?

Her fingernails were just as colorful with designs painted on them but also had little gems attached. Amir had decided to go for the flash, as well, with a bright pink ring finger and bright pink tips in what they informed me was a reverse French manicure. Who knew there were so many fucking terms for something as simple as nail paint?

Nail polish? Nail art?

Whatever.

I'd never really thought about getting my nails done – though I did indulge in pedicures for my sore feet – but now that I was seeing how cool they could be, I was considering joining them on their next outing and getting some cool design that could be seen from the crowd when I was on stage.

"That tickles!" Issa squealed as she tried to squirm out of my hold, but I just rolled forward until my body weighed down her legs and kept her in place so I could continue my inspection of her feet and toes.

"I never knew toes could taste so good," I said, sucking her big toe into my mouth before releasing it with a pop.

"You're gross," she said half-heartedly.

"How did wedding planning go today?" Cyrus asked.

He was on his back with Issa's head on one shoulder, Amir snuggled on his other side.

"Overwhelming," Issa admitted with a sigh. "I had no idea how much went into all that."

"It didn't help that my mom went full *Big Fat Greek Wedding* on her," Amir said with his eyes closed and a soft, happy smile tugging up those delicious, full lips.

"It's *My Big Fat Greek Wedding*," I corrected. "And what do you mean? Was she overinvolved?"

Issa shifted a little and the muscles in her legs went tense below me.

Abandoning her feet, I pushed to my haunches and stared down at her. I'd been so tired when we'd rolled into the driveway.

After a few orgasms and some pack time, I was wide awake and full of energy. "I'm sure Amir can talk to her. She seems like she's the motherly type and wouldn't take offense to being told she's going overboard."

Another of those shifts and she was having difficulty maintaining eye contact.

"That's kind of the problem," she admitted softly.

She had worked so hard to come out of her shell and Amir had helped her break through so many emotional boundaries and walls so she could open up to us and tell us how she truly felt.

"I didn't really have a mom. I had an incubator then I had nannies. It's…I like it. Don't get me wrong." A smile bloomed on her face. "And she said I'm just as much her daughter as…well, her daughters. But it's going to take me some time to get used to that."

"Hey, you learned to trust us, and you were scared of alphas when we met you. There's no rush," Cyrus said, running a hand over her hair before tugging her closer so he could plant a kiss to her forehead.

"I know," she said, shimmying closer to him and drawing her legs up until one knee was crossed over his groin, resting just above where Amir's was resting over Cyrus's thighs. That alpha couldn't move if he wanted to…

But why would he want to?

"I did decide that I want something more casual and lowkey, not a whole lot of guests since I don't really have much family left or any friends other than you four and Aryn. And I definitely don't want one of those big, poofy gowns like they forced on Cora."

Three matching growls lifted on the air at the mention of how Cora's life could've turned out had Enzo's brother and his pack not decided to try to use Pack Alvarez's only omega daughter as leverage.

"My mom offered their house and property, but I told her we hadn't made any decisions," Amir said before releasing a jaw cracking yawn.

"You two need to get some rest," Enzo said, finally speaking up from his place on the other side of Issa.

"Why? You three are the ones working to support all of us," Issa said, wiggling against him.

He raised a hand and swatted her ass hard enough to earn a surprised yelp.

"It's temporary. And I think I can speak for everyone when I say we're content with you and Amir being naked and fucking when we get home. Gives us even more to look forward to," I said, attempting to wedge myself between Issa and Enzo and settling for resting my head on her thigh.

I supposed I could always move to the other side and spoon Amir through the night. But I was still awake, damn it. And the other four were sinking into the mattress, their eyes closed, their bodies relaxed.

For a second, I toyed with the idea of playing with one or all of them the second they fell asleep, wake each of them up with my dick. But Enzo was right – we all needed our rest. I'd just have to count sheep.

Or maybe I'd count how many orgasms we each had during Amir's last heat.

Damn it. That did nothing but make me hard as granite.

Eventually, my mind began to slow enough that I was able to picture how our omega and beta would look all dressed up for their wedding. I hadn't yet asked whether we would be allowed to participate in the ceremony, but just like with every aspect of our relationship, I'd leave that decision up to Issa. She deserved nothing short of controlling her own fucking life.

Right. Like she's controlling her life now.

Like we reminded her on a regular basis, this was all temporary. But fuck...we still hadn't caught a single sniff of that cocksucker, Antonio.

Amir and Issa agreed on a date just over a year from now, so I could only hope this shit would be resolved by then.

Fuck, Enzo's brother had his own people looking for him, scouring streetlight and security cameras, searching for any form of electronic or paper trail.

Nothing. Fucking nothing. How the hell was someone like him, someone who craved money and power able to stay off the radar? No way in hell was he living off grid like a homesteader or some shit.

As my brain chased my thoughts like a dog chasing its tail, sleep finally dragged me under.

The next time my system went back online, the mattress jostled below me, and my dick jumped to attention at the prospect of sex going on inches from me.

And was severely let down.

It was only Cyrus climbing from the almost empty bed. Apparently, we were the last two to wake up after our late night of fun. And honestly, I could have slept a little longer after staying awake close to two hours longer than everyone else.

"What time is it?" I croaked out as Cyrus shuffled toward the door, his bare ass on full display.

Damn...when was the last time the two of us had fucked around. Now that Issa was not only willing but loved having sex with us, the two of us hadn't felt the need to seek our release with each other. Didn't mean I wasn't still highly attracted to the levelheaded and sweet natured alpha.

"Just after eleven," he said, glancing back at me and smirking when he caught me ogling his ass.

"Love you, Cy."

"Love you, Ax," he said before stepping from the room.

I needed a shower but really wasn't ready to wash the scents of my pack from my skin. Amir's chocolate and strawberries mixed so beautifully with Issa's warm, comforting sun-dried linen. Enzo and Cyrus were there, too, though a little faint since I'd spent my time fucking and pleasuring our omega and beta.

Sitting up, I threw my legs over the side of the bed and rolled my neck and shoulders. My muscles were tight and tired, but I had to work tonight. I needed to get in a workout, needed to eat, needed to practice the new choreography.

I was only in one group performance tonight. I had convinced the other guys to start doing solos to showcase their specific talents. It was a shame to see their skills go to waste by getting lost in the group dances.

Searching through the pile of clothes on the floor, I snatched my boxer briefs up and dragged them over my ass before leaving the room in search of copious amounts of caffeine and food. Normally, I would have worked out before eating breakfast or drinking any coffee, but my brain and body were equally exhausted.

Would missing one workout really be that big a deal?

Eh. There were other ways to get my heart pumping and my muscles straining. Better, more fun ways.

The moment I stepped out of my room and the warm smell of coffee wafted up my nostrils, the decision was made: Coffee first. Fuck my omega and beta second. And I'd make damn sure it was a hell of a workout for all three of us.

CHAPTER 42

<u>Issa</u>

It had been over a month since my asshole former alpha tracked me down and showed up at the club. Over a month since Amir and I had been on lockdown, only allowed to leave with armed guards.

Over a month of fighting the feeling I'd lived with my whole life, the feeling that my life was no longer mine.

Once again, my every move was being dictated by an alpha.

Not that my alphas were doing it out of spite or a need to control me.

It felt more as though Antonio was once again in control of my life, my actions, my choices since he was the reason I was back to being unemployed, back to sitting at home while waiting for my alphas to return.

At least I had my omega here with me every day. And neither of us had grown tired of the other's company yet. And he couldn't hide it if he had grown bored with me since I could literally feel his every emotion in my chest.

Since that day at the nail salon, we'd gone back twice more simply to change the designs. It felt frivolous but amazing at the same time. And every time the two of us came back with something new on our fingers or toes, Ax would go crazy and demand he nibble on my toes like a damn foot fetishist.

Not that I was complaining. It tickled, but oddly sent heat coursing through my body.

Oh, who was I kidding? Everything my pack did made me hot. It was like their scents alone were the best kind of aphrodisiac. Their grumbled words, their growls, and their purrs were like a vibrator to my clit.

I was a woman lost to my guys and madly in love with all four of them.

"I don't feel like sitting around the house all day again," I pouted as the alphas drank their coffee.

Amir was busy making pancakes…in nothing but a pair of boxer briefs that showcased his tight, muscular ass and outlined his beautiful cock. I sighed internally as I fought the urge to play with him all day instead of leaving the house.

But we could always make love when we got home. Or in a dressing room as we'd done in the past.

"Abdel and Oscar are already outside so let them know where you want to go then let one of us know where you're heading and when you get back home," Enzo said before lifting his mug to his lips.

I sighed and dropped my chin on my arms folded on top of the table. "I hate Antonio."

My life had become a total fairy tale before he'd reappeared. Sure, I still dealt with PTSD, but my nightmares had become few and far between with my pack cuddling me in the pack bed every night.

I'd had a job. Was making friends. Had a pack who didn't solely dote on our omega, but treated me like a princess, as well. It drove me a little crazy that all four of my guys were more protective of me than our rare designation of an omega.

But I understood it.

Amir wasn't small by any stretch of the imagination. And he hadn't hesitated to jump into the brawl at the club to protect our alphas while I'd cowered by the bar.

But really, what the hell could I have done short of getting in the way or distracting my pack? I would have never forgiven myself if they'd been hurt because they were more worried about protecting me than themselves.

"Bain's been keeping me updated. His people might have found your former beta," Enzo announced, yanking me out of my inner turmoil.

My head popped up. "They found Carlos? Where? Is he okay? Did he find a new pack?"

I hadn't really had anything against Carlos other than the fact I hadn't chosen him. But he'd never been cruel to me. The only thing I felt mildly resentful about was that he'd left me alone with Antonio.

A growl rumbled from Ax.

Turning a frown on him, I shook my head. "I can literally feel that possessive rush, alpha. I don't want Carlos. But it's nice to know he's not dead."

"He has a new pack with an omega and two alphas. He's about an hour away. Bain's sending someone to chat with him, see if he's had any contact with Antonio or if he might be aware of anywhere that shit stain might be hiding," Enzo said, completely ignoring the banter between Ax and me. "I know you're tired of hearing it, but this is –"

"Temporary. Yeah."

I knew I sounded bitchy. I sounded bitchy in my own head. But it was so hard to continue pretending to be happy when my life was once again being controlled by that...*shit stain*. Enzo had called it right.

My pack lead tilted his head and rested his forearms on the table. "Do you two want to come to the club tonight?"

I popped up so fast I was pretty sure I strained a muscle. "Seriously?"

He held up a hand. "Let me make a few phone calls and ask if Bain or Ghazi can send a few more guards to keep an eye on the room before you get your hopes up. But if we have enough backup...you two can come hang out, do some dancing, watch Ax strip."

"For fuck's sake–"

"*I do not strip*," the four of us said in unison, repeating the same words we'd heard a dozen times.

Amir and I erupted into giggles while Ax smirked and shook his head.

"Fucking brats."

* * *

"Is this too much?" I asked Amir, turning side to side in the mirror.

Ax, Cyrus, and Enzo had left for work on their motorcycles a few hours ago. Now, Amir and I were getting all gussied up for our first night at the club since Antonio had shown his stupid face.

"You're so fucking beautiful," he said, sprawled on my bed the way Ax used to before I'd accepted the fact he and my other two alphas wanted me for more than a roommate.

Smiling at him in the mirror, I tugged on the top of the dress in an attempt to cover more of my cleavage.

"Oh, hell no. Leave those girls on display."

"So our alphas will get all growly and possessive?" I asked with an eye roll.

"Yeah." That one word sounded more like *duh* with that tone of voice. "Think of all the fun we'll have when we get home tonight."

With my hands still on the strap, I tugged the top back down. "Good point."

I'd chosen a dress I hadn't had a chance to wear yet. I tended to wear jeans or a reasonable skirt when I worked as a server, but tonight was about having fun with my omega and, hopefully, my alphas if they had time, as well.

We had both gone all out, although Amir had had to put in a lot less work. His mane of curls took him the most time. I'd curled my long hair and left it in big waves down my back, then smoked out my eyes before slipping on some blood red lipstick.

All that was left was jewelry and my heels. I opted for a simple chain with a single diamond and a pair of solitaire earrings. "Is the necklace too much?"

Amir's eyes jumped to mine and a solacious smile stretched across his beautiful tan skin.

"Focus, omega," I teased, sliding my feet into a pair of strappy black four-inch heels. "Is this too much for the club?"

"You sure you don't want to stay home tonight?" He wasn't asking because he was concerned about us being in public. Why would he be when there would be six damn armed guards along with the usual bouncers and security keeping their eyes on us.

No. He wanted to rip the dress off me and stay between my thighs for the rest of the night.

"Save all that energy for when we get home." A wry smile kicked up one corner of my mouth. "Or at least until we sneak into one of our alpha's offices again."

Amir rolled from the end of the bed and extended his elbow, escorting me from my room and downstairs where Abdel waited by the door.

"Ready?" Abdel asked. His constant scowl deepened when he caught my appearance, but he quickly averted his eyes.

"You don't like my dress?" I asked when I was close enough.

"Not if it will cause your alphas to act foolish."

Amir winked at me as I laughed, and we followed him through the front door and to the waiting SUV. Oscar was already behind the wheel with another SUV in front of his.

I thought six armed guards was a bit of an overkill for the two of us. Even if Antonio showed up, no way did he have the balls to try anything again, not after seeing how viciously my pack would fight for me.

The ride to the club was as uneventful as I'd assumed it would be. And a crowd was beginning to form a line to the front door. If I'd been working tonight, I would have made a killing in tips. I always did on the weekends, and Saturday nights tended to be the best.

"Omega Rivera. Beta Rivera," the bouncer greeted us as our entourage escorted us in like we were royalty being surrounded by freaking secret service or something.

Did royalty have secret service? And why the hell was that the question that was now stuck in my head?

Oh shit. I was anxious. Scared. I was worried my mere presence would cause my pack drama. Again.

It felt like from the moment I'd met my alphas, I'd brought them nothing but chaos. They'd never complained about it or me, had never begrudged the way we'd met or the fact there had been two incidents because I was working there. But I felt guilty, nonetheless.

"There they are," Aryn called from the bar as we approached. "Missed you, girl. I was wondering if you were ever going to show your face again."

I stepped up onto the foot bar along the front and leaned forward, turning my cheek for a kiss and nuzzle from the female alpha and the first friend I'd made since escaping Antonio. Well, the first friend outside my pack.

"Missed you. I want to come back to work but…"

Aryn waved her hand in the air. "Girl, I get it. I wouldn't want you two out in public without a few bad asses watching over you, either." She glanced up at Abdel who was within touching distance, his back to me while he faced the crowd. "How the hell did they find so many hot alphas to guard you two?"

"I think a few of them are packless if you want some intros," Amir offered.

She scoffed. "My pack is more than a handful."

That answered the question I'd had when I'd first met her. I'd wondered whether or not she had a pack at home waiting for her. She was so sweet and protective, she absolutely deserved as much love and happiness as possible.

"What can I get you two?"

"Hey! We've been waiting," a male beta said to my right.

Aryn turned a scowl on him. "And you're going to wait some more. Keep it up and you'll wait all fucking night."

When she turned back to me, her smile was back, and humor danced in her eyes.

"Dirty martini," I said.

"Shots," Amir said.

"We can't just drink shots all night. Order a big boy drink so our alphas don't get all pissy when we act like drunken fools," I teased him, curling into his side when he wrapped an arm around my shoulders.

"Fine. Draft beer. Dealer's choice."

Aryn shook her head. "You know it's dangerous to let a bartender choose your drinks, right?"

"Eh. I trust you."

"You're lucky you're mated to my bosses," she teased before getting to work filling our orders.

The place was filling quickly, the music thumping through my chest like a second heartbeat. I could feel my alphas' concern through the bond, but I could also feel their love. Amir was there, a bright ray of excitement and sunshine as he moved around to my back, wrapping one arm across my chest as he swayed his hips against my ass and encouraged me to move with him before we even hit the dancefloor.

Aryn slid our drinks over, then slapped my hand when I tried to hand her some cash from my clutch. "Put that away!" she admonished before winking and walking down to the row to the waiting patrons.

I'd make sure Enzo forced my tip on her later.

But now? I wanted to have some fun and pretend I didn't have a past, pretend Antonio didn't exist, pretend I'd grown up as a normal beta and was out with my omega for a night on the town like a regular pack.

"Hey," Cyrus said, hurrying over to us and pressing a kiss to my lips then moving to do the same to Amir. "Stay close to the guards. Let them know if there are any problems. Alert them immediately if you so much as catch a whiff of Antonio's scent."

"I know. We'll be fine."

He raised one brow at me, then glanced over my shoulder before winking down at me and moving into the crowd.

I wasn't sure whether he was looking at Amir or checking in with one of our guards, but I wasn't worried about tonight. Now that Antonio knew I was no longer an easy target, that not only did I have a pack who would burn the world for me but that I was no longer the same broken and subservient beta he'd tried to break, there was no chance in hell he would make another appearance here.

He was a typical bully. He wouldn't attempt anything knowing my alphas were here, knowing so many sets of eyes were on me, knowing that he couldn't win. People like him went for soft targets, they threw sucker punches and attacked from the shadows.

"Dance or people watch for a while?" Amir asked, his glass of beer in one hand as he settled the other on my lower back.

I lifted my martini glass to my lips and downed it in two swallows before turning and setting the empty glass on the bar. "I'm ready to dance."

As Amir held up his glass to get Aryn's attention before setting it on the bar for her to put away until we returned, Abdel turned and looked at me over his shoulder. "Alpha Enzo told me to tell you to slow down."

My brows puckered before I looked around. I couldn't see him so he must have watched me through one of the cameras. I had no idea which one he was watching, so I looked at the closest one and stuck out my tongue.

For the first time since I'd met Abdel, the corners of his lips twitched in what could almost be considered a smile.

"We're going to dance. Join us."

"I don't dance, but I'll be out there with you," he said, his serious expression back in place.

Of course, he didn't dance. Even if he was an expert at breakdancing, he wouldn't do anything that might divert his attention from any threat that might be in the crowd.

I wondered how Amir and I looked to the crowd as our little

entourage followed us through the throng of people and kept a barrier between us and anyone who might get too close.

No point in dwelling on that. I couldn't control the situation, nor could I control other people's opinions.

Amir's hands landed on my hips and dragged me closer until we were pressed as close as we could be with our clothes still on. His erection pressed against my stomach.

I smiled up at him. I swore my omega was always ready for a little play, always ready to make love to me no matter where we were or what we were doing.

As promised, Abdel stood sentry without so much as swaying to the beat. We'd taken a place close enough to the stage to see Ax dance without hindering our view of the others. Sure, Ax tended to steal a majority of our attention, but the others were so damn talented, and I'd gotten to know a few of them fairly well during my time serving tables here. They were sweet and respectful, and a few of them were actively seeking either a pack or an omega.

I glanced at Abdel, over my shoulder at Oscar, then to the men flanking the floor like a group of…bodyguards. Because that's exactly what they were. I couldn't help but wonder if the people giving them a wide berth and watching from the corner of their eye knew how much firepower was in the club.

Were my two regular guards single? I could always play matchmaker and try to set them up with one or more of the dancers. And a few of the dancers were betas so all the better.

Ax and his male dance review put on an amazing show as usual. Amir was pulled on stage this time for some extra attention from Ax and his crew – much to the delight of the crowd – and I danced with my omega until sweat trickled down my back and between my boobs.

The two of us did enough shots to earn ourselves a healthy buzz before Enzo announced it was time for us to head back to the pack house when he caught us trying to sneak away from our guards to replay the first time we met in Cyrus's office.

"That was so much fun," I slurred, leaning heavily against Amir's shoulder as Oscar drove us home.

"I'm surprised you remember much," Oscar muttered from the driver's seat.

"Hey! I'm not that drunk," I whined.

Amir huffed a laugh. "You're pretty toasty, beautiful."

I turned my head to look up into his face and giggled when it took my eyes a second to focus on only one Amir instead of the double that my alcohol hazed vision tried to show me.

"Okay. I'm a little drunk." I held up my hand, putting my forefinger and thumb an inch apart.

So I was *a lot* drunk. And tired. And my feet ached.

But I didn't regret a single moment of the night. For the first time since that disaster of a night, I didn't feel as though I was suffocating, as though my world had once again been turned on its head by an asshole alpha.

The smile on my face stayed there even when my eyes fell closed, when the door opened beside me, and when I was hoisted into strong arms and carried inside while being cocooned by the sweetest perfume in the world.

CHAPTER 43

<u>Amir</u>

My mom let Alysia leave school early so she could be a part of today. Since Issa hadn't had a chance to make friends during her years with her family then her former alpha, the only two women who would have attended while she tried on dresses were her sister Cora and the bartender Aryn.

When I told my beautiful beta I'd invited my mom and sister, she'd actually gotten excited and beamed brightly at me. Honestly, I'd been a little worried it would make her anxious with so many sets of eyes on her and so many opinions.

Mom tried to shoo me out the door, saying it was bad luck or whatever. But not like we weren't already bonded. I had seen Issa in every possible way, had explored and tasted every inch of her body. There wasn't a damn thing my girl could do that would make me love her any less.

Though I *was* falling in love with her more every single day.

Shit, I was falling in love with all four of them more every day.

My alphas were amazing men as it was, but watching them with Issa, the way they cared about her, the way they protected her made me adore them all that much more.

"I'm so excited," Alysia said, clapping her hands together lightly.

"Don't overwhelm her," I reminded them quietly.

My family – or at least the women in my family – tended to be forthcoming with the excitement and affection, something that had been new for Issa. She'd been gracious and tried to hide it, but I'd noted how tense she grew every time someone other than her pack tried to hug her.

The sound of a curtain being pulled back preceded the attendant who was helping Issa into the dresses.

And when my girl stepped around the corner, a burst of perfume exploded from me and saturated the air.

Shit. I should have doused myself in scent blockers before we left because no way would the filtration system in here be able to keep my pheromones from setting off any omegas or alphas who might be here, as well.

"Wow," Alysia said barely above a whisper.

"Issa..." Aryn started then trailed off, her alpha pheromones mixing with my perfume. I knew the alpha wasn't romantically interested in my beta, but a person would have to be blind to not see how stunning my girl was.

Mom was surprisingly quiet, and when I turned my eyes to her, she was carefully wiping tears from below her lashes.

This was the third dress Issa had tried on but only the first she'd actually let us see. According to her, the other two weren't right.

But this one?

She'd chosen a satin, floor length gown in a soft rose color. The front dipped in a cowl neck style, showcasing a mere hint of cleavage. And when she turned to get a look in the mirrors surrounding the platform, I got a glimpse of how low the back of the dress dipped.

The material clung to her body in a classy way, making her look sexy yet elegant.

"Are you going to wear a veil?" Alysia asked.

Issa looked at her in the mirror, only then noticing our reactions. A watery smile pulled up her lips as tears glistened in her pretty light brown eyes.

"I hadn't planned on it. I have an idea for my hair, but I think I might put a flower in it or something."

"May I show you something?" the beta stylist asked.

"Of course."

She disappeared and I pushed to my feet, circling the platform to get a full three-sixty view. This was where she belonged, on a pedestal like the fucking princess she was.

Nah. She was a queen. *My* queen.

"It is taking everything in my power to keep from bowing at your dainty purple painted toes right now," I admitted as my cock strained against my jeans and begged to be released.

And inserted into my beta.

For the rest of the day.

She wrapped her fingers in my shirt and tugged me closer, bending at the waist so she could press a kiss to my lips before stepping back as the stylist returned.

"I've seen worse," the attendant said with a giggle. She stepped onto the platform and toyed with Issa's hair before placing something in the makeshift hairstyle.

When she stepped away, Alysia squealed, my mom let out a soft *aww*, and Aryn sniffled.

The adornment was some kind of comb or clip, was covered in pearls and rhinestones, and was glamourous and elegant.

Just like my Issa. My fiancée.

And in less than a year, my wife.

"It's perfect," Mom said, pushing to her feet and raising her phone to take a picture.

"It really is, Issa," Aryn confirmed.

She was struggling to keep the tears from rolling over her lashes. Just because she was an alpha didn't mean she didn't have emotions. Kind of like I was an omega but not small and sure as hell not meek or submissive.

Issa turned back to the mirror and tilted her head to get a better look. "It's so beautiful."

Her hands smoothed down the dress and she turned and looked over her shoulder in the mirror.

"Do you think the back is too…flashy? Or skimpy?"

"You look absolutely stunning, *Kori*. I can't wait for your alphas and your new fathers to see you," Mom said, speaking to Issa, not me.

Tears glimmered in my beta's eyes again as she turned and looked Mom in the eye. "Thank you so much for being here. And for…just being. Being you. And being so nice to me."

Mom wrapped her in one of those big, smothering motherly hugs and patted her back lightly before letting her go.

"You inherited a family when you fell in love with Amir. We're not going anywhere. And I dare anyone to come near you when I'm around."

Aryn huffed a laugh then covered it with a cough when my mom turned a glare on her.

Mom was not only an omega, but was as small as Issa, maybe smaller, though definitely curvier after having four kids and being spoiled by her alphas. But she had that stereotypical Greek temper and would go toe to toe with a grizzly bear over any of her kids.

And that now extended to Issa.

* * *

Mom and Alysia pulled from the lot while Aryn waited until Issa and I were safely locked inside the SUV.

As if Abdel and Oscar wouldn't blast a hole through anyone who tried to hurt either of us.

But she was Issa's friend and was watching over her like the rest of us. She wanted our girl safe. And, while I didn't know the alpha well, that definitely endeared her to me.

How could I not love someone who loved Issa?

"I can't wait for the next year to pass," Aryn said, ducking to press a kiss to Issa's cheek. "You're going to be the most beautiful bride." She turned to me. "And you are the luckiest bastard in the world."

She'd told us she had a pack, had even spoken about them affectionately, so this felt more like a best friend warning the fiancé to be good to Issa.

And I loved Aryn even more for it.

"I *am* absolutely the luckiest man on this planet."

Aryn gave me a side hug – avoiding rubbing her scent glands anywhere on me – then stepped away with a wave as I climbed into the backseat beside Issa.

"Home or the nail place again?" Oscar asked. There was humor in his voice, even if his face remained neutral.

"I'm not ready to go home yet," Issa admitted. "But it's too soon to get our nails done again."

Since we tended to use the SUV with the guards during our outings, our alphas had been taking their Harleys to work every day. I couldn't wait to finally get my Thunderbird delivered to the pack house so I could get back to work on restoring her, then finally take my girl on a joy ride.

Of course, the joy ride would either have to wait until Antonio was no longer a threat or would include a guard or one of our alphas.

"Want to go shopping? Or we could have an early dinner? You boys hungry?" I asked Abdel and Oscar.

Abdel shot a scowl at me over his shoulder at being called a boy, especially since he was not only close to my fathers' age but a humongous, brooding alpha.

"We go where you go," Oscar answered, glancing at me in the rearview mirror as he pulled into traffic.

"Food sounds good. Something hot and greasy. Bar food or comfort food. I don't feel like going to a stuffy restaurant today," Issa answered, snuggling into my side as I tightened my arm around her shoulders and nuzzled my cheek against the side of her face.

"Anywhere in particular?" Oscar asked.

"Nah. You guys pick this time. You have to have a favorite," Issa said, resting her head against my chest with a wistful sigh.

My sweetheart was happy. I loved moments like this, loved when she was able to simply relax, when we were able to enjoy each other's company without thinking about that fucking threat constantly looming over our heads.

Her head. Not mine. That mother fucker was after Issa.

And according to her, there was literally no reason for him to be interested in her any longer since her fathers were dead and there was no power or wealth attached to her name.

The only reason he would still be sniffing around her was to control her, to continue his own form of abuse.

Or maybe for revenge.

Cowards like Antonio weren't brave enough to go after the people who'd ended his opportunity to become some high roller in the criminal world, so he would go after Issa instead. He would punish Enzo and his pack as well as my alphas by hurting or killing Issa.

"My mom owns a diner," Oscar announced nonchalantly as he guided the SUV down the four-lane road bisecting town.

"Ohhh. Yes, let's do that," Issa said, leaning forward and tapping Oscar on the shoulder. "I have so many questions for your mom."

She smiled up at me and winked.

Both guards were pretty quiet, merely staying in the shadows and answering any questions we shot their way with monosyllabic replies.

And since they were so secretive and closed off, Issa and I had made a game out of teasing them and trying to get them to open up to us, even going so far as threatening to make Ax pull one of them on stage the next time we visited the club.

Oscar had smirked. Abdel's permanent scowl had grown deeper, and a light growl rumbled from his chest.

The diner was quaint and not very busy. But the two guards ushered us toward the back of the room, putting themselves between us and the windows, exits, or anyone who might so much as pass our table.

Yeah, they were keeping both of us safe, but I could tell it was starting to grate on Issa, like she retreated a little into her old ways any time anyone acted as though there was a constant threat.

Because of the way she'd been raised, the way everyone in her life had treated her before our pack, she didn't realize how common it was for alphas to be uber protective of their beta *and* omega, regardless of their gender. It was in an alpha's genetic makeup to protect those they cared for.

Turning my head, I opened my mouth to remind her this was all temporary, but snapped it shut. She was tired of hearing those words from our mouths, tired of being reminded that her life was currently out of sorts because of the same fuckwad who'd abused her.

It was temporary. I had zero doubt her sister's alphas would move heaven and earth to track that fucking alpha and end his life.

Then, we could go back to living our own lives the way we wanted.

CHAPTER 44

<u>Issa</u>

By the time we finished eating – and I'd had the opportunity to chat with Oscar's unbelievably sweet beta mother – the sun was setting. There would still be a few more hours before the alphas would return, but at least I hadn't spent the entire day in front of the TV.

I still had that warm fuzzy feeling deep in my heart that had started at the dress shop. It was so nice to have women in my life, women who cared about me. I had Cora now, sure, but now I had a mother figure, sisters, and even a best friend.

Never in my life would I have thought I would have become so close to a female alpha. Hell, I would have never guessed I would become close to any alpha, yet here I was, surrounded by them every day and loving every minute of it.

Even Abdel and Oscar had wormed their way into my little circle of trust.

"Somewhere else or home?" Oscar asked as he waited for traffic to clear enough to pull onto the main road.

"I think I'm ready for a bath and some old reruns," I said as I cuddled into Amir's side.

Would there ever come a time where I didn't constantly crave his touch? Omegas were built to crave physical affection, but I was beta.

Yet I couldn't get enough of his sweet touches, his embraces, his kisses…

And all the other fun stuff we did to pass the time while waiting for our alphas…and then again when our alphas returned to us.

"You in an eighties sitcom mood or black and white mood?" Amir asked.

I hummed in thought, then glanced up into his face. "I'm thinking maybe some older movies instead of a sitcom tonight. Oh! What about *Pretty Woman?* Or *You've Got Mail?*"

There really was no point in even making suggestions because Amir always went along with anything I wanted, no matter how hard I pushed him to pick for the night. He always teased that he spent more time staring at me than the show or movie, anyway.

We were still about ten minutes from home, but I was already planning my shower instead of a bath, my pajamas, and the snacks I would lay out on the coffee table for the impromptu movie night.

Not really a movie night since it was only the two of us and we would probably end up falling asleep during at least one of them. But it felt like a perfect ending to such a perfect day. It was right up there with the day Amir had officially proposed to me.

An *omega* proposed to *me*.

So many times, I'd wondered how I had been blessed with this life after the nightmare of the first twenty odd years of my life.

"Do we have any candy?" I asked, tilting my head to look into Amir's face.

"I'm sure one of our trusty babysitters wouldn't mind running out for us," he teased, raising one brow as we waited for the response we knew was coming.

"Not babysitters. And not a food delivery service," Abdel said in his heavily accent voice.

Both our bodies shook with a giggle.

The SUV turned into our driveway, then stopped suddenly, causing both of us to lurch against our seatbelts.

"What the f—"

BOOM!

Glass exploded from Oscar's window and sprayed across the cab, pieces slicing across my cheek as I threw up an arm to block whatever the hell had just flown into the driver's side.

My brain was slow to catch up, thinking a rock or bird had flown through the window and smashed the glass.

But that didn't explain the loud boom or the warm, wet liquid that had splashed my cheek and forearms.

"Put it down!" Abdel bellowed as I blinked slowly, raising my head to look around.

"Oh my god," I cried out.

Oscar was leaning to the side, blood trailing from his head and pooling on the center console.

And outside the door stood an alpha with a mask covering his face, a gun pointed directly at me. Or maybe Amir.

"Put your fucking gun down or they both die."

He didn't need to wear a mask. I knew his scent and voice. Both haunted my nightmares.

Antonio.

We didn't have a gate surrounding our property or loads of guards walking the perimeter. It was just Oscar and Abdel protecting us.

Oh no. Oscar.

My heart thumped painfully as my eyes darted from Antonio, to Oscar, to Abdel's gun pointing at my former alpha, then back again.

"Which do you want to die first?" Antonio asked.

"You pull that trigger, you fucking die," Abdel growled out as his alpha hormones filled the cab with strong pulses of burned rubber and something spicy like cayenne.

"Which of the two are you willing to sacrifice first? I might die, but you'll have to bury the omega or the beta, as well."

Trembles started in my roiling stomach and worked their way to my fingertips and toes. My vision blurred with fear and the tears that welled in my eyes.

He was here for me. And he was threatening to kill my omega. He'd already killed Oscar and the alpha was only doing as he'd been paid to do, keep the two of us safe.

Keep me *safe.*

This was my fault. All of it. The big guard's death, the gun pointed at Amir, the drama that had occurred at The Vault.

And all because I'd dared to build a normal life with men I'd fallen in love with.

"Stop!" I screamed when Antonio positioned the gun until it was pointed at Amir's head. "What do you want? Tell me and it's yours," I promised.

Even if it meant handing myself over to him. Even if it meant sacrificing myself to keep my omega, my fiancé safe and alive.

"Get out," Antonio said, his voice deceptively calm. "Now."

"Don't you fucking move," Abdel said, never peeling his eyes from Antonio or lowering his gun the slightest.

He needed to calm down before he got Amir hurt. No way would Antonio simply shoot and kill me here and now. He wouldn't get the revenge he wanted if he killed me then Abdel killed him.

Oscar moved, the slightest twitch of his arm that laid limp on the seat. I sent up a prayer he wasn't dead. Not that he could help in his condition.

But I didn't want the death of someone on my heart, even if I would only feel the guilt for a short period before Antonio was done with me.

Amir was behind me, his scent bitter with anger and fear. But I could feel his hand against the small of my back, could feel him slowly moving and shoving something into the waistline of my jeans.

It was hard and plastic and a little cool. His phone, maybe? Why was he sliding his phone into my pants? He would need that the moment Antonio dragged me away.

Blowing the bonds wide open, I sent every ounce of fear and dread to my alphas, doing the only thing I could for now to let them know we were in danger.

But the club wasn't nearly close enough and they wouldn't have been on their way home being as it was still early in the evening.

At the realization that no one would get to us on time, I flooded the bonds with every ounce of love I felt for all four of them. I wanted them to carry that with them long after I was gone. I wanted them to move on, to maybe one day find another beta who needed their love and care as much as I had.

"I'm not going to count. Either get your skinny ass out here or watch your omega die."

"No!" I screamed out and began to scramble away from Amir, struggling to undo my seatbelt with shaky hands.

"Beta Rivera–" Abdel started, but I cut him off.

"Protect my omega," I said.

"Leave your fucking phone," Antonio said as I tugged away from Amir's arms and pushed my door open.

Reaching into my purse, I started to pull it free, but he snatched the bag from my trembling hands and tossed it onto the seat, his gun still aimed at Amir's head. All it would take was one twitch of his finger and my entire world would crumble.

His hand curled around my bicep and yanked me away from the open door before I was pushed toward the back of the vehicle. Another set of arms banded around mine, locking them to my side.

Who the hell was this? I didn't recognize the scent, but he was an alpha if I was correct about his size and the signature floating around him and into my nostrils.

"Issa!" Amir bellowed, crawling through the open door and reaching for me as Abdel lunged from his side and positioned himself directly in front of my omega.

Good. At least my love would be safe, no matter what happened after I was dragged away from him.

"I love you," I whimpered as I was dragged backward to a car parked perpendicular to the driveway. My driveway. *Our* driveway.

I wanted to take a moment to memorize the outside of the house, to stare into Amir's beautiful green eyes, to soak up every bit of his presence as I could before I died.

Because I had no doubt I wouldn't live much longer once Antonio and the thug behind me drove me away from the only place, the only people, where I'd truly felt was home.

Amir's face crumpled as tears rushed down his cheeks, his arm outstretched as though reaching for me.

He knew he couldn't get to me. Knew there was no way to get to me without one or both of us dying right here in the driveway. Then our alphas would lose us both in one night. They would come home to us dead in the driveway.

I didn't want to leave him. I didn't want to say goodbye to my alphas. But there was a small part of me that was happy they'd intentionally sought an omega just for me. They'd fallen as hard for him as I had.

They would still have him once I was gone, once I was dead and buried.

Nothing more than a memory.

Those trembles that had started when my brain caught up to the situation continued to make me feel as though the ground itself was shaking below me. My heart thundered painfully behind my ribs as the asshole behind me kept that same iron grip around me until I was tossed into the passenger seat.

Not the backseat. They must not have been worried I would dive from car first chance I got as if I was some kind of daredevil who could tuck and roll on the highway like a stuntwoman.

The other alpha climbed into the backseat, a gun appearing in my periphery and aiming at Amir and Abdel as Antonio settled behind the wheel, the engine humming softly, and hit the gas so hard the tires squealed against the asphalt.

My stomach lurched with my body as I was pushed against the seat with the speed my former alpha was driving.

I didn't bother with the seatbelt. If we crashed and I died…that had to be a better death than anything Antonio had planned.

"What was the point of the mask? They'll know it was you," I said, my voice breathy and holding a tremor as the fear and unknown of my immediate future forced blood to whoosh in my ears and adrenaline to burn through my veins.

"Plausible deniability," the asshole in the back said with a chuckle.

I turned and glared at him as he pulled the mask off his face. I still didn't recognize him, even with his face uncovered.

Looking at Antonio's profile, I pushed the fear aside and smiled. "They'll find you. They're going to hunt you down and kill you. Doesn't matter whether I live or die. They're all going to kill you. My pack. Cora's pack–"

His arm whipped out and his hand cracked against my lips. They throbbed with my heartbeat, and I could taste the coppery tang of blood, but he hadn't loosened any teeth, merely split my lip. That was nothing compared to how he used to treat me.

Spitting the blood welling in my mouth onto the floorboard, I swiped the back of my arm across my lips.

Fuck him. I would never again allow him to see a moment of weakness from me.

As he continued to speed away from my house, my only true home, my family, and pulled the sedan onto the on-ramp for the highway, a buzzing started in my back.

Not in my back. *Against* my back.

I'd been right; Amir had slipped his phone into my pants as though he'd known Antonio would demand I leave mine behind.

And why wouldn't he? It would have been so easy for my alphas to track me, to track my phone.

Just like they would be tracking Amir's.

A flood of emotions rushed over me and through me. They were not only coming from my own hope that Ax, Cyrus, and Enzo would find me before it was too late, but the rage and reassurances pouring through me from my pack.

They were coming for me. Just like I'd thought before, my alphas, my pack, my family would burn the planet to the ground to find me.

And they would rip Antonio to pieces the moment they got their hands on him.

CHAPTER 45

<u>Ax</u>

One moment I was wiping away sweat, the next, it felt as though someone had punched a hole through my chest as a fear unlike anything I'd ever experienced blasted through my heart and straight into my bloodstream.

That fear hadn't come from me. And it sure as fuck hadn't come from my other two packmates.

Something was wrong. Something was wrong with Issa. She was in danger.

Still shirtless, I sprinted from the dressing room and shouldered Enzo's door open without bothering to punch in the code the same moment he was racing toward it, his bike key in hand.

"Issa!" I barked out, swiping my own key from his desk.

Neither of us sought Cyrus. He would have felt the same terror we had felt. He would be on his way to the Harleys parked out back.

People cursed and screeched as we shoved them out of the way in our hurry to get outside and on the road.

We had no idea where she was, but we had to get to her.

"It's Abdel," Cyrus yelled as he ran through the backdoor. "She's on the move. Amir put his phone in her pants. He's tracking it now."

There was a grim look on his face, and I feared what that look meant. But for now, all I could focus on was getting to my girl.

I could not fail her.

I could not fucking lose her.

Cyrus's eyes were unfocused as he looked across the parking lot and listened to the guard on the other line.

My patience snapped.

More like exploded into tiny cinders on the wind.

"Fuck! Where?" I yelled, the sound echoing off the brick building and asphalt parking lot.

"Pull up the app," Cyrus said as he jogged across the space between us and threw a leg over his own bike. "She's on the move. On the highway heading north. Not more than twenty minutes from here."

Twenty minutes my ass.

With the bikes and the lack of heavy traffic, we could close the distance in no time. We just had to avoid getting smeared on the highway in the meantime.

Not bothering to wait for my packmates, I pulled up the tracking app connected to all our phones and pinpointed Amir's. Issa's was at the house, meaning that fucker had taken her phone away.

But our omega must have foreseen exactly what he would do and made sure there was a way we could track her once she was driven away from our property.

After tonight, there was as a very high probability I would demand both Amir and Issa had some form of device inserted into their skin or maybe under a crown in their teeth.

Anything to be able to keep an eye on them in case something like this happened again.

Our pack might not have made enemies like Bain's, but he was still family. Meaning someone could come after our beta and our omega to get to them.

Or some asshole could simply try to steal one of them away for no other reason than their own sick motives.

The vibrations below me and the wind whipping across my bare chest, shoulders and arms, and sending my hair behind me did nothing to distract me from my single-minded focus.

And that focus was getting my beta back and killing Antonio.

Cyrus hadn't confirmed it had been her former alpha, but he didn't need to. Who else would have any reason to fuck with our pack? Who else would have passed a rare male omega and taken our beta?

Though she was fucking gorgeous. Stunning. Heartbreakingly beautiful.

The cars flew by in my periphery. Horns honked periodically as we weaved in and out of traffic, barely missing a few bumpers by inches in my haste to catch up to Issa.

And then what? Not like we could run the car off the road. Even if we were in a bigger vehicle, we couldn't risk hurting our girl.

But at least we would know where the hell she was. We would stay right the fuck behind them until they had no choice but to pull over.

And then I would rip that mother fucker's head from his shoulders with my bare fucking hands. I would make him suffer for thinking he had any right to breathe the same oxygen as Issa let alone daring to put his mother fucking hands on her.

CHAPTER 46

Issa

I was wedged as close to the passenger door as possible, keeping as much distance between Antonio and myself as I could. The jerk in the back smelled heavily of cigarette smoke and cheap beer.

No idea how I could tell it was cheap other than he smelled... sticky.

Like the smell of the trashcans at The Vault at the end of the night.

The entire cab of the older model sedan was filled with their scents, of smoke and alpha hormones. And it turned my stomach and filled my throat with bile.

"I'm going to throw up," I blurted.

There was a glimmer of hope that if I threatened to puke in the car, Antonio would pull over and I could make a run for it or wave down some help.

Surely, someone would see two giant alphas chasing after me and either stop to help or call the police.

But Antonio made a dismissive sound in the back of his throat as though he either didn't believe me or had no intention of pulling over any time soon.

Probably best for him. Though it sucked for me.

Best for him because I was not the weak, broken beta he knew from before. I would fight tooth and nail the second I was able to get out of this car. I would scream and flail and fight until either he gave up or someone stepped forward to help me get away from my fucking captors.

How the hell was I here again?

And had he killed Oscar?

My heart ached at the thought someone might have died simply because they were supposed to be protecting me.

I had balked at the idea of having armed babysitters everywhere I went, had almost pitied Cora for having to live behind the heavily guarded walls that surrounded her estate.

But if we'd had manned gates at the start of our driveway there was no way Antonio would have had the balls to attack us the way he had.

"You shot Oscar when he wasn't looking," I blurted, turning in my seat to look at him then at the jerk behind me.

"That the dead fuck's name?" Antonio said, smirking as he shared a look with the alpha in the backseat.

"You're a coward. You knew if you'd waited until they were out of the SUV, there wasn't a chance in hell you would survive in a fight against them. You snuck up and shot him through the window instead of going toe to toe with him like a man. You threatened my omega instead of challenging Abdel because you knew he would sacrifice his own life before ours."

A growl lifted on the air, sending the fine hairs on my arms and the nape of my neck to stand on end.

"Careful, beta," Antonio growled.

He turned a glare on me long enough I grew nervous. His eyes needed to be on the road being as he was pushing the sedan over eighty miles an hour with quite a few other vehicles around us.

I turned in my seat and stared through the windshield, still pressed as close to the door as possible, my arms wrapped around my middle.

"They're going to kill you," I muttered.

Both alphas scoffed.

"Even if they don't find me. Even if you kill me and dump me somewhere no one will ever find me, my pack and my sister's pack will track you down and kill you. Both of you."

I glanced in the side mirror as though I could see the alpha in the backseat…

But instead caught the distinct single headlight of a motorcycle. Then another.

It wasn't just one, but three. And they were whipping in and out of traffic, growing closer by the second.

My alphas.

The phone in my pants, the one Amir had shoved back there without Antonio knowing. They had used it to track me and were so damn close.

They could catch up to me but then what? Not like I was some stuntwoman who could jump through the window and onto the back of one of their bikes.

Think, Issa.

I couldn't bring attention to the fact my alphas were flying up on us. Antonio would intentionally try to hit them or run them off the road. And since they were on two wheels instead of four, they would have nothing to protect them if they were to crash.

Especially since Ax refused to wear a helmet because *it messed up his hair.*

Biting my lower lip, I nearly broke the skin as I worried it and searched the vehicle for…what? What exactly was I looking for? No way in hell would either of these assholes leave any weapons where I could reach them.

There had to be a way to…*damn it.*

A way to do what?

Distract them. I could distract them. But then what?

I still couldn't exactly leap from the passenger window and onto the back of one of their bikes or into their arms.

And we were on the highway doing…

I glanced toward the speedometer as discreetly as possible and sighed. He was only doing seventy now instead of the eighty plus he'd been driving at originally.

Did that mean he was so stupid as to think he was in the clear?

Let him think that. If he let his guard down, that would give me and my alphas some way to end this with as little bloodshed and flaming car crashes as possible.

Without turning my head or bringing attention to myself, I let my eyes roam the entirety of the cab, finally landing on the emergency brake between us.

After another quick glance in the side mirror to make sure my alphas weren't too close but close enough to get to me before Antonio could kill me for what I was about to attempt, I reached down, pulled the e-brake at the same time I threw the car in neutral, then slammed into the dash as the tires began to squeal against the pavement and the smell of burning rubber filled my nose.

While Antonio cursed and struggled to keep the car under control, I lunged for my door, popped the lock and threw the door open.

We were still going entirely too fast, but no way would I stick around to see what my former alpha would do after my little stunt.

The highway was a blur as I stared at it then closed my eyes and threw myself from the passenger seat, immediately wrapping my arms around my head in hopes of minimizing the damage, at least to my head.

Broken bones and road rash would heal – brain damage wouldn't.

As my body was jostled, rolling and bumping against the asphalt, I squeezed my eyes shut and clenched my teeth against the pain tearing through my arms, my legs, my back.

Whether anything was broken, I wasn't sure, but there was definitely skin being torn away.

Horns blared. Tires squealed as people slammed on their brakes. But I kept my eyes squeezed shut and prayed anyone who might have been following us closely didn't run me over before those three motorcycles made it to me.

When I finally stopped rolling and bouncing, voices made it through the blood rushing through my ears and my heart pounding like a damn bass drum in my head.

Hands smoothed over my head and hands, and I instantly batted them away, ignoring the pain in an effort to keep Antonio from dragging me from my alphas again.

"Issa – Issa!" Cyrus's voice was raised over the cacophony of sounds invading my senses. "Stop!"

My eyes were wide as I stared into his face. "Am I alive?"

His lips quirked into a sad smile as he forced me to stay lying on the asphalt, headlights illuminating both of us.

"You're still alive, sweetheart. Don't move."

"I'm fine," I grunted as I tried again to sit up.

But my head spun, and it felt as though my body, or maybe my mind, was shutting down.

"Fuck! Baby girl, open your eyes!" Ax said, his voice deep and guttural, as though his emotions were clogging his throat the same time a growl worked from his chest.

"Did you catch him?" I muttered as my lashes fluttered in an attempt to open my eyes.

"Bain's men are dealing with him."

I forced my lids up and my eyes met Enzo's. All three of my alphas were kneeling around me, their expressions varying from enraged to downright grief stricken.

"I'm not dead," I gritted out. But I no longer tried to push to sitting. That hurt too much and made my head spin and my stomach roll. "You look like you're looking at my corpse."

I tried to huff a laugh, but even that hurt.

My alphas' scents surrounded me as their hormones exploded from them.

A broken, stuttering purr was coming from my left, where I'd seen Cyrus.

Sirens wailed in the background, barely making it over the sounds of engines running, feet hitting the pavement, then somewhere in the distance…

My eyes flew open at what sounded like fireworks. Or like several engines were backfiring in rapid succession.

Bain's men are dealing with him.

Hopefully, by dealing with him Enzo didn't mean they were literally firing their guns right there on the highway for anyone to see.

Even if they were able to take off before anyone caught sight of their faces, those who'd been close enough when I'd thrown myself from the car would know I was somehow connected, that my pack was somehow connected.

And the last thing we needed was attention from law enforcement over a death – *two* deaths counting the asshole alpha who'd helped Antonio – in the middle of a now congested highway.

"Can you keep your eyes open for me, sweetheart?" Cyrus asked. His warm, wet scent washed over my face and coated my tongue as I took in deep breaths, trying to ignore the pain igniting my nerve endings.

"I'm trying," I forced out through lips that were growing numb.

That can't be good.

Shock. It had to be shock. It didn't feel as though I'd broken anything, and I couldn't clearly remember whether I'd hit my head.

But damn…I had really thrown myself from a moving vehicle.

The sirens grew closer and blue and red flashed across my closed lids or my alphas' faces when I was able to peel my lids open for a few seconds at a time.

My alphas' scents faded a touch and growls lifted on the air the same time fresh beta scents surrounded me and hands began to smooth over my head, my neck, my arms and legs.

I was trying so hard to stay awake, to open my eyes and keep them open as a thick collar was wrapped around my neck and I was carefully lifted onto some kind of hard board.

Then I was being lifted again and placed on a stretcher before being wheeled to the waiting ambulance.

"You can't all fit in here," someone said.

My lips twitched in humor as I pictured my alphas trying to crawl into the back of the ambulance with me.

"The motorcycles," I muttered.

My lids fluttered and I looked into the face of a young male beta donning a paramedic uniform.

"What was that?" he asked, leaning close and turning his head so his ear was close to my mouth.

"They can't leave their motorcycles. Someone will steal them."

The paramedic huffed a chuckle and repeated what I said to the alphas.

"Fuck the bikes. I'm not leaving you, baby girl." That was definitely Ax.

Focusing on our bond, I sent each of them, including Amir who felt as though he was losing his mind, love and comfort. As far as I knew, I would be okay.

Unless of course there was some kind of internal bleeding I was unaware of...or maybe brain damage.

But again, I didn't feel as though I was seriously injured, just a little shaken up from the chaos of the past thirty or so minutes.

"Oscar?" I asked.

"We don't know yet. Abdel said he was alive when the ambulance took him away."

I blew out a sigh of relief.

"You can follow us, but there is no way to fit all three of you in here with us," the paramedic said, inserting as much authority as he could into his voice.

I had a feeling this poor guy was more than used to dealing with overprotective alphas on his job.

A constant growl filled the interior of the ambulance. I lifted my hand and reached for Ax. His big, warm hand wrapped around mine.

"Go. Meet us there. I'm fine."

His face filled my vision, blocking anything else.

"Oh. And call Amir and let him know I'm okay. And check on Oscar."

I blinked rapidly, trying my damnedest to keep my eyes open and on Ax's face, even when his own beautiful eyes glimmered with tears.

"Why the fuck did you jump out of that car?" he said, his words choked.

I tried to shrug but couldn't with the way the medics had me strapped to the backboard. "So he wouldn't ram into you guys when he noticed you chasing after us."

It sounded completely logical to me at the time, and it still did as I said the words to him.

He could be mad at me later. For now, I desperately wanted to close my eyes and sleep until whatever hurt so badly healed.

CHAPTER 47

<u>Cyrus</u>

Four of us huddled around Issa's hospital bed, waiting for her to wake up, to open her eyes, to hear her voice.

According to the ER doctors and nurses, she'd only broken two fingers, had a crap load of road rush, and would be extremely bruised.

Other than that, she had zero brain damage according to the scans, and no other broken bones.

I counted that information as nothing short of a miracle. No way that car had been going any slower than fifty or so miles an hour before the door was shoved open and her petite body came rolling out.

"Jumped out of the fucking car," I muttered, running both hands roughly over my face.

We were all exhausted. We'd been in this hospital for hours, in this room for nearly as long. Amir continuously had to swallow back whimpers and whines as he clung to Issa's small hand.

Ax and Enzo...

I would have thought Enzo would have at least been able to keep his shit in check being pack lead and all. Ax was the one who was led by his emotions more often than not.

But both men couldn't sit still, pushing to their feet to pace the length of the larger pack room before dropping onto their chairs again.

Back and forth. Back and forth.

"I'm a badass," Issa muttered.

All four of us stiffened and turned wide eyes on her.

Amir leaned forward. "Issa? Are you talking in your sleep?"

"Open your eyes, beautiful," I said, looming over her opposite from where Amir was hovering.

Her lashes fluttered and it took a few tries, but she eventually opened her eyes then squeezed them shut.

"Too bright," she muttered, her brows furrowing and causing a crease between them.

Enzo quickly moved across the room and dimmed the lights so she could still see us without being bombarded with the glaring fluorescent lights overhead.

"Better?" he asked when he returned.

She opened one eye tentatively, then finally opened the other and sighed.

"Were you talking in your sleep?" Amir asked again.

"No. I'm a badass. I jumped out of the car like in the movies."

Her voice was a little hoarse since she'd been asleep for so long. Or unconscious.

We were warned she had suffered a concussion, but they'd monitored her the entire stay and reassured us she wouldn't suffer from any lingering effects.

"You could've gotten yourself fucking killed. You should have waited for us," Ax growled from the foot of the bed.

I shot him a look, but he was busy staring at our beta.

"If I'd waited, you could have gotten killed. Did you think he would just pull over and let me out when he saw you?"

Ax opened his mouth, his lips moving like a fish, before he closed it and scowled at her.

None of us liked the fact she'd done something so stupidly reckless and potentially deadly, but she had a point. Even if we or one of Bain's men had started firing at Antonio or whoever that fuck was in the backseat, we could have risked hitting her, or getting her killed when the car lost control.

Whether she was right or not didn't make the whole situation any less terrifying. We'd come far too close to losing her.

"What about Antonio?" she asked.

When she tried to sit up, Amir climbed into the bed beside her and coaxed her onto her back, resting his chin on her shoulder and nuzzling her cheek as the softest whimpers left his chest.

"Bain's dealing with him," Enzo said. Or rather growled since neither he nor Ax had stopped since we'd felt her fear through our bonds.

"And the other guy? There was another alpha."

"He's dead," Enzo said, his arms crossed over his chest.

"So why are you looking at me like you want to throttle me?" Her voice grew smaller, and it took every ounce of control to keep from lunging at our pack lead and beating the shit out of him.

But Enzo's face instantly softened, and he sighed heavily. "I don't want to throttle you. You know damn well I would never hurt you."

"Then why do you look so pissed?"

"You jumped out of a moving car on the fucking highway. It's *our* job to protect *you*, not the other way around," Ax answered on Enzo's behalf as though they were currently two halves of one brain.

"Can we talk about this when we get home?" Amir asked through a whine.

He nuzzled his cheek against Issa's, pressing kisses to her throat, her cheek, her temple, anywhere he could get to without over-whelming or smothering her.

. . .

IT WAS two more days of monitoring before the doctors agreed to release Issa to us to go home. I was more than ready to have her back in our house, behind closed doors, and lying in the pack bed surrounded by her omega and alphas.

It had been quick thinking on Amir's part to shove his phone down the back of her pants. Otherwise, we wouldn't have been able to track her the way we had. Who knows where that fucker might have taken her or what he might have done to her.

She'd still gotten hurt, but it had been her own doing when she'd lunged from the fucking passenger side door.

I still couldn't believe she'd done that. Ax and Enzo growled any time it was brought up, so she threatened to sleep in her own bed alone if they didn't chill out.

Not that I believed that threat for a second. Though she was a beta, she'd been more affectionate, even more so than before. She was constantly touching one of us, asking one of us to snuggle or hold her.

And none of us had a single fucking complaint. The three of us alphas had taken off a few days to watch over her and make sure she didn't get up and move around too much.

Just because she'd only broken the two fingers didn't mean she needed to put too much stress on her battered body. She didn't have the accelerated healing of an alpha or an omega.

And just like when we'd first had contact with her, her bruises, cuts, and scrapes would take a few weeks to be fully healed.

We had nothing but time now.

That fucker Antonio wasn't dead, not *yet*. But he was no longer a threat. Bain and his pack were taking their time punishing him with the promise that one of us had the pleasure of pulling the trigger when it was time to put him down like a rabid fucking animal.

At the moment, we were all crammed into the pack bed, some eighties sitcom playing softly in the background, takeout containers littering the end of the bed and nearby surfaces, while Issa and Amir snored softly.

That had been too close. In a span of moments, we had come so close to losing Issa.

Fuck. We could have lost them both had Abdel not kept his head and focused on protecting Amir. A small fact that had pissed Amir off enough that he'd demanded his father fire him.

Didn't happen. In fact, we had personally hired him on full time to stay in the house until he found his own pack.

And Oscar didn't die, nor had he suffered any damage to his brain. His recovery would take longer than Issa's being as he'd been shot in the head, but, thankfully, the bullet had missed his brain and the bullet hadn't gotten lodged in his skull.

"We should see if they'll push up the wedding," Ax said out of the blue.

Both Enzo and I frowned at him.

"Put it off longer?" I asked.

"Nah. Sooner. I want them married. I want to celebrate and have a fucking party. And put all that bullshit behind us."

I glanced in Enzo's direction, but he was staring down at Issa with nothing short of love in his eyes.

"She'll want to go back to work as soon as possible," I said.

We'd discussed possibly asking her to quit working at the club, but we also knew there wasn't a chance in hell she would give up the sense of independence without a fight.

Hell, she'd only been away from her part time job just over a month while we'd looked for Antonio and had been going out of her mind with boredom.

Hence her and Amir's constant shopping trips, manicures, and visits with his parents.

Ghazi, Myer, and Athena had come to the hospital the moment they'd figured out where the ambulance was taking her and then came here every day since we'd brought her home, bringing home cooked meals or takeout while Amir's sisters busied themselves with tidying and minor household chores as though the four of us couldn't leave her side long enough to run the dishwasher.

There was nothing physically keeping us from leaving her side – we just didn't want to.

The wedding was planned for about a year from now, but I could see why Ax wanted to move shit up; that had been entirely too close for comfort.

Not that Amir and Issa having a wedding or even a marriage certificate would change a damn thing about our relationships or her place in the pack.

But we...*she* absolutely deserved something beautiful, a celebration, a big ass party complete with a DJ, flowers, and any kind of food she wanted.

Fuck, I would have a variety of food trucks parked along the curb if that was what she wanted.

"We'll bring it up to them, see if that's what they want." Enzo lifted a hand, halting whatever Ax was about to spout. "Their choice, Ax. I'm fucking serious. Don't start pressuring her about anything."

"What about talking one of them into carrying a pup for us?" Ax said, a wide, shit eating grin on his face.

My nostrils flared as I inhaled deeply before blowing it out slowly. "She has no desire to be a mom. Or at least to get pregnant. And it's still pretty early to start talking about adding kids to our pack."

Not that I wasn't dying to see either of their bellies rounded with one of our babies, or that I wasn't more than ready to see little pink or blue toys littering the house.

But no way in fucking hell would any of us push that on her. We understood. We truly did.

Conversation ceased and I swore all three of us focused all our attention on the sleeping duo, on the way Issa's dark lashes fanned over her cheek, on the way Amir kept a tight hold on her even in his sleep.

He was still beating himself up that she was taken instead of him. Didn't matter how many times we all told him how well he'd done by putting the phone in the back of her pants, or how he'd remained calm and had been able to help us track her.

There had to be a way to reassure him, but we all knew it wouldn't come from us. It would be up to Issa to convince him he'd done exactly as he should have by ensuring they both remained alive and that we were able to get to our beta before it was too late.

CHAPTER 48

Three Months Later

<u>Issa</u>

*H*ow had they talked me into this?

Not only had Amir and I agreed with Ax's excited and rambling plea to bump up the date of the wedding, but I'd allowed them to help in the planning.

I'd thought Athena was a lot. She had nothing on my alphas.

The only high point was they hadn't invited hundreds of people.

But they had decorated the entirety of the house – literally the whole house including the bedrooms and bathrooms – as well as the yard with thousands and thousands of fresh flowers and flickering candles.

At least they'd listened to every bit of input I'd given them. The flowers were in soft blush and lavender tones, the candles were all ivory, and the guys all slept together in the pack bed while I'd spent the night alone in my own room.

It had felt so weird sleeping alone after spending so much time surrounded by the scents and warmth of my pack, but it was one of those things I wanted to do, one of those little superstitious things betas often did before their wedding.

And I wanted to feel as normal as possible for once.

Not that anything about our pack was normal, and that was completely fine with me.

Amir and I had asked our alphas if they would walk me down the aisle the way fathers often did when giving their daughter's hand in marriage. The beatific smile on Ax's face had been enough to melt my heart.

Apparently, they'd already talked and had hoped Amir and I would invite them to be a part of the ceremony in some way but refused to pressure me.

As if I could do something so important without them playing a part.

I hadn't seen any of them since last night, since they each stood in a line and kissed me goodnight before I'd spent some time pampering myself in the tub in my ensuite bathroom.

Now, I sat in front of my vanity as Cora helped attach the jeweled hairpiece I'd chosen the day I'd picked my dress with Aryn, Amir, Athena, and Alysia.

That had also been the day all our lives could have changed irreparably and irreversibly.

But that memory wasn't welcome in my head or heart today. All that mattered was we were all together, all safe and in one piece.

Even my bruising had faded, though I did have a few faint scars that had to be covered with concealer since my dress exposed so much skin. I knew my alphas and Amir wouldn't care about the marks, but I didn't want anything to mar this perfect day, including bad memories.

"Have you seen my guys yet?" I asked Cora when she stepped away to check her placement in my soft braids.

A soft smile pulled up the corners of her lips when she met my gaze through the mirror.

"Your guys look amazing. They're dressed in their tuxes and Ax even pulled his hair back. Although Amir left his crazy mane loose."

"Per my request," I said with a chuckle.

I loved my omega's hair. I loved the feeling of his soft, silky curls running through my fingers.

Especially when he was nestled between my thighs, his tongue in my mouth as he fucked me, his hair creating a curtain around us…

"Girl. You're lucky you're not an omega."

I frowned at my sister's reflection.

"You're flushing and your pupils just blew wide. If you were an omega…" She gestured toward where I sat with my dress smoothed down under me and I caught her meaning immediately, causing my flushed cheeks to blush a deeper shade of pink.

"Cora!" I whisper-screamed, pressing my cool hands to my cheeks.

It wasn't exactly warm outside, but the alphas had turned on the AC, determined to make sure everyone was comfortable if they ended up mingling inside the house.

As though we'd invited a hundred people instead of maybe twenty.

I'd actually begged to cut the list more when I'd spotted Amir's guest list. He had a huge family, and they were all overjoyed he had not only found a pack but was actually marrying his beta.

Apparently, every single one of his family members held the same belief that designations didn't mean anything when it came to finding your forever person.

And the two of us had not only found our forever person but forever *people*. We had each other and three alphas who adored us.

"Are you nervous?" Cora asked, stepping back to check her hair and makeup in the other mirror hanging over the double sink.

"I wasn't until you asked. Thanks a lot," I teased, pushing away from the vanity and standing. "Is everyone ready?"

"I'm pretty sure your alphas have been waiting outside your door for the past hour. Or more," she said with a chuckle.

"They're ridiculous," I said, hurrying across my room and pulling it open a crack to find exactly as Cora said – my alphas leaned against the wall looking absolutely edible in their tuxes.

"They're in love," Cora said, pulling the door open further so she could step out and make her way down the stairs. "I'll let everyone know you're ready," she called over her shoulder as she carefully descended the stairs in her lavender heels.

She'd chosen a lavender dress to compliment the soft rosy blush color of my gown, hers matching my décor.

I had gotten a glimpse of the decorations before I'd been sequestered away by Cora before the alphas had seen me, but I couldn't wait to fully see the damage my pack had done in the form of money spent. There had been no reason to go so overboard, but I wouldn't stop them from following their instincts, from protecting and spoiling me and Amir.

Actually, their instincts were supposed to be protecting and spoiling their omega, but Amir had taught me to simply enjoy every-thing they did for me and give them my heart in return.

Oh, and my body.

But I would have given all four of my men my heart, body, and soul even if we'd simply donned nice clothes and had a judge or other officiant come to our house to declare me and Amir husband and wife.

"Wow," Cyrus said, taking my hand and bending so he could press a kiss to my knuckles. "You look so beautiful."

"You really do," Enzo said.

Ax remained silent, his eyes wide as he scanned me from head to toe, his lips parted as though unable to speak a coherent sentence.

And man did I get that sentiment. All three looked amazing. And Ax *had* pulled his hair back and tamed it into a neat ponytail at the nape of his neck.

Since I'd chosen the style and decorations for the ceremony, I'd let Amir decide on the guys' attire. Not that there were a whole lot of choices.

But he'd gone with simple black tuxes with white shirts and black bowties.

"You guys…you all look so handsome," I said as my smile grew.

That snapped Ax out of his silence. "Oh, please. I look hot." He tugged on his lapels and smoothed his jacket before extending his elbow. "You ready to marry our omega?" His voice was softer, sweeter, just like the look on his handsome face.

"I'm so ready," I admitted.

I was still a little nervous, but not about the marrying part. I was nervous I would trip and make a fool of myself or stammer over my words. There wasn't a chance in hell I could ever doubt how I felt about my omega or my alphas.

Cora appeared at the bottom of the stairs and raised her brows, so I shot her a smile and a thumbs up.

This was it. I was ready.

The guys would escort me downstairs, through the house, and down the makeshift aisle Athena and Alysia had designed alongside Cora and Aryn. I really didn't know what I would have done in such a short period of time had it not been for the women in my life, with my new mother-in-law, my new sisters, my only biological sister, and my best friend.

Cora hurried away and my alphas guided me down the stairs, ensuring I was steady on my heels on each step.

The trip to the backyard was a blur; all I could focus on was the ridiculous number of flowers and candles everywhere. All this had to have cost my alphas a fortune.

Once the French doors opened, the soft music filtering to my ears and I caught sight of Amir in all his glory waiting for me under an arch made entirely of fresh flowers…

All thoughts of cost, fears, memories, nightmares, and my past floated away like a wisp of smoke from an extinguished candle. All that mattered was the man grinning at me with the most heart-warming smile and the three alphas surrounding me on my left, my right, and following closely behind.

The guests who'd been invited – coworkers, Cora and her pack, some of Amir's family, and even my brothers – all stood when Cora spotted me and pushed to her feet.

Smiles were on most faces, but there was only one I could focus on.

It felt as if I was floating down the beautiful ivory runner covered in petals scattered by Annalise and Amini.

Our alphas handed me over to Amir then took their place near the officiant. I might have been mistaken, but all three looked a little misty eyed as we were told to repeat after the beta guiding our vows.

The moment we were announced legally married, Amir wrapped his arms around me, dipped me backward, and sealed his mouth over mine, deepening the kiss regardless of who was watching.

I didn't mind. If our guests didn't like this beautiful show of affection, they could close their damn eyes.

We were nearly skipping back down the aisle, our hands clasped tightly, and led the entirety of the group to the tables set up around the lawn.

The guests chatted as the caterers Athena had found on such short notice served our food.

Once dinner was over, it was time to party. And party we did.

Ax had a blast showing off. Amir and I danced until I gave up and kicked off my heels. Cora and her alphas danced with my pack. Even my brothers seemed to be enjoying themselves, though they barely spoke to me.

It would take time to build a relationship with them the way I had with Cora. We had all been raised by the same jackass tyrants and had a whole lot of habits and twisted ways of thinking to break.

But we had time now. I no longer had to worry about Antonio or anyone else out there with some messed up vendetta.

I could live my life with my pack, enjoy my life with them, love them as deeply as possible while continuing to heal from those parts of my past that sometimes still reared their ugly head in my memories.

Eventually, the party slowed, and the guests left, leaving behind more gifts than twenty people should have brought.

"My family sent them," Amir explained when I gawked at the massive pile in the living room.

"That's going to take us forever to open. What in the world could they have bought? Not like we're newlyweds setting up our first pack house."

Amir exchanged a cryptic look with my alphas but steered me toward the stairs before I could question them.

It was time to consummate our marriage. And there was no way that would happen without all five of us naked and in the bed together.

CHAPTER 49

<u>Issa</u>

I had only gotten through a few of the presents in the two days since our wedding. Most of them were simple, things like crystalware, jewelry, and such. There was also a load of envelopes that felt thicker than they should have if they'd only contained simple cards, making me worry his family had stuffed money in them.

Today, we were heading to Amir's family's home. My new family's home.

A smile pulled up my lips as I braided my hair away from my face then applied a coat of mascara.

"You almost ready, sweetheart?" Cyrus asked from the bathroom door.

"Yep. Just got to put my shoes on," I answered.

My guys were all in jeans, t-shirts, and hoodies since the weather had taken a turn toward cooler since it was still early spring.

I was dressed similarly but had chosen a sweater over a tank top instead of a hoodie.

Cyrus leaned against the door, his arms crossed over his chest, and watched me with a sweet smile.

"What are you looking at?" I teased him as I tugged on my boots.

Amir had bought them for me as a prewedding gift after the last time I'd gone to his parents and ended up stepping in a steaming pile of horse poo. We'd all gotten a good laugh at that, especially me when I whined so much Amir had ended up cleaning said poo from the bottoms of my sneakers.

"Why do you look so fucking hot in everything you wear?" Ax said as he pushed past Cyrus to get to me.

He instantly bent me backward over his arm and started nibbling on my neck, sending chill bumps rising across my body when he brushed across any of my bonding marks.

"We're going to be late!" Enzo called from downstairs.

I swatted at Ax, trying to wiggle from his hold. Instead, he lifted me in his arms and carried me bridal style from the room and down the stairs like I weighed nothing.

"Can't have you scuffing up your new boots now, can we?" he said as he ran his chin over the top of my head.

"They're supposed to get scuffed, dumbass. They're for stomping around in mud and horse shit," Enzo grumbled.

"Nice," Cyrus said with a shake of his head.

Amir had a few gifts stacked in his arms as he waited near the garage door for us with a smile adorning his gorgeous face.

"Are we opening more gifts at your parents'?"

He shrugged up one shoulder. "Mom said something about wanting to see you open a few of these."

"She worried about what the rest of your family sent?" I joked as Ax set me down in the back seat of the SUV before climbing in beside me.

So far, the few things we'd opened had been beautiful and innocent.

"Something like that," he said after depositing the boxes into the hatchback and taking his place on my left.

Both Ax and Amir had their fingers twined through mine, resting my hands on their thighs so my arms were spread out. I liked it so much better when we were all piled together on the bed or even the couch.

But I loved their touch, regardless.

Amini and Annalise were outside playing when Enzo pulled the SUV to a spot beside the other vehicles. All three of Amir's parents were home as well as his sisters being as it was the weekend, and this was a mini family get together.

Unlike the other times when we'd arrived, Amini and Annalise simply raised their heads and looked in our direction with smiles. I'd grown used to them squealing and giggling with joy and running at us the moment we pushed open our doors.

"There's something else I wanted to tell you. Or rather give you," Cyrus said.

"*We* wanted to give you," Ax corrected.

I looked from Cyrus to Ax and back. "What do you mean?"

Amir opened his door and stepped out, offering me his hand and leading me to the fence keeping the horses from running loose. Our alphas flanked us on both sides and little feet hit the ground hard as Amir's two youngest sisters ran to catch up.

"What are we doing?" I asked.

We were here to visit with his parents, yet I was being led to the pasture.

Amir smiled and jerked his head toward where Princess Fancy Pants and Pearl paced and waited to see if we had treats for them.

When I turned my head toward the mares, I realized there were two more horses grazing nearby, one so black it was almost blue, the other a tiny bit smaller and brown with white fur around its legs like socks.

"What…" I couldn't form the question.

"These are our wedding gifts to the two of you," Cyrus answered my unspoken question.

"Wedding gifts?" I asked when I struggled to make sense of what he was saying and what I was seeing.

There were only two horses here before. I knew that because I'd asked. I'd ridden with Amir the day he'd proposed to me.

"You get your pick of the two," Amir said. "The alphas wanted to get us both something and saw how you lit up with the horses."

"We've already hired someone to set up the property with secure fencing, build a barn with stalls, the whole shebang," Ax said.

"What?"

The guys exchanged a look.

"You okay, baby girl?" Ax asked, a crooked grin pulling up one side of his lips.

"You got me a horse? You got *us* horses? As a wedding gift?"

I felt silly repeating the facts back to them, but I was having a hard time making it all make sense.

Moving closer to the fence, I stared at the two new additions and smiled as they both sauntered over, the smaller of the two making a beeline straight to me and nudging her way past Pearl and Princess to stop directly in front of me as though claiming me.

Just like my alphas had done before I'd acknowledged it.

Tears blurred in my eyes as I lifted my hand and rubbed between her ears.

"What are you going to name her?" Amir asked as he wrapped his arms around me from behind, his chin resting on my shoulder.

"I have no idea," I said through a watery laugh. "Maybe I'll let your sisters come up with something."

"You realize his sisters are the ones who came up with Princess Fancy Pants, right?" Enzo teased.

"I can't believe you got me a freaking horse," I said as realization and excitement settled in and pushed away the disbelief and shock. "I love you guys so much."

Leaning my head back, I dropped it against Amir's shoulder as he nuzzled my neck and I continued to scratch my horse between her ears.

I really did need to come up with a name for her so I wasn't constantly referring to her as *my horse.*

"I literally know nothing about taking care of her," I said, looking at first Amir over my shoulder than to each of my alphas.

"I do. And we've hired a ranch hand to help out during my heats or if we need to go out of town for anything."

A giggle burst from my lips. "You hired a ranch hand? For two freaking horses?"

It was all so absurd and over the top.

But couldn't the same thing be said about my pack?

After all, I had a beautiful omega who had taught me how to love and be loved, who taught me how to ask for what I want. I had three alphas who were fully devoted to both Amir and me, not just our omega.

I had an alpha who danced like he was part cat, part water, and a whole lot of parts sex god. I had an alpha who was so freaking sweet and patient and kind. I had an alpha who would literally rip his chest open and present his heart to me. To any of us, really.

In a year, I had gone from a broken beta who didn't believe I was worth more than my past to a beta with four men who loved me and had zero problem showing me every day.

I was officially married, was officially Isabelle Rivera of Pack Rivera, and was building a close relationship with my sister after being estranged most our lives.

In a year...I had been gifted with the most perfect pack and the most beautifully perfect life I could have ever dreamed possible.

FROM THE AUTHOR

FROM THE AUTHOR

If you loved Issa's story of discovering her inner strength, finding her pack, and building a loving family, I would love if you could take the time to leave a review on your favorite site.

For cover reveals, early sneak peeks, and free novellas, make sure to subscribe to my newsletter here.

9 781949 447989